RELIABLE IN BANGKOK

An Asian Thriller

by
Valerie Goldsilk
& Julian Stagg

This novel is entirely a work of fiction. The names, characters and incidents portrayed in it are the work of the author's imagination. Any resemblance to actual persons, living or dead, events or localities is entirely coincidental.

First published by Thaumasios Publishing Ltd. in 2018 under the title 'The Reliable Man'.

Second edition published by Thaumasios Publishing Ltd. in 2021 as 'Reliable in Bangkok'.

Copyright © Valerie Goldsilk and Julian Stagg 2021

Cover design by Mark Hevingham

No part of this book may be reproduced or transmitted in any form without permission in writing by the publisher.

The Reliable Man Series

Reliable in Bangkok
Reliable in Jakarta
Reliable in Hong Kong
Reliable in Danang
Reliable in New York
Reliable in London
Reliable in Manila
Reliable in Lapland (Short Story)

The Inspector Scrimple Series

Classified As Crime
Dragon Breath
Perfect Killer
Fatal Action
Random Outcome
Yellow Hammer

Other Books by Valerie Goldsilk

The Oldest Sins
Negative Buoyancy
Sins of Our Sisters
Sins of Our Elders
White Bishop

About the Authors

Valerie Goldsilk is English and has lived in Hong Kong for over thirty years. She is now retired but used to run her own business, traveling frequently around Asia working with factories. Her better half is a former Hong Kong police inspector.

Julian Stagg is a British investment banker who, after a thirty-year career as an adviser, entrepreneur and investor, can still be found plying his trade in the City of London.

Authors' Note

This book was **previously published** under the title 'The Reliable Man', originally written by Valerie Goldsilk in the early 1990s.

This new edition has been revised and slightly edited for length and to be appropriate for a more contemporary readership.

DEDICATION

To SC - for allowing Bill to borrow your body.

To DL - for parts of the story which I have embellished.

To PC - who explained to me all about the Pattaya German mafia and the Filipino hitmen who were brought in to take them down.

To the Gough - sorry about your exit!

And to my brother Ted - who never did get to have any companions as exotic as the Four Seasons.

"This story has no moral. If it points out an evil, at any rate it suggests no remedy."

'The Unbearable Bassington' by H.H. Munro

"Fiction is a process of producing grand, beautiful, well-ordered lies that tell more truth than any assemblage of facts".

Julian Barnes

1

It was one of those clammy Bangkok afternoons. The 'Miami' had never been a deluxe hotel, but I'd chosen it for reasons of nostalgia and to provide the cover I wanted. It was as low key as one can get. I was on my first girl of the day when the door burst open and a strange man poked the muzzle of his revolver into my ear. I stopped moving and decided to listen to what he had to say. He wasn't wearing an Armani suit or a gold Rolex, so I assumed he was the hired help and had some message to deliver. I didn't like the idea of that. Nobody, to the best of my knowledge, had been privy to my movements.

"What your name?" he demanded, breathing tooth decay into my face, smelling like an exhumed corpse. I watched the sweat from my exertions drip onto the girl's breasts. My erection subsided and slipped sadly from within her. It's funny how the hardest men turn soft in the face of death. I told him my name.

"You give her one thousand Baht," he ordered.

The girl, not un-gently, pushed me away then slipped from the bed. She pulled on her clothes quickly and found my wallet, a real Louis Vuitton, not a street stall imitation. She extracted the money hurriedly, uncomfortable at the situation but no stranger to opportunism. I studied her with regret. The man stepped back and said something to the girl in Thai. She replied then gave me a grin of apology and a wave before she slammed the door. A thousand Baht was good going for ten minutes work.

She had been sitting next to me in a Nana Plaza beer bar. We'd played a form of noughts and crosses on a plastic rack and I'd lost five times. After four beers I decided it was time to get my hands onto her lithe, impudent body. It was a shame we'd been interrupted. I'd just been getting into my stride.

The room was dank and gloomy. A hospital bed took up most of the space. The gun threatening me was a tarnished Smith and Wesson Revolver. It looked like a snub-nose Model 10, well used and badly maintained, and had probably been floating around South East Asia since the Vietnam War. He held it easily like a man pointing a finger at something funny. Sitting naked on the edge of the bed with a wilting erection, I must have been an amusing sight.

The visitor, who had spoiled the mood of my afternoon, was large and muscular. His teeth were chipped and dirty brown. A gecko crossed the big damp patch on the wall behind his head. He had a squint in his eye, perhaps earned from a lifetime of looking at people over the edge of rusty gun-barrels.

"Were you looking for me?" I asked.

"You come from Hong Kong?"

"Yeah. Have you come to rob me or do you hope to improve your conversational English?" I was working out the distance separating us and coming rapidly to the conclusion that I had no sensible choice for action. He did not answer me.

"You like Thai lady?" He grinned for the first time since we had met. It was not the sort of smile that won friends and influenced people. "You big man. Lady like big man." He gestured in the relevant direction with his lethal finger.

"Put on clothes, *falang*."

I obeyed. He was the one calling the shots. Or holding the gun at least. I pulled on a baggy pair of linen trousers and a pink and yellow batik shirt.

"What's your name then?" I asked, trying to lighten the atmosphere in the little room.

"My name Kronk," he said. With his left hand he fumbled in his shirt pocket and extracted what looked like an envelope, which he threw at my feet. I picked it up. Turning it over in my hand I noted the name and crest of 'The Oriental Hotel', that grand old dame of Eastern hospitality. It was not the sort of hotel I imagined my new friend had ever stayed in as a paying guest.

I tore open the envelope and looked inside. It was made of a pale-yellow vellum. The only contents were a picture of a Chinese man in a pale blue suit, the sort stitched up by a cheap Hong Kong tailor and worn with white socks, sitting by a computer terminal. He wore a foolish grin under bottle glasses and sported a receding chin crammed with buckteeth. He looked like the studious nerd-son of a middle-class family, one of a thousand accountants, bankers or lawyers I had come across in Hong Kong, but I had an idea he wasn't any of those.

"My boss think you go looking for this man. You stop looking now or I kill you. Not your business."

His words troubled me. I was here for work, but this wasn't it. I shook my head.

"I don't know this man, nothing to do with me. Tell your boss I'm not interested. Who is he, by the way?"

Kronk looked puzzled then said, "My boss *chao por*, okay?"

I knew the expression. It meant 'influential person', what we might call a 'godfather'. It made sense to me. What I didn't understand was why his goon wanted to warn me off looking for a man I genuinely didn't recognise. I studied the picture again. After ten years in Hong Kong, telling Chinese faces apart was not a problem and this face hadn't crossed my path. I considered the possibilities and decided I had no wish to cause offence, certainly not the sort that spat fire from a Smith and Wesson Model 10.

"No problem," I said. "I take holiday. Thailand beautiful country. Ladies *suwai mak mak*."

"Many beautiful ladies here, he said, leering offensively. You do more *bumsing*. Good for man, I no kill you." Already it seemed the Germans were leaving parts of their language lying around like discarded beer bottle tops. *Bumsing* was a German gutter word for copulation. Hordes of German tourists came every year to the Ancient Kingdom of Siam on cheap package tours and a sizeable community had fallen in love with the place and settled here. A lot of the bar girls, adapting to the demands of the marketplace, already spoke better German than English.

Kronk decided he had given me enough advice for one day. The gun vanished into the back of his pants. He gave me another glimpse of his chipped, rotten teeth and left the room nearly as quickly as he had arrived, leaving a faint shadow of decaying body odour behind.

His visit made me uncomfortable. A man of his limited talents should not have been able to find me. Whoever he worked for knew my name, where I was staying and a good deal more. It was time for me to move on. I bolted the door and packed my big black overnight bag, conscientiously folding my Hugo Boss suit while dumping most of the other items into it carelessly. The overnight bag felt heavier than usual because of the false bottom containing the tools of my trade.

Outside the door of the Miami the *soi*, a side-road which led down to the main Sukhumvit thoroughfare, was cluttered with fruit stalls and three wheeled motorised rickshaws called *tuk-tuks*. They were cheaper than taxis, able to weave through the stagnant traffic more easily and driven by mad young men intent on killing themselves and their fares. Four of them, lounging about on the curb, spotted me and waved and hollered.

The air was sultry, filled with dust, dirt and the miasma of exhaust fumes. It was the distinctive, foul, street smell of the 'the City of Angels'. There was nothing quite like it, the true smell of the Exotic East. And there was no city quite like Bangkok.

"Patpong," I said to the first *tuk-tuk* driver.

"One hundred Baht."

"Twenty Baht". One could have almost jogged from the hotel to the red-light district if it wasn't for the risk of carbon monoxide poisoning. We settled on Fifty Baht. I had climbed onto the plastic seat ready to get a lung full of grime when I noticed Kronk standing on the streetcorner. He grinned when I spotted him and I nodded coolly in return. The tuk-tuk lurched forward and we were off fast and furious, missing Kronk by inches as the driver swung the vehicle into the afternoon traffic.

We weaved through taxis, trucks, battered

Japanese saloon cars and other tuk-tuks, then turned into an alley, scattering two old ladies and three scruffy chickens. We re-emerged on another large avenue and melted into the flow of cars.

Finally, we reached Patpong, the famous three streets that made more money in a week than all of the Northern provinces made in a whole year. Like the whore it was, Patpong was still sleeping in the late afternoon sun.

I stopped the tuk-tuk by the MacDonald's and walked to the 'Bobby's Arms', a pub that provided a cool and solidly British atmosphere. I'd been coming to Thailand from the British colony of Hong Kong, a two-hour plane trip, since 1983. The pub was as typical of Thailand as sun, sand and sex. Tourism was the country's major official source of foreign revenue, worth billions of dollars. The tourists enjoyed the imitation bars and restaurants that made them feel at home while they were at the other end of the world. A lot of these places were owned and run by expatriates: Brits, Swedes, French, Germans and people of every nationality under the sun who had been gripped by the gentle kingdom, married one of its daughters and never gone home.

The latest Test Match ran silently on a television screen suspended from the ceiling. I pulled back a stool and ordered a Singha beer and a packet of Marlboro Lights. The local Krong Thip cigarettes guaranteed smokers an early death from bronchitis and were intended only as a last resort. The beer was better. There were three other customers. One sat further up the bar reading the *Bangkok Post*. We nodded at each other, politely. The place was quiet and calm, away from the hustle of the streets, the smog, and the humidity.

Leaning against the bar with one elbow, an eye on the Test match, I considered whether to stay another night in Bangkok or go straight down to Pattaya, the seaside resort that made Sodom and Gomorra look like Quaker settlements. There had been no real reason to remain so long in the capital except that I wanted to make discreet enquiries about what I was letting myself in for when I got down to the coast.

I had my back to the TV when someone came up next to me and said, "Fancy bumping into you here. Thought you would have gone back to the UK by now." Turning around I found a familiar red face grinning at me.

2

Robin Keller looked ten years older and thirty pounds heavier than when I'd last seen him eleven months previously in the Officer's Mess of Tsim Sha Tsui Police Station. It had been someone's farewell drinks party and there had been serious drinking around the bar that night. Keller looked as if he hadn't stopped boozing since.

"Hello Robin," I said. "What are you doing here? On long leave?" I shook my head as he proffered his Benson & Hedges.

"The wife and kids have gone back to the UK, so I've taken a few days off to rest and relax. Get away from the daily grind. You know how the Force is. Gets you down after a while, you need to get away to forget it all. Either that or you start taking things too seriously, like that bugger who shot himself in his flat in the Hermitage."

I knew what he was talking about and so had the copper who'd taken his service revolver home for an intimate tête-à-tête.

"Been here long?" I asked.

"Not long enough by far," he replied with a lewd grin. "Who can get bored of paradise? There are seven thousand working girls in this part of town alone. I know I'm just an old fat fucker, but this place makes a man feel good and young again."

He chortled like a naughty schoolboy. I looked him up and down. I couldn't say either adjective looked appropriate at the moment. Thailand might have refreshed the inner man, but it just made the outer man look fat and forty. He was barely older than me.

"When you're bored of Bangkok, you're bored of life," I said. "Didn't Samuel Johnson say something like that?"

"That's about it," he said heaving himself onto the barstool next to me, adjusting his belly over his belt buckle. "You should have seen the little honey I pulled out of Queen's Castle last night. Sweetest little pussy you can imagine. Only been working four weeks, she told me."

"Come on, Robin that's what they all say," I commented. It made me queasy to imagine him grunting over the girl as she contorted her angelic face to make believe he was giving her pleasure. "How's your marriage?"

"Been on the rocks for a long time. She always hated Hong Kong," he said. "She found out about this Filipina *Amah* I'd been seeing, so she's taken that as an excuse to spend a lot of time back in England. With a mortgage on the house and the kids at school, I can't afford to get divorced."

He looked over his shoulder nervously as if expecting someone, then asked: "What do you do these days? Are you on business here?"

"No, mate, same as you, taking it easy and enjoying the fleshpots."

"By yourself? I normally see you hanging around with Julian McAlistair."

"Might catch up with him later in the trip, but for now, yes. I was just thinking about going down to Pattaya. Now I'm a Financial Adviser I've got one or two clients I'm seeing here."

"Well, I haven't got a penny to invest," he said, draining his beer and ordering another. "You know how it is in the old 'Farce'. The moment you get your salary it's already spent. No, you spend it even before you get it."

"There's always some money to be found somewhere. Even if it's in the Duty Officer's safe," I said, reciting a line I had fed to thirty expats this year. "Put it aside at the beginning of the month when you get paid, then have someone pick an investment fund with a good yield."

"Be realistic," he said defensively. Once you've paid the bills and the wife, there's barely enough left to have a few beers."

A few more people came quietly into the bar and ordered their first wet one of the day. I looked at Keller, trapped in a job that had lost its challenge. That had been me a couple of years ago. When he first arrived in Hong Kong, he'd probably been full of drive, ready to take on the whole Triad underworld. Then beer, the mundane reality of the job and a nagging English wife had reduced him to what he was now, an overweight, middle-aged man with responsibilities from which he could only hide once in a while in the fake glitter of a Patpong bar.

He'd started off badly, already burdened with a fiancée when he joined the Police Force as a Probationary Inspector. Mildred was a hawk-faced and demanding woman who moved to join him in Hong Kong when he passed out from Training School. Unhappy at her life in the colony as a bored expat housewife, she became more and more of a shrew. It was a depressingly common story. Keller was always to be found in the Mess drinking at five past five, reluctant to go home, until eventually he graduated to the bachelor pleasures of Wan Chai.

There had been no serious woman in my life when I came to Hong Kong. I'd never looked back since getting off the plane. White women couldn't compare to the silky charm and natural femininity of Chinese girls. After ten years in Asia, white women appeared the size of wrestlers, smelt like Billingsgate market and spoke back to you with the force of a right hook. Out here we preferred out women gentle and loving. Or paid them to pretend to be.

"You should have a word with someone at Immigration and tell them never to let your wife back into the territory."

"Those idiots at Immigration? You must be joking." He finished his Singha beer and ordered two more for us. I thought I caught a tremor in his hand as he picked up his glass.

"Beer. At least you can rely on a good cold beer. Won't fleece you for money or nag you to death if you come home late and worse for wear. You're looking in good shape, Bill," he said ruefully, grabbing the roll of fat around my middle and giving it a bit of a jiggle. "Not like me. Not much fat on you. How old are you now?"

"Thirty-two," I replied. Unlike Keller my waist was still firm. My job demanded that I kept reasonably fit and in shape, so I worked hard in the gym. But I was nowhere as young and healthy as I had once been. When I stared into the mirror, holding my razor, it wasn't the slim nice fellow who'd once been there, staring back.

"Where are you posted, Robin?" I asked, trying to change the subject. It was starting to depress me.

"ADVC Ops Yuen Long. Not very exciting but you don't get a choice, do you?"

Being posted as Assistant Divisional Commander to a small town in the New Territories was a dead-end job. Once even a sorry excuse for a copper like Keller would have escaped it, but as the Force sought to promote more and more indigenous officers, expats like him were being used simply to balance the books.

Hong Kong had changed a lot in the last few years. The shadow of China, which was due to take back the Territory in 1997, cast a chill over the old colony.

"What made you leave the RHKP?" he asked me. I had a ready answer for that, and it was close enough to the truth:

"I'd had enough of the arse-lickers, incompetents, back-stabbers and 'by-the-book' wankers that seemed to make up most of the senior ranks. Plus I wanted to make some serious money. You'll never get rich in the Civil Service unless you're on the take. And we missed all of that. We arrived too late."

Keller looked uncomfortable. He nodded. "Did you hear about this Chinese Superintendent? He was supplying under-age prostitutes to Jockeys in exchange for racing tips."

"Good scam, until you get caught," I said. Once the RHKP had been a hotbed of corruption. To their credit, after a particularly egregious scandal, the authorities had cracked down hard. The Independent Commission Against Corruption, or ICAC, had made life so uncomfortable that eventually the police had mutinied. A typically British compromise had calmed things down. Past failings were forgotten, but any new ones were rooted out with alacrity. There was still the odd bad penny, but the majority of policemen were straight now. They let their waywardness come out in drinking and whoring instead.

"You had two good postings with Headquarters units, didn't you? SDU, the anti-terrorist boys must have been fun, then VIP protection?"

"It was all right. It was a laugh, but it didn't lead anywhere. Where's the future in being a colonial policeman anyway? Sooner or later I would have ended up in an admin post unless I wanted to wear two-pips and a bar forever."

"The way things are now," he said, "I'll be wearing three pips until I'm sixty. Then I'll vamoose off to the Philippines or somewhere cheap and sit on a beach watching the sunset with a Flip in one hand and a San Miguel in the other."

It was a nice dream, but he had to believe in something. I hoped things would work out for him. Not many jobs available for a penniless policeman over forty.

His tale of woe had run its course. We watched the cricket in companionable silence and I thought about the things I had to do in Thailand. After a few beers he said:

"Do you fancy a massage up the road? The early afternoon girls are great at the 'Mon Chérie'."

He looked as if he couldn't wait to get underneath the soapy body of a teenager trying to feed her family. I thought about it and decided that, having been disturbed the last time, it probably wasn't a bad idea. I had a load to get off my mind. We walked up the street where stalls were already being set up ready to sell anything from T-shirts to bootleg videos and tapes, counterfeit wallets and bags. The shutters were coming off a few Go-Go bars. When we got to the 'Mon Chérie', we came through glass swing doors and took an escalator up to the first floor. A man in a dinner jacket greeted Keller with the warmth reserved for regular customers.

"Try number 23, she's got a very slim waist and big firm tits. And she doesn't mind giving a blow job," Keller advised.

The place had been around for years. A musky smell, the residue of a decade of salivating men, pervaded the furniture. The girls would be the newest thing in here. They turned them over rapidly. When girls had been working for too long, they got a vacant look in their eyes. The punters complained, even though they were the ones responsible for putting it there.

We went over to the bar and ordered a drink while we made up our minds. The bar and several threadbare sofas faced a large plate glass window behind which the girls waited to be chosen by customers. Sitting in the 'fish-tank', they could not see us but we could see them. There were at least twenty-five of them on carpeted steps, some watching television, some knitting, others chatting or filing their fingernails. Just another day in the office. We had a range of all shapes, sizes and ages to choose from.

Keller wandered over to the glass inspecting the merchandise. "How about Number 61. She good?" he asked the Manager.

"Very good. Very good," the manager said, as if he would have admitted anything else. "Come from Chiang Mai. Good blowjob. Like big man."

"OK," said Keller as if the last sentence had decided him. The best salesman always flatters his customers. He turned to see if I had decided yet. Number 23 wore a plain pink dress that showed an interesting cleavage and had a tiny mouth painted with red lipstick. Pink meant she would do anything I wanted, which suited me fine, so I indicated to the manager that she was the one for me. The girls in white only gave a body massage, the ones that wore red did everything except make love. It seemed strange to me that if you were going to rub your naked body over punters for cash, that you wouldn't let him prod you with his cock for a few Baht extra. But women were funny about that, everywhere in the world.

The girl appeared a minute later. She had an armful of towels and lotions and I was looking forward to a soapy sensuous hour or two. Keller had disappeared already with Number 61. Mine told me her name was Nid and giggled appealingly. She led me up a flight of stairs and along a corridor with rooms on either side. Hers was the second from the end. There was no outside window and the room was dominated by a double bed lit by a pale red light. It was clean though a little shabby, like the rest of the establishment. It would be owned by a syndicate of local businessmen and make millions, but there was no point in wasting money on fixed assets when the girls had all the liquid assets under control.

In the corner was a shower and a large tiled area on which lay an air mattress where the customer would recline while the girl soaped her body and then rubbed her breasts, stomach and pubes all over him. I walked over to the bed and started to unbutton my shirt, thinking about Keller's drab existence. But for a quirk of fate and a man called Bolt that could have been me. There were better men than Keller stuck in the same rut. I had my back to the door. I heard a murmur of voices, a male talking with the girl and then somebody came into the room. I turned, naked except for my boxers, and found myself facing two Asian men. One looked hard and menacing. I'd never seen him before. He wasn't holding a gun, which was good, because twice in an afternoon was a record even for me, but he looked like he could use his fists. I recognised the second man, and my heart sank.

3

"No massage for you today, Mr. Jedburgh," the tall thin man in a costly suit and round steel-rimmed glasses said to me. He was Hong Kong Chinese, in his mid-thirties and I knew him well enough to curse Keller under my breath.

What bothered me most was the thought that he had set me up, because I couldn't see how else I would have found myself half-naked and facing hired muscle for the second time that afternoon. He should have been more loyal to an ex-colleague. The next time we met, I promised myself, he would regret it.

"*Gam ngaam ah*," I said in Cantonese expressing my sarcastic surprise at seeing Sebastian Tse in a Patpong massage parlour. It made sense since his boss was the sort of man who might have shares in this kind of cash cow. "Can I put my clothes back on before you shake me down? You can see I'm unarmed."

"You better had," Tse said, looking me up and down. "Mr Tang is looking forward to seeing you again, but not like that I fear."

"Hasn't he heard of the telephone? People use

it to make appointments. What are you doing in Bangkok anyway? I suppose Mr. Tang is next door having a rub down from Number 69."

"Upstairs," Sebastian said, by way of an order, not information. He spoke excellent English. He had studied Accounting and Finance at some University in Canada and probably even had a Harvard MBA.

Traditional Chinese families sent their children overseas to be thinly veneered in a Western education that would fool foreigners into believing they were dealing with someone who shared their values and desires. But a few years of study at business school couldn't outweigh a culture that has developed independently for three millennia. Scratch Sebastian and underneath you would find the face of a Mandarin from the Ming dynasty.

"Are you his bodyguard?" I asked the other man. He was wearing a leather jacket, jeans and a scowl.

"This is Captain Suvilit. Royal Thai Police. Anti-Drug Squad," Tse explained.

"We are well connected, Sebastian." Suvilit glared at me. He'd understood the insult.

I finished buttoning up my shirt. The unpleasant scenario, on top of my encounter with Kronk, was making me feel decidedly irritated. I took my time. There was no way I could have fought my way out of the warren of the massage parlour and with Sebastian having brought a bent policeman as insurance, I would only end up in jail if I tried.

Sebastian and the Captain waited patiently like Roman legionnaires, waiting for Christians to finish their prayers before escorting them into the arena and a friendly interview with the lions. When I'd taken as long as I could, I followed them through a fire door and up two flights of stairs.

"You should be careful in these places," Sebastian said. "It is easy to catch AIDS these days."

"Your boss has an interest in this place?" I asked. He nodded. "Then I can be certain every one of the girls will be diseased."

"That's not a nice thing to say, Bill. You know, we are businessmen. It would be bad for business if customers complained, but we can't stop AIDS."

"I'm not bothered about AIDS. I've never met anyone who has AIDS. That's seven years down the line if it comes. And I don't sleep with little boys or inject drugs. You pay your money, you take the risks. Don't tell me you've never had a hostess girl from the 'Volvo' night-club or your boss's 'New Empress Club'?"

"That's different. They are Chinese girls." He spoke with the smirk of a man who probably believed that the Chinese race was genetically incapable of being infected by the disease. It was a common misconception.

We'd arrived outside a door barred by a metal

gate. Beyond it, a desk so shabby it could have been Hong Kong Government issue dominated the room. On the desk stood the kind of telephone that I thought had gone out of service with the demise of black and white movies. Two stained beige settees formed an L-shape around a coffee table with a cracked glass top. Incongruously, on the table stood an unopened bottle of Remy XO Brandy and a quartet of glasses that still dripped water down their sides. I was disappointed. Tang was usually seen in better surroundings.

I dropped my bag on the unswept floor expecting at any moment to be attacked by a rabid rat. There was another door leading to a second room. I watched it expectantly while Sebastian poured us a drink each. We sat quietly. I enjoyed the quality of the liquor, hoping the glass would not give me a cold sore.

Captain Suvilit chucked the brandy back like a man used to drinking cheap vodka, then continued staring at me as if trying to memorise each feature of my face. Or perhaps he was trying to measure me up for a charge that would put me away for a lifetime. I wasn't too happy with his presence, as the police here took drug smuggling seriously and the prisons were full of Europeans and Americans. He sat still but looked very shifty for a man of the law.

"How are the 14K and the Sun Yee On?" I said, making small talk. "Are they still murdering each other and their families as an alternative to birth control?"

"Mr. Tang will not be long." Sebastian said ignoring my comment.

As predicted, his boss arrived a few minutes later. Tang Siu Ling was a small, stoutly built man with the flabby cheeks and double chin of the successful Hong Kong entrepreneur. His hair gleamed with traditional hair oils and his thick black spectacles made him look like a myopic toad that no princess in her right mind would kiss or mess with.

He came into the room and smiled at me genially as if I had come to tell him that his horse had won at Happy Valley. He was not Cantonese like the majority of people in the colony where he lived, but a Chiu Chow, a region in China that had sent its children all over the world in search of prosperity. All over South-East Asia, from Penang to Jakarta, Ho Chi Minh City to Manila, the Chinese had settled in hope for a better tomorrow and, being gifted traders, had mostly done well.

The majority of the ethnic Chinese in Bangkok, some settled for two or three generations and controlling extensive businesses, were Chiu Chow, which explained Tang's presence in Thailand's capital. In Indonesia the wealthy Chinese merchants had been persecuted and thousands murdered during riots in the early 1960s. On the whole they tried their best to blend in without losing their racial purity.

I stood up because there was no need to be impolite to him yet. He shook my hand.

"Mr. Bill... How do you pronounce your name?" he asked. He spoke good English but not the transatlantic perfection of his right hand man

"It's a small town in the Scottish Borders. Most people try to pronounce it like Edinburgh, but it ends in 'burr' like the rough edge of metal that has a tendency to scratch, or the prickly thing that sticks to your clothing."

"I have never heard of this place. Edinburgh I know. I went there on holiday once. Did you enjoy one of the pretty little girls downstairs?" Tang came from an age that had studied hard, knowing English to be a necessary adjunct to a good commercial future. The accent was harsh, but his usage and fluency were impressive.

"Your messengers didn't give me a chance," I replied bitterly.

"Then we must make sure that Sebastian gets you your money back," he said sensibly. "We are a commercial enterprise and cannot have disappointed customers. We rely on word of mouth for business."

Sitting down opposite me Tang placed a black plastic briefcase on the desk. I noted his watch, a diamond-encrusted Bulgari, which contrasted with his casual slacks and Fred Perry shirt.

"Have some more brandy," he invited.

"I've had enough. What do you want with me?" I was getting irritated now and I didn't care who knew.

He looked positively embarrassed. I didn't know why, because he was a callous, selfish, and greedy creature. And powerful. He was the acknowledged leader of the Wo Hop On Triad, not the largest but one of the more influential Triad factions in the territory. They controlled nightclubs, prostitution, loan sharking, gambling, dangerous drugs, most other dubious means of turning a fast buck and of course an endless list of entirely legitimate business ventures such as transport companies, couriers, pet shops and dry cleaners.

"I want to give you a chance to make some money," he said politely.

"Not interested," I said.

"Jedburgh, I am offering you a job and will pay very well." I took a breath, then told him what I thought:

"First I don't need a job, I have my own business. Second, I'm on holiday and third, any job that you need doing will be completely illegal or dangerous. And if you want a *gwai lo* to do it, it'll be both."

I wanted to let him have a few more choice insults but my tone had been rude enough, so I stopped there. Tang was an important man in the Hong Kong community: on the council of the General Chamber of Commerce, a Vice-

Chairman of the *Po Leung Kuk*, the Society for the Protection of Women and Children, on nodding terms with Legislative Councillors, and one of those irritating men that were too distant from the actual commission of crime to be ever nailed by the authorities. In short, not someone to idly jostle in the cafeteria queue.

"I've been told that you are very direct. I can see it's true. Please stop thinking so badly of me. I am a businessman and I spend my time making money. Money is very important. It is the only thing that can ensure your family's happiness and give you a good life. Money makes life worthwhile. Don't you agree?"

"I don't disagree. Money is pretty damn important."

"But you are telling me that you don't need my money. You can't tell me that you have enough money. Nobody has enough money. I don't have enough money. Li Ka Shing, Y.K. Pao, they don't have enough money. I know you need money because I have been checking. You are how old now? About thirty? Most people, Chinese men, will be married already with children. They will have some property and a beautiful car. And how about you? What do you have?"

It was a rhetorical question, which I felt sure he would answer in due course. Tang was not the type of man who went into any venture half-cocked. If he wanted me for something he knew as much as there was to know. But I hoped there were some things he didn't know about me - however much money had been flung around researching my background.

He came around the side of the desk, shaking his finger at me. "Not a pot to piss in," he said, triumphant at his command of the idiom and went on, "I know a lot about you. We have a lot of friends in the Police" He smiled coyly. I knew what was coming. Some bent Station Sergeant was a little bit richer from a bit of file copying in his spare time.

"So you've read the whole of my P-file from when I was in the Force. How clever of you. Why my file?"

"I was looking for something special. Some people remembered you and mentioned your name. Yes, yes, very interesting reading." He turned the pages. Over an eight-year period my file had attracted an extensive collection of other people's assessments of me. Some of those had been written by complete morons. Others were not far off the mark.

"'At times he can be incredibly selfish and arrogant which puts doubts on his ability to work well in a team,'" Tang began to tell me about myself. That was Ross Templer.

"'Inspector Jedburgh has a good grasp of Cantonese and gets on well with his junior officers although at times he is unorthodox and does not obey or seem to know the regulations of the Police General Orders manual. I have had to reprimand him several times for setting a bad example to his men. He usually shows respect to his senior officers but can be rude and too direct.'" That sounded like K.K. Tong, a nervous and self-important paper shuffler who had objected to me wanting to do the job rather than scribbling minutes into his pale blue Investigation Files.

"Here is a good one. 'Senior Inspector Jedburgh was today commended for good leadership and quick reaction in a hostage situation. His dynamic intervention resulted in the arrest of two men who will be charged with a number of firearms related offences and the robbery of a goldsmith shop in Yau Ma Tei.'"

Tang was enjoying himself. It gives quite a feeling of power to have a person's life in one's hands. I noticed that Suvilit was listening with interest.

"You are clearly a capable man. You are a very good shot. You are fit. You are intelligent. You are a highly trained specialist who worked in G4, the VIP Protection Squad, and the Special Duties Unit at Fanling, our famous Flying Tigers. And before you joined the police you were an officer in the British Army for three years."

He was right. If I had been writing my resume that would have been a pretty good summary. I was proud of my time in the RHKP. It had made me the man I was today, for better or worse. Tang sat back down in the chair and Sebastian poured him a glass of brandy and refilled my glass.

"The real reason that I asked for your file," Tang said, finally getting to the point, "is that you speak fluent German." He smiled like a benevolent uncle telling his favourite nephew that his education was being paid for. I waited for the next insight. I had no idea where the whole thing was leading.

"Born in Germany," Tang had flicked to the front pages. "Father Major James Jedburgh, Coldstream Guards, mother Cynthia. Lived in Germany until the age of eleven when you went to school in England. After school joined the Army Intelligence Corps, Short Service Commission. Then applied to the Royal Hong Kong Police Force.' Since you were assigned by G4 for VIP duties for any German speaking dignitaries, I presume you speak perfect German, correct?"

"I suppose so."

"Then you can help me with my problem."

He produced a brand-new burgundy passport, the new European standard, from his case. It seemed absolutely genuine. I opened it up and recognised my likeness on the inside back cover. It was the picture that had been glued into my P-file. I had short-cropped hair and wore a grim expression, probably taken after a morning of monotonous square bashing under the firm tutelage of the Chief Drill and Musketry Instructor. My date of birth was correct, but the given name was one Karl Graunitz, born in Munich.

I could have told him I wanted nothing of his dirty schemes, but he was clearly a man who went to meetings well prepared and something told me he wasn't going to take no for an answer.

4

Up until now, Sebastian had looked smug and bored as Tang described my service history. He had read the textbook before and knew the salient points. Now it was his turn to continue with the lecture.

"Your rent has not been paid for two months and last week, before you went to Thailand, you sold your car. There are less than five thousand Hong Kong Dollars in total in both your current and savings accounts. The records on your financial consulting company, Finpro, show that you have been operating at a loss since you set up the business. You cannot even afford an office." I nodded, because all that was supposed to be true. I wasn't going to tell him anything different.

"For a man of thirty, you have very little to show," he continued, looking down his nose at me through his glasses. "Everybody in the world respects a man who is successful. You are not successful in business. Mr Tang is offering to pay you ten thousand US dollars for a simple job. He wishes you to pretend to be German."

He looked at me triumphantly, and demonstrated he'd at least learnt something from his time studying in the States:

"This is an offer you cannot refuse."

I thought about it. There were a lot of Germans in Pattaya. A German passport might come in useful. I was always in need of fake identities. Ten thousand dollars for a short job, if it came with expenses, might be useful. But it didn't do to look too eager."

"So, ten grand is the carrot," I said slowly. I pointed at Captain Suvilit. "Is he the stick?" Tang looked puzzled until Sebastian explained in a quick burst of Cantonese.

"There's no stick, no stick. I'm sure you'll agree," Tang laughed.

"What is he doing here then?" I demanded.

"Just a friend."

"Who works in the Anti-Drug Squad of the Thai Police, which suffers from so much corruption that it rotates its senior officers every three months?"

Suvilit's eyes flashed at me. Tang shrugged his shoulders.

"You may think that the Captain might arrest you on suspicion of selling heroin if you do not agree. They are very strict in Thailand about foreigners selling drugs. The courts are very busy, and it takes a long time to apply for bail." He paused and I admired his skill. This wasn't his first attempt at blackmail and he was good at it.

"You don't have to think these things. It is not necessary. I am offering you two thousand U.S. Dollars now and eight thousand when you come back with the information I want."

"You're a slimy Chinese toad," I informed him.

Sebastian jumped to his feet. "Don't talk to the boss like that. You stupid *gwai lo*. Be grateful for the crumbs falling off the master's table."

"Is that a Chinese proverb?" I said.

Tang said calmly: "Ten thousand US is a lot of money. Eighty thousand Hong Kong Dollars. It's a lot of money for a simple acting job."

"Think of all the girls and beer you can have," Sebastian added patronisingly. I had to admit that I was curious. I wasn't half as outraged at the idea of working for Tang as I pretended to be. It just didn't sound like my line of work.

"What's so special about me speaking German?"

"Brandy." Tang wagged a finger and Sebastian poured another round.

"Do you know the expression Right of Abode?" Tang asked.

"I've heard it on television."

"Hong Kong's future is not very secure. Many people are worried and they work harder than ever to make money. Hong Kong people are industrious, that is the Chinese way. Everybody loves Hong Kong but many people are looking for a secure future. They want right of abode in other places to protect themselves in case the

Chinese make it harder to earn money in the future. To have right of abode you need two things, a passport and money. Money is the main thing of course. With money you can always buy a passport. Like that one." He pointed at the passport that lay on the table between us, the one that claimed I was Karl Graunitz.

"Is the passport stolen or a counterfeit?" I asked.

"A perfect copy. No immigration official has ever stopped anyone carrying one of those passports. They are beautiful and very expensive. Made in Thailand by a Hong Kong man. Just as I told you, people are willing to pay a lot of money for them. Not just Hong Kong people who want a safeguard. Mainland Chinese who want to go to Canada and America. Vietnamese, Thai people. Anybody who wants to go into a country unnoticed. It is a good investment. Good quality is expensive, yes."

"You make these and sell them?" I asked. This was getting more interesting. I needed to get into a country unnoticed more often than he could imagine. "Which nationalities?"

"Several European countries now that their passports are the same. Australian, Canadian, American. British too, but they are not very popular. Hong Kong people have no confidence in anything British anymore."

"How much?" I asked.

"A hundred thousand Hong Kong Dollars."

I knew, because I frequently bought counterfeit documents, that he would be selling them for a lot more than that. He just didn't want me to realise their actual value.

The telephone rang. It was more of a strangled rattle than a ring. Tang answered it. He yelled *'wai'* down the phone then listened for a moment.

"*Ho, ngoh yat jan lei*, I'll come in a minute," he said. "I am going for a meeting. Sebastian, you tell Jedburgh the entire story and then come to see me at Haak-Gau's house." He turned back to me. "This is your chance for the big money. And enjoy the girl."

"I didn't say I would do whatever it is you want."

"Come, Bill. Don't be difficult," he said jovially. "I will pay you well. How about twelve thousand US? My final offer." His eyes flickered in the direction of the silent Thai policeman. I had never had any direct dealings with Tang before but his cunning and duplicity were qualities admired even by the Chinese police officers with whom I had worked. I nodded warily.

"I seem to have no choice, but I need to be sure the plan works before agreeing to the proposal. Just to be sure the remuneration is appropriate."

Tang looked delighted, like a casino operator who has just watched the ball land on '0' when the roulette tables are loaded. He knew I was hooked. He'd probably have been prepared to go to fifteen, but I couldn't be bothered with the game.

"We should go somewhere more civilised than this place to discuss matters," Sebastian suggested. I had no objection. The drab room was getting on my nerves. There's only so much slumming that a person can take.

Tang left with Captain Suvilit. They had made it fairly clear that I had no choice in the matter. If the policeman's services were required to put pressure on me later, they believed I would not be difficult to find.

If I really wanted nothing to do with Tang's plans, no crooked policeman or the threat of time at the notorious 'Bangkok Hilton' prison could persuade me. I knew a few people in Thailand myself who would help me out. However, an altercation with the law at this stage of the proceedings was something I needed as much as genital warts.

The Shangri-La Hotel, Sebastian's idea of somewhere more civilised, had enormous panoramic windows that looked out over the *Chao Phrao*, the River of Kings. He explained that Tang kept a suite there and rooms for his associates. The next hotel further along the river was The Oriental, reminding me that I would have to pay a visit there soon to investigate my mysterious gunman and his envelope.

They were serving high tea in the lobby. We ordered a pot of Earl Grey from a waitress whose legs would have fetched her a fine price had she been willing to bare them on a Patpong bar top.

"As you heard, Bill," said Sebastian with cool familiarity now, "Mr. Tang has been dealing in the manufacture and sale of counterfeit passports to interested parties. We were making them here in Bangkok because it is safer and cheaper than Hong Kong and a good distribution centre. It is potentially a very lucrative business especially because our product is by far the best on the market." He paused as if he were a Marketing Manager giving a corporate update.

"Why are they the best?" I asked, professionally curious.

"It is not easy to make good passports. You have to understand the texture of papers, the watermarks, the laminate, the printing has to be accurate to the thousandth of an inch, the ink has to match and with some new models they have bar codes designed to be scanned by computer. There are security features such as intaglio printing on the front and back of paper, and the inks react if they are tampered with."

He poured our tea into china cups, like a mother hen. He was a true bureaucrat. They existed even in Triad gangs. He winced when I added milk – like most Chinese he drank his black. The bergamot flavouring worked its way up my nostrils and extinguished the smell of the massage parlour. A string quartet was trilling from the speakers. Patpong seemed a world away. Sebastian slurped his tea in the approved Cantonese manner and continued:

"Luckily we had working for us an old man who was a true artist in forging documents. As is the Chinese tradition, before he died the father passed all his skills and knowledge to his son, who being a modern man was interested in studying computers and going to the States. Mr. Tang arranged for all that and for the last two years since returning from his studies the son has been designing computer software to make counterfeit passports accurate to the smallest detail through digital processing. He has also blended these modern ideas with the old techniques he was taught by his father. The Forger, as we call him, is a very intelligent and creative man as you can see from the quality of the passport Mr. Tang showed you."

He was leaning forward over the low table, speaking in a hushed voice. We appeared like any number of conferring commercial men contesting the details of a scheme that would yield stunning profits for all parties involved. I glanced around the lofty foyer wondering how many other groups were discussing schemes as illegal as this.

"Why did you have to go through that charade with Robin Keller?" I asked. Sebastian looked irritated that I had changed the topic suddenly. "What have you got on him that he'd help so willingly?"

"We threatened to expose details of his private life that would probably end his career. We needed someone who knew what you looked like and whom you would not mistrust, to bring you to a convenient place for a conversation."

"Always up for a little bit of blackmail, you Wo On Hop boys," I said, dropping a dollop of clotted cream onto a warm scone. He flinched imperceptibly at the mention of the name of his Triad, as if I had mentioned gang-rape in a cathedral.

"All that is irrelevant to your assignment. Three months ago the young Forger disappeared with all the hardware from the factory. Our sources tell us his work is still turning up in Bangkok. They are being sold in small quantities by a gang of criminals based in Pattaya."

"And that's who you want me to go and become pally with?" Now there was an interesting coincidence. Or perhaps not at all.

He nodded.

"What happens once I'm pally with them? I grab your forger, shoot all of them and bring him back to you?"

Sebastian smiled, quick and impatient. "These Germans control Pattaya. They have many connections. They bribe the police; they run the bars and clubs. We think they kidnapped our forger and stole all the machinery."

"Perhaps they just offered him more money?"

"Don't be stupid. He is Chinese," said Sebastian.

"He won't work for foreigners, even for more money. They must be forcing him." He paused to let the waitress refill the pot. I watched a slim boat flash past on the water outside and wondered when the smog that hung over the city would blot out the sun completely.

"Mr Tang is offering you twelve thousand U.S. Dollars to go to Pattaya and gain the trust of the Germans. You will offer to do business with them and when they trust you must find out where our man is making the passports. We wish to know as much about the set up as you can discover: who the bosses are, where and how they work. Once you have given us this information, your job is finished. We will make arrangements to reclaim our property. There will be no requirement for you to do anything else. We have special people who will take of the rest."

"As simple as that," I said. Sebastian did not appear irritated at my British sarcasm. Neither his Chinese upbringing nor his expensive North American education had made it easy for him to detect the Anglo-Saxon subtleties. He simply nodded.

"You understand why a German will be trusted by them?" he asked. "They are like the Chinese, they believe that they can trust their countrymen."

"I can follow the reasoning, but your plan stinks like a Mong Kok street hawker's *chau dau foo* bean curd."

It was so simplistic it was hard to take seriously. But then I'd heard more ridiculous operational briefings from senior police officers readying to resolve a hostage situation. The Chinese were not tacticians, they were stronger at strategy. So perhaps it was true. I decided to reserve judgement until later.

True to his Chinese character, Sebastian misunderstood my comment. "There will be no more negotiation on the fee," he said sharply. "You will go to Pattaya tomorrow. A girl will come with you. She is an actress, daughter of a former associate of Mr Tang, his protégée in a manner of speaking. Mr. Tang trusts her and you can use her to pass information back to us. Please treat her with respect. She will keep an eye on you and it will make you look more serious if you have an Asian wife. You will have passports that will identify you as Mr and Mrs Graunitz. In this brown envelope is an advance of two thousand dollars and some spending money."

I took the handy little package. I had decided to accept the job already for reasons that were entirely personal. My actual business was in Pattaya and it seemed to involve the same Germans that had stolen Tang's forger. The idea of some female company was both appealing and irritating. She had better have some wits about her, and a decent figure. It could turn out to be an interesting ride.

I stroked the rough grain of my face and sighed. "I'll do it. What about the rest of the details?" I asked.

"In here," he tapped another envelope on the table top, "and the girl will tell you anything else we know." He slid over the envelope. "Where are you going to stay tonight?"

I gazed out of the windows, thinking that, since Tang's money was an unexpected windfall, I should squander it rapidly. "The Oriental, I think."

He blinked rapidly but only said: "The girl will look for you there tomorrow morning. If you have disappeared, you know we can always find you." He had lowered his voice half an octave to create what he thought was a sense of menace. I pulled open the second envelope he had given me and extracted a black and white photograph.

"That's the Forger," said Sebastian.

"I thought it might be."

It was exactly the same picture that Kronk had shown me earlier in the day.

5

By nine o'clock I'd started on my second bottle of Bollinger. From my table there was an excellent view of the river. What looked like a temple stood on the other bank edged by a thousand light bulbs while, downstairs on the open-air veranda, diners romanced each other in a setting that had changed little since the days of Somerset Maugham.

I'd decided to spend Tang's money wisely. I had taken a deluxe room at The Oriental, then booked a table for one at 'Lord Jim's', the hotel's fine dining restaurant. I had my Boss suit pressed by the valet, donned a comfortable pair of matching brown brogues that would have been approved by the old Colonel of my Regiment and a fancy chromatic silk tie that would have made him wince. I'd stayed in the hotel before and found the service consistently commendable: the chambermaids even laid out your toiletries on a starched white cloth by the washbasin and your slippers by the bedside.

'Lord Jim's' was neither inexpensive nor run of the mill. The waiters were attentive and helpful.

I had started with a sliver of gravlax then feasted on the medallions of veal, let my taste buds quiver, had my glass refilled frequently with a 1982 Chateau Haut Brion and thought about death and making money.

At the table next door an American matron with a voice that could have shattered glass was trying to interest the restaurant at large in the story of how she had left her first husband. Had she been my wife, they would have found her garrotted, hanging from the canopy of the bridal bed on the first night of the honeymoon. I eavesdropped cheerfully and chucked down the champagne.

"Of course Marvin was a rich man, but he couldn't give me what I wanted," she was saying, as the waiter approached me with the humidor. I chose a Romeo y Julieta Churchill, instructing him on the size of the cut.

The bill came to 13,000 Baht. Waiting for the change I tried calculating how many girls I could have in Patpong for that if the average cost were 700 Baht a night. In a court case I'd once attended, the defence counsel had asked the female witness, an aspiring model and blackmail victim, if being promised a house and a car for two acts of oral and two of sexual intercourse were not a bit above the market value? Haughtily, she had pointed out that she wasn't a prostitute. The brief had been too polite to suggest that they'd already established what she was; they were just discussing her pricing policy. What made one girl worth 700 Baht while the next one got a diamond necklace or a townhouse?

The change arrived. The answer was eighteen shags and enough left over for a blowjob. I sat and watched the tender blue smoke curl around me, reflecting that there would be plenty of time for all that later. For the moment I wanted to know who had sent me the note in an envelope with the hotel's logo.

In the Mens Room I splashed some water onto my face. It was a good face I decided vainly, listening to the alcohol talking rather than looking at the reflection in the mirror. Already some distance from the sallowness of youth, but not yet affected by the gravity of middle age which padded the skin, creased it and dragged it down. I ran a damp hand through the black hair that had fallen over my right eyebrow and straightened the tie. My eyes looked grey in the bright lights of the mirror, peering out over strong cheekbones, more Norman than Anglo-Saxon. Were they cruel eyes, I wondered fancifully? Girls told me I looked stern and forbidding, not someone who suffered fools gladly. Irritable more likely, since most girls sooner or later made me lose my patience. A suntan was needed, I decided. There should be time for that in Pattaya.

"Can you tell me how many suites the hotel has?" I asked the girl downstairs at Reception who was working on the computer screen checking the bookings. There was a slight slurring of my words as I spoke. I had drunk the champagne quickly and was feeling its effects.

The girl was pretty in a well-cut uniform, even prettier than some of the girls working in the bars up Suriwong Road. The hotel receptionists generally came from well-to-do families with connections. She smiled helpfully. I hoped she couldn't read minds and see the filth in mine.

"Sorry, sir. We have so many."

Her English was excellent, spoken with that gentle inflection that was so appealingly Thai. She was still looking at me helpfully. Perhaps she actually believed I was a decent young executive, a trifle drunk and somewhat lonely. She turned to retrieve a leaflet with all the room rates. There was a whole list of suites ranging from The Royal Suite, which was unpriced, down to the Executive suites on each floor at 7,000 Baht a night. I gave the receptionist my warmest, soberest smile, took the leaflet, explaining I might switch to a suite later and decided to have a little walk around the building hoping that something interesting might turn up.

Kronk had said the man he worked for was a heavyweight, an important Thai who, if he were actually staying at The Oriental, would be in one of the best rooms. But which one? This wasn't some provincial joint that kept a suite or two in case the odd VIP turned up. Even the standard rooms were pricey. I guessed he would probably be in one of the Authors suites, each named after a well-known writer who had frequented the hotel.

There were two wings to the hotel, the River and the Garden Wing. I took the lift to the 15th floor. The 16th floor was the Royal suite and only accessible by private elevator, so I decided to give that one a miss for now. Facing the lifts on the right was a set of swing doors that led to the fire stairs. I looked up and down the corridor, found nothing, then descended the stairs to the next floor down. There was no hotel security about but I walked carefully.

I checked more corridors for the next fifteen minutes wondering if all this legwork made sense. It did, because finally I came across a man, sitting in a chair placed outside one of the rooms. He was reading a paper with less than full concentration. If he wasn't a bodyguard then I was the Queen of Sheba.

The guard had not seen me, so I slipped back into the fire stairs, ran down one floor and came up again in the elevator.

As the doors opened, I found the bodyguard diagonally opposite me. He lowered his paper and gave me a sharp glance. I ignored him and with the rag doll walk of a genuine drunk, which came naturally, headed for one of the rooms at the end of the corridor. I pulled out my key, stood back from the door and compared the two sets of numbers painstakingly.

Ostentatiously, I found they did not match. The man watched me with amused disdain as I staggered back to the lift. Our eyes met and I shrugged. He was squat whereas Kronk had been muscular, running to fat with not much of a neck to boast of and his teeth - a few were missing - were a mouldy black that made him look unwholesome. Dentistry in Thailand was obviously a dying profession. He wore a black suit that looked tight around the shoulders and arms. He was swarthy like a man used to waiting in the sun while his employer had meetings in air-conditioned offices. Underneath his jacket was the malignant growth of a concealed weapon. There was a good chance that this was the room I'd been searching for. It was the 'Graham Greene' suite.

To make sure, I checked the remaining floors but found nothing else of interest. I crossed the glittering lobby, nearly sober again, resolving to come back for Toothless at a more convenient time.

Fifteen minutes later, I was sitting in the 'King's Castle Two' Go-Go bar on Patpong One. I watched a couple of girls doing double takes when they saw me. There was nothing quite like wearing a suit for getting noticed in Patpong.

It was one of the best bars on the strip, zinging with teenage energy and full of the prettiest dancers. What was it like to know that you were young and beautiful? At seventeen you still believed that life would last forever.

A couple of years of hard work and the bright girls were ready to retire. The majority ground on until there was nothing left of their bloom, or went overseas, or married. It wasn't too bad a life on this street. I'd heard of brothels on the outskirts of town that purchased, deflowered and imprisoned their girls, even imported girls from mainland China, probably with passports crafted by Tang's forger. Condemning what was going on around me seemed self-indulgent. These girls were feeding themselves and their relatives and every trick they turned trickled down into the wider economy. Not to help them do so would be rude. Some of them might starve.

"Last time you come you look like poor man, now you look like rich man. You buy me drink," somebody shouted in my ear. The music was guaranteed to keep conversations simple. I looked around and found El sitting on the stool next to me. She was a little pocket rocket, originally from Chiang Mai. Tonight she wore a virgin white bikini and three inch matching high heels which were a present from her Italian boyfriend, who visited three times a year to roger himself silly, bearing the latest fashions for his one and only love. The rest of the time other men brought her gifts and were grateful for her charms.

The first time I'd been with her we'd walked across the road to the seedy but convenient Rose Hotel. She'd clambered onto my cock and ridden me like a berserk Lady Godiva. She was wetter than an autumn day in Yorkshire and tighter than Marlon Brando's belt. Two years on the *Reeperbahn*, the Hamburg red light district, seemed to have done little damage, physically or morally. I was so impressed I took her for dinner and made a point of seeing her at least once every trip.

The name of the game in Patpong was fun but you had to know what you wanted. It was too easy for the inexperienced tourist to be chosen instead of doing the choosing. A smile, a nod, the girl comes and drapes her young body around you and it becomes hard to say no to the drinks and the bar fine. The opposite trap, which I had frequently fallen into myself, was to drink through the night, only to find that the prettiest things had all gone home with faster and more sober men, leaving you to the mercies of dawn, your right hand or maybe an off-duty Mama-san making her way home.

Already it was a busy night, with not a seat free. Men of all ages, shapes and sizes, mainly whites, some Chinese and a few blacks off a ship, sat around the centre bar. Down the middle was a T-shaped stage on which the girls danced and messed around. The music was loud and upbeat.

The atmosphere was buoyed by latent lust. The girls scampered about, happy that the pickings were rich, and their mood brought in more men who could sniff the ambience while walking past on the street.

To get the best out of Patpong you had to decide the shape, size and personality of that evening's dream woman. Then you had to have a yardstick that made choice easy and simple. The fun had always been in the hunt. Going from bar to bar until you found the personification of the vision in your mind without being sidetracked.

If you were aching with lust for a woman who would not have you, the best cure was a week in Thailand. Amongst the thousands of girls going with foreigners, there would always be one who resembled your love and could remove the ache from your groin. Frequently I had come across girls who could have been twin sisters of women I knew in Hong Kong, bedded them and returned home with a wolfish smile of secret satisfaction.

"Why you look so serious?" El demanded punching me hard on the thigh. The cheer must have slipped off my face. I'd started thinking of the work that had to be done and Tang's odd request.

"Too tired to smile."

"Too tired. Too much fucking with other girls."

"Yeah, too much fucking. Too many beautiful ladies and not enough time. Not enough money."

She jabbed me in the ribs this time and scowled playfully at me, feigning jealousy.

There was a tap on my shoulder. I turned. A young honey I hadn't seen before held out her hand. As I reached out to shake she pulled it away and brushed her fingers against my nose. Then she turned and scampered off giggling.

"You like her?" El said. "She my sister. Only 17. She come to Bangkok one month only."

"She's learning quickly." I studied the girl as she began chatting to a broad-shouldered youngster with a baseball cap reversed on his head. On the cap, in yellow lettering, it read 'USS Nimitz'. The sailor, fresh-faced and with biceps that spoke of empty evenings on a ship spent pumping iron, sat down dragging the girl onto his lap. She pulled off the cap and placed it on her own head.

"You wait for her dancing. I teach her. She very sexy dancer."

"Too late, she's already found a boyfriend," I told El.

"No problem, I tell her you good man, she go home with you." I shook my head, smiling. It wasn't my day for taking on the USS Nimitz. There was a certain unwritten code of conduct between girls on 'prior claims'. Inevitably there was some bitchiness. It could not be avoided in any environment where young women worked together.

I was suddenly reminded of the girl I would

be meeting in the morning. Would she be tough, practical, or simply an irritation? I had become accustomed to independence and most women rapidly became a burden to me. In my life women were for recreation. The best I could hope for was that the girl wished on me by Tang might be attractive and amusing. I hoped she'd possess redeeming features and could provide me with more entertainment than aggravation.

Another beer appeared in front of me. "You having good time?" asked the manager, a young man with a scar on his cheek that could have passed as a dimple. He leant across El, nodding pleasantly, shaking my hand.

"*Sabai, Sabai,*" I said. It was a Thai expression implying enjoyment and happiness. We had been introduced months before, but I had forgotten his name.

I enjoyed the action for another ten minutes. Then I paid my bill, slipped five hundred Baht into El's cleavage and left. I hadn't seen what I was looking for. In the final analysis, that's what made places like Patpong boring - all your body's desires could be fulfilled here if you had the time and the money but what I really yearned for was the pleasure of the hunt.

6

In 'Pussy Galore' my hunt found its fox. She fitted the image I'd created in my mind, only she wasn't available. As I sat staring, the Mama-san came and took her off to meet a trio of young handsome lads, all of whom had sharp angular features with long hair and big Mediterranean noses. French, I judged, working in Asia for two years instead of doing their national service. You recognised all the different types after a while. I watched for the period it took me to smoke another cigarette. The boys were making their final choices and I could not fault their taste. The girl got up and went to change into her street clothes, which meant I'd missed my chance. It didn't matter; she'd be back tomorrow and available to the first man willing to pay the bar-fine.

Checking the room I spotted someone familiar. Another face from Hong Kong. It was Scrimple. The last time we'd met was in a Wan Chai girlie bar. He'd just been transferred out of CID after an incident where, in the course of an arrest, another Detective-Inspector had been shot by a well-known Triad. It had not been Scrimple's fault, nor even his case, but facts were not always relevant when the senior officers of the Force reached their decisions. Scrimple had unofficially taken the blame, sentenced by the gossip in the Superintendents' Mess.

He'd always had a reputation in the Force for being bad news. A week before that incident, his best friend had committed suicide for no apparent reason. Scrimple had discovered the body. The suicide was played down in the papers and attributed to work pressure and oppressing debts. I'd never heard the real story but I thought it unlikely. Most young Inspectors lived beyond their means without worrying about it. There was always a fat gratuity at the end of each contract.

A well-nourished gut was the most noticeable feature of Scrimple's otherwise bland personality. Still, he looked fitter than the last time I'd seen him. Sitting beside him was another familiar face, Bob Kenworthy, well-built and good looking with the sort of designer stubble favoured by pop stars like George Michael. Although casually dressed he gave the impression that he took care of his appearance and favoured designer brands. I watched them. They were already drunk, five or six beers ahead of me.

Scrimple had his hand down the front of a girl's briefs while she was whispering lewd suggestions and her price tag into his ear. The disco music started up again. A bevy of bare bodies filled the dance floor, swaying their slim hips to the beat. Downing another beer I felt that familiar feeling of physical detachment creeping up on me. That level of intoxication that made the nasty, brutish world appear a thoroughly splendid place. Two more beers then I'd slow down a little, I wanted to be drunk, not incapable of action. On my way back from the toilet I stopped to say hello to Scrimple.

"How are doing, mate," he said and burped.

"Not bad, not bad," I shouted.

Scrimple turned to Kenworthy and shouted in his ear: "This man left the Force. Bloody good decision. We should have left the Force. Too bloody late now. Can't do any other job."

"You can't do any job at all," his friend observed, intently watching the pair of breasts gyrating close to his eye-line. The girl was on his knee.

"Fuck off, Kenworthy. You're not such a shit-hot copper yourself." He turned back to me and continued: "Kenworthy's been interdicted for nobbing some Superintendent's teenage daughter who's still at boarding school and her Mummy found out."

I grinned. That sounded like Kenworthy. "That's what comes from sleeping with white women."

"Exactly what I said," Scrimple nodded.

"You take what's on offer," Kenworthy said

philosophically. "But a shag's a shag. Leave me alone for a moment you little devil." He tipped the girl off his lap. "I've had a few good years in the Force if they decide to kick me out. Can't complain. What are the salaries like in the commercial sector?"

"What do you think of this one? Look at these knockers. They'll do me all right." Scrimple interrupted, admiring the merchandise he was fondling.

"You're too pissed to shag anybody. Anyway it's too early to pull a slapper. Drink your beer," Kenworthy said grinning. The girl got the hint, hopped off and left for better pickings. "We've already had two birds each in the afternoon."

I sat down next to them.

"You bastard, where did she go?" Scrimple said.

"So what do you do now?" Kenworthy asked me.

"Sell investment advice to expats who earn more money than they can spend. Financial consultancy."

"Make much money?"

"Not enough. There are too many other people doing the same thing in Hong Kong. I'm surviving and I work for myself."

"You probably don't have many customers in the Force given the salaries they pay us."

I nodded. Compared to the private sector, the Government was always a poor paymaster. Even though there had been a big pay rise recently, most younger coppers just spent more. Only when they reached the ranks of Chief Inspector and above did people start worrying about having nothing put aside. Even though it was over five years away, the uncertainty of what would happen to their jobs after the handover in 1997 was already making people edgy, especially those who were married with children. I'd had this conversation a hundred times before.

Scrimple explained he'd just finished a nine-month tour with the Police Tactical Unit, where he was banished after CID.

"Great crack. You spend 3 months training at Fanling, getting fit, riot drills all that crap, then they send you on attachment to the Districts where we just do anti-crime operations and go on the piss all the time. I lost twenty pounds during training then put it all back on again." He looked into his glass and found it wanting. "I need another beer."

"Do you miss the Police at all?" Kenworthy asked me.

"Do I miss the Royal Hong Kong Police? You must be joking. I don't answer to anyone except myself now. And what interests me now isn't putting in an eight-hour shift but making some serious money." I spoke with sincerity. Things had changed a lot in my attitude since the day I resigned the Queen's Commission and then donned the olive-green uniform and black Sam Browne of 'Asia's Finest'.

"Got a card? I might be on the streets looking for a job soon. I'll be fucked if I'm going back to UK to freeze my balls off." I took a business card from my wallet and passed it over. I enjoyed the financial consultancy work that provided me with a cover and an official income. It wasn't complicated. It was basically selling life insurance products. Most of my clients were old acquaintances or strangers one met in clubs or bars.

"What's with the suit and tie?" Scrimple asked. This is Thailand. Nobody wears a suit and tie."

"What the hell do you know about dressing up, you fat slob? You'd be in trouble if the winter uniform didn't have clip-on ties," Kenworthy said amiably. Scrimple replied with obscenities and demanded to know if we'd have another round. His mate shook his head.

"We're going to check out the 'Rome Club'. You coming with us, Bill?" he said. We drank up, paid up and left.

"I prefer to choose my girlies with their clothes on," said Kenworthy shouldering through the crowd. "Leaves more to the imagination, having to wait and see what you're going to get into. If you've got the eye for it, you can tell from the way they move and dress if they're any good in the sack." It was an interesting theory but I wasn't sure if I agreed. I'd slept with a few stylish dressers and awesome dancers who turned out to be less exciting than a textbook on double-entry book-keeping.

We threaded our way through the unrelenting touts towards Patpong Three. The best way was not to amble but stride out with a determined look ignoring their badgering suggestions of massages and endless pussy shows. Going up a dark staircase into a dimly lit club was an invitation to getting ripped off. The majority of Thais were friendly and helpful, but every society has its share of thieving scum who prey on the foolish.

"I thought the gay bars are on Patpong Three," Scrimple said, as he stumbled against a street hawker's stall of coloured beachwear.

"That's right," I said.

"You queer bastard, Kenworthy. I always knew there was something perverted about you. Why are we going to a gay club?" Scrimple demanded.

"It's a discotheque with good music. There's usually a very mixed crowd, some expats, young trendy Bangkokians, tourists..."

"A transvestite floor show and some gays," I added. Kenworthy nodded mischievously. Scrimple didn't look convinced. We walked on along the crowded pavement.

"Last time I came here I pulled the daughter of the French Ambassador," Kenworthy said, smiling at the memory. "What a filthy little slapper she was. She put her tongue in places that I never knew existed. Teach them early in France."

There was a short queue outside the 'Rome

Club'. A banister ran along the front of the building creating a patio. The throbbing bassline of disco music could be heard from where we stood. Young people, mainly Thais, sat smoking, drinking and chatting. Unlike Patpong One there wasn't any noticeable hustling going on. It looked more like young, newly rich Bangkok out for a night of fun. It was impossible to tell which girls worked in hotels and offices or were supported by their parents and which girls had made their money laying on their back. Not that it mattered.

A party of argumentative Indians were in front us in the queue, reluctant to pay their entrance fee. I glanced around. Opposite were several gay Go-Go bars and Cafes with suggestive homosexual names. I noticed a tall effeminate Thai boy wearing an ostentatious turban sitting at an outside table of a cafe called 'Telephone'. Talking intimately with him was a familiar face.

The way Robin Keller was leaning forward touching the boy's arm made me realise what it was that Sebastian Tse had on the jaded policeman.

7

Kenworthy was reaching for his wallet, asking how much the cover charge was, when I tapped him on the shoulder saying I would catch up with them later. The gay cafe where Keller and the boy were sitting was no more than forty feet away. There were knots of people milling about and Keller, preoccupied, had not spotted me. I stood behind a cigarette vendor's stall and considered what to do.

A pockmarked creature asked me if I wanted to have a little boy; good, clean no have AIDS. Curtly, I shook my head. Keller was leaning close to his turbaned companion who was dragging at a cigarette in a slack-wristed way. I was surprised that a man like Keller would sit in a public place with an obvious queen. In Hong Kong, according to the old statutes, the act of buggery and other sexual acts between men still carried a long prison term, and there were always on-leave coppers in Bangkok. Hell, I'd bumped into three of them myself without even trying. He must be drunk, mad, or both.

I had nothing against homosexuality, despite

not being that way inclined. Sexuality was a dial, not a switch and mine had been locked in the vaginal setting for a long time now.

I knew gay men had to hide their feelings in a world that was still hostile to them, but sometimes you could still tell. Nothing as obvious as having an effeminate manner but little things that might add up to a question mark: the way a person spoke about other men and women; the way his eyes moved when a good-looking man entered the room; the fact that he was seen around girls, but never with one.

But Keller had always seemed to be the classic example of a standard copper. A man of limited ambition and intelligence. Someone to be counted upon in the Officer's Mess or for beers with the boys around the girlie bars of the Wan Chai district. Not someone you'd expect to meet sweet-talking a nancy-boy on the streets of Patpong Three. Perhaps it was Bangkok that had dredged up a frustrated passion in an otherwise commonplace man. Bangkok with its intense excesses and an environment that refused no desires. Or he could have always known he was gay and simply carefully hidden his true desires to avoid arrest. A special unit of the Hong Kong police, the SIU, kept a close eye on the homosexual scene despite difficulties in prosecuting offenders. I wondered how Tang had got his claws into him.

As I watched, Keller touched the boy's face. He

said something to him then got up and walked into the cafe. The boy in the turban began powdering his nose from a gold case. Keller had disappeared into the back of the darkened room. I drew out my wallet. There was a button-down pouch for coins. This is where I kept a condom and two innocuous coils of fishing wire. I took one of the coils, palmed it and followed Keller, threading my way through unoccupied tables until I found the toilet sign.

There were five urinals and three cubicles. A strong smell of excrement pervaded the room. A filthy towel lay draped across a washbasin. The toilet reeked of disease and decay. I took in the scene and noted with satisfaction that we were alone. No blowjobs being given in any cubicles. At the far urinal stood Keller relieving himself. His eyes were closed, his forehead pressed against the wall. His cheeks were red; he hadn't been sober for hours. His eyes remained closed when I went and stood next to him. His senses were dulled by the alcohol, his concentration was completely taken up by the act of urination.

The fishing line was 18 inches long and had finger loops knotted at either end. I slipped one end into the loop of the other forming a noose. I checked the door. At that moment Keller opened his eyes and recognised me. I took two swift steps that brought me behind him and pulled the garotte over his neck, jerking him away from the wall.

The garotte was tight in an instant. He didn't have a chance to make a sound. His eyes bulged in panic. I grabbed him by the belt and dragged him backwards into the first cubicle, kicking the door shut. He twitched feebly in resistance. If I failed to loosen my grip he would be dead within 15 seconds. His hands scrabbled at his neck. That was the beauty of the garotte. If taken by surprise the victim panics and wastes the critical seconds during which he could still free himself by doing the wrong thing. He should have been fighting me, attempting to hit me in a vulnerable spot that could result in me slackening the tension on the thin tough nylon. But by now the fishing line had sunk deep into Keller's flabby skin. Impossible to get a finger under the line. His last chance was to strike at my face, elbow me, stamp on my foot, but already it was too late.

I pushed him down onto the toilet seat, wedging his large rear into the bowl and released the pressure on his neck. With the lack of blood to the brain he must already have been blacking out. Like a dark mist descending across the moors on a cold November day.

His mouth closed and opened in quick succession. The lungs that had been straining against the blocked trachea managed to drag down some air. I watched his eyes for a spark, ready to tighten the garotte at the first hint of resistance but he had lost the will to fight. I remained cautious; a sudden jerk would tighten the noose and have him struggling for air. Keller's face spoke of terror and the alcohol would have evaporated with the fear. I leant close to him and said:

"What's the game, Keller? Setting me up for a meeting with that shithead Tang? How much did he pay you?" He couldn't speak so I slipped a finger under the line and loosened it some more. He began shaking and hyperventilating. I slapped him hard on the side of the head.

"Or has he been blackmailing you, threatening to tell people that you're a queer? Is that it? You've been helping out Mr. Tang for some time because you're frightened of anyone finding out that you like screwing little boys?" I spoke in a fierce whisper, keeping an ear out in case anyone else came into the toilet.

His flies were still undone. There was wetness all down his trouser leg. He tried to speak. Finally he managed it: "Didn't have a choice. Believe me. They forced me. Didn't think it mattered. Just offering you a job. They said."

I jerked on the garotte and snarled: "You could have told me what was going on. Don't you have any loyalty to an old mate? I don't need a slime like you packaging me up for Tang because he knows things about you or you owe him. You're scum. Selling out a man you used to work with. You have no respect for friendship. Loyalty to your friends. That's the most important thing after money in this world."

"I didn't mean it. I've just got too many other problems," he gasped.

"You're pathetic."

"I had to do it. Don't take the job if you don't want to."

I smiled grimly. "It's too late for that."

Keller was coming back to life, trying to get hold of my arm and stand up from the toilet seat. He sagged back down when the fishing wire cut into his skin again. I wasn't sure what to do with him. I was angry and I'd promised myself revenge. It only took me an instant to make up my mind.

8

By half past twelve I stood crushed in a corner of the 'Peppermint Lounge'. From where I stood, I had a clear view of most of the room. Julian McAlistair had once called this vantage point 'the natural Boys' Corner'. Every disco, every bar had one. It had to be close to the supply of beer and afford the best view of the dance floor, without being in the mainstream of traffic. 'Peppermint' was wall to wall with wild partying people. This was the place everyone came to when the go-go bars closed. This was the place where the music belted out loud and fast until the night was gone. Everybody was alive, high, beautiful, bopping to the music.

Nobody cared about anything except the present. The walls throbbed. This year it was my favourite place in the world. It was Bangkok at its best. The club stayed open until five in the morning unless there was a new police chief letting his name be known or it was the bi-annual review of the squeeze money during which period the constabulary punctiliously enforced the laws that prohibited all night entertainment until an agreement suitable to all parties had been reached and the money and alcohol flowed freely again.

I downed two Singha beers in quick succession and felt the earlier pleasant dullness of the brain slowly ooze back. My chat with Keller had been more than sobering. I let my eyes trawl around the room stopping whenever a pretty girl held my gaze firmly.

As it got closer to two o'clock 'Peppermint' became more and more crowded. People pushed through the revolving doors onto the heaving dance floor. Many of the girls were from the surrounding clubs, already off-duty after a short time with a customer, or not working tonight. Some girls were not dancing girls, perhaps they worked in 'Members Only' hostess clubs or were secretaries and students out for a fun time. It was impossible to tell the difference in the haze of the smoke and the energy of the night.

I watched the characters that Asia had attracted to its playpen. A guy in a beaded waistcoat and long braided hair danced with a white girl who had a gold stud in her elephantine nose. A tall handsome black man jived sleekly with a girl whose skin had the ochre lustre of a healthy Chinese beauty. She was nearly as tall as him and raven hair fell straight down to her waist. Besides them schmoozed a couple I recognised from Hong Kong. A fresh-faced English lad, in slacks and a striped red shirt, a young broker or banker, with his arms hugging tight a small Eurasian girl whose hourglass figure I had admired several times as she stood behind the front desk of the Mandarin Hotel.

The disc jockey whacked on John Cougar Mellencamp, the song called 'Cherry Bomb', one of those that brought up a memory surge of old wild good times, one of my first trips to Thailand, a holiday to tell your grandchildren about as long as grandma wasn't listening. Little had changed in Bangkok except the prices and the damage to my body brought about by an excess of booze, birds and blow. Why did the fun things in life age a man so much? Why did beer make the eyes bloodshot, cigarettes give you crow's feet? Why did you need to have a good clap doctor on speed-dial?

Close to the revolving door I spotted El. Now in an orange dress topped by a matching hat she stood out from the crowd like a rabbi at an Irish wake. She was holding a man's hand now, and the man was Kenworthy. They must have met at the Rome Club.

He spotted me, then pushed through the crowd dragging the girl behind him. She held onto her hat valiantly like Mary Poppins being pulled into the skies by her umbrella. I couldn't hear what Kenworthy said at first. Finally, he leaned in close and asked me where I had disappeared to.

"Saw an old mate. We had some things to

talk about," I said truthfully. "Where's your fat friend?"

"Decided to run back to 'Pussy Galore' and grab one of the girls he fancied before they closed."

I looked at my watch. It was quarter past two already.

"This is El," Kenworthy said jerking his head at the girl by way of introduction. She smiled shyly pretending not to know me. I played along.

"Nice hat," I said.

"Nice arse," Kenworthy shouted in my ear.

We appraised her as she stretched herself over the counter to shout at the barman, letting our eyes glide over the small tight rear. "I'd do that," he confirmed leaning close to my ear.

We were shouting rather than talking. A speaker hung exactly above our heads. I nodded. I could have told him she had a great body and a few things more. But that would spoil his fun. When you took a working girl home you might consider that she'd been with a thousand men before but, then and there, she was yours and you put all the rest out of your mind because you were living in the present, living for the here and now.

Kenworthy saluted me with his bottle of Kloster beer. The tequila ladies in front of us decided to move on, perhaps over to the 'King's Lounge'. Then over their heads by the door I saw the girl from 'Pussy Galore' who had left with the long-haired Frenchman. She was still with him and I got the feeling they had not been back to his hotel but spent the time dancing or drinking while he tried to do his utmost to persuade her that he was too romantic and sensitive to hand over cash for an act of love. The young Frenchman could not hide the dazzle in his eyes, the realisation that he could have any woman that pleased and if he were adventurous, anything that he dared. It was an intoxicating thought. I looked forward to depriving him of his evening's work. There were plenty of other girls for him to choose but he happened to be with the only one I wanted.

She sat on a stool against the far bar while he stood next to her. She did not speak. She smiled whenever he whispered or caressed her, which was often, while he swigged from a bottle of Kloster, nodding his head in time to the music. It took fifteen minutes before she eventually got up to go to the toilet. I lit another cigarette then pushed through the crowd after her. The Frenchman had turned his back to order another drink.

The little corridor by the toilets was busy and I was buffeted several times while I waited. When at last she came out she did a double take finding me in her way.

"I saw you before. You are very beautiful." I said in Thai. She stopped, inclined her head with surprise and suspicion, then asked if I spoke Thai.

"*Nitnoy*, only a little bit." Close up she was still pretty and her chest held the promise of soft comfort.

"Is that your boyfriend?" I jerked my head in the direction of the bar. She nodded without making a move to get past me.

"I know he paid for your bar-fine but I like you very much and want you to come to my hotel with me."

She smiled, embarrassed at my directness. "Cannot. Already have man. Tomorrow I go with you. Not tonight."

"What's your name?"

"My name Tuk."

"Tuk, tomorrow I go back to Hong Kong. I stay at The Oriental. It must be tonight. Maybe you tell *him* tomorrow." That impressed her. I looked wealthy. I was wearing a smart suit. I was staying in one of the most expensive hotels in town. Obviously she was interested but she liked the handsome young Frenchman. She shook her head firmly. There should be honour among whores. "I tell him already I go with him." She put a hand on my arm, trying to get past.

Somebody put a hand on my shoulder. Tensing, I brushed it off, feeling angry at the intrusion. I turned and found myself staring into the face of my competitor. He was about my height and flushed with anger.

"Leave the girl alone. This is my girl," he ordered in an accent that confirmed his Gallic origins. I did not like his attitude and I did not like his accent.

"We were just discussing some business," I said politely, dropping my cigarette butt on the floor and grinding it with my toe.

"Just go away," he snarled, and I really believed he was jealous. He gave me an audacious little shove which helped me reach a decision. With a snappy nod I butted him hard on the nose. He howled in pain, both hands reaching up to the injured spot leaving unprotected his groin into which I drove a merciless knee. He sat down on the floor with a bump. Blood began to well out from between his fingers but the pain in his crotch would have been more acute. He began whimpering, which made me change my mind about kicking him again. He didn't look as if he would be coming back for more.

I glanced around. A tight crowd kept their distance from me; nobody seemed ready to interfere. I pulled out some banknotes from my wallet and dropped them in the boy's lap. He'd paid the bar-fine after all. Whatever was left over would compensate him for the broken nose. Crouching down next to him I took hold of his chin and said: "Buy yourself another girl, you rude little Frog. Be more polite next time and it won't hurt so much."

I took the girl's arm. She didn't resist when I pulled her into the crowd.

Outside 'Peppermint', *tuk-tuk* drivers milled

around their vehicles waiting for business. Further along I saw Kenworthy and El boarding a machine. He looked intent on getting her home.

"Where we go?" the girl asked me.

"Oriental Hotel."

"Cannot take lady." She hesitated. She knew the better hotels wouldn't admit street girls, even with guests.

"No problem," I said. This wasn't the first time I'd done this.

It was a fast but expensive ride down Suriwongse Road. The driver demanded his fare based on the quality of the destination, not the distance of the journey.

The lobby was sleepy. We got as far as the lifts when a night porter intercepted us. He looked pointedly at the girl's clothes and their contents. Bringing back women to The Oriental had to be done discreetly, expensively or not at all. Before he could say anything, I pulled out six five hundred Baht notes. I looked around. The lobby was empty. That was nearly one month's salary for him, to be earned in the blink of an eye.

"I forgot to register my wife," I said confidently in Thai. I was already in the lift, with Tuk cowering behind me. The porter looked confused first, then puzzled. The doors slid shut on his indecision, but the money had vanished fast into an inner pocket.

"First time I come here," the girl said when we got into the room. She explored its size, checked out the view of the river, kicked off her high heels and flopped onto the enormous bed.

"You very rich man?"

"Not rich enough."

"I think you not good man. You hurt young boy. You know Thai boxing?" She pouted but she was impressed not frightened. My normal fighting technique was *Wing Chun* Kung Fu, learnt from a *sifu* in Hong Kong but I'd spent a few weeks at a Thai boxing camp during my long leave once.

"*Nitnoy*. You want to eat?" They always wanted to eat. Room service delivered fried rice and fruits fifteen minutes later which didn't go badly with the mini bottle of Champagne I opened. There would be hell to pay in the morning, my head would be screaming.

"I think you very dangerous man," she said. I laughed unlacing my shoes.

"I'm only dangerous to stupid Frenchmen who annoy me."

"He was a nice man," she insisted, a fork full of fried rice hovering by her mouth. It did not bother her to eat my food while insulting me.

I plumped up the pillow and watched her finish the food. She stared me in the eye and hurled one of the white linen napkins at me. I stretched out next to her on the vast bed. The chambermaid had turned the bedsheets down nicely and laid an orchid on each pillow.

"Now I take shower," Tuk said. She turned

and walked to the bathroom. I listened to the hiss of the shower while finishing off the champagne, wondering idly about the hair on her mound and the firmness of her breasts. After she had showered, she sat on the edge of the bed wrapped in the damp towel with her fine charcoal hair tied in a bundle on top of her head. The bathroom was steamy. I showered cursorily, then brushed my teeth, impatient to get on with the carnal act of physical gratification.

"What do you like?" she asked

"Play with yourself."

And she did, obediently, unselfconsciously, she stretched and spread her long, firm, smooth legs. Where the thighs joined together there was a diamond of tender hair guarding a little bulb of a clitoris, which she began to caress with one fingertip while with her other hand she held back the folds of skin around it.

The towel slipped apart as she arched her back a little in enjoyment, dipping her finger in her mouth to wet it, tracing circles around the pleasure point. She had done this before many times.

I felt myself getting hard. I rested the tip of my cock against her opening and at the right moment slid into the slippery, comfortable space. She yelped with surprise as if she had forgotten there was a watcher, embraced me with her legs, pulled me into her, firmly impaled herself onto me. I bucked hard into the moist flesh, turned on by the visible pleasure she was having, hoping I could hold it, control it until she could come. We thrust, heaved and panted against each other, concentrating on the end of the journey, the burst of sunlight at the end of the tunnel.

Her mouth was open, her eyes rolled up with only the whites visible. She gasped loudly three times and squeezed hard with her legs. This was my signal and I let go, for several shuddering pulses, the relief unbearably sweet. She clung to me until it was over for both of us.

"I don't like baby. I take pill tomorrow," she said pragmatically. There was a sheen of perspiration across her forehead. Gently I extracted myself. I lay back and closed my eyes. I had enjoyed that. As she lay on the big bed, a post-orgasmic flush across her amber chest and cheeks I kissed her softly on the mouth. Even a hooker needs some tenderness.

"You want me to stay?" she asked. I shook my head. There was some work to be done and I had no further need for her. Perhaps, I told her, I would come looking for her again another time.

Wearing a pair of jeans and the smelly T-shirt from earlier in the day I took her downstairs to make sure she did not get bothered by the hotel staff. A taxi driver ran over for the business when he saw us at the doors. I patted Tuk on the bum, kissed her on the cheek and went back to my room where I had an ice-cold shower and drank two glasses of Evian. It was four in the morning when I took the lift back to the floor where the bodyguard should by now be waging a losing battle against weariness outside the Graham Greene Suite. With luck he had already lost and was snoring a treacherous sleep.

In the silence of the little hours the lift doors opened raucously. Bright-eyed in front of me, and staring straight into my face, was Kronk.

9

We were both surprised. I'd expected a sleepy guard sitting in a chair by the door trying not to nod off, jerking his head up each time the neck muscles relaxed into sleep. The doors of the lift closed behind me and we confronted each other, three feet between us. I raised my hands, palms facing forward to prove that there was no threat.

"I want to talk to your boss. It's about the man in the photo you showed me."

"He sleeping."

"Wake him up and tell him the *falang* wants to speak with him."

Kronk shook his head slowly. He drew the same tired Smith and Wesson from a holster at the back of his trousers.

"You turn around," he instructed. I obeyed on the assumption that, without a silencer, Kronk was unlikely to shoot me in the back in the corridors of a luxury hotel. He rested the muzzle of the weapon on my spine while he patted me down for a weapon with his left hand. I had been taught that being so close to your adversary was careless. The instructors, two dour professionals from the SAS who took us gung-ho lads from the Special Duties Unit of the Royal Hong Kong Police only half seriously, advised that when you were close up to a suspect you should completely dominate. Get your adversary to squat or lie down, if possible, with a knee in his back. Kronk had picked up his techniques from the sort of American cop shows where the hero wore stubble and designer clothes and the guns shot blanks.

When he was satisfied that I was unarmed he stepped away again to ponder whether he should disturb his master. He was still within an arm's length of me, so I turned on my heel and hit him hard in the throat. My timing was good; he staggered from the blow to the Adam's apple. It was an underrated target area and could easily kill a man, but I had held back because, as much as he had pissed me off earlier, it didn't suit my plans to kill him. I spun further and stepped behind him, got my left arm around his neck and twisted the gun up and out of his fingers as taught. He bucked against the stranglehold, which made me shift my balance. I recovered, got one knee right up into the base of his spine and forced him down onto the ground. He was a strong bastard, but I had practised the moves many times. The gun was still in my right hand and I juggled it until I was holding it firmly. Then I jumped off him and waited until he caught his breath and sat up.

Kronk stared at me with venom, rubbing his throat, through which rattled laboured breaths. The next time he burst into a hotel room while I was hammering away at a girl there would be little mercy from him. I had made an enemy for life - which was relative depending on how long either of us lived.

"Come on. Open the door," I said.

He got up with difficulty and approached the door. The moment that he turned the handle I kicked him hard in the buttocks. That sent him reeling into the well-lit interior of the suite's reception room and sprawling onto the floor. There was no one else in the room but the lights were on. It was ostentatiously furnished. A closed door led to the bedroom. The remains of a lavish midnight feast lay on a delicate side table and the air was heavy with stale tobacco smoke.

Shutting the door behind me, I locked it, in case the other guard returned. By now Kronk was back on his feet. His eyes spoke of murder, but he knew that this time I was in control. I smiled, pointing at the far corner of the room.

"Stand there," I ordered. Reluctantly, he complied. I went to the bedroom door and put my ear against it. Coming from inside the bedroom I could hear moaning, indicative of sexual activity. Somebody else was going to be interrupted with their trousers down for a change. I glanced quickly over my shoulder to ensure that Kronk had not moved. He glared at me like a schoolboy punished by the headmaster. Carefully I twisted the handle and slid sideways into the room.

The bedside lamp was on, shedding light on a revealing tableau. Facing me at a slight angle was an attractive Thai girl. She was naked except for long raven hair as she knelt on the king-size bed, being buggered by a trim middle-aged Thai man. The girl hadn't noticed me. She was resting on her elbows whimpering under her breath at each thrust into her abdomen. The man froze as he saw me. There was neither fear nor embarrassment in his manner. Nothing nervous about the way he spoke, even though a white stranger had walked into his bedroom holding a gun. I admired his style.

"Who are you?" he demanded in excellent English. His eyes flashed venomously. The girl looked up at the sound of his voice. A damp sheen glistened on her face. Her eyes were glazed as if in pain or from drugs or drink. The man extracted himself from her with the casual air of someone zipping up their flies in the lavatory. He pushed the girl aside as if she were an unfinished meal and he had lost his appetite. She rolled into a silent ball and lay still.

On the floor I noticed a crumpled tube of KY jelly next to jockey shorts and grey silk underwear that had been torn from its owner. A lone high-heeled court shoe lay discarded under a chair. I hadn't answered the man's question because I was assessing what I saw.

"Do you know who I am?" the man said standing up and reaching for a towel. His accent was recognisably Thai now. I watched his movements carefully. The prone girl appeared to have passed out.

"General Charoenchati. I hadn't expected a man like you to be employing a neanderthal like Kronk, but now some things are a bit clearer."

"What is it you want? You are the Englishman I sent Kronk to deal with this afternoon. Was my message not clear?" He lit a cigarette and stared hard into my eyes. The top of the lighter snapped shut in the quiet room. I gestured with the revolver.

"Let's go in the living room and talk. Nice girl, General. Where did you find her?"

He answered irritably. "It is called 'The Abbot's Club'. Not a place for foreigners. You can get your girls from Patpong."

"If all the girls are as pretty as her, I think I should try it." The General continued studying me coldly. I had moved away from the doorway and suddenly Kronk appeared framed in it. He looked helplessly from me, to his gun, to his master.

Moving carefully, we all stepped back into the living room and I faced both men across a solid dark coffee table. General Charoenchati seemed obliviously to the fact that he was wearing barely any clothes. His face displayed a noble arrogance, the result of being born into one of the kingdom's favoured families. His manner implied that he had the habit of command, accustomed to being obeyed. It was hard to guess his age, but I supposed him to be in his fifties.

"Now you can put away the gun. Unless you want to kill me," he said.

"I don't. I want to ask you some questions." I laid the weapon on the table between us, daring Kronk to make a grab for it. I knew I'd be faster than him and probably so did he. It was possible that he wasn't smart enough to realise. The General must have had the same thought because he said two sharp words in Thai and Kronk relaxed visibly.

"Who told you where to find me?" the General asked as he leant forward to flick his ash into an ashtray beside an empty bottle of Chivas Regal. It was littered with cigarette butts, some imprinted with crimson lipstick.

"I found you myself," I said. "I'm a smart, resourceful individual and I used to be a policeman, General. I know who you are because you are a well-known personality, but I do my best to remain anonymous. Why should you think it necessary to send me threatening messages and how did you find me?"

"If you are a smart man, then you should understand my message," he said. "I am disappointed that you have come here and threatened me. Not many people are that brave. Not in my country. Even you should know that, even if you are a *falang*."

"You are right," I said smiling. "I'm here because I know your reputation. I want you to explain to me exactly why you sent Kronk to warn me off."

He said, carefully: "You have an interest in the man in the picture. I want you to lose your interest. Very simple? My interest in him is different from yours. If you cannot understand my warning then I will order someone to kill you."

His calm menace was impressive, I had to admit. This was the real thing. His was no idle threat or empty talk, despite my bravado. However, in my case I had a few aces up my sleeve, not least of which was the fact that if anyone was going to do the killing it was going to be me. I had no qualms about that sort of thing either. I leant forward and stared the General hard in the eyes.

"I am a reasonable man, General, and I do not wish you to order my death. I don't want to know what your interest is in that man. I simply want to know why, according to your information, you believed I had one that conflicted with yours? Because I had never seen this picture before until Kronk showed it to me."

The General raised an eyebrow and pondered my question, clinking the ice cubes in his empty glass. In my book he was an entirely more frightening person than Tang or Tse who lacked the intelligence and clout to truly scare me. Whereas Tang was crass, *nouveau riche* and clever, Charoenchati was smooth, cultured and cunning. In the final analysis both were greedy, selfish and highly dangerous men.

"My friends tell me that you are in Bangkok to work for a Triad boss, Tang Siu Ling, from Hong Kong. You are going to locate a skilled forger for him and bring him back to Hong Kong to make passports. I have other plans for this forger. You and your Chinese boss would do well not to interfere."

That stumped me. Charoenchati knew of my meeting with Tang before it had occurred. I suspected Captain Suvilit might have a number of people providing him with brown paper envelopes stuffed with Baht. Given Charoenchati was that well-informed I wondered whether he might also know the real purpose for my visit to Thailand. I'd have to give it more careful thought. In the meantime, I decided to play along with his version of the story.

"Your friends must be gifted with the ability to see into the future. When Kronk came to see me, I was doing nothing else except enjoying my holiday."

The General shrugged.

"Only after your man here threatened me with his rusty revolver," I continued, "did I get an offer from Tang to do some work for him. Frankly, I haven't made up my mind what to do, since I'm not really fond of the man."

A look of confusion crossed the General's features, then he seemed to make sense of what I had said and barked some words at Kronk, who replied sheepishly in Thai.

"Given the circumstances," I said, "and your special interest in this forger, I think I could easily be persuaded to drop this whole matter and just go to Pattaya and lie on the beach."

"You will not go to Pattaya," he commanded in a low voice.

"If you insist. I'll go to Phuket or Ko Samui instead. But I really wanted to visit some of my friends in Pattaya."

"There are girls everywhere in Thailand. They will all be your friends for a thousand Baht."

So far, given that I'd been holding a gun on him, he'd been punctiliously polite and controlled. But Asian people had volatile tempers and even the most sophisticated men had the capacity for violence. I was making him look foolish in front of his servant.

"It would have been better for you if you had taken my advice in the first place. To come here was a very stupid thing," he said.

"I think you understand my position, General. I was confused and I wanted to clarify things by talking to you face to face. Like yourself, I am a businessman. I have no interest in working for Tang nor in giving you offence."

"You have already offended me enough."

"I accept that. Now, can we agree that if I don't go to Pattaya, you will be happy?"

He did not reply. He simply stared at me with mean brown eyes, letting me know that the only thing that would satisfy him now would be for me to turn the gun on myself and pull the trigger.

"Very well," he said finally.

"And if I do go to Pattaya?"

"Kronk will kill you," the General said with finality.

I hated being pushed around. I'd been willing to give the General face and forget about Tang's proposal, but I was not going to walk out of this room feeling that I had been intimidated.

"What will you give me in return for the courtesy of obeying your instructions?" I asked.

He lit another cigarette and considered me with amusement. "You are asking me for money?"

"I'm doing you a service. Services are usually rewarded."

"I am rewarding you with your life."

"I'm not some shit-bag little street trader you can threaten with big words. You want to kill me, try your best. You want my cooperation then ask me nicely and show me your gratitude."

"You are a fool. An arrogant Western fool," he said with finality. For a minute we sat in silence playing the staring game. I was waiting for Kronk to make his move. Things had not gone the way I wished them to. It was too easy in life to make enemies and this was one I should have avoided. But we all have some fatal pride in us. A man like Charoenchati could have been a useful ally rather than a bitter foe, but I had chosen to saddle this horse, so I had to ride it.

"What's so special about this little forger?"

"Nothing, he will be killed."

"Lots of killings on your agenda, General."

"That is life in Asia. Now what is your choice?"

"It's up to you. I'd like to go home." I was beginning to mellow. I didn't need the money. I had found out as much as I was going to. My head was starting to ache from the drink, so I reined in my pride. "I'm going to leave and I'm not going to interfere in your plans for killing. That should make you happy. But if I look over my shoulder and see Kronk there, I'll shoot first."

"You speak like the mouse who is about to be crushed by the elephant's foot."

I nodded amicably and picked up the gun. His eyes followed me with interest.

"Oh, and I am going to keep this battered old revolver because I think you should buy Kronk a new one. Bangkok can be such a dangerous place and a man should have a good weapon - not a rusty old antique."

Slowly I backed out of the room watching them both carefully. I shut the door and ran to the fire stairs. When I got back to my room, I bolted the door and considered what had been said. General Charoenchati had lost face, but he should be content because I had agreed to do as he demanded. Perhaps, despite his obvious urge to kill people, he might let me be. Until the moment when he realised that I was not going to change my plans.

I still intended to go to Pattaya.

10

On the assumption that the General would not imagine I was staying in the same hotel, I considered myself safe for the time being and went to bed, but not before placing the revolver under my pillow. It was not until the telephone rang that I woke from a deep alcoholic sleep.

"Could I speak to Mr. Jedburgh, please," a woman's voice said slightly hesitant. She had a strong French accent and for a moment I was disoriented. I looked around the room and my eyes focused on a half-filled glass of water on the bedside table.

"This is Jedburgh." The sound from my throat sounded alien, a husky croaky sound that told me there had been too much tobacco the previous night. I drained the glass and fished the Smith and Wesson from under my pillow.

"My name is Simone de Marelle, may I come up to your room?" The sound of her voice was unfamiliar. It was a nice voice: young and sensuous and French.

"Come up," I said. "I have no idea who you are, but..." I found myself speaking into dead air:

she'd already hung up the phone. My mouth still felt dry and the previous night's excesses were throbbing in my temples. I checked the Rolex on my wrist. It was nearly noon. In the bathroom I found a soft thick robe, with the hotel's name on its pocket. I looked into the mirror and saw a strange, unshaven man facing me with crows-feet around his eyes. Before I had finished gargling with Listerine, in lieu of toothpaste, the doorbell rang. I picked up the revolver, checked the cylinder and approached the door cautiously. Through the spy hole I could see the outline of a woman with black hair cut around the ears.

The girl in the doorway of my hotel room appeared entirely Asian. She was beautiful by any man's standards. She smiled and blinked long eyelashes at me, taking in my disheveled appearance. Her high cheekbones and Chinese features told me she was not a Thai. My eyes dragged themselves reluctantly away from her face and behind her to ensure there was no hidden danger. My sluggish brain was reminding me that there was a man in the hotel who had threatened me with death.

"May I come in?" she asked in that sultry French accent again. I simply nodded and stepped back, trying to hide the gun behind the folds of my robe. She walked past me and into the room heading for the sofa. I watched her firm bunched calves undulate. She was short, but a pair of 3-inch heels brought her up to a perfect height. Elegantly she turned and settled herself on the cushions, crossing her legs smoothly in a way that showed breeding.

"I'm sorry to wake you up," she said, looking concerned and amused.

"Not at all. I'm sorry I look so terrible. It was a long night."

"May I smoke?" she asked

"Of course." My befuddled senses finally realised who she was. She wasn't a present from Father Christmas unless Santa was Chinese, bespectacled and used a lot of hair oil. "Tang sent you?"

She laughed, making the large round silver earrings flap against her face. "I thought you were expecting me."

"I was expecting someone. I wasn't expecting you."

"Is that a compliment, Mr. Jedburgh?"

"Call me Bill. It's early for compliments, but I suppose it was. I associate Mr. Tang with sleaze and violence, not elegant young ladies like yourself." Her face took on a look of concern.

"What do you mean by that?"

"Another compliment I suppose. Coffee? Something to eat?"

"Just coffee." She extracted a cigarette from a packet of Virginia Slims with a long ruby red fingernail, setting it on fire with a Dupont lighter that made an expensive click as the flame shot up.

As I ordered room service on the telephone, I studied the woman on my sofa. She wore a pale cream suit that came to just above her knees and seemed to have curves in all the best places.

The cheekbones were high, the nose dainty, her skin was slightly bronzed and she was darker in complexion than Hong Kong girls. Her lips were full, generous, painted in a glossy red that promised passion. Her accessories were simple, apart from the earrings, a gold necklace, a Cartier handbag and watch and a diamond ring that could have been a gift from her mother or a lover. It was a pleasant picture to wake up to.

"Were you painting the town red last night?" she asked, smiling mischievously.

"It's very odd listening to your accent and yet you are so Asian."

"Yes, it surprises some people."

"It's very pleasant."

"Another compliment. Please be careful. I'm just like any other girl. I love sweet talk and if you carry on I'll start to believe it."

"I don't have a reputation for being charming," I said, re-arranging my bathrobe with care because she was starting to turn me on, "but you do intrigue me. I'm struggling to work out where you're from."

"Were you disappointed that I wasn't a tall, sexy European woman when you opened the door?"

"On the contrary. I was relieved. When we spoke on the phone I thought you were French. I don't care much for white women."

"I find that hard to believe," she said coquettishly. "I'm sure that's just some line you keep for us innocent Asian girls."

There was a knock on the door and the waiter wheeled in my food and her coffee. I'd ordered Eggs Benedict for both of us, two glasses of freshly-squeezed orange juice and some croissants. It smelled excellent and in my experience was an effective hangover cure. Once I had tucked into a few forkfuls I was able to converse more coherently.

"It's a shame that you are here because of Mr. Tang. I don't particularly like him."

For the first time she looked upset. Insulting Tang was offensive to her and I needed to know why. Until I understood her role in the affair, I would have to be careful in my dealings.

"I have temporarily agreed, against my better judgement, and not without some coercion, to assist Tang Siu Ling," I said. "He told me that I would be accompanied by a young lady and I am delighted it is you. But you should know that I am not happy with the situation."

She nodded, her fingers hesitating over the pack of Virginia Slims. She decided against another smoke, instead sipping from her coffee, waiting for me to continue. I buttered some toast and ate it slowly. Breakfast is an important meal when one gets up late in the day. I watched her and she watched me back with no hint of embarrassment.

"I was warned that you were an irritating person to deal with," she said at last in her soft, sexy French accent.

"What else did he tell you?" Everybody loves to hear stories about themselves.

"You drink and spend your days whoring with bar girls," she said. "You're washed up and virtually broke, which is why you are doing this job and that I should be careful because you have a way with words but can become violent."

"Other than the washed-up part, which is gratuitously offensive on Tang's part, that sounds generally close to the mark. What would make you agree to spend time with a fellow like me?" I asked, offering her a piece of buttered toast which she declined.

"Uncle Tang asked me to assist him and I like to please him."

"Uncle Tang?" I said, curious, because I couldn't see any trace of amphibious reptile in the woman in front of me.

"He's not my real uncle, but he has done many things for my family and took care of my education when my father died. I am indebted to him." She paused for a moment then added: "I am sorry if you feel uncomfortable working for him."

I shrugged. "Don't worry, my decision has been taken. I just wanted to you to know why I'm annoyed."

"Uncle has given me clear instructions. I'll come along with you and pretend to be your wife. I am to keep you out of trouble and to make sure you are doing what Uncle Tang is paying you to."

"And what do you think he is paying me to do? You do realise that Tang Siu Ling is a well-known figure in the Hong Kong criminal fraternity?"

"How dare you. I have known him for a long time and he is a businessman, a successful businessman." She looked affronted, but I suspected, despite her protests she knew exactly what kind of business he was involved in.

"As a former Inspector in the Royal Hong Kong Police I can tell you that his only interest in business is crooked. A few acts of kindness to your family will not change that. Let's change the subject since we will be spending a lot of time together. Tell me about your parents. Where does this odd French accent come from?"

"My father was a Chinese Thai and my mother was half French half Chinese Vietnamese. When my father died, my mother took me back to France and Tang helped to support us. Four years ago, she died and Uncle Tang suggested I should move to Thailand and help him with his business interests here."

"So what do you do exactly?"

"I assist his manager in running the office."

"You speak Thai?"

She looked rueful. "I'm learning. It's hard, but I'm getting better. We mainly use Chiu Chow in the office. I speak a little Cantonese too. Uncle Tang tells me you can speak Cantonese," she said. "They tell me all Hong Kong Policeman are made to learn it."

"I get by. I can also speak a little Thai, and French, for that matter. So what shall we do today, Simone?"

She gave a sweet innocent smile and lifted up her hands in a typically Gallic gesture.

"I thought we'd take a car down to Pattaya after breakfast and see what's going on," I suggested.

"Were you holding a gun when you opened the door to me just now?" she asked.

"Yes, it was a gun. I try to be careful when I deal with men like your Uncle Tang."

"My suitcase is downstairs. We can go whenever you're ready," she said suddenly more business-like. We agreed that she'd go down to the lobby while I packed up. She stood up and smoothed down the texture of her skirt. She held out her hand, the palm slightly upwards in a friendly intimate gesture. I took it and we shook hands.

"To a successful business relationship, Bill."

"To a successful relationship. I hope we will enjoy each other's company. There should always be a little pleasure in doing business."

"You are a bad man," she teased, the emphasis

was on 'man' and she left the room before I could open the door for her. Quickly I packed my belongings. The one good suit, now crumpled, my two ties, jeans and casual shirts. Finally, on top of it all I tossed the rusty Smith and Wesson because it had to remain handy from now on until I could find a more appropriate tool.

The Model 10 was easy to conceal with reasonable power in a small-size weapon. It brought back memories of the dainty underpowered guns we used to carry in the Force. It sounded and felt functional which was the main requirement from a weapon. I had difficulty extracting the six .38 Special cartridges because the ejector rod seemed too short and I had to tip the revolver muzzle up. The rounds looked healthy. I'd rather have had a stainless-steel Model 60, which was better in moist environments, but you took what you could find. The way things were developing I would need something more serious, preferably an automatic, although for the time being this pocket revolver would do. It should not be too difficult to snap up a weapon of more recent vintage when I had a chance.

In the shower I considered the girl. Simone, a sensuous name. I reminded myself not to be fooled by the attractive packaging. She had some quality, and she knew it. Given her closeness to Tang, I wasn't going to be able to sweet-talk her into trusting me. It would be hard to penetrate her aloofness and in doing so I would be playing with fire.

Heading downstairs with my luggage, I found Simone sitting in the lobby next to a big Samsonite suitcase designed to be tossed around by airport baggage handlers. I paid the hotel bill and arranged for a car to take us down to the coast. There was no sign of Kronk or his boss.

The taxi was new and had air-conditioning. We stowed the luggage, settled ourselves on either side of the backseat. It took an hour just to get out of Bangkok. The traffic as ever was appalling, with cars mingling everywhere.

By the time we finally hit the main road, I was certain that a grey Mercedes with shaded windows was carefully following us.

11

The taxi made good speed as soon as the traffic cleared up and I settled back to doze off the rest of my hangover. I wasn't in the mood for chatting and in Pattaya I would need a clear head. I arranged myself in such a way that I could observe Simone surreptitiously through half-closed eyes. She was one of the most beautiful women I had seen in a very long time. I was always attracted to Thai Chinese features and her quarter of French blood added to the allure. I watched her contentedly until I drifted into a half sleep.

The next time I woke we were already a long way from Bangkok. I watched the countryside flash past: flat arable land with hills in the distance and the occasional village with stone and wooden houses. Men and women were going about their business, on foot or motorbike, or standing under small timber shelters waiting patiently for a bus.

"Why were you smiling?" Simone asked, breaking the silence.

"I was?"

"You were smiling in your sleep," she said.

"I was dozing and reflecting on unimportant matters."

"What sort of unimportant matters?"

"Women, relationships, love, lust," I replied.

"You are a lonely man, aren't you? What woman did this to you?" she asked casually.

"No one in particular. Just a long chain of them."

"It sounds like a terrible sad, story."

I laughed and rearranged myself on the seat so I could see her better, glancing through the rear window as I did so.

"A car has been following us since we left Bangkok."

She looked alarmed. "What do you mean?"

"A few hundred yards behind us there's a grey Mercedes."

"How do you know it's following us? Other people might be going this way. It's the only road to Pattaya and Rayong."

"It pays to be paranoid when people are out to get you. Do you think your Uncle Tang might be making sure we are going in the right direction?"

"Why should he do that?"

"Because if our circumstances were reversed, I might do the same." I doubted it was anyone sent by Tang. He had already planted an efficient tracking device on me in the pleasing shape of Simone. I had a shrewd idea it could be Kronk.

Simone pulled out her handbag and twisted

up the red lipstick she found in it. "I think you're trying to impress me with how dangerous our job is. Uncle Tang warned me you would try to play mind games on me."

It seemed to me that Uncle Tang had been working hard in the mind games stakes himself. She seemed to be completely in his thrall. We lapsed into silence again.

"Have you ever been married?" I asked her sometime later.

"What makes you think that?" she said sharply.

"You have an attitude which women often acquire once they've experienced the dubious joys of matrimony."

"You mean I sound cynical?"

"You have to live closely with a man before you fully appreciate our failings."

"I don't agree. I have never been blind to men's faults. But yes, I was married once. I still use my married name, de Marelle."

"And now?"

"Now I do as I please," she said firmly. "Have you never come close to settling down with someone? You're not young anymore."

"I'm too selfish and independent to commit to a permanent relationship. Perhaps I'm waiting for the right woman to make me change." It was a good line and had worked on women many times in the past. They all believed they might be that woman. Simone however looked unimpressed.

"You men, always wanting to present a challenge for a woman. It would be better if you were sincere and treated us well, then we'd take you more seriously."

"It sounds like your husband didn't treat you with the respect you deserved."

"He was French. I discovered they treat women as poorly as Chinese men do. You are expected to be beautiful in public, smile and flirt with only him, then cook and make children. I was young. I thought if a man was handsome and he treated me like a lady, that would be enough for a lifelong romance." She sighed. "I was wrong."

"The French are like that. Once passion dies, the quotidian, everyday life, takes over until some new passion awakes them again."

"True. I left him when I found out he was sleeping with another woman: white, haughty and married." Simone smiled wistfully in remembrance, then used the opening to question me in turn. "How are the English? Are they a passionate people?"

"We're usually cold and reserved, and because of the climate we are terrible lovers, appallingly lazy in bed. Englishmen prefer the company of other men. It's easier for us to communicate with them. Women are an inconvenience, like a beer gut. Just something that one acquires as part of getting older."

"That's it then," she said, laughing. "I'll avoid Englishmen, now that you have warned me. Probably better to avoid all men."

"If that makes you happy," I said, looking into her eyes with a challenge in mine.

She met my gaze for a moment, then looked away. We didn't talk again until we saw the sign that welcomed visitors to Pattaya.

"Where are we going to stay?" she asked.

"A hotel complex called the Sport Resort. It's off the main tourist beat, very clean and orderly, run and owned by some Germans."

"How do you know?"

"I've been to Pattaya many times. I know of the place. I also know that the Germans who control the city, bribe the police and manage most of the clubs, use the Sport Resort as a legitimate business front. They have one of the best-equipped gyms in town there. A lot of the big bodybuilder boys work out in it. When they aren't out collecting the squeeze money or forcing women into prostitution, that is."

"Are the Germans gangsters? Like in America?" she wanted to know.

"Similar. They're well-organised: drugs, prostitution, blackmail, extortion and it seems they are venturing into forgery."

I looked at her as I said that. From her reaction she didn't seem as if she was fully aware to what extent Uncle Tang made his money in these areas as well.

"Is your German good enough to fool these people?" she asked.

"I think so. I'll put on a heavy Bavarian accent, which should be fairly convincing. Here we are."

The taxi pulled into a gravel forecourt surrounded by chalets with quaint bamboo roofs. As we did so a man came out of a large building which I guessed was the gym. He must have weighed over 250 pounds. Long blond hair, like a Swedish schoolgirl's, hung down over enormous shoulder and back muscles. A small plane could have landed on the broad expanse of his tanned and oily chest and his biceps were the size of my thighs. He wore tight black cycling shorts and a string vest that stopped short of his stomach muscles, which looked like an aerial photograph of a Himalayan mountain range. Clipped to his waist was a pager the size of a cigarette packet. He gave us a long hard blue-eyed stare as he swung himself onto a motorbike, a powerful customised chopper with a polished chrome petrol tank.

"Why is he so big?" the girl asked.

"He's on the juice. A few more like that and Hitler would have won the last war." She looked puzzled.

"Steroids and growth hormone injections," I said. "Makes the muscle grow much faster and bigger than normal."

"I've never seen someone with such big arms," she said. Her voice was tinged with fascination and disgust. The large blonde man left in a swirl of dust and engine oil.

"One part of your body can never get larger when you take steroids," I said.

"Let me guess," she joked, "the brain?"

"That's why you need to be naturally well-endowed," I said.

"Twin beds," she instructed the Thai receptionist when we checked in. Our passports, proclaiming us to be Herr and Frau Graunitz, were photocopied and the numbers noted. I had total confidence in their quality.

"I hope you don't mind sharing a room with a stranger," I said as we walked past the open-air coffee shop and bar along a well-tended tiled path towards our chalet. Beyond was a kidney-shaped swimming pool. The place looked immaculately kept. Except for the white flabby complexions on display in the pool it was a pleasant environment.

"It would look very strange if husband and wife didn't share the same room together, Bill," she said. "I'm not an innocent girl anymore. And we're here for work."

When I closed the door, she pointed to the bed closest to it and said pleasantly: "That's mine, Mr. Jedburgh. Please stay in the other one unless I specifically invite you over." It would be hard to get a good night's sleep lying within three feet of her, but there was plenty of time.

"I need a shower," she said. I tipped over the

contents of my bag while she disappeared into the bathroom and began sorting through my dirty clothes. I figured being German the place would operate an efficient laundry, literally and metaphorically.

No woman that I knew could spend less than half an hour in the bathroom, so I shouted through the bathroom door that I'd be by the pool having a drink. I wanted to examine the lie of the land. I tucked Kronk's Smith and Wesson into a bum bag which I belted around my waist and wandered back to reception with my dirty laundry in the bag provided.

In the shade of the open-air bar, I ordered a beer and glanced around. I spent a fair amount of time in Pattaya and I didn't want to run into anyone I knew. The fake passport might stand up to scrutiny, but someone who knew me as Bill Jedburgh would be hard to explain away.

A trio of teenage German girls lay beside the pool. They were at that age where they knew men were interested in them but hadn't quite figured out how to handle it. Beside them lay a man, perhaps their father, reading the German tabloid *Das Bild*. The headline said 'Another Minister in sex, drugs, scandal' next to an unrelated picture of a blonde with enormous breasts. I wondered if I'd ever get to see Simone's. They had looked good through the thin fabric of her jacket, and in sensible proportion, unlike the model in the paper.

The man reading the paper had an enormous, rounded, beer belly that swelled over the top of his trunks. Too much rich German beer and not enough extra-marital sex. At the next table was a gang of young men in their late teens and early twenties. They looked fit, firm and tanned and each had the same sort of pager on his belt as the giant blond biker we'd spotted coming out of the gym.

"*Guten Nachmittag*, Herr Graunitz," a voice behind me spoke in German. "May I welcome you sincerely to the Sport Resort? I am Max Gruber, the Director of the hotel." He was a slim man in ironed jeans and a loose white shirt. We shook hands politely. He had the creased, brown, features of someone no longer in the prime of youth but who took care of himself. "Is everything satisfactory?"

"Just perfect," I replied in the same language, putting on a heavy Bavarian accent. My father had been attached to the British Consulate in Munich for three years while I was at primary school. The accent still came easily.

"*Bitte*, please join me for a beer, Herr Gruber," I said.

"A small glass of Schnapps, perhaps, Herr Graunitz," he said, slipping into the chair beside me. "You are Bavarian?"

"Originally, but I have been in Hong Kong for many years."

"And your wife is Asian?" he asked politely,

summoning over a waitress, who fawned attentively in front of her boss.

"She's Chinese, but she studied in France."

"I must confess, I had the door to my office open when you checked in. She is a very attractive lady."

"Thank you. *Zum Wohl!*" His drink had arrived and we toasted each other.

"What brings you to Pattaya?" he asked.

"Partly pleasure," I said, enjoying the quality German beer. "It's a friendly place for people like us. But I'm also here to discuss investment opportunities."

"What is the nature of your business?" he asked, taking an interest. "I might be able to assist you."

"I've a number of interests, mainly involving real estate," I said, wanting to keep things suitably vague.

"Property is always the best choice in Asia," Gruber said, with a knowing look. "Are you looking into purchasing condominium, bars or something industrial?"

"I have an open mind," I said, hoping to reel him in. "I sometimes like to be a bit more adventurous. I suppose you have been in Pattaya for some time?"

"Four years," Gruber said, toyed with the empty shot glass. "I came out from Germany with a group of like-minded... investors. We have a lot of connections around town now. I'd be happy to be of assistance."

"It would be appreciated. It's always better to deal with one's own people."

"*Richtig*, one cannot really trust the Thais. Behind their warm smiles and soft manner, they can be quite deceitful," Gruber said, lowering his voice. His voice was melodious, like a songbird sitting on a tree. But there was something ingratiating about his smug manner that made me want to push the jagged edges of a broken beer bottle into his face.

"You run a hotel, Herr Gruber," I said. "What do you think of Pattaya's prospects in the leisure industry?"

He looked troubled and shook his head. "The tourist business is regrettably in decline. People prefer the cleaner, quieter beaches of Koh Samui, Samet or Phuket. We feel that Pattaya will become less of a resort and more of a commercial and industrial centre. They are developing the port further north. But of course, there will always be the beach."

"And the girls," I added with a smile. "I am always interested in those."

"There are girls all over Thailand. If there is demand, there will be supply. You are a businessman you know how it is." He stood up. "I must go to attend to my matters. Let me know if I can help you in any way, business or," he paused and gave me a shady look, "pleasure."

"*Das ist sehr nett von Ihnen*, It's very kind of

you, Herr Gruber," I said and stood up to shake his hand. He gripped mine hard and bent his head down for an instant then snapped it back up in the traditional gesture of respect known as a '*Diener*'.

It had been a fortunate meeting. I hoped I would not have to seek out the men that I wanted to meet. Gruber would bring them to me, because he was part of their set-up. I had to hand it to Tang, it had been a good idea to come as a German and to stay in the wolf's lair.

12

I was on my third or fourth beer when Simone appeared, walking along the poolside. She had changed into a light orange cotton dress that complemented her alabaster skin and drew long lustful stares from the men by the pool. One of the youths at the next table gave a low whistle and leered at her. I ignored my desire to get up and break his arm. It was nice to have one's woman, even if she wasn't exactly mine, admired by others.

"You look very nice, my dear," I said, rising to kiss her on the cheek. I felt a slight pressure against my jaw and as we separated, she smiled, her teeth sparkling. She ordered a vodka lime soda and asked me what we were going to do next.

"I thought I'd have a shower now that you've vacated the bathroom. After that I'll hire a motorbike and we can take a spin around town."

"Bill, I'm wearing a dress. I can't get on the back of a bike."

"Sure you can."

She didn't seem to be impressed with the idea,

but I had made up my mind. I missed the thrill that came from riding a big heavy machine.

"Boys will be boys. Haven't you grown out of motorbikes yet?" she said.

"It's exciting," I replied.

She laughed, tossing her head back. At least she found me amusing. Make a woman laugh and you were halfway there.

"Don't we have work to do?"

"I've done my work for the day. Business first, pleasure second."

"What do you mean?"

"While you were washing your hair, I was making contact with the local community." I told her about my talk with Gruber.

"After our ride we could go for dinner at a restaurant that's run by an amusing French fellow."

"It sounds interesting, do I have any other choice?" she said coquettishly.

"You can stay here and go to bed with a good book."

While I showered and shaved, I thought about what I had to do and how having the girl in tow might affect it. I was planning to see two of my closest friends while I was in Pattaya, Julian McAlistair and Harry Bolt. They both knew more about my business than was strictly good for them or me and I didn't want either of them to feature on Tang's radar. That was a risk if Simone came with me and reported back to him. On balance I thought it was a small one. They were both well connected in Thai society and McAlistair's sprawling house was heavily guarded. He lived a good forty minutes by car outside Pattaya, much closer to Rayong. On a fast bike the journey would be a lot less.

Once my chin was smooth again, I returned to the bar and found her deeply engrossed in a Catherine Cookson novel, sipping occasionally at her drink.

"Ready to ride," I asked, "or has the good book won?"

"Let's go," she said and stood up. The sun was waning and the air had cooled slightly. As we walked down to the courtyard, I caught Gruber bending over the computer in reception. His eyes flickered over us briefly and I gave him a brief wave. We took a taxi down to the beach road where motorbikes are for hire. At Soi 18 I knew a man who always kept one or two beauties back for his best customers.

"Where's the black Goldwing?" I asked the man, who was picking his teeth and scratching his rear simultaneously.

"No have now, have accident," he told us.

"Shit," I'd come close to a few accidents on the back of that bike myself. I cast my eye over what else was available.

"You take this one. Very fast." The man slapped the saddle of a Kawasaki CBX with an engine that could have powered a car. I inspected the machine and found it pleasing. The petrol tank and bodywork were painted dark blue. The tyres looked new with plenty of tread.

We haggled for a while and agreed on a thousand Baht a day for ten days. Simone was looking at the bike as if it would come to life and leap on her.

"You're crazy," she said defiantly.

"Never been on one of these before?" I asked. "There's always a first time. Come on you'll love it."

I swung my leg over the bike and fired it up. As I turned the throttle half an inch, the pitch of the motor escalated and I smiled with anticipation at the thrust contained between my thighs.

Simone was still hesitating. Finally, she accepted she had no choice. Tang had told her to stick with me. She arranged her skirt, swung her bag over a shoulder and got on the pillion wrapping her arms tightly around my waist. Neither of us was wearing a helmet. I felt her breasts push up against my back, her inner thighs against the back of mine. There was a warmth everywhere our bodies met and a sweet tingle in the pit of my stomach. I let the engine growl a few more times, engaged the clutch and pulled into the Beach Road traffic.

It was beginning to get dark. Lights were coming on. At sea, beyond the dirty strip of beach, lay motorboats and jet-skis. The sunbathers had packed up an hour earlier and the drunkards and whoremongers were beginning to emerge.

There were a lot of Baht buses - pick-up trucks with benches in the back which served as taxis - ferrying tourists from their hotels to the sights of 'the strip', where seafood restaurants jostled alongside go-go bars and there was late night shopping.

I dodged between little Hondas ridden by Western men of all ages in shorts and flip-flops. Each had a girl on the back, holding on tight like Simone. No man went without in Pattaya. The air was filled with a muggy stench and the honking of horns. We drove carefully to avoid the people ambling along, families promenading and single men hunting for the right bar, while the girls made themselves easy prey or called out to stragglers. A few of them smiled and stared at me, assessing the competition in the shape of Simone.

People smile a lot in Thailand. Everybody seemed friendly. We rode past Soi Diamond where the open-air beer bars were already filled with early evening drinkers. Further down the road was the 'Marine Bar', dominated by a Thai boxing ring that had nightly shows where the fighters pounded each other in front of an appreciative crowd. Above the 'Marine Bar' was a disco, not unlike but three times larger than 'Peppermint' in Bangkok. Here things got busy after three in the morning and the action didn't stop until dawn. Further down the strip we passed the 'Simon Cabaret', already filling up with people who came to watch the transvestite show.

I turned left and we drove through the Arab quarter, strains of strange music coming from their collection of wooden beer bars. Then I turned right onto the Jomtien road where the traffic thinned out and the night began to envelop us. The big bike, growling into the cool evening breeze as if to demonstrate its potency, shot up the steep hill to the Royal Cliff Hotel.

When we got to Jomtien Beach I opened up the accelerator and let the beast show its true form. I felt the adrenaline in my blood, my heart beating with the thrill of its velocity. I held onto the bike like a mad cowboy on an untamed bronco, clutching the handlebars as the tornado tried to tear me from the saddle. I could sense the helpless alarm of the girl behind me and felt the anxiety in her arms as she squeezed my waist so tight it was difficult to breathe. Any words she tried to shout were lost in the tempest of speed. I hunched over the petrol tank, praying there were no stray dogs on the road or drunken lovers while continuing to turn the throttle until it could go no further.

The speedometer needle wavered close to the edge, but I could not see properly through the tears that were streaming from my eyes. We raced into the darkness, following the spot of yellow light thrown in front of the wheels by the Kawasaki's twin headlamps. For a timeless moment the machine and the road blurred and the ecstasy of potential danger engulfed me, until suddenly I lost sight of the road.

Blackness jumped up in front of me. Panic slammed into my chest. It wasn't the right time to die. The road reappeared. The bike decelerated rapidly as I shifted down through the gears and brought it back to forty miles an hour, wiping the back of my left hand across my face. I could hear the hammering of the blood in my head then heavy blows landed repeatedly on my right shoulder. I turned my head slightly and the girl was screaming into my ear, demanding that I stop.

I slowed the Kawasaki to a standstill. My shirt was soaking wet from perspiration, from fear and exhilaration. The bike rocked to a stop. She leaped off the saddle and stepped up close to me, her hair wild and distraught, her eyes blazing fiercely in the semi-light. Her hand went back and shot forward suddenly, striking me viciously across the face.

"Are you crazy? she yelled. "I want to keep my life. It's the only one I've got." I watched her as she fought to calm down, still gasping for breath, her chest and shoulders shaking. Eventually she said, "Don't you ever do that to me again."

I said nothing, just looked into the sky where the stars were as clear as crystal. It was a beautiful night and the fresh smell of greenery came off the trees that lined the road, mingling with the tangy gusts blowing in from the sea. In the distance glimmered the lights of Jomtien and Pattaya and next to me stood a woman who was furious, but all the more attractive in my eyes because of it.

13

We stood in silence for a minute or two. I watched her in profile. The experience had demonstrated her vulnerability but the way she had handled it proved to me she was endowed with inner strength. The engine continued ticking over with a gentle growl. I looked out across the water thinking how women were odd, quirky creatures. Finally, I spoke:

"I didn't mean to frighten you. I just like driving fast."

"Well, I don't," she said and walked away from me to the side of the road nearest the sea. After a few minutes staring into it, she came back.

"I'm sorry I hit you," she said. "I hate it when I lose control. Shall we get on?"

I nodded. The episode had broken some ice between us. She got back on the pillion and we rode at a leisurely pace for another ten minutes until I pulled up in front of a heavy electronic iron gate.

"Is this where your friends live?" Simone asked, with awe in her voice. In Asia, when you are rich, you are insanely rich, and Julian McAlistair had married into some mad money. He and his wife could afford whatever their hearts wanted and everything that their bodies required. The millions were hers. She made it and he spent it, while she was out making even more.

We waited for the security guard to emerge. He must have recognised me, because the gate slid back smoothly. I gave him a wave and noticed that next to a two-foot truncheon he wore a revolver on his belt. McAlistair had told me on my last visit that there was a pump action shot gun in the guard's hut and a direct line to the nearest police station as well, just in case.

The drive wound through clusters of trees and bushes, past a tennis court, a mini golf course and an out-house for the servants with three garages on the ground floor. Julian and Marjorie's bungalow was enormous. It sat directly on a pristine beach with the sea about thirty yards from a terrace that commanded the sort of view people die for in California.

Standing in the open doorway to great us was my old friend and former colleague. He was wearing a pair of rugby shorts, tight over thick muscular thighs, and a string vest that had seen better days which displayed the faded Chinese characters for 'Hong Kong Police Athletics Club'. When we came to Hong Kong as Probationary Police Inspectors, he had been one of the skinnier men in the squad. It would have been easy for a man with no responsibilities to go physically to seed after leaving the Force, but he had managed the opposite. Now he had added a good fifty pounds of muscle, sported a healthy suntan, and looked like a model for an aerobics video, lean muscular and in fine shape.

"You're looking disgustingly healthy for a man who sits at home and does bugger all," I said. "Got any beer for a thirsty man?".

"It's a tough life," he agreed grinning, "but some of us deserve it."

I introduced Simone. He looked at the girl with curiosity and the eye of a connoisseur. Two years of marriage had not changed his interest in the opposite sex.

"It is rare that I see Bill with such a classy woman," he said holding her hand a little longer than necessary.

She laughed, taken in by his looks and his warm personality. McAlistair had always been a man of culture, which made him no less of a copper. He had been educated at Sherborne, then read Philosophy at Cambridge. After graduating he had travelled the world for a year and then had taken a commission in the Royal Green Jackets, where I'd first met him on a training exercise. He was always larger than life and much less successful than me at keeping his wilder side out of the spotlight. There had been some incident involving the colonel's wife. His conduct was deemed entirely unbecoming and he was kicked out of the regiment.

An uncle then offered him a job in the City.

He stuck it for three weeks until a slightly more senior trainee stockbroker tried to pull rank on him. McAlistair broke the boy's nose, handed in his resignation and wandered down to Grafton Street to apply for the Royal Hong Kong Police. The Superintendent seconded to the London office was not too bothered about the colonel's wife or a caution for assault. He needed twelve Probationary Inspectors and McAlistair looked like the sort of man who could represent law and order on a sweltering day in a Kowloon Public Housing Estate.

"McAlistair is a poet," I explained to Simone as he led us through the house.

"I read poetry," he clarified, "but I write prose. And pretty mediocre prose I have to confess."

"You write?" Simone said.

"I spend my lonely afternoons supervising the gardeners and writing mystery novels."

"You must be very successful if you can afford this house?" she said.

"Sadly no, I haven't sold a single one yet. I had the great fortune to marry a girl who was not only pretty but also very smart. It helped that her father was smart before her, of course."

Stepping onto the terrace we were confronted by an evening view of millions of twinkling diamonds in the distance; the dark mass of the sea contrasted with the white sheet of the beach. A small staircase led down to the sand. There was a rattan couch where we sat and an armchair. Next to the armchair stood a small side table which held a Toshiba laptop, an ashtray and a pipe rack with a tin of Navy Cut tobacco.

On the other side of the chair was a drinks fridge. He opened it and passed me a bottle of cold San Miguel beer, the genuine article smuggled in from the Philippines, not the pale imitation brewed under licence in Thailand. He poured a vodka, lime soda for Simone and took another beer for himself.

I closed my eyes and sighed in appreciation. With the soothing movement of the tide and the gentle crashing of the waves I was reminded how wonderful it was to have money and to spend it on personal pleasures.

"Where is Marjorie?" I asked.

"Taking care of business. She went to Bangkok this morning, should be back soon. Just bought another building. Can't stop the woman from making money." He shrugged his shoulders. "There's not enough hours in the day to spend it."

"I'd lend you a hand," I offered.

"I would appreciate that. You know me. I have simple tastes," he raised the bottle by way of salute. "To drink and the other two pleasures."

"How's the writing going?" I asked, gesturing towards the laptop.

"Good news. Brilliant news. This is number two. My first novel's finally been accepted by the publisher in London. Six thousand copies in hardback. Foot in the door. You are looking at the new James Clavell."

"How much money will you make out of that?"

"Oh, nothing, a pittance. It's fame I want. I want my name on every airport bookstand from Jakarta to Toronto. "These are the best years of my life and I intend to enjoy every second of them," he said. "Not long now and I'll be an internationally famed author much in demand on the talk show circuit, arbiter of good taste and reluctant sex symbol."

I gave Simone a long look at this outpouring of ego and she giggled.

"What's your book about?" Simone asked.

"Oh, sex and violence. And violence and sex. One should always write about familiar things. Bill knows nothing about anything, which is why he always had to copy from me in his police exams. And he's an alcoholic. I would advise you to have nothing further to do with him. Another vodka?"

McAlistair was a charming host but as a copper he could be savage and brutal. Once, when he was a Regional Crime Unit Inspector, I watched him interview someone suspected of raping schoolgirls. When the man wouldn't confess, McAlistair beat the rapist unconscious with a telephone book, which left hardly any visible bruises, then went out drinking with me and ordered his sergeant to page him when the man was ready to sign the confession. Three hours later we interrupted our evening to take a taxi back to the police station and charge the offender on six counts.

The conversation lapsed for a while. There was an idyllic quality about sitting on the veranda on a perfect evening, with a close friend, a woman who was more than simply beautiful, and a cold beer. It was easy to forget that the world was evil, or that life could be nasty, short and brutish.

I took out my cigarettes and McAlistair tossed me a solid gold Dunhill lighter from his little writing table. I turned it over in my hand and read the engraving: 'Now tell us where you hid the money' - followed by the date some three years previously when the Independent Commission Against Corruption informed him that he was no longer suspended for having 'assets not commensurate with his official earnings.'

The witch-hunt had been spun out of rumours and jealousy, although McAlistair had brought it on himself for the most part with his extravagant lifestyle. The black BMW 323i, grey Armani suits and gold Rolex gave off an image that most people felt uncomfortable with in a junior expatriate inspector. His cocky and sometimes superior attitude had not helped matters either.

Unlike ICAC, McAlistair's friends understood that the car, the clothes and the watch were gifts from his girlfriend, a Cathay Pacific flight attendant who was the only child of a wealthy widower with a substantial and diverse investment portfolio. McAlistair and Marjorie had met in a taxi queue, both heading in the same direction. Six months later she had secretly moved in with him and loved him with the passion that Asian women reserve for their men.

On the day that ICAC gave McAlistair the all-clear, I organised a party that moved from bar to disco to pub to bar to restaurant. Starting out as a group of thirty-three, we slowly dwindled to five, sitting on Repulse Bay beach around a crate of Scotch, as the sun peeped over the horizon like a curious child. Everyone else had been lost along the way: under tables, in toilets, in love hotels. The uniforms had arrested two of their off-duty colleagues for being drunk and disorderly and three for getting involved in an argument with a taxi driver.

"We need to talk some business, Julian," I said.

He nodded and reached for the pipe. He packed it deliberately with Navy Cut and then spent a minute bringing it to glow. Simone had her eyes closed and looked as if she had dozed off. We walked back to the house and up a spiral staircase to his study.

There was a wonderful abstract painting - all reds, blues and black in sweeping brushstrokes - on the wall facing the sea view. A large desk dominated the room. More books were stacked on shelves from roof to floor. There was a computer, phone and facsimile machine. McAlistair closed the door and gestured me towards an armchair.

"Where did you find that little thing?" he asked. "She's a bit too classy for you. You've always been the master of quantity not quality."

He walked over to the picture and swung it aside. Behind was a wall safe, from which he extracted a pile of letters. They were from my two banks in Geneva and the one in Liechtenstein.

"That's all," he said. "What's the job you're doing in Pattaya? Do you need some help?"

I explained that it had to do with the Germans and I was intending to infiltrate their gang.

"Dangerous," he said. "They don't mess around. We don't get any bother out here, but in Pattaya town they have their shitty little fingers in a lot of pies. Once in a while someone upsets them and they wind up dead. Drug overdose. Police turn up: 'Oh dear, another one of those stupid drug addict tourists or whatever. Case closed. Thank you very much Mr. Kurt or Hans for your donation to the police widows and orphans' fund'."

"You've told me as much before on the phone."

"I'm telling you again, but I know it's your job and God bless you," he clapped me on the shoulder to relieve the burden of his words.

"I think it's about time you slowed down," he said. "Spend some of that money you have been making. Get yourself a nice house like mine here. There's a lovely shack half a mile down the beach just coming onto the market. Marjorie will negotiate a big discount for you."

"What's the asking price?"

"Nine million Baht. It's not as big as this place but you could probably find some willing girls to fill up the guest rooms.

"Might consider it."

"Don't wait too long. You snooze, you lose," he said. "I'm going to London to launch the book next month. Why don't you come with me and we'll do some serious partying? Madrid, Paris, Rome. A little holiday. I'll pick up the big bills. Marjorie likes me to go away from time to time."

"Go to Europe and chase white women?"

"Sure, we'll go to all the chic places. Work our way through the Michelin guide. Pick up girls in Saint Tropez. Gamble and lose in Monte Carlo."

"Sorry, Julian, you know Western girls leave me cold."

There was a copy of the previous day's *South China Morning Post* lying on the floor next to the armchair. I picked it up and read the lead stories. Since we had left the police, law and order in the Territory seemed to have deteriorated. There was an item about a man who had been shot with a crossbow bolt as he stood waiting for a bus. The police described it as a case of mistaken identity. I knew better but would not be calling them to give my statement.

"We had some fun in Hong Kong back in the

day," McAlistair said wistfully. He nodded at the newspaper. "Strange things happening there nowadays. There was something in the paper last week about Victor Mok Bun disappearing while on leave."

"Tall skinny guy with a twitch in his left cheek. Used to be a course instructor at PTS when we were there?" I said.

"Yeah, then he spent four years as the Force's forgery expert in CCB. Hong Kong's authority on counterfeit bank notes and he's vanished without trace."

"That's interesting," I said, meaning it. "I'm surprised they let the press get hold of that."

"Probably a leak. That sort of thing would go on the teleprinter and anyone with access to the TPM messages would know."

"One other thing," I said. "You're the man with the connections. How's the black market for guns these days?"

He gave a disparaging shrug. "You know how it is. Anything that money can buy is available in Thailand."

"Any chance of getting a Glock 17, Browning Hi-Power or a Beretta 92SB?"

"Nothing like being demanding. What's wrong with a good heavy revolver?" He considered for a moment drumming his fingertips on the desktop. "I know the sort of thing you want. Automatic, big magazine. No identifying marks and you'll make it disappear once you've made use of it."

I nodded. I passed him the old revolver, which I'd taken from Kronk and brought with me. If McAlistair got me something better, I'd have no need for it and he could trade it in.

When we got back to the terrace we found that his wife had arrived.

"Jules, you did not tell me we were having visitors tonight?" she addressed her husband with a chiding smile. "You men talk business and leave this lovely lady alone?" She greeted me warmly. We had known each other a long time and she had even forgiven me for breaking several of her friends' hearts. Turning to Simone she wagged her finger.

"This is the worst man I know. He always talks nonsense to a woman. Don't believe a single one of his words."

We returned to our seats and got fresh beers. I studied Marjorie. She had not changed much in the four years since we first met. Tall, slim, supremely elegant, exquisitely cultured, she was to me a rarity, an attractive woman and a gifted business person. When her father had died, she gave up the idle, glamorous existence of a stewardess and took on the task of running her father's companies.

After resigning her job, she suggested that McAlistair did the same and they should get married. Trying to dissuade him, I took him for a weekend in Manila. After he turned down every little hooker I lined up for him, from Mabini to Makati, I told him it was time.

Marjorie possessed a natural gift of taking the correct risks and making the most profitable decisions. Now her business interests concentrated on property and the export of garments. She had the right connections and enough money to see her investments grow. She and Julian were living the life of Riley and it suited both of them. His wife gave him the freedom he needed, and he gave her the respect she demanded. They were a perfect couple.

14

Outside the house, next to my bike Simone said to me, "I think you're drunk."

"I should hope so, that's the point of drinking alcohol."

She gave me a contemptuous shrug and a frosty look that women often used on me. This time she mounted the bike immediately and gripped me firmly around the waist. Again it felt good. A familiarity was growing between us. I wanted that familiarity to become a scorching passion. I was thinking along these lines on our ride back to Pattaya, not really concentrating on the road. We were travelling at a gentler speed than our outward journey, although in the sparse traffic I was still leaving most cars behind.

We'd been riding for about half an hour when something came up fast behind us, its headlights banishing the shadows in front. We were approaching the spot where the road forked, both roads leading into town. I turned off left, up the road I'd taken earlier which led past the Royal Cliff Hotel. The other car followed closely. I dashed a look over my shoulder. Only the dark shape of the vehicle was visible, about three yards behind me. Like a dark barracuda opening its serrated jaws, the grey Mercedes from earlier in the day was closing in.

Dying wasn't in my plan for the evening. Things had been going very nicely. I intended to spend a few hours over dinner with Simone, trying to entice her into bed. The sudden appearance of the Mercedes annoyed me.

I yelled at her to hold tight and, not waiting for her arms to tense, jerked open the throttle. She let out a short, low scream as the acceleration tried to separate her from me. The Kawasaki reared like a horse. The Mercedes dropped behind rapidly in my side mirror. It wouldn't be enough. The road was about to become tricky ahead and they would catch up.

We sped on, my eyes streaming with tears and straining to see all the contours of the road. Then, out of the darkness came the stretch I had expected. It sloped steeply and curved away into the unyielding night and the engine howled as I went from fifth right into second.

I was jolted forward onto the handlebars. I had no other choice; it had to be slow and careful. I flicked the pedal back up to third gear feeling more confident. Already I could sense the other car on my tail again and feel its headlights boring into our backs. My eyes were streaming from the wind and my muscles were tensing to keep control. They were coming up at speed, secure and threatening in the safety of their German saloon. I gauged our relative distances with several swift glances. Then I pulled right to the inside of the curve, slammed on both front and rear brakes and, skipping the clutch, jumped back into second gear. The engine barked its disagreement.

The Mercedes shot past me, wheels already locked and burning on the asphalt. Two wheels hit the off-road gravel and the saloon swerved madly in continued forward motion.

I threw the bike to the left to steer around it, hoping that the girl had not leant the other way. The bike wobbled. The car, slewing on the tarmac surface, missed my right knee by an inch and we went bouncing into the off-road vegetation.

Amazingly the Kawasaki, hopping wildly across the ferns, stayed upright. We hadn't hit any rocks or potholes, only little bushes. I fought for control like an urban cowboy whose electronic bull had gone haywire. The back wheel flicked around without grip until I remembered to release the throttle and we slowed down a little. We were still parallel to the road, so I hauled the handlebars to the right and let the wheels leap back onto the tarmac. At which point the engine died.

I looked back. The Mercedes had stopped twenty yards behind us. It had been my fault that the engine stalled: on the last jerk my hand had released the clutch. The doors of the car began to open as I jabbed the starter button. If they opened fire Simone's body would take the first bullets and I would die next.

Thankfully, the engine fired up again. The tyres gave off a noise like a thousand rats being clubbed to death and we began putting distance between us and the Mercedes with its murderous occupants.

Back at the hotel, I cut the engine. My face was dripping with sweat. It had been hard work. Simone was trembling. She gave me a terrified look, leaped off the bike and ran towards our room. I heaved the Kawasaki onto its stand and patted the leather like a cowboy would have patted his horse after braving a stampede. Simone was waiting outside our door. I put the key in. She pushed past me and locked herself in the bathroom.

After I had stripped off my sodden shirt and dropped it on the floor, I poured myself a neat Black Label, lit a cigarette and thought things over. Whatever had made me idly part with the Smith & Wesson earlier? Apart from Simone it was the only thing I wanted to sleep with that night.

Whoever had been in the grey Mercedes had intended to kill or seriously injure us. Unless there was an unknown factor that I was missing, it was most likely Charoenchati's men. I had promised him not to come to Pattaya on the pain of death and it made sense that Kronk would keep the General's promise to see me dead.

My mind revolved, re-running events. We would have to be careful but there would be no change of plan. A general did not call off the battle and go home when his advance platoon encountered sniper fire. There was money involved and I had no intention of calling it a day.

It was quarter past nine when Simone emerged from the bathroom in a robe. She looked pale but wore the smile of a little girl who was making the best of the fact that her favourite pony has been put down for the best of reasons.

"It's all right. It's over," I lied. "They won't come again."

"I was scared", she sighed, perhaps angry at her own frailty. "I thought we were going to die." She buried her face in her palms for an instant, then looked up. "Being with you is very demanding."

"Don't blame me, blame your Uncle Tang."

"I'm just not used to this excitement," she said.

"You'll get used to it. Unless you want to leave?"

She shook her head, "I can't. Uncle Tang would be angry. Since my father died Uncle Tang has taken care of everything for me. He told me that was what he had promised my father and a promise is a promise."

"There's no such thing as a free meal," I said.

"Your Uncle Tang has not been taking care of you for purely altruistic reasons."

"Whatever you think," she said angrily, "you have to understand Asian culture. I have obligations to him. If he asks for favours I cannot refuse him."

"I'm starving," I said. "Let's go and eat."

As I explained to Simone, that there was no better way to forget a frightening experience than good food and expensive red wine. While she got ready, I considered my choice of weapon. I wasn't going to be at ease with anything less than a small machine gun under my jacket but the best I had, now that McAlistair had my revolver, was my Mikov switchblade. I had bought it as a young boy in Germany. It had been made behind the Iron Curtain in Czechoslovakia and had been a constant companion down the years.

I rang down to reception to ask if Herr Gruber was still there. As we went through the lobby, he came around the counter with a big obliging smile on his face.

"*Guten Abend*, Herr und Frau Graunitz. Going for dinner so late?"

I nodded curtly. "Herr Gruber. How are your security arrangements here?"

"Excellent of course. We have never had anything stolen from the compound," he said with conviction. I believed him. Only a fool of a thief would risk the wrath of the Germans. It was not petty theft that I was concerned with, but rather the danger of a murderous assault.

"My wife and I had some trouble at the petrol station. A misunderstanding with some young Thai men." I cocked my head in the direction of Simone who was studying a travel brochure. "I'm a bit worried they might have followed us. They were being threatening."

Gruber looked disdainful. "You are perfectly safe. Safer than any of the five-star hotels. We had an attempted burglary once. My security guard shot him dead. We don't want any of our guests feeling unsafe. The local criminals keep away from the Sport Resort now."

He grinned in a way that made made me wonder if it might not have been Gruber who had shot the potential burglar in the head. I thanked him. It seemed unlikely that the grey Mercedes and its occupants would get into the compound. I explained this to Simone. She had changed into a white dress with blue polka dots. I didn't recognise her perfume, but it smelled expensive. As she mounted hesitantly behind me on the Kawasaki, I resisted the urge to glide my hand back along her bare brown thigh.

A peaceful, romantic, dinner was what I had in mind. Everybody needed to relax sometimes. I rode cautiously and I could tell that Simone was nervous by the way she held me close. It was beginning to feel good.

The small courtyard of 'Café de Marseilles' held only three other vehicles. It was tucked down an ill-lit *soi*, away from the garish waterfront nightlife. Dedicated patrons knew where to find it. The proprietor was a jovial Frenchman, Marcel Charpentier. He was a bull of a man with a full grey beard and a platter of eccentricities. He was a champion of the good life who directed the theatre of dinner from his chair by the bar with all the passion of his race. He rolled his eyes at Simone when I introduced her, like a chef pleased with the gourmet's choice of dish.

"You are the man who always dines by himself," he said. "We French have always understood that a beautiful woman adds extra savour to the taste of the food. *N'est-ce pas, Madame?*"

Simone thanked him for his compliments in perfect French. The host nearly fell off his stool with delight.

"You are the most delightful lady to come to my restaurant for months," he purred. "These fat German ladies have no class. They don't appreciate the food. *Ils sont degoulasses.*" He waved towards four stout ladies who looked like the Valkyries' older sisters.

"You must have the oysters. They are delicious tonight and," he winked, "very nourishing for young lovers."

Life can be harsh and unpleasant. I took my pleasures where I found them. It was nice to have, from time to time, a fellow traveller as enticing as Simone to share the hardships and joys of the journey. We passed the meal in friendly conversation. She talked, I prompted. Matching me glass for glass, she became more forthcoming. She enjoyed reading books, playing badminton and shopping with her friends. While I didn't consider myself an expert on anything but sex and weaponry, I spent a lot of time on planes and on the beach, reading books and magazines to pass the time. We discussed a little literature, some politics and relationships.

"How about your husband. How did you meet him?"

"Uncle Tang introduced us. Whenever he has businessmen to entertain he calls me and asks me to accompany him and bring a girlfriend. We would have a very fun evening, dine in one of the famous restaurants, go dancing in 'Bubbles' or 'Diana's', you know, what rich people do."

"Did they talk business?"

"No, of course not. They were interested in our bodies, not our brains, but I never let them touch me more than I had to. One day Uncle Tang called me and told me he had some customers in town from Europe and we had Thai food. That's how I met Max. He was French." She paused. "I had never had a boyfriend, not even slept with a man yet because for us Asian women it is something special." A light burned in her eyes at the memory, it wasn't the reflection from the candle. "By the end of the evening I knew I wanted to be with him forever. Uncle Tang said it was not good to marry a foreigner. But he agreed that Max was a good choice: rich, not too young, respected in his business. Well, I didn't care, I was in love."

"So what happened?"

"I went out with him every time he came to Bangkok. He visited me every month. And then, one day with a diamond ring he proposed marriage. I don't know if he really loved me or not. I think he loved me. But I still don't know." She fell silent for a while gazing into the darkness of the ocean. Her cheeks were flushed from the wine and she had probably drunk more than normal.

"In the end he turned out to be a disappointment?" I prompted.

She smiled sadly. "I went to live with him in Marseilles. After six months I could not stand it. He drove me crazy. He was too possessive. Too emotional. He stayed out all night drinking and gambling and when I told him I had enough, he beat me. Uncle Tang said all foreign men treat Asian women badly. They think we can be bought like bargirls."

"He would say that. But look how happy McAlistair and his wife are."

"I saw that this evening. Do you beat your girlfriends, Bill Jedburgh?"

"Only if they ask me to."

"You can be cold sometimes. Typically English perhaps. You like to hide your emotions. No involvements. Is there a good man inside there?"

I thought about it. I was a good friend and a bad enemy. The wiring in my brain which allowed me to kill dispassionately made friendship something that developed slowly and turned swiftly to hate when my affections were betrayed. The wine led me to be more candid than I would ordinarily have been.

"I'm very selfish," I admitted. "Most of my encounters with women are shallow by choice. There have been a few women that meant more to me than that. But they always told me afterwards that I'm a good friend but a terrible boyfriend."

"That's complete rubbish," she said sharply. "Have you never loved a woman so much that that you could not bear to be without her even for a minute? Didn't you ever love a woman so much that you'd do anything for her? Die for her. That your heart exploded every time you saw her."

"No. I had a Springer Spaniel once. She was called Jenny."

"Don't change the subject," she said, trying to exploit my uncommon frankness. "You must wish that you could love like that?"

"Sure. But I don't live in a fairy tale. My life is real. I admit I'm a bit cynical but then I've been knocking around for a while. Women like that are rare, and men need physical release far more frequently."

"Then I am very sad for you," she said. "To

really love, you must be vulnerable. I think you have spent your whole life trying to become invulnerable and this *carapace* you have grown has not made you happy."

We ordered coffee and Charpentier came over with two espressos to enquire why we had left some cheese. As a Frenchman he found it hard to believe that a *patron* could ever be full. Only one other couple was still dining. They were a young European pair who whispered to each other over clasped hands and looked as if they were on their way to some long forgotten hippy commune. I watched them, noting the feeling that flowed between them. In some fashion, Simone's words had got through to me, and for an instant I wished that she and I could reach that stage in a relationship.

I dragged myself back from the brink of sentimentality. Charpentier was telling Simone that Pattaya was a sorry place. He was thinking of leaving, opening up a restaurant in Koh Samui where the beaches were cleaner, the nightlife healthier and the gangsters less demanding.

"Have you had trouble with gangsters here?" I asked. He shrugged.

"The Germans think they can frighten everybody and buy the town. They are the new Nazis."

"They don't frighten you?"

"I have told them what they can do with their heads. *Salles boches*. I still remember what they did to us during the war."

It would be interesting to have a further chat with him, I thought. He knew more about Pattaya than McAlistair and might be able to give me useful intelligence.

I studied Simone's profile as she watched Charpentier return to his seat at the bar. It was wholly oriental with soft contours and flawless skin stretching from the forehead across the delicate bump of a nose, the gentle slopes of her cheekbones, the hot crimson of her liberal lips to the firm and sculptured chin. There had been several women in my life as beautiful as her, in some respects more perfect, but I could think of none at that moment more exquisite, more delectable, more endearing.

"What are you thinking about?" she asked.

"You, men and women. The differences between the sexes. How we speak a different language using the same words." I had also been conjuring up images of Simone undressed, marvelling at her bared breasts, admiring the sublime symmetry of her sex.

"Men and women being different is a fairy tale encouraged by men so they can live by double standards," she said. I could see her point.

"Let's go and dance," I suggested.

"Where?" she asked.

"The 'Marine Disco'. It's busy until the sun comes up. You'll hate it. You'll have to protect me from all the little prostitutes."

"Do you think I haven't seen all that before?"

she said accepting the challenge. Charpentier simpered over Simone as we left and we told him we would be back soon, because the meal had been sublime. He glowed with pleasure.

15

In the courtyard my bike was standing by itself. I didn't notice the only other parked vehicle until I heard a sharp intake of breath from the woman on my arm. It was the grey Mercedes. Like a beast of prey it had successfully hunted and finally cornered its quarry. The doors opened. Kronk emerged from the driver's side, grinning, ugly and with a look of determination in his eyes.

"You very trouble man, *falang*," he called, coming towards me. "Now I kill you." Kronk was holding a large knife with a serrated edge. On the other side of the car stood his partner, Toothless, baring what was left of his molars in amusement.

I needed to deal with Kronk, or he would continue rearing his hideous head. I shook off Simone's arm and faced him.

"You want to die?" he asked

I didn't waste my breath replying. From my pocket I quickly pulled the Mikov. It snapped open with a comforting click as it locked firm. Kronk looked irritated. The odds had evened up a little. It would have been easy for him to shoot me, but he wanted to make a point with his knife in my guts. Our contest was now personal. I watched his fierce angry eyes as we circled each other. In the periphery of my vision, I noted that Simone had turned back into the restaurant to fetch help.

"Simone?" I shouted without looking back.

"Yes?"

"No police," I said, making my voice was as commanding as I could. She didn't respond.

Kronk and I moved anti-clockwise. More than an arm's length separated us. He wanted me facing the light from the house before he would lunge. Experience had taught me in similar stand-offs that the first move had to be his. I had trained for this type of close combat and felt confident. I tested my stance, dipping slightly in the knees, ready to move either way. Both our knives were held with the blade facing up. I held mine loose; Kronk gripped his tight, his thumb resting on the blade. He could go for the left or the right with an upward drive into the ribs. With his left forearm he would shield any move from me.

A flicker of uncertainty crossed his face. He was disconcerted by my relaxed stance. He wanted me to tremble or run. We stopped circling as he reached his desired position. I stared into his eyes for another ten seconds, willing him to come at me, until he lost patience. He was a fighter, an aggressor; he could not stand

and wait.

With a brutal cry, Kronk feinted left and moved his blade right. I stepped back, dipped somewhat, tossed my knife into the left hand and arced the blade upwards, catching his attacking wrist on the edge of my weapon. The steel bit into him and he dropped his knife. At the same time my right fist hit him on the jaw and he staggered. I tossed my knife back into the right hand, closed on him with a leap and drove the blade up to the hilt in his thigh.

I saw the terror in his eyes as his momentum carried him backwards as he fell. He landed hard, smacking the back of his head on the concrete. I landed softly, cushioned by his body. I pulled the knife out of his leg muscle and placed it against his jugular. When I looked up, I found myself staring into the single eye of a Colt Automatic. Toothless was standing over me nervously, unsure of his next move.

There was a shout from the direction of the restaurant. Charpentier was standing beside Simone with an ancient shotgun trained on Toothless and me. The rest of the staff and the last remaining guests watched on in horror.

"*Arretez*. Stop. Drop the gun. Drop the knife," Charpentier ordered and repeated his words in Thai. If Toothless dropped his automatic I was happy to drop my knife. Kronk groaned and made a useless attempt to heave me off. I nicked his neck, which produced a rivulet of blood that dribbled down his shirt. Toothless stared at me and then at Charpentier, considering his options with the speed and precision of a drunk man trying to open his front door. He could shoot me, but might hit his partner, then he might get shot by the irate landlord. At last, the automatic fell from his hand. Still kneeling on Kronk's chest I gripped his Adam's apple between thumb and forefinger then cleaned the Mikov on his shirt and dropped it to my right out of reach of both of us.

Charpentier came down the stairs cautiously. I looked up at Simone and noted her tense frightened features. I gave her a ghost of a smile and a hint of a wink. She frowned.

"Get off him, *Monsieur*." Charpentier commanded. I obeyed and there was an exchange in Thai between Kronk, Toothless and the Frenchman. I stood well back. Kronk struggled to his feet with the help of his partner. A garish black stain had spread down his trousers, but there was no arterial bleeding. It had been a straight stab to debilitate the muscle. I had no intention to wound him mortally once he'd been disarmed. I didn't want to burn all my bridges with his boss.

"Who are they? Were they planning to rob you?" Charpentier asked suspiciously.

"Let them go, no police. It's better that way," I said. "I'm sorry for causing you trouble."

Charpentier considered the situation then

spoke in Thai. Kronk limped towards the Mercedes supported by Toothless.

Charpentier watched the two get into the car, wary in case they tried to pull a fast one. The Mercedes reversed slowly onto the main road and took off at speed. When it was out of sight, he lowered the shotgun. The young couple were still frozen in each other arms. It made a touching, somewhat pathetic scene. Charpentier told them he had foiled a robbery and they were safe now. They nodded and left hurriedly while I kissed Simone on the cheek by way of thanks. She had been quick in fetching the reinforcements.

"He said they are only interested in you." Charpentier said.

"Thank you for your help," I said, picking up the automatic. Toothless had dropped it at full cock, so I removed the magazine, ejected the round in the breech and handed it to Charpentier. It was a wonder it had not gone off. Some people wielded guns without understanding the dangers of mishandling them.

"I am not used to this," he said, when we went back inside to the bar. "This is your business, I think. They were not simple robbers."

"Can we have a cognac? I will tell you the story."

He nodded and poured three large glasses into cognac snifters. I carried one over to Simone who had sat back down on our old table. She initially waved it away, then reconsidered and sipped it nervously. Her hand shook slightly as she did so.

"Now I understand why Uncle Tang chose you to come here," she said. "He told me you were trained to take care of yourself."

"It could have turned nasty if you hadn't got hold of old man Charpentier and his siege gun."

She regarded me for an instant. There were two emotions churning inside her: repulsion at my cold brutality in stabbing Kronk, but also admiration, acknowledging that I had kept her safe. She could not reconcile the two feelings and it made her irritable.

Sitting on the bar stool I sipped my glass of Remy Martin and thanked the landlord for his intervention. Simone was staring out of the window, distant in her manner. I made up a story for Charpentier, similar to the one I had told Gruber.

"Yes, you had better be careful," Charpentier suggested, regarding me over his half-moon glasses. I got the feeling he did not believe me and was looking through me into my dark world.

"You were saying something about the Germans before. Do you think they could be working with these guys?" I asked.

"It could be. Many Thais are on their payroll."

"How many Germans are there involved in this? Who is their boss?"

He shrugged his heavy round shoulders. "Twenty or thirty perhaps. I do not know. I want nothing to do with them."

"Do you know who their leader is?"

"There is a man called Schwartz," he said. "He has a big house near Chonburi. I have heard that he is their leader, but no one ever sees him in Pattaya. I know that the police close their eyes, *comme on dit*, to their blackmail and prostitution. They are not nice people." Charpentier shrugged again and his eyes stared off into the distance. Maybe in memory of days in the French Resistance, when Germans in staff cars and smart black uniforms were his enemies. I had disrupted the calm atmosphere of his restaurant.

I resolved to come back the next day and speak with the Frenchman again. We said our farewells and left. I retrieved my Mikov flick-knife from the bushes as we left. The automatic, Charpentier had impounded, which was fair.

Simone seemed pensive and I was exhausted. It had been a long day and I wanted nothing more than an undisturbed night. By the time we got back to the Sport Resort it was late. I parked the bike cautiously and nodded at the guard standing by the reception desk. Except for his uniform and friendly smile, he could have been a bandit from the hills resting his palm on the grip of a big-holstered revolver.

"Who were those men?" Simone demanded, drying her hair as she stood wrapped in a bathrobe. I was already in bed, clothed in shorts and a T-shirt for her sake. "They were not sent by Uncle Tang." Her voice had a hint of uncertainty. "Were they sent by the Germans?"

"No, the Germans are protecting us here because Gruber has smelt the possibility of making some money from me. Those men are the competition."

She looked puzzled. "I don't understand. Whose competition?"

"I'm not sure either. Nothing is as simple as it is in the movies. It doesn't have to be just us and them. There are other parties involved."

"Do you think they are interested in the Forger?"

"I assume so, or maybe they really don't like me hanging around with an attractive woman and are taking it personally."

She sat on the edge of the bed and dropped the towel into her lap. "I don't feel safe. I'll have to call Uncle Tang."

"Tomorrow," I said. "Uncle Bill will take care of you tonight." I heard her snort in mock disgust. But my weapons were close at hand, the door was bolted, and I'd slipped the guard two hundred Baht to watch our bike. It was the best I could do. I'd carry on worrying tomorrow.

16

Leaning over me was Simone holding a cup of something wet and warm. In my dreams she had been as well. I felt drained and weak and the texture of my mouth was like the inside of a cement mixer. She looked fresh and wonderful in the morning light and I wanted to pull her down and bury my nose in her cleavage.

"Tea or coffee?" I queried. My eyes were like a new-born kitten's in the sun and I seemed to have lost my sense of smell.

"Tea, two sugars."

"I don't take sugar," I grumbled

"That figures," she said, "given that you are not being very sweet with me this morning."

I took the cup anyhow. It was nine o'clock and I wanted to get a few things done today. I was in the mood to bring the battle to the enemy.

"I'm going down to the pool to have breakfast," Simone said and left. I figured she wanted to make a private call to Tang and tell him the latest developments. That was fine by me. With what had happened to us, I was earning my money three times over. I poured the rest of the tea down the sink and pulled an orange juice from the fridge. Then I called McAlistair.

"Got my gun yet?" I asked.

"For fuck's sake, Bill. I've only just got out of bed and finished having a swim."

"You rich idle bastard."

"Yeah, yeah. Did you shag her?"

"No."

"Thought it was on the cards last night. You're losing your touch."

"We only met yesterday morning, she's a nice girl."

"Is she? I thought in your eyes all women are equal."

"Well, some are more equal than others."

We arranged to meet later at a place called 'Wee Jock's'. It was a replica Scottish bar run by an authentic Scottish owner. Like most Scottish pubs it was long on alcohol and short on female companionship, so I'd managed to avoid it on previous trips to Pattaya. Plus, it was full of Scotsmen. Even though I was named after a town in the Scottish borders, I was as English as they came. McAlistair of course considered himself a Scot, even though his accent was posher than mine.

"Marjorie's not working today so she wants to take your little lady-friend shopping. I thought that was an excellent idea. I've got a little treat for you. Especially after you bummed out last night," McAlistair said.

"Women, I hope?" Enforced celibacy wasn't helping my mood. There had been far too much water under the bridge since my encounter with Tuk in The Oriental.

"Sharp man. I'll have seen my contact about your hardware by then. And Harry Bolt is coming to town. Keep yourself available. He wants to have lunch tomorrow."

I put down the phone and prepared myself for the day. My eyes looked bloodshot. I wondered how Kronk was feeling this morning. It would be best if we disappeared from view for a while. Maybe change hotels, to somewhere more anonymous. There were plenty of those in town. Once I had showered, I went down to join Simone by the pool. She gave me an awkward smile as if she felt guilty about reporting back to Tang. I looked at her breasts, nodding to myself. That's what I really wanted for breakfast. Instead my subconscious ordered two soft-boiled eggs and a *Broetchen* - a fresh crumbly German roll.

"We're going to check out after breakfast," I said.

"Where are we going?"

"Don't know yet. First we need to get some more information about the Germans from our dear friend Charpentier, then I thought we could go down the beach and catch a bit of sun. Might as well enjoy ourselves while we are here. After lunch we're meeting McAlistair and Marjorie. She wants to go shopping with you."

"I haven't got enough money to shop," she said showing a new side of herself. She was embarrassed. But then judging by her wardrobe, maybe she needed a lot of money to shop.

"We'll put it down as expenses." I gave her ten thousand Baht from my wallet. She pocketed it without a blink like any good housewife.

"What did Uncle Tang say?" I asked. Simone looked guilty again, then decided to be honest.

"He isn't happy about the incident with the Mercedes and the man with the knife, but he has confidence in you. He says you don't have any other choice."

"Then he and I agree for once."

My eggs arrived and I cut the bread into soldiers, spraying crumbs all over the tablecloth. Dipping them into the egg yolk I enjoyed my food quietly. Looking up I realised the girl was watching me with an odd expression. I smiled. After two cups of coffee I felt ready for the day. Returning to the room we packed quickly, paid the bill and arranged to pick up the bags later.

I told Simone to wait and knocked on Gruber's office door. He was on the telephone ordering fish in German. The window looked out over the swimming pool and I could see a pale woman with lards of flab which drooped over the edge of her bikini bottoms, testing the water with her toes. She lowered herself onto the edge of the pool and slid in like a monster seal.

Gruber slammed down the telephone in a gesture of rebellion at the mundanity of his occupation.

"You slept safely last night?"

"Comfortable but I am afraid that I am checking out this morning."

He looked upset. I went on. "An old friend has come into town and he has a condominium that he keeps for his holiday use."

"Ah, of course. Where does he live?" he inquired as politely as he could.

"Near Wattana Beach, a new complex."

"I know it. The views from the flats are lovely. Then are you still interested in meeting my associates to discuss business?"

"Yes, that's what I wanted to ask you about." Gruber looked relieved and made a show of pulling open a Thai Airways diary.

"They have suggested this evening. Is that convenient?"

"*Ausgezeichnet*," I said, in my Bavarian accent, "that is really excellent news. I am looking forward to meeting some more of my countrymen."

"Do you know the '*Strammer Max*' cafe near the Montien Hotel?" he asked. I recalled a German bar in that vicinity, so I nodded.

"We have a *Stammtisch* there. How about eight o'clock?" Gruber was so obliging it made my skin crawl and my sixth sense uneasy. It seemed all a bit too straightforward. Introduce myself as a fellow German, express an interest in doing business here. Meeting arranged.

I hoped I was getting together with the right set of German gangsters. The Italian mafia was a collection of different gangs that split the profit areas between themselves. Maybe the Germans were no different. What was the likelihood that a pie as lucrative as Pattaya would be controlled by a single group? After some consideration I concluded it was pretty high. I needed to find the man called Otto Schwartz. If Charpentier was right, he was the Chief Executive, the *Geschaeftsfuehrer* of the gang.

Simone was leaning against the motorbike. I drew her towards me and managed to kiss her very quickly on the lips. She jumped back and looked very annoyed.

"That's for saving my life last night and bringing me a cup of tea this morning." This brought a faint smile to her face.

"Now you've got lipstick on your face," she said. When I rubbed my lips a red smudge transferred to the back of my hand, which excited me more than it should. She was wearing tight Calvin Klein jeans again and a plain white shirt with lots of pockets that made her look like a freshly trained stewardess from Singapore Airlines on her first leave in springtime Paris. She hid her eyes behind a pair of Armani sunglasses.

We drove leisurely in the direction of the beachfront, my right hand on the throttle and my left resting casually on her knee. She didn't object, holding me loosely around the waist. The air was hot already, but not too humid and the smell of the sea and the stench of petrol fumes mingled. The roads were not busy yet. On the left we passed the *'Strammer Max'*. *Stramm* meant strapping in German, but the cafe shared its name with a well-known German dish - a fried egg with ham on brown bread. Like all its competitors, the name was intended to attract expats and tourists by evoking nostalgia for the old country, whichever one that might be.

We rode through the quiet streets. The bars and restaurants which had been gaudy and enticing the night before, now looked shabby in the daylight. Finally we reached the *'The Café de Marseilles'*. An old rusty Toyota was parked in the courtyard. I noticed a dark patch on the asphalt from the previous night.

A blackboard displayed the figure of a running chef holding a tray advertising *'le petit déjeuner'* French breakfast of croissants and coffee. It made my mouth water despite having just eaten. I went up the steps and found the door locked. Cupping my hands I peered into the house, found only darkness. This did not feel right. Somebody had arrived in the Toyota and set up the blackboard but now the doors were locked and there was silence. Sniffing the air I detected the familiar odour of gas. I began walking away.

Just as I made up my mind to smash the pane on the front door, a tremendous pressure slapped me on the back. It was stronger than any typhoon I had ever experienced, and propelled me forward into the courtyard flinging me onto my face. Then came a scorching heat and a resounding thunderclap that stung my ears.

I lay dazed for a minute. The Kawasaki had been knocked over by the blast and Simone was sitting on the asphalt staring at me. The air was filled with the smell of burning wood. Unsteadily getting to my feet I helped her up and brushed the dirt from her arms. The restaurant door hung open, off its hinges, and the windows were shattered. Flames were shooting out from inside, eagerly lapping up oxygen in their desire to become a crackling good blaze.

"Go down there," I ordered Simone, pointing at the main road. "I'll be with you in a moment." I saw her mouth move but I couldn't hear her - my eardrums were still useless. I shoved her away.

Sprinting up the stairs again, I kicked the remains of the door aside and ran into the main dining room. It was like jogging into a sauna. Tables were turned upside down, glass lay strewn over the floor, tablecloths burned with a foul stench emitting billows of smoke. The swing door to the kitchen had disappeared. On his back, on the black and white tiled floor, I found Charpentier. There was not much left of him. He was charred and bloody. You didn't have to be a detective to understand what had happened.

The restaurant was mainly wood and the flames were engulfing me in a smoky embrace. I began to cough. I sprinted back through the dining room holding my breath, trying not to stumble on broken furniture. As I did so, the upper part of the bar collapsed. Glasses crashed inches away from me. A second later I was outside, had picked up the bike and pushed it quickly towards where Simone was standing.

"What happened?" she wanted to know.

"On the bike," I commanded, punching the starter with my thumb, pausing only to make sure she had a good hold of me before gunning the machine away. Looking back, the windows were pumping out charcoal smoke. We were a good two hundred yards down the road before a second explosion went off. There must have been some propane canisters in the storeroom.

My main concern was not to be at the scene when the police and fire service arrived. They would keep us as witnesses and, when they found suspicious circumstances, would consider us as suspects. That would disrupt my plans. I could do nothing to help Charpentier, except discover who had terminally revoked his restaurant licence. When I found that out, I would repay the debt I owed him from the previous evening.

The two possibilities were that the Germans, annoyed at his refusal to pay their extortion money, had decided to make him an example to other hold-outs, or that Kronk had taken revenge for Charpentier's interference in our fight.

Swiftly, giving it plenty of throttle, I rode towards 'Wee Jock's'. The traffic was beginning to congeal with the approach of the midday sun. We passed three policemen on motor scooters going the other way and I heard in the distance the discordant jangle of a fire engine. It surprised me how quickly they had responded.

"I think I'm getting used to this excitement," Simone said clicking her lighter into life, while I chained up the Kawasaki outside 'Wee Jock's'. "I'm not even shaking. Look!"

She held her hand horizontal for me to check; her face was flushed though. I'd decided that wherever the sun was - below, above, beside or behind the yardarm - we both deserved a drink after our narrow escape. I did not like the look of a man blown apart. There were cleaner, more honest ways to die.

17

The boast of 'Wee Jock's' was real home cooking, genuine ale, and friendly waitresses that let you drink in peace. The walls were covered in Scottish gewgaws and there was a noticeable tartan tinge from seat covers to the food menu. In the corner a trio of young men in crew cuts were playing darts. A lanky westerner, the colour of processed bread, was following the darts match. He was clutching a pint of the dark brown bitter the Scots call 'Heavy' and muttering support for each player's shots. He was as bald as a honeydew melon and dressed in a singlet and khaki shorts. His prominent Adam's apple stood out like a cannonball on a skating rink. A dimple-faced barmaid wearing a T-shirt bearing the legend 'Scotland for the World Cup' smiled and served us a couple of brandies.

"What do you think happened?" Simone asked, watching me down the first brandy in one and order another. Her hand covered mine in concern.

"They surprised him as he was opening the place up, before any of the staff arrived.

Whacked him on the back of the head, maybe shot him, who knows. Then turned on the oven to full and lit a candle or something. Closed the doors. Ten minutes later the kitchen goes boom and so does the landlord."

That morning's copy of *The Nation*, a Thai English language paper, was on the bar and I flipped through it idly. Amidst the usual stories about the King and Queen, army generals threatening to withdraw their support from the Prime Minister and more projections for excellent economic growth, there was a report of another foreigner found dead from a heroin overdose in Pattaya. It was a young reporter from a Hong Kong newspaper on holiday and with no known history of drug abuse. He had been found with a piece of rubber tied around his arm and a dirty needle in his vein, face down on the pillow of his room in the Diamond Hotel. That put the annual death toll of single male tourists to thirty already. The police refused to comment.

The doorway darkened and a chap walked in parking himself at the bar. He wore a well-nurtured gut and had big sleepy eyes that made him look like a weary old basset hound. His face and hands were lobster red. He waved at the skinny old-timer who idled over with his pint and they greeted each other in impenetrable Glaswegian. From what little I could understand, it appeared that the lanky one was Wee Jock, the owner.

"We'll be meeting a guy called Harry Bolt tomorrow," I said to Simone.

"Another friend?" she said as if I'd exceeded my quota. "What does he do? Does he also live in Thailand?"

"No, he's an investor. Made his first million before he was 26 by selling blank videotapes to the Arabs. Now he's probably selling them guns or penicillin. Or oil. That's the sort of scheme he cooks up."

"Why are all your friends successful and rich but you are not?" she asked.

There was an implication of failure in her question. I couldn't tell her the truth, because as far as she and Uncle Tang were concerned I was a penniless expat. I contented myself with:

"I'm happy with what I have achieved so far."

Simone considered my answer. I interested her, I frightened her, but she did not yet admire or respect me. A lot more work would be needed before she fell breathlessly into my arms and between my sheets.

I checked my watch and indicated that I wanted to leave. I was early for the meeting with McAlistair, so there was time for the beach. A few rays would top up my fading tan nicely. With luck Simone could be persuaded to strip down to her swimsuit and I could ogle her physique.

The beach was crowded. Apart from the European holidaymakers there were plenty of bar girls topping up their tans, in anticipation of dancing later on stage in their bikinis. Simone found a free pair of deckchairs under a ragged shade. Immediately people descended on us asking to be paid for the chairs, offering food, drink, knock off clothing and massages. Life for a poor Thai was one long hustle. Simone handled them with what I assumed to be the polite aloofness of the upper classes and we were left in relative peace.

"Aren't you going to sunbathe?" I asked. I had stripped down to my bathing trunks and taken out a small bottle of Coppertone.

To my disappointment, she shook her head. The only thing she took off were her sandals. I let the heat suffuse my skin and watched the action around me. Simone adjusted her sunglasses and addressed herself to her Catherine Cookson novel.

Half an hour later, I awoke from my sweaty doze. Simone had her eyes closed and her book was face down on her chest. Smearing some more suntan lotion across my thighs, I watched a chubby Chinese tourist in a harness hanging on for grim life behind a speedboat that finally whisked him up into the air at the end of a ragged parachute. When I followed his progress, I noticed that someone had been watching us from further along the beach. It was the bodybuilder with the ponytail from the Sport Resort gym. He was sitting, on a tiny towel, glistening with oil that was being rubbed into his shoulders by two giggling Thai girls, neither of whom looked older than fifteen, in brightly-coloured swimsuits. One girl, holding high a family size bottle of suntan lotion, was massaging his left shoulder while the other worked on his right. I didn't know how long he had been watching us, but it made me uneasy.

I put on my clothes, skin sticky against the cotton, woke Simone and we rode back to 'Wee Jock's'.

The fat Scotsman with the basset hound face was still keeping close to the bar. He held a sandwich in one hand and a beer in the other. He and Wee Jock were having an animated discussion about Scottish soccer. The darts players had retired to a table and they eyed Simone with palpable lust.

The feral growl of a sports car outside announced McAlistair's arrival. Through the open door I glimpsed a red Porsche 911 with tinted windows. When he entered the pub, the fat Scotsman said:

"It's that rich bastard from up the road."

"I've come to see the scrawny Scot who thinks he runs an alehouse." McAlistair answered clapping them both on the shoulder.

He introduced us. The fat Scotsman was Angus Donnelly, a golf course designer based in Singapore who was working on a project on the outskirts of Pattaya. Golf – popular with rich locals and tourists alike – was rapidly becoming a major money-earner in Thailand. Wee Jock leant forward and tapped me on the knee.

"All these stories yon man comes out with about Hong Kong when he's had a few bevvies. I don't believe any of them." He regarded me slyly.

"You're right to be wary," I said. "Romance at short notice is his specialty. Old Julian here had a great career ahead of him in the Force: promotion, excitement and endless sex. He turned it all down to become a married beach bum."

"And I love it," McAlistair said, then added: "and I love my wife," just as the lady herself, who had followed in her own car, came into the pub.

"I've come to take Simone shopping, Bill" she said. "I hope that's OK?"

"If that's OK with her," I said. "Julian and I will look after ourselves and have a few beers." Simone gave the impression that she'd had enough of dodgy Scottish bars and my company. Once they had departed in Marjorie's dark blue Mercedes SL and he'd downed a beer, McAlistair turned to me:

"Come out to the car. I've got your present."

We sank into the yellow leather seats and I inhaled the aroma. The Porsche was an impressive beast. I ran my thumb over the gear stick and stabbed the CD player into life.

"Where are the CDs?"

"In a rack in the boot, you twat," McAlistair explained turning the stereo off again. He looked at me seriously. "There was an explosion this morning which destroyed that French restaurant you like. They say that the owner's burnt body was found inside and a gas leak is suspected. Weren't you going there last night with Simone?"

"Last night and this morning, which is when it blew up in my face." I told him what had happened, omitting the fight with Kronk because I did not want him unnecessarily worried.

"Anything to do with you?" he asked.

"Not sure. It might have been the Germans and I have made them my business. I've got a meeting with them this evening."

He put the car into gear. He dropped the clutch and it leapt onto the road in between two Baht buses.

"Like my little baby?" he said patting the steering wheel.

"It's a beauty. Stands out from the crowd."

"That's the way I like it. Have a look in that bag under your seat."

I was impressed. In fact, I was delighted. McAlistair had found me, in such a short space of time, a handgun that suited my instincts perfectly. It was a Glock 17, Austrian made, a weapon that we had carried and trained with in the VIP Protection Unit of the Royal Hong Kong Police. Holding it in the open palm of my hand I felt like a batsman weighing his bat at the beginning of the new cricket season. It was familiar, comforting and for the first time in a while I felt back in control.

He leant across me and opened the glove compartment, dropping in my lap a hard leather Sickinger holster, which was moulded to sit discreetly over the right kidney.

"You should go into business," I said.

"This is business," he said and named his price. It wasn't cheap, but the goods were the best quality. There were two spare clips and a couple of boxes of ammunition in the bag.

"Put it on the tab," I said.

I examined the ammunition, whistling with approval. They were German 9mm Parabellum MEN *Deformationsgeschoss* – hollow points. They had a very light tip which covered an axial cavity resulting in damaging expansion once they hit their target. They were excellent for deflating tyres, even better for exploding peoples' heads. In most countries they were illegal unless you worked for the state.

This Glock was relatively new. With a 17+1 magazine capacity, accurate sights, good handling characteristics and a weight of only around 800 grams that made it practical enough to carry concealed, it was a working man's tool. If you were in my line of work, that is. I checked its action, loaded it, slipped it into the holster and clipped that into my pants, pulling my shirt loosely over it.

When I looked up, we had driven out of town and we were racing into the greenery. We weren't heading towards his house, so I wondered what he had in mind for the afternoon.

"This place I'm taking you to is an exclusive gentlemen's country club that provides rest, relaxation and sporting activities for weary executives. Wait till you see the girls. No German bully boys or English squaddies in this club," McAlistair explained as if reading my mind.

"Will they let the likes of me in?" I asked. I was conscious I was dressed more like a beach bum than a business executive and my clothes still smelled of smoke from the fire at the French restaurant.

"I'm a valued member. I'll vouch for you. This is the best club you will ever see in your life."

"Sounds fascinating. Who owns it, not the Germans obviously?"

"49 percent is owned by our good friend Harry Bolt, which is why it's called the Bolthole. It's a very lucrative concept."

Talk of girls made me realise that I was incredibly horny. Too much staring at Simone's tits without being allowed to get my lips around them, I told myself, as we drew up at a heavily guarded gate. McAlistair waved a membership card to gain access. We followed a wooded driveway for half a mile until we arrived at a vast building in the style of an English country manor and rocked to a halt on the gravel, next to a stone fountain of Cupid balancing on one foot. At any moment I expected Jeeves to emerge from the front entrance.

18

The concept was indeed very Harry Bolt - chauvinistic, luxurious, discreet, and totally civilised - the perfect hideaway for men who hated slumming it. The architecture was colonial with an air of home counties: dark wood panelling inside, pale marble floors, lofty interiors and pictures of previous glories. The main hall brought to mind, in its grandeur, visits to my grandfather's club in St. James's Square. A wooden ceiling fan lazily stirred air which was already comfortably cool from hidden air conditioning vents.

A pageboy, impeccable in black trousers and white uniform top, complemented by pristine gloves, opened the oak door. The pageboy turned out to be a politely smiling girl. Another girl, older and wearing silver braid on her epaulettes greeted McAlistair with deference and ran his card through the machine then asked him to sign the book. She must have pressed a hidden bell because in an instant a young European in the traditional dark manager's garb emerged from a door. He had the good looks of a continental movie star and the manner of a man whose ancestors had been hoteliers since the renaissance. He turned out to be Swiss, which explained matters. McAlistair introduced me as a close friend of Mr. Bolt. He eyed me professionally and commented with a grin: "I see you adopt the same dress code as Mr Bolt."

Harry deliberately dressed like a bum, but I had to say my current attire was pretty rank.

"I have had a difficult morning," I explained. "If you can find something more appropriate and put it on Mr McAlistair's account, I will gladly change."

"I will see what I can do," he said. "Some clubs would not admit you dressed like this, but on the instructions of Mr Bolt we have very few dress rules, except for our staff. Our principal rule is that we permit no women and children on the premises, except of course our own staff who have been trained to give a select service for our discerning members."

"Sounds like heaven on earth," I said.

"There are few complaints, as you will realise when you see our ladies," he said. "We also have extensive sporting facilities and a French chef." He looked me up and down with a professional eye.

"I will arrange to have a new polo shirt and chinos waiting for you in your room when you have chosen a companion," he said, and smiled modestly.

We had a beer in the 'Sportsman's Bar'. French windows overlooked a terrace with an aquamarine swimming pool fringed with palms. Two girls in identical red bikinis, that hid little and showed lots, dangled their bare legs in the water. Beyond the pool, carefully tended grass undulated up to the horizon with the occasional pole and flag to indicate the location of the golf course. Holding my drink and stepping out onto the chimney-red slabs of the veranda I could see two people with tennis rackets walking in the direction of some grass courts.

"Not cheap," I said. A middle-aged man with grey hair, sitting at the end of the bar with a whisky and soda reading the *Financial Times*, looked up. Behind him was a rack containing recent editions of most of the world's great newspapers. There was also a copy of *The Sun*.

"This is as good as The Oriental," I said, admiringly.

"Better, much better. There's a gym upstairs with a resident trainer and dietician. Some people come here and lose ten to fifteen pounds in two weeks."

"From eating healthy food or shagging themselves stupid? What's the score on the girls? I need you to find me a little tart I can abuse for an hour to relieve my sexual tension."

"That's more like the Bill Jedburgh I used to go out on the pull with," he said. "I was beginning to think Simone was making you go soft."

"You can't talk, I said, "with your millionaire lifestyle."

"Let's be clear," he said, taking another sip of his beer, "the fact that Marjorie and I love each other does not stop me sleeping with anyone, just as long as I'm discreet. And if I thought your Simone was in the least interested in me, I would shag her in a heartbeat."

"That's two of us, then," I said. "But you need to get in line."

"Hi Julian," an American accent said beside us. I turned and found a tall, trim white woman in a tracksuit standing beside McAlistair. She had freckles around her nose, California blue eyes and long blonde hair. She put an arm around my friend's shoulder in a friendly gesture that wasn't too intimate.

"Mandy, meet the rudest, most horrible and racist, women-hating man you will ever meet," McAlistair said by way of introduction. She shook my hand firmly, as if she had been taught in high school that it was a good way to make first impressions count. I wasn't interested in western women as a rule, but she was in very good shape.

"Bill Jedburgh. Nice to meet you, Mandy. Where are you from?"

"I'm from Oregon. I'm the resident dietician. It's a pleasure to meet you, Bill," she said, looking me in the eye as if to prove that inside that strapping body she was more than my equal.

It was something that had always irritated me about western women. They invariably had to prove they were better than men. I preferred my women gentle, vulnerable, confused and in need of someone to take care of them. For me that was the natural order of things. But when I met women like Simone, I realised that Asian women could be just as complex. I was too old to rethink my lifestyle choices, but perhaps I was becoming a little more nuanced as I got older.

"You didn't see me drink this beer, Mandy," McAlistair said.

"That's two demerit points for you," she said with a smile. "One for drinking alcohol and the other for trying to hide it. Are you coming to work-out later?"

"No, we thought we'd take it easy today."

I studied her as they bantered. Her complexion was tanned and healthy but her forearms were muscular and the texture of the skin seemed rough and dry. She was older than she looked. Her appearance was the product of good nutrition and exercise, the American dream.

"Woman in the bar. Not allowed that," I complained after she'd left.

"What you mean is she was wearing clothes and she wasn't Asian," Julian said, finishing his beer. "I know what you prefer, but there are quite a lot of men, myself included, who occasionally like a bit of white meat in their diet. Anyway, let's go and find a dish more to your liking."

Down a corridor labelled West Wing we found the massage reception room. The room we entered was a far cry from the worn down carpets and dim red lighting of the 'Mon Chérie' where Keller had taken me. It was decorated in dark green with deep pile carpets, dark brown leather settees, and hunting prints on the walls, lending it an air of seriousness. The Manager was a mature woman, perhaps in her late thirties but still a beauty. She put her hands together and raised them to her forehead in the traditional *'wai'* greeting. McAlistair and I returned the compliment.

"You have any preferences, sir?" the lady asked.

"Any recommendations?" I turned to McAlistair.

"We'd like to see the video of Sunny for my friend, and please call Linda for me, Pi Noi." Mrs. Noi bowed in acknowledgement.

Along one side of the room was a white screen. No vulgar two way mirror in the Bolthole. An attendant brought us some drinks. Mrs. Noi installed the cassette and dimmed the lights and a pretty round face appeared in close up on the screen. The camera drew back to reveal a young girl, in her late teens, in Thai garb. She curtseyed and *wai'd* at the same time then addressed the screen in fluent English: 'Welcome to the hospitality of the Bolthole. My name is Sunny and I am here to make your stay happy and relaxing'.

"Yes, I want her," I whispered into McAlistair's ear.

The picture faded into a view of the sea and an empty pristine yellow beach. It wasn't a beach that I recognised. Perhaps the video had been shot on Koh Samui or some other island that, being less accessible, still had sand and sea as pure as the people in paradise. Now the girl was wearing a silver swimsuit, sparsely cut, that hugged her figure closely. The zoom pulled her in close. Her long charcoal hair looked damp and waved around her shoulders in a mild ocean breeze. The scene changed to what looked like the lobby of a large hotel. Sunny, dressed in a blue velvet dress, matching court shoes and sparkling jewellery came gracefully down a long winding staircase. She walked past the camera through two glass doors that were opened by butlers and towards a car which looked suspiciously like McAlistair's Porsche. It looked even better on film than in real life. Now it was by the fountain outside the Bolthole. The girl slid out, careful not to let her knees lose touch with each other. She looked straight at us and said 'I hope to see you soon'.

"Very artistic," I applauded.

"Very naughty," McAlistair assured me.

Sunny proved to be as much and more than promised. Five minutes after seeing her acting debut I was holding her slim waist and she was unbuttoning my shirt telling me that she had been in London the previous month, but it was too cold for her. She put me through my paces until, at last, my tension was released across her thighs and stomach. An hour and a half later I was back in The Sportsman's bar, released, relaxed and mellow, freshly showered and in clean Chinos and a Polo shirt.

"Nice little rub down?" McAlistair asked. He looked gleaming from his own encounter.

"Outstanding, lovely little girl. No bullshit. She didn't bat an eyelid when I put the Glock on the bedside table."

"I imagine she's seen a weapon or two since she's been working here," he said, sipping his drink.

"Not too many, I hope. She's a sweetheart."

"Well, don't say that your mate McAlistair doesn't take you to the best places."

A foursome of diminutive Japanese golfers sat at a table near to us and twittered. Golf chat was the same the world over. Apart from them there was a certain genteel calm in the bar, like the mess of a regiment that had just been withdrawn from the front line. We sat in comradely silence for a while then decided to make a move.

"A word of warning about the Glock," McAlistair said. "Don't use it unless you have to and don't get caught with it by the police. The Thais might be warm and friendly towards innocent tourists, but they can be hard crazy bastards. I wouldn't want to see you in the 'Bangkok

Hilton'." He used the traditional nickname for Klong Prem Prison where not a few Westerners were serving long sentences for drug smuggling or fraud. He'd reminded me that things were getting a little hot for me in Pattaya.

"How many rooms do they have here?" I asked.

"Forty, fifty. Mostly suites."

"Any chance of me staying here with Simone?" He thought for a moment.

"In the main house, not a chance. You heard the manager. But there are some luxury chalets a few hundred yards down a track. I might be able to arrange it, especially as you're a mate of Harry's."

The manager was more than willing to bend the rules, as long as Simone did not come into the main building. The chalets were two-bedroom bungalows, perched among trees on a slope that looked down onto the golf course and the swimming pool. I took a key and told them to expect me in the late evening.

"What's the arrangement with Marjorie?" I asked, as we got back in the Porsche to leave.

"Said I'd call her on her carphone."

"Carphone," I repeated in amazement.

"Have you ever tried doing business in Bangkok without a carphone? With the way that traffic has been seizing up, no serious wheeler-dealer like Marjorie can live without one. They don't work that well, but once in a while you get through. He opened the armrest behind the gear lever, pressed a speed dial and handed me the Motorola handset. I put it to my ear, listening to the electronic hum of the ionosphere, rushing, buzzing and beeping until it formed into a long uninterrupted tone which meant that I probably hadn't got through. I pressed the redial button. On the third attempt, I heard a faint ringing noise and then heard Marjorie's voice. I explained to her that I had a meeting and that I would pick up Simone later from their place. She started to ask me something, at which stage the great satellite in the sky decided we had spoken enough and cut us off.

"Do me a favour, Julian," I said as the wind whistled around us as he got up speed. "Take me to the Sport Resort first so I can pick up my bags."

It was quicker than I'd expected to get back to the hotel. I asked McAlistair to park a hundred yards from the entrance. The Porsche was distinctive and I didn't want Gruber or his cronies to see us together. We perched Simone's Samsonite behind the seats and put my bag in the boot in the front – being a Porsche the car had a rear engine - then went on to 'Wee Jock's'.

I agreed with McAlistair that he would take Simone's luggage back with him and I would persuade her to stay at his place that evening. I brought my bag in with me and we had a quick beer before he headed back home. He said he was going to write but I figured he'd probably fall asleep on the veranda. It was hard work doing nothing all day.

I glanced around the room after he left. There were no familiar faces, only familiar types: beach bums, Thailand flotsam, bachelor tourists, and a few businessmen down from the city for the weekend. There were several girls, dark skinned and casually dressed in jeans and flip flops. Nothing to please the senses after an afternoon at the Bolthole. It didn't surprise me to see Angus Donnelly swaying mildly on the same spot where we had left him three hours earlier.

"You ever been to Singapore?" Donnelly asked. "Just moved my office there. Better place to work. Wife's from Singapore." He pulled out a cracked wallet and a photo of his wedding. "That's the Mrs - she's Hokkien Chinese. Got a nipper on the way. Angus junior." He looked sombre and sober in a Tartan kilt, the girl looked decent and delectable in her bridal dress.

"Christ, I'm mortalled," he said, finally lighting a Salem cigarette at the fifth attempt. He had reached a bridge too far, even for the nation that had built most of them around the world. "Where you staying then?"

"Sport Resort. May be moving to the Bolthole."

"That's one of my babies," he said, slurring with pride. "Put a lot of water onto that course. That's what the Nips like, lots of water, sand. You play golf? You should come up to Singapore and play on my course there. I'll give you my card. Ah, I left the fucking things in the hotel."

His podgy fingers crammed his wallet back into his baggy shorts with some difficulty.

"I canna wait to get out of Pattaya. It's a pisshole. And there some fucking arseholes around this town an'aw," he went on.

"What do you mean?"

"Everything you do you've got to pay squeeze money. Building anything in this country, even golf courses, is a fucking nightmare and this town's the worst. They're so fucking corrupt it's a fucking joke. You ask Wee Jock, he's been here ten years."

"Do you have any dealings with the Germans?" I asked, seeing an opportunity to get some intel.

"The Germans can fuck right awf." He took a deep swig of his beer as if they were too appalling to talk about and he had to wash out his mouth. "Two more days I'm here then I've got a project meeting in Indonesia. They're getting keen on golf. Good for tourists."

"You're making a few pennies then, Angus."

"I'm deeing arright. Used to be a footballer ten years ago. Came to Hong Kong to play football. Dinnay even know where Hong Kong was."

His eyelids fluttered for an instant and it looked as if he was on the verge of a power failure. It was time for me to move on so I told him to take care and went out to my bike. The Germans raised their hydra heads everywhere I looked. It was time someone made an effort to lop them off.

19

Evening had spread its cooler balm over Pattaya and the town was gearing itself up for another night of carnal commerce. After 'Wee Jock's', stepping into the *'Strammer Max'* was like being whisked from Clydeside to Kiel. The furnishings were all zinc and pale wood. In England it would have passed as a café. There was no bar to stand and lean at in that time-honoured Anglo-Saxon tradition.

Some of the tables were occupied by couples or middle-aged families with teenage children tucking into Wiener Schnitzels. On the *'Theke'*, the bar, stood a large contraption from which the beer was tediously drawn slowly into tall decanter-shaped glasses with little paper napkins around their base.

From the speakers on the wall, Peter Maffay, a popular German rocker could be heard singing one of his old songs called *Ich will Leben* - I want to live.

In an alcove was the *'Stammtisch'* - the table reserved for regulars and the landlord's friends – where I found Gruber and his companions. They were playing *Skat*, a popular form of German whist. Gruber came to his feet, clicking his heels together in greeting.

"Herr Graunitz, *darf ich Sie vorstellen*, may I introduce you?".

My muscle-packed friend from the beach, his hair now decently tied back in a ponytail, was seated opposite me. His name was Wim. His pecs were barely restrained within a grey T-shirt. From the openings in it sprouted a thick sinewy neck that would have made a bull proud and bulbous arms criss-crossed with elevated veins. A tattoo of the Pink Panther in a top hat, cigarette holder with smoke curling off the end was nicely drawn on his left forearm.

Next to him on the bench sat Harald. He looked cold and mean with very dark hair closely cropped to hide the fact that he was going bald. His suntan was deep and his skin was taut across the cheekbones. Firmly-etched crows' feet, and two vertical lines running down on either cheek, put his age over forty, but he was trim and healthy and greeted me warmly.

I felt uncertain of my status, like a rabbi dressed as a Catholic priest, invited to have an informal drink with former members of the Waffen SS. Reminding myself they were just a bunch of exiled bank robbers, lording around in a corrupt seaside resort, I studied both Wim and Harald at length.

"You are from Hong Kong, Gruber here tells

me," Harald said, shuffling the pack of cards then carefully slipping them back into their box. His was a Hamburg accent. I nodded.

"I saw you on the beach with a nice little mouse," Wim said, "She's not from here or I would know her." He grinned as if every woman in the region had to be approved first by his cock.

"My wife. She's Thai."

"A nice little mouse," he repeated, using the German slang. It explained a lot that, for us Brits, women were feline. To Germans they were rodents.

Gruber stood up. "I'll leave you to talk business." My beer arrived together with three glasses of Bismarck schnapps, clear and lethal in little solid shot glasses. Wim's beer glass looked small in his hand. I noticed evidence of recent bruising across his knuckles. I did not envy whoever had been unwise enough to place his face in the way of the fist earlier.

"*Zum Wohl*," Harald toasted and threw the fiery liquid down his throat. He sighed and savoured his beer. "Nothing like German beer, is there, Herr Graunitz?"

"*Besser gibts nicht*, nothing better," I agreed.

"Here in Pattaya we Germans are very influential," he said, leaning towards me conspiratorially. "We know about, or are involved in, everything that happens in this town. Three quarters of the bars and clubs are owned and managed by people from our country. We have an understanding with the police, who, in exchange for our financial support, respect our business initiative. If you are interested in doing business around here, we are the only people you should talk to."

He had spoken quietly and in German. I considered my best approach. His speech had been very direct, as expected.

"I'm not interested in buying a condominium or opening a girlie bar in Pattaya," I said, in accented English. "I was given the name of Otto Schwartz by a contact in Hong Kong as a good person to deal with. Do you know him?"

Harald's eyes sharpened. "We are familiar with Herr Schwartz. But he doesn't get involved in much commercial stuff these days. Who recommended that you speak with him? We have a number of business contacts in Hong Kong. Was it one of them?"

"I cannot say. You will understand that discretion is always necessary in such things."

Harald shrugged to show his indifference. "That makes it difficult for me to be open with you. Why don't you contact Herr Schwartz directly?"

"I don't know how to contact him. I only know his name." I fixed him with a stare that implied I was just as tough as him, which in a way I was. I could see him trying to work out if I was the soft businessman that Gruber had led him to believe, or somebody altogether more dangerous.

"Tell me the business you are interested in," he said at last, "and I will find out if Herr Schwartz might want to speak with you."

"I want to bring dancing girls into Hong Kong. My associates and I are opening a bar in Wan Chai. I need ten and they will be replaced whenever their visas expire. I need a regular supply and a reliable partner who can make all the arrangements at this end."

"Your wife is Thai, is she not able to help you in finding girls and arranging things?"

"My wife's not a bargirl. She can't help me with the documents and the visas and the extra tips that must be paid."

"Otto Schwartz isn't really interested in the export business," Harald laughed. "Nor are we. This is our little kingdom here, not Hong Kong. Will they fuck, the girls, or just dance? What will you be calling your club?"

"Club '*Sanssouci*'."

Harald smiled and I saw he got the allusion. He nudged his companion, "You don't understand that Wim do you?"

"I don't speak Chinese," Wim said irritated, sensing he was being made fun of.

"Frederick the Great called his palace in Potsdam *Sanssouci*. What does it mean Herr Graunitz? Without care and worries, right?"

"I'm going to the piss house," Wim said and stood up.

"The girls will mainly dance and talk to the

customers," I went on as the big man left, "but if anyone pays, they can be released. Most of the bars there now bring in girls from the Philippines but they lose out on a lot of revenue from the sex by overcharging. I want the girls to give professional service, so that the expat businessmen will regularly come into the club and have a beer and some quick executive relief before going home for dinner. If the girls have been working in the clubs here, they'll know what turns a man on and they'll do it well. It's simply good service that's needed."

"So that is your business plan?" Harald asked. I looked serious. Off the top of my head, worked out while being kneaded by the proficient Sunny in the Bolthole, it was as good a scheme as any. I'd spent some time working on an SDS Vice squad and understood the idiosyncrasies of Hong Kong law when it came to the sex trade.

Harald picked up his box of cards and dropped them into the palm of his hand. He shuffled them for about ten seconds, laid twenty down in two orderly rows and turned over four at random. They were all aces. He smiled.

"Good?" He brushed them back together into a pile. All this time I'd been watching him impassively. "In Germany I killed two people. So I can't go back," he said, matter of fact.

Tapping my lower lip with my index finger, I looked around for the waitress.

"You are not interested in why I'm a murderer?" he asked.

"A man's past is not important. What matters is whether he has learnt the lessons from it to influence his future. But if it amuses you, tell me."

"I was young; and I wanted to be rich. I bought drugs wholesale, adulterated them in my mother's guest-room and sold them in packets at a higher price. When the police came I knew who had informed on me. My sister and her boyfriend. Five years in prison. When I came out I shot her three times in the face and her husband - they had got married while I was in the slammer - twice in the heart. Then I emptied their bank accounts, got on a plane and came to Thailand. It makes you feel powerful to kill someone, did you know that?"

"I'm a businessman. I don't need to kill people. Do you think you or Herr Schwartz would be interested in working with me?"

Harald's tough man act was beginning to irritate me. Not a shoddy bank robber but a murdering drug dealer who cheated at cards. I wondered how he'd feel if I pulled the Glock and put three bullets into his face like he'd done to his sister.

"Herr Graunitz, I think you are probably a nice man. You come here asking for Otto Schwartz wanting to do some whoring business. I don't know you from Adam. Herr Schwartz doesn't know you from Adam, but your business sounds interesting. If I were Herr Schwartz I'd like to find out some more about you and the people you associate with first."

"I'm willing to tell him whatever he wants to know."

"But not me?"

"If you're willing to deal with me on this and have the connections, sure. I'd prefer not to say who suggested Herr Schwartz's name but that, you must agree, is only politeness."

"My interests and those of Otto Schwartz are the same, actually," he admitted. I tried to hide my relief. At least I hadn't been barking up the wrong tree all this time.

"So what shall we do? If neither of you is interested in my little whoring business, as you call it, then I'll take it elsewhere and spend the rest of the day relaxing by the pool."

"In Pattaya, there is nowhere else you can take your business. As in ancient Rome, in this little seaside town all roads lead to us."

"I see you spent your time in jail wisely and read a lot."

He nodded and gave me a small, lukewarm smile. He said, "Gruber tells me you've checked out now. Where can we find you?"

"I'll find you. We are staying with some friends of my wife's. They have a condo further south."

Wim came back with a fresh beer in his hand, followed by the waitress to see if we wanted another. I declined. I had said my piece and today I'd drunk too much beer already. I'd be growing a belly like Angus Donnelly soon.

"In case we misunderstood each other," Harald said lightly, "your Hong Kong connections are useless here. You would not be the first person to make that mistake. Here in Thailand, we are the people who decide what is what. You can't mess around with us. You can't mess around with Otto Schwartz. If you ever think you can, go down to the police station and ask them about their file on mysterious deaths. Wim could help them a lot with their enquiries, but he doesn't. We call him The Exterminator."

I glanced at Wim who was grinning inanely. So much for him liking mice.

"As I said, I am here because I'm a businessman," I emphasised.

"I really hope we can do business together," Harald said, bringing our conversation to an end. "After all, you are a fellow German. You don't look stupid and you don't look like a man who shits easily in his pants. Don't try to be tough with us. I'll talk to Herr Schwartz and leave a message with Gruber tomorrow lunchtime. *Zum Wohl.*" He waited until I'd raised my shot glass and we downed them as one.

20

The golf ball flew straight and true down the fairway, wavered momentarily as a small breeze caught it, and then gravity tugged it down pleasingly close to the green. It was barely eight o'clock in the morning and I stood on the first tee indulging in a rare pastime. I was trying to concentrate, but my mind kept going back to a dream from the night before in which Simone had finally succumbed. I had slept alone in the chalet beside the golf course, which perhaps explained my obsession with her. Only small scenes remained vivid, it had been one of those dreams, but they kept on returning with a nagging and erotic persistence.

My swing was acceptably smooth despite having not played for a year or so. I was alone on the course. Just myself, the morning, the trolley with clubs and the recollection of my nocturnal fantasies. There was a gentle breeze wafting across the fairway tempting one to forget that in only an hour it would be hotter than the temper of a woman scorned. The ball lay comfortably on the well-tended grass. I chose a 9 iron and chipped it onto the green but there was too much power in the stroke and it bounced a yard away from the hole then rolled on until it was stopped by the small lip on the edge of the green. Jogging along the edge of the golf course was the slim figure of a woman in a yellow tracksuit. A yellow headband held back long blonde hair. There was only one white woman on the premises. I wondered if she was coming to disturb my reflections.

I sunk my put and carried on to the next tee, got the wood out and prepared to address the ball.

"Bill, hi, you must be one hell of a keen golfer to get up so early and hit the golf course," Mandy said with syrupy American familiarity.

"Good morning," I said, mildly irritated by the interruption. Turning I leant on my club. "I'm just a holiday golfer. I like the relaxation of the game. It's early for what you are doing as well. A little bit too energetic for me."

"Got to shake up that metabolism. You look in good shape, Bill. Work out much?"

"Not religiously but on most days."

I wondered if, in a country which men visited to indulge themselves in the charms of Asian women, she was lonely. It wouldn't be the first time. I'd met many attractive Western girls around Asia who couldn't get a decent date given the competition. She'd be wasting her time with me, but perhaps I wouldn't be wasting my time with her. McAlistair's reference to white meat had penetrated my subconscious.

"What about alcohol. Would you fancy a drink with me sometime?" she asked, as if my thoughts had been written on my golf bag.

"Does that represent healthy nutrition?" I quipped. She smiled like a cheerleader who had been asked if she liked the back seats of cars.

"We're all allowed a bit of carbohydrate sin from time to time," she said smartly. She was batting her eyelids at me like they were a semaphore.

"Why not," I said, deciding to play along. "Let me get hold of you when I've finished here."

"Ask the guys at reception to page me," she said. "So long then, got to keep my heart-rate up."

"I'd be glad to oblige you with that."

"You cheeky Brit," she laughed and cantered off.

Without doubt she had a great figure, I thought, watching her rear-end as it got smaller. It might be an interesting exercise in depravity to let her seduce me and sleep with a white woman once again. It wasn't altogether unattractive; it would be something different for once.

An hour and a half later I'd done nine holes and shot an unimpressive 52, but it had been fun. I dropped off the clubs at the caddy shack and went to the breakfast room. There were a few men dining in silence. The comforting smell of bacon and eggs hung in the air reminding me unaccountably of my schooldays.

The waiter poured me a cup of English Breakfast tea and took my order. After my little walk following the white ball, I was starving. I looked around and noticed the pleasant result of another house rule - no girls at the breakfast table. In my experience women tended either to chatter during your hangover or steal those parts of the newspaper you were just about to read.

I glanced through the morning's *Bangkok Post* and came across the small paragraph I had been expecting. They had finally found Harry Keller's body. He was described as a middle-aged tourist found hanging from a fishing line in the toilets of a bar frequented by homosexuals and transvestites. He had not been discovered until a bad smell attracted the attention of the staff. The door was locked from the inside and police were considering the possibility of suicide.

I had not made much of an effort to cover up except for removing my fingerprints and climbing over the top of the cubicle. If they preferred suicide to murder that was fine by me. For the life of me I couldn't understand how a man strangled himself with a fishing wire. But the Thai police, like all forces in the world, would prefer to keep their detection statistics up - an unsolved murder didn't help the figures.

I checked the obituaries but there was nothing for me there, or in the *South China Morning Post* either. Business was slow this month. Not to worry. I already had enough going on to keep me busy.

The marmalade was thick and traditional. I was spreading it on my last piece of warm toast when McAlistair came in wearing a black tracksuit with red Adidas trimmings. His cheeks were crimson and his hair damp.

"Been in the gym?" I said.

"Yes, but I've also got something for you."

"Half a million dollars? Your wife wants to have a second husband?"

"No, on both counts, but the word on the street is that the French restaurant was blown up by the Germans. Charpentier was adamant that since the French had won the war and were better lovers, he wouldn't pay protection money to a crowd of neo-Nazi thugs. So they shut him down permanently."

"A man of principle, now sadly, a dead man of principle. Even if it was Churchill, not De Gaulle, who won the war. Who told you this?"

"My friend who owns the Wai Hotel, who also happens to be closely related to the current police chief."

"The police know that the Germans did it?"

"The Germans are not too subtle about this stuff. They haven't hidden their involvement in a fire since they burned down the Reichstag."

"And why doesn't the police...?" I left the sentence unsaid. "Yes, stupid question. I must tell you about my dream last night. I was shagging Simone on the back of my bike."

"She's not very happy with you," he said.

"So why is my darling annoyed with me?" I asked.

"Perhaps she missed you when you didn't come to pick her up. She said something about having to accompany you everywhere. Marjorie explained to her, without being too blunt, that you are the sort of man who isn't used to being accompanied by women."

Dislodging a loose strand of bacon with a toothpick, I nodded.

"Where are Marjorie and Simone then?"

"The wife's gone up to Bangkok to see the bank and your little darling is sitting in my car." I looked at him questioningly.

"No women on the premises!" McAlistair reminded me.

"This is really a great club. Remind me to tell Harry."

We drank another leisurely cup of tea. Then the whirlwind that was Harry Bolt finally arrived.

"Waiter, throw that man out," I said as he came through the swing doors.

"Bugger off, you little git, I own this place." We laughed and grabbed each other's arms and shook hands, because it's always good to see a man you like and trust.

Harry Bolt looked like a scruffy bricklayer's assistant from Neasden whose flight to the Costa del Sol had been diverted. Covering his bald head was a baseball cap, reversed in Nikki Lauda style. His pale, chubby cheeks and neck were covered in a fair stubble. The shirt he wore looked like it had been stolen from a sleeping tramp and his shorts were as faded as the British Empire. But the dynamism of the self-made man, shone from his bright blue eyes.

"Hello, son. Like my little place, do you? More tea, please."

He yelled at the waiters like a medieval squire, clapping McAlistair on the arm. There was nothing working class in Bolt's background, but he enjoyed slipping into his accents.

"There was a nice bit of totty sitting in your Porsche outside, McAlistair," Bolt said, his eyes wide open in exaggerated query.

"Nothing to do with me. Ask him. I'm a happily married man."

I explained Simone's provenance without too much detail.

"Ready for a day on my little boat?" Bolt asked me, slamming down his china cup on the tabletop and waving us to action. He swept out of the breakfast room and McAlistair and I followed in his wake.

Outside, Bolt stepped up to the passenger side of McAlistair's convertible, offered his hand over the rolled-down window, and said: "Hi, I'm

Harry."

The girl looked up and shook his hand. For the first time since I knew her, she looked ill at ease. Bolt had this effect on people.

"This is Simone, my accountant," I said.

"How convenient. I'm just looking for an accountant. My last one got arrested. Do you know anything about corporate taxation for foreign companies in Laos?"

Simone blushed and shook her head. Turning to me he said seriously: "Well, it's very simple, Bill. I'll only make the offer once - I shall trade you my four girls for your accountant."

I looked at Simone, shrugged and said: "Done."

She was confused. She wasn't sure what to make of a man whom I had told her was incredibly rich but was dressed in clothes that would make a beach bum blush. There was a quality about him that made him immensely likeable socially. People trusted him and all of a sudden found that he owned them. In business dealings he had no morals and all profit belonged to him. But if a person was in his circle of close friends Harry would move heaven and earth to protect them - as long as it also suited his designs.

"Come Simone," Bolt said. "I'm going to introduce you to my assistants."

"Assistants?" Simone said.

"Yes, they assist me in making life worthwhile and pleasurable. They're very effective assistants."

21

When Harry Bolt decided that the time had come to settle down, he flew to the north of Thailand with a local negotiator and purchased from a backward village four teenage girls. The families, scratching a living from the soil, were happy to sell a daughter for fifty thousand Baht. Bolt packed the girls off to a private school, had them educated, groomed and pygmalionised. When they were ready he installed them as his attendant princesses and went everywhere with them.

Harry pulled open the Porsche's door and let Simone step out. We walked over to where his giant jeep was parked.

"Ladies," he said, "you remember Bill. This is his friend Simone."

The girls all greeted her warmly as Bolt introduced them one by one. First there was Winter: cool as a Siberian morning, until she got drunk. Tall, skinny with legs that went on and on, the tiniest behind and hair cut in a German helmet bob style. Her hair was charcoal as were the eyes that dominated her face and froze any man who tried to hold her gaze.

Second there was Spring: petite, vivacious, child woman, wild, always leaping about, giggling, playing tricks. The colour of her skin was darker than the others, her nose and chest not as prominent and her hair was tied up pertly in a ponytail that emphasised her school-girlish looks.

Third, there was Summer: comely, voluptuous, tempting with extreme curves rarely seen in an Asian woman. All hips and breasts. Her shape was not unlike Simone's, although the hourglass was even more accentuated. She reeked of sensuality and female allure. Her mouth was full and demanding. Her eyes deep and warm. Her fresh skin was a rich oriental ochre that you longed to lean forward and stroke.

Finally there was Autumn: she had Chinese blood, which made her skin pale compared to the rest. The long straight hair hung down the back of a figure which was divine in its closeness to a classical ideal. Her legs, not too long, her hips not too heavy, her chest not too large, her face the archetypal Asian beauty, perfect in its simplicity.

I smiled indulgently. They were marvellous ladies and the nicest thing about them was the strong affection that I knew they felt for Bolt. Sooner or later, he expected them to yearn for independence and he would release them from their obligations. But they were still all young, none of them twenty yet, and since I had known them, no other man could even crawl close to the pedestal they reserved for their master. You could feel their loyalty like the searing heat of the desert sun.

Bolt took them wherever he had business; they had become an extension of his image. It pleased him to spoil them. They spoilt him in turn, avoiding generally the petty squabbles and vain jealousy that often surfaced when girls were thrown together in constant company. Today they were wearing identical blue and white striped shirts and matching shorts. Like a doting parent Bolt treated them all with equal favour, so on each wrist flashed the same elegant Cartier watch, on each neck an identical pendant fashioned from a wine-red ruby.

Simone agreed to ride with Bolt and clambered up. The ladies were already giggling. It promised to be a day of high spirits. Briskly, Bolt wheel-spun his Jeep out of the courtyard in the direction of the main road. McAlistair and I followed in the Porsche.

After half an hour we were close to the sea. An old man with two fruit baskets hanging from a pole across his shoulders leapt into a ditch as the Jeep hurled around the corner into a dusty side road that led to a jetty and a speedboat with a Yamaha outboard engine.

I had never been on Bolt's yacht before, a vessel as charming as his ladies, strong and sleek as a dolphin. It was a Riva 20 Corsaro, built in a Savona shipyard near Genoa, with engines capable of 32 knots and a crew of two. He had taken delivery only a few months before and still displayed the excitement accorded to a recent acquisition. It was white with black trimmings. Bolt had christened her 'The Four Seasons' in honour of his girls.

"Autumn, let's have some beers for the boys." Bolt said when we reached it. Sometime later I was sitting in the cosy stateroom, which doubled as Bolt's seaborne office, and was sipping my first drink of the day.

Simone was on the rear deck where the girls were basking in the sun and playing cards for unstated sums of money. Like all Asians, men and women alike, the Thais had a passion for gambling. Autumn and Summer were rubbing Hawaiian suntan oil into each other's polished skin. Spring had released her hair from the confines of the elastic band and begun brushing it with an item that looked like a metal hedgehog.

Bolt inserted a videotape into a machine, which connected to a three-foot screen, and we watched football for an hour. He was passionate about the game.

"How's big business?" McAlistair asked at some point after Arsenal scored a goal.

"Getting bigger," Bolt said. "Let's go and eat." On a table outside someone had dished up a buffet of diverse delights. Dipping a copper ladle into the traditional lip-scorching *Tum Yang Gung* soup, Summer was filling little bowls. Simone and Winter had their heads close together, already bosom friends.

"Bloody women. Never stop gossiping," Bolt muttered amiably patting Spring on the behind so she scampered out of the way and he could sit down. "Thank you, darling." He accepted the bowl from Summer.

I didn't care much for the *Tum Yang Gung*. It made my eyes water and my palate numb. I filled a plate with little titbits and walked over to Simone.

"Have you eaten?"

"Yes, thank you." Her smile was very warm and it surprised me since I thought she was still annoyed. I had not taken the time to speak to her yet. Winter sensed something and rose quietly. I took her place.

"I heard that you were upset with me," I said

"I am. You tricked me into spending the day with Marjorie and then avoided me. Why did you do that?"

"No special reason. Once I had my meeting with the Germans there didn't seem any point in going all the way back to McAlistair's place to pick you up."

"Uncle Tang told me to stay with you at all times, to keep you out of trouble and away from other girls," she said accusingly.

"And to spy on my every move."

Simone looked offended. "I am here to help your cover story so the Germans don't get suspicious."

"I suppose that's Chinese reasoning. A man with a wife is more decent than when he's without one."

"I don't know about Chinese reasoning. Last night I felt you were trying to stop me from doing my job. If you don't want me to help you I'll tell Uncle Tang and leave."

"Don't leave, I enjoy your company."

"Why?"

"I like you."

"That's all?" Her vanity was pricked.

"No, there's more. But not now." I smiled mysteriously.

"Fine. Don't do again what you did to me last night. It made me lose face in front of Marjorie and her husband. I looked very stupid not knowing what was going on."

"Okay but trust me a little. Some things are easier if I do them by myself. I don't have to hide anything from you or Tang. I'll tell you what I have been doing but I want you to do me a favour. Don't involve my friends in this business. Don't tell Tang that you met McAlistair or Bolt. They have nothing to do with this project. They are simply friends."

She nodded. I offered her a papaya as a token of our understanding. She leant forward and kissed me on the cheek to show me she appreciated what I had said about liking her.

"I wish you had nothing to do with Tang. Then you would be perfect," I said and squeezed her hand. After a few more plates I began to feel decidedly languid. I reclined, resting my head on Simone's thigh. She didn't object but took up her discussion with Winter again, who was speaking to her in rapid euphonic Thai, with an occasional burst of Chiu Chow when Simone failed to keep up.

My mind tiptoed lightly around recent events without reaching any firm conclusions except that the issues were still muddy. Only one thing was certain: I was either going to come out of this with a lot of money and a job well done, or not at all.

"What's on your mind?" Bolt said leaning over me so that condensation from his beer dropped onto my face.

"Women."

"You still haven't got your priorities right. First money, second business, third beer, fourth mates, fifth sports, sixth women." He inclined his head, "Let's talk about about money and business."

"Might as well, I wasn't getting anywhere thinking about women." I sat up and patted Simone on her bare thigh, taking a long lustful look down the front of her shirt. She frowned.

"I'll be back," I said using the macho voice.

Bolt led the way into his cabin and closed the door. He adjusted the air-con and absently pulled the videocassette from the machine, tossing it onto the floor to join the others. He opened and shut several cupboards without finding what he was looking for. I reached forward and offered him some of my cigarettes. He took a long deep puff.

"Bill, tell me what sort of job you're working on at the moment."

I looked out of the window and watched the blue smoke curl up along the glass. "I thought after the first few times you preferred not to know any details."

"This time I'm interested."

I considered. Bolt was a man I trusted. Mainly I trusted him because he was an old friend who valued the meaning of that little word. We knew things about each other's affairs that could destroy both of us. He had gambled high in taking me into his confidence once. He had read my character, correctly, so the gamble had paid off, changing the course of my life. Perhaps he could help me deal with a Gordian knot that I was still not certain how best to slash.

"Tang Siu Ling hired me to locate a former employee of his who appears to be working for the Germans here forging passports."

For a second he looked baffled. "Since when have you become a private detective in the employ of Triad scumbags like Tang?"

I grinned at him. "Circumstances made me a helpless victim of blackmail." I explained what had happened. Harry Bolt had a mind as sharp as a draughtsman's pencil. The incongruities in my story leapt up at him because he knew me too well.

"That's bollocks. What you just told me might be true but it's just a red herring. You're not here in Pattaya to find some lost little Chinaman who has been abducted. You kill people for money. Now tell me who you're really after?"

I took a minute to work out where to start. Harry had finally found some beers in a cupboard and handed one to me. It was warm and wet.

"Here's what you don't know," he said. "General Charoenchati owns the other half of the Bolthole. He's one of my most valuable business connections in Thailand."

Things suddenly started to resolve themselves. I began to suspect I was in the clusterfuck because of my old friend Harry Bolt, almost the only person in the world who knew my alternate identity as the Reliable Man, the highest priced assassin in Asia.

22

A lot of blood had passed under the bridge, even though it was just a few years and a dozen or so kills, since my first job. My first contract as the Reliable Man. The first time I had killed a man in cold blood, for money. It had not worried me. I had thought the whole scenario through from a policeman's point of view. I had looked at the elements of incriminatory evidence, the loose threads that invariably allowed detectives to unravel a case and find the perpetrator. I analysed the risks, minimised them through careful planning and considered it a fair proposition.

The idea of murdering a stranger didn't bother me at all. Had never bothered me then or since. If I felt uncomfortable with the victim, or the circumstances were too risky, I refused the job. My greatest advantage was that I knew how the law investigated crimes. There were a series of common-sense diktats which made assassination a relatively risk-free occupation. Following these painstakingly was the element of professionalism, which made the occupation lucrative.

Harry Bolt and I had known each other for

about two years at that point. McAlistair had introduced him to me while we were still both coppers. They had been at school together. Bolt was a shaft of startling sunlight outside the routine of my work and my tired circle of policemen friends. It was a relief to talk to someone whose view of the world was wholly profit-driven, whose morality revolved entirely around himself, whose conversation went beyond the constraints of cop-talk.

When he had enough of me moaning perpetually about being broke he asked me, hypothetically, if I would kill someone for money. I knew the answer. Definitely, if there was a lot of money on offer and I was certain to get away with it.

"How could you be certain to get away with it?" he asked.

"You have to know what you are doing," I had said, listing the points that came to mind. Never let yourself be identified or linked to the crime. Don't use an obvious or traceable murder weapon. Don't leave forensic evidence that can be built up into a picture of the murderer. Don't have personal contact with anybody connected to the job. Work alone at all times. Don't be specific with clients about time, location or any details of the job. Distance yourself as much as possible from the scene of the crime. If possible, prevent any investigation in the first place by making it look like suicide.

"So why don't we test your theory," he said with a smile on his face, "with a little practical exercise?"

Over a curry and several pints of Carlsberg we worked out the perfect assassination. Bolt's eyes gleamed. Later I realised what a power junkie he was. He loved manipulating people, being in control. The thought of ordering an execution gave him a tremendous charge of adrenalin. I didn't know then that, true to form, he had been contemplating the concept for some time. He just hadn't known that his collaborator would be me.

It wasn't the first time I had killed, although I didn't tell him that. When you tell someone you used to be a policeman in Hong Kong, almost the first question they ask you is 'Did you ever shoot anyone?' The truth is that as a copper you go out of your way to avoid it. Not just because it represents a failure of policing, but because of paperwork, the bane of a policeman's life, especially in the RHKP. Simply drawing your gun from its holster had you bogged down in administration for days.

No, I had killed in Northern Ireland. A Provo bomb-maker with a desire to cause carnage and an undercover operation that had gone badly wrong. It was 1982. Most of the British Army that wasn't protecting the Rhine from Russian invasion was in the South Atlantic and I got a lucky break. My Commanding Officer called me in. He was reading my service record and muttering to himself.

"Jedburgh," he said, as I saluted smartly, but with a sense of apprehension, "at ease."

He paused, as if trying to get the conversation off on the right footing. "We have an opening, and I have reluctantly come to the conclusion that you are the best person we have to fill it. I do that against advice from the Adjutant, who thinks you are a disgrace to the Intelligence Corps, and of the O.C. of your unit, who says you are a natural intelligence analyst and who doesn't want to lose you." He straightened in his chair. "I have a short-term vacancy in the Det. You know what that is?"

"14 Intelligence Unit. Based in Northern Ireland. I was thinking of applying once I'd extended my commission. You shouldn't let me anywhere near it without a year and a half of training and a selection course in the Brecon Beacons."

"Which is why I don't want to regret this."

Three weeks later, and I was regretting it as well. Cursing my lack of experience and the fact that I was supposed to be babysitting a desk in a cubbyhole in Derry while people with more experience and training were out in the field. Instead, I was facing a man in a greasy set of overalls with a package wrapped in newspaper that might have been fish and chips, but I knew was several pounds of Semtex.

"Just stand there and don't let anyone out," the guy had said, before disappearing around a corner of the seedy industrial estate we had been surveilling. He was SAS and had turfed me out of the car, thrusting a Browning Hi-Power into my hand, telling me not to attract any unwanted attention.

The subsequent enquiry exonerated me. I had shot to defend myself when the bomb-maker had pulled a revolver. I saw the look in his eye, a bead of sweat on his forehead and as his finger tightened on the trigger, I shot him in the face. I was exfiltrated from the province that evening and two months later my short service commission ended and there were strong hints that I should probably look for another career.

"Frankly, Jedburgh," the CO said when I returned to the unit, "somebody in Horse Guards just wants a veil drawn over matters. You're a good lad, and in this case you're collateral damage. Come and have a drink at the house before you leave."

I knew exactly where his house was. I'd been there in the afternoon with his wife a couple of times. She thought I was a good lad too.

A few months later I was a Probationary Inspector in Hong Kong.

Which is how I knew, when Harry asked, that I would have no trouble killing someone. I had been offered counselling by the army, but I could honestly say that I had never lost a minute's sleep over the man I killed in Derry. His bomb would have murdered hundreds of people, so it was a righteous kill in that respect, but even so I felt nothing. It was a job, just like killing for money would be a job.

A week later, Harry asked me my definition of a lot of money. I suggested half a million US Dollars, but we agreed that would price me out of the market. We chose eighty-eight thousand, a lucky Chinese number, and I found myself thinking and talking about it seriously.

Two weeks later I flew to the Philippines. In my shirt pocket was one of those chunky Montblanc pens that aspiring executives favour. Bolt had bought six of them on the Moscow black market during a business trip, 50 US dollars each, cash. They were relics from the cold war, beautifully crafted and ingeniously designed. They fired a microscopic needle which left a puncture mark so minute that no medical examiner would detect it unless they had been told what to look for and where.

The needle contained a droplet of ricin, a derivative of castor oil seeds, four times more lethal than cobra venom. Striking a main artery, the victim would display the symptoms of a heart attack and die within fifteen seconds. His death would appear natural, the beauty of which was that without suspicious circumstances no overworked police force would open an investigation file.

A band called 'Bahala Na' was playing in the 'Euphoria' discotheque of the Manila Intercontinental. At a quarter past twelve the dance floor was packed and I was bopping with a girl called Peachy. A rat-faced Indian man in a pink tie was dancing beside me, leering over a slimmer, sexier dance partner. He had made the fatal mistake of cheating Bolt over a minor business deal.

I was waiting for the strobe lights which came on for fifty seconds every few minutes. As soon as they began to flash, I twisted the cap of the Montblanc pen so that the nipple came out and cupped it in the palm of my right hand. As the strobe effect finished and everyone's eyes were taking time to readjust, I inserted the needle into his inner thigh. He was on the plump side, from too many curries, and was sweating obscenely. A moment later he collapsed. Eventually the couples around him noticed and the music stopped. Two young medical students tried to resuscitate him and by the time the ambulance arrived, Peachy and I had left the bar and were on the way back to my hotel room.

Harry paid me US$ 88,000 for my efforts and the Reliable Man was born. As Harry said: 'If a secret identity is good enough for Superman or Batman, then you fucking need one too.' Originally my jobs had come through Harry spreading the world, but it was now well-known in the right circles that if you needed a professional hit and you had the money, the Reliable Man was your best option.

Only Harry Bolt and Julian McAlistair knew my secret. If you wanted to contact the Reliable Man, you placed a carefully worded obituary in the *South China Morning Post*, the *Bangkok Post*, or the *Straits Times*. The obituary should give a fictitious name of an elderly person who had died at the age of 57 from consumption. The obituary would list a contact telephone number to call if one wanted to donate flowers.

Once I noticed the age of death and checked the wording was correct, I'd get in contact with my prospective client from a public phone box using a voice changer. I would give clear instructions as to what information I needed in order for me to assess the viability of the commission and to identify the target they wanted eliminated. This file was sent by courier to an address in Thailand. Before it could be delivered it would be intercepted and find its way to McAlistair via a bar in Pattaya where Julian sometimes drank. Julian would pick up the parcel and check it hadn't been tampered with, re-package it in case there were hidden tracking devices, and send it back by courier to a serviced office address in Hong Kong.

A dozen deaths and a couple of years later I had earned over a million bucks and what was left, after expenses, was distributed in discreet bank accounts around the world. I'd learned a lot as a result of tactical drinking sessions with a friend in the Commercial Crime Bureau and taken advice from Bolt on money laundering.

I was still careful these days but had noticed the occasional cockiness that leapt onto my back like a tempting devil. That sort of cockiness had resulted in acts like Keller's death. But for selling out a former colleague, he had deserved to die.

23

"When General Charoenchati told me that he wanted a man called Otto Schwartz killed," Harry said, "I recommended he use a professional and told him how to contact you. It's too much of a coincidence that you've turned up in Pattaya now. Am I right?"

"I spoke with a man in Singapore who couriered me the details of the target. I had no idea that Charoenchati had anything to do with it."

"Makes sense," Bolt interjected, "just as you don't want anyone to know who you are, nor does the man paying for the kill."

"The advance was telegraphed into one of my accounts and I agreed to get on with things. Then for some absurd reason Tang hits on me to come out here and infiltrate the Germans to find his forger so I reckoned I could kill two birds with one stone. Find the forger, hit Schwartz, right? Then Charoenchati found out somehow that I was going to do the job for Tang and threatened me with one of his goons to lay off."

"He had no way of knowing you're the Reliable Man," Harry said. "No way do I tell anyone, especially not my business partners. I might need you to slot them."

"Obviously, he was warning me off. I wasn't going to say anything, so I agreed to stay away from the Germans which of course I haven't done, because I had a job to do. I just didn't realise it was for him."

"Charoenchati heard about the Saudi killings and thought they were the work of a Middle Eastern hit man. He wanted someone professional and discreet. I suggested if he called your number, he'd get a reliable man."

I remembered the killings Bolt was talking about. That had been six months ago in Bangkok. Wearing a red wig and with my face swarthy from make-up to look like an Arab, I had shot two Saudi diplomats in the street who were involved with arranging jobs for Thai workers abroad. They had fallen foul of someone higher up in their organisation and a bullet each had cancelled their visas.

"Do you think it's wise playing smart with both of these people?" He spoke as a devil's advocate although he knew that if I wanted to handle things in this manner, nothing would change my mind.

"We'll see how things work out."

"I might have another job for you. It might change your perspective, but I'd have to check with the other party first before I can talk."

I laughed. "I'm really a bit too busy this week,

Harry. Let me put this one to bed first and then we'll talk."

"No hurry. The faster you kill Schwartz the better, though," he said with a venom that I wasn't used to from him.

"Why?"

He looked grim. "This morning I was told about the death of a friend of mine. They found his body in the surf on Jomtien Beach, face down in the sand. Another mysterious drug death," he said with sarcasm as heavy as his monthly bar bill at the Singapore Cricket Club. "The police said he'd been drinking and then took a dozen Dexies which flipped his heart out. Crap. Everybody knows that Dexedrine's one of the Germans' trademarks and they'd been shaking him down hard lately."

He paused and jabbed a finger hard into my chest to make his point. His face had turned into a red mask of anger. "Nobody goes around murdering friends of Harry Bolt. Kill Schwartz, because he's behind all of this and kill whoever actually did the dirty work if you can find out."

"Who was your friend?"

"A small fat Scotsman called Angus Donnelly," he said. "I've known him for years in Hong Kong. I own part of his company. He designed golf courses. He did the course at the Bolthole."

I wasn't listening anymore because my temper also rose suddenly like a typhoon from nowhere. The bastards. I took several deep breaths while

Bolt watched me with interest.

"Fuck," I said. "I was with him last night. I had some beers with him."

"He was a bloody good lad." Bolt walked over to the closed door, popped his head around it and told one of the girls to bring us some more cold beers.

"You want to be careful of that bird." He jerked his head in the direction of the door, meaning Simone.

"I'm keeping an open mind."

"For you, women are always a nightmare. I've been saying that for years and have always been right. Be careful."

"She doesn't know too much. Tell me, why does Charoenchati want to have Schwartz killed?"

"I get the impression that it's something to do with national pride besides personal profit. For the last few years, they've let the Germans get away with murder and the rest in Pattaya. Somebody might have said to the General, 'these *falangs* are getting a bit too serious and organised'. Underneath the gentle smiles the Thais are a proud people. If there's going to be corruption they want to benefit from it. You know how this country works, half a percent of the population owns ninety-five percent of the wealth. Charoenchati is a major player; he might get mixed up in politics soon. It's useful to have a guy like him on your Christmas card list."

"I think I've offended him already."

He tossed a beer can at me then popped the ring pull on his own and took a swig.

"Not a good idea at all. You have this habit of rubbing important people up the wrong way."

"Tell me something new. I'm too old to change."

"At least you now have enough money to enjoy yourself in the process," Bolt said. "Having a good time, getting laid a lot, getting pissed, having enough money not to worry, leaving a mark on the world. That's what life's all about."

"We can't all make the world a better place," I said with a twinkle in my eye.

"Killing Schwartz will make the world a better place."

I nodded. It was this journey forward that kept exciting me. The growth of my retirement fund, the tension of planning a hit, the pressure of executing it and then the euphoria of completion. It was like sex but so much better because it was so much more dangerous. It required control as well as a certain madness. Gunning people down in the street was an adrenaline rush but unnecessarily risky. And I wasn't doing it for fun. Purely for pecuniary gain. Because I wanted a lot of money, had few scruples and could think of no other job that suited me better.

"It's not a good thing, pissing Charoenchati off," Bolt said. I agreed. Kronk turning up everywhere, hot for my blood, was an inconvenience. How had he been able to know so quickly where Simone and I were? It was just one of a number of things that bothered me. The other was how Charoenchati had got the picture of the Forger.

"Do you want me to speak to Charoenchati?" Bolt asked

"Not for now. I'm not prepared to compromise my anonymity. I'll work something out. It just needs a bit of thought."

"Fine. Just make sure you think fast and stay alive." He gave me a hard punch on the arm to show me that he cared.

When we got back onto the rear deck Bolt snuggled himself between two of his girls. I joined McAlistair who was gazing pensively at the setting sun.

"Beautiful, I wish I had the words to describe it," he said, like the crap author that he was.

"You will, you will."

He sighed, then turned and patted me in the small of my back to check if I had my Glock on me. "Great little piece that. I wouldn't know you were carrying. Is it comfortable?"

"Like a mattress with a broken spring. You get used to it when you have no other choice."

"I'd like to know what you're really up to here, Bill. It would be good material for a new book."

"Confidential. I'll tell you when we're old and grey."

"Not long to wait then."

I told him about Angus Donnelly's death and what I knew. When I finished he only said: "If any of those rounds in that Glock are going to be put to use in Pattaya you know where I'd like them to end up." Then we sat in silence.

The warm languid mood of the afternoon had long gone. A briskness was whisking over the ocean and I no longer wanted to be on the boat. I had things to do, decisions to make. Events were tugging me back into the centre of the current. Action was beckoning like a shore-bound siren with a lethal smile and a languid wave.

I tapped the crystal face of my watch at Bolt and he got the message. The girls began packing up after which we made our way back to the Bolthole. McAlistair told me he'd see me later in the week. Harry said he and the Four Seasons would be in The Oriental in Bangkok. Then both cars disappeared in a cloud of dust flung up from the fast-spinning rear wheels.

24

Simone looked at home in the elegant surroundings of the chalet. The wooden floor and bamboo fixtures spoke of quality. The living room had a comfortable, luxurious atmosphere, dominated by a semi- circular sofa with deep royal blue cushions facing the balcony. Siamese historical scenes graced the walls. The bedrooms were identical in size, each containing beds large enough to get lost in for a month. She stepped out onto the balcony for a cigarette while I dumped her bags in a corner and fetched two glasses of water. The smell of woodlands hung about pleasantly. A hundred yards away down a moderate slope was the third tee. We could still see a pair of golfers struggling back to the main building in the gathering dusk. I sat in one of the rattan chairs, resting my feet and nursing a glass of whisky. Walking past me, Simone gave my hair a ruffle.

"Which bedroom is mine?" she asked.

"The one that I'm using. I want to sleep with you."

She sat on the broad arm of the chair and

cupped my chin in her hand. Our day together had softened something between us.

"I'd like to sometime," she said. "Very much. But not this time." She kissed me on the mouth. A warm, moist kiss that I could feel on the back of my scalp and in the tips of my toes. My barometer of desire shot into the red for a few heartbeats.

She got up and left me with a smile, but her female musk lingered around me, mixed with the aroma of her cigarette. I wondered if she might be playing with me. If so, this was a game I might lose. For a minute or two I sat letting the tension subside.

I got up to pour myself another whisky, contemplating an evening deadening my heartache with liquor. There was an envelope that I had overlooked on the silver message tray by the door. It was from Mandy requesting me to call her as soon as I got back.

The old Jedburgh reasserted himself. If Simone remained a fortress unconquered then I'd just have to go and pillage another, more compliant, village. I tried to remember the American girl, but although her attractive blonde figure jumped easily to mind, my testosterone levels didn't rise accordingly. I tried to remember back to before I had first come to Hong Kong. I'd had a steady girlfriend as blonde and white and sporty as Mandy. Try as I might, I couldn't remember what sex had been like with her. I only knew that, since I had started sleeping with Asian women, I had no desire to look elsewhere. Maybe that was why I was contemplating Mandy. She was not a rival in any way to Simone or any of the other women I chose to sleep with, but she would help to pass the time and might have interesting gossip for me. She must know people around town.

Simone had emerged from the bathroom and was trying to dry her hair and smoke a Virginia Slim at the same time. She wore an oversized white bathrobe that hid most of her body.

"By the way," I said, but the noise of the dryer was too much. She smiled and turned it off. I went on, "Remember that Scottish guy in the pub. The fat one?" She nodded.

"They found him dead this morning on the beach."

She dropped the hairdryer in surprise and stammered some words.

"Rumour is that he had some problems with the Germans and that's the way they often execute someone. Fill him with drugs and dump him in the sea."

She studied her feet for a while. They were exquisite feet but then at this moment everything about her was. I went to the minibar for some mineral water. I'd had enough alcohol.

"He was funny and now he's dead," she said, with a catch in her voice. "So many people are getting killed here. The Frenchman and now…"

"It's a hard game people play here. Your Uncle Tang plays the same sort."

"No!" she said, angrily, "he doesn't do that sort of thing. He's not a killer. He may be a tough businessman, but to be successful you have to be tough."

"His sidekick Sebastian Tse arranges all the nastiness," I said, carefully and took a swig from the small Perrier bottle.

"Bill, stop it. I won't talk about this anymore. You want me to doubt Uncle Tang and what he does. You want to confuse my loyalties and yes, you have been succeeding, a tiny little bit. I'm really sorry about the fat guy. Perhaps we should just get this job done and get away from these Germans."

"I don't think so. I think someone has to stop them."

"And you believe you're the one? Don't be silly. This is for the police to settle."

"This is Thailand, Simone. You know better than I do that isn't going to happen."

She stared at me for a moment then looked resigned.

"Well, maybe Uncle Tang will do something about the Germans," she said.

"Maybe. After all they stole his forger."

"He's not really a forger," she said angrily. "He's a computer scientist who writes important programs for Uncle Tang's companies."

I was starting to understand why even the

evillest of men seemed to have a loving, gullible, woman at home. If a woman wanted to believe in a man's goodness in the face of facts, she would always find a way to persuade herself.

I said, half to myself, "If you're rich and powerful like Tang it's easy to be kind to a few people in return for their loyalty and devotion. Murderers and politicians love and hug babies, that doesn't make them good or honest men."

She stood up and the hair dryer clattered to the polished parquet floor again. Then she stormed off into her room. Our conversation was over for the moment.

It was her loyalty to Tang that bothered me. Already she knew a bit too much about my private life. A feeling inside, which I wanted to believe, told me everything would be all right if I could only cut her away from this childish worship of a man I despised. The door to her bedroom was locked. I tapped on it with my fingers.

"I've got to go to a meeting. Lock the front door and don't open it until you're sure it's me."

Dropping the empty Perrier bottle into a wicker basket I got the things that I wanted and left the chalet. The front hall of the main building was quiet and even more scholastic now that the sun had gone. A different girl sat at the reception desk, no less pretty than her colleague. She pointed out where the phones were. It rang five times before Mandy's congenial voice answered. She asked me what I'd been doing.

"I was on the beach and went out on a boat with some friends."

"Do you still have some energy left to party?"

"Don't know about dancing on tabletops until dawn but I could do with a nice dinner."

"Are you free tonight, Bill?"

"I'm free most nights when dinner involves pretty girls."

She chuckled and called me a gallant Englishman.

"How about a drink somewhere first?" I thought quickly and decided that the Wartsteiner beer from the previous night had left a favourable impression. It wouldn't matter if the Germans saw me there. They might have some news for me. "How about the German bar on the Beach Road near the Montien Hotel? It's called *'Strammer Max'.*"

There was silence from the other end, then she said, "No, I don't like that place. Look why don't you come over to my condo? I've plenty of wine and I haven't had a chance to show off my cooking skills for a while"

"Fine by me."

"I'll put a lean steak on and toss up a healthy salad."

She gave me directions. It was a new development near Jomtien, easy to find. Her apartment was on the top floor. When I hung up I wondered what I had let myself in for. This was likely to turn into a big seduction scene and I wasn't sure how ready I was for a blonde caucasian. It would have been better if Simone had given in to my advances. I might not have been this easily tempted by Mandy.

Since I wasn't going to drop by the '*Strammer Max*' I decided to have a quick look at the Sport Resort. I got on my motorbike and rode the half hour into Pattaya town.

Gruber was still in his office. Perhaps filing another two notches into his desk now that Angus and Charpentier had been removed, victims of the Teutonic bulldozer. We exchanged pleasantries, his more sincere than mine and he confirmed that my meeting with Otto Schwartz was fixed. His boss was keen to expand into Hong Kong. He'd been talking about it for some time even before I came. He was willing to spend an afternoon listening to proposals. I noted how Gruber, for the first time, had referred to Schwartz as his boss and not as his associate.

25

Mandy came to the door in white Lycra pants that were tighter than a Yorkshireman's fist. On top she wore a grey silky item with thin straps that fell off her shoulder every time she moved. She also wore fluffy Mickey Mouse slippers and a gold Bulova watch.

I apologised for being late and followed her firm posterior into the living room. The Bolthole must be a generous paymaster, I noted, glancing around at the furniture arranged with female self-consciousness. The style was mainly white, light and airy. There was a three-piece settee in cream linen, a twenty-four-inch Sony TV, a deep plush wall-to-wall carpet that came up to my ankles, and top-lit prints of impressionist paintings in wooden frames. Stepping past a cabinet laden with duty free bottles, I studied the books on her shelves. There was a lot of literature on exercise and nutrition, specialist texts as well as fashionable diet books; two Linguaphone courses, Thai and German, looked neglected next to the usual collection of airport romances and a stack of old Cosmopolitan magazines. Dotted around the room were eastern artefacts like Chinese opera masks, Wayang puppets and tea sets giving an unobtrusive dash of traditional East meets modern West. I made appreciative noises, admiring the decoration.

Sliding doors opened onto an ample balcony. A rattan chair hanging from a chain in the roof swung lazily in the evening breeze. The view was down over the empty amber of Jomtien beach, miniature deckchairs and folded umbrellas just visible by the lights cast from the houses along the road. She handed me a glass of Californian Cabernet Sauvignon.

"Are the steaks spoiled?" I asked

"Everybody is late in Thailand. I was waiting for you before putting the steaks on. Did you have a productive day?"

I shrugged noncommittally. She was sitting in the corner of the settee, sipping white wine from a tall crystal glass. At the other end of the room, some twenty yards away the table was laid for two, a family size wooden bowl of salad stood next to the open bottle of wine in a silver cooler. Low soul music came from one of the four speakers dotted around the room.

"Do you enjoy living in Thailand?" I asked.

"Can't complain. I'm doing fine for a little girl from Hicksville, Nowhere. I might get bored in a year or two. Then I'll just move on. I get offers all the time. I'm good at my job, you know, Bill. You ever been to the States?"

"Never. I went to Canada on exercise once when I was in the Army."

"Oregon is a pretty wonderful State, a bit like Canada. But I couldn't wait to leave. You have to see the world when you're young." She laughed, showing her perfect ivory teeth. She reminded me of an old girlfriend. They say owners grow like their pets. That one had a horse.

"And how young *are* you?" I asked, genuinely curious. I was pretty good at guessing the age of the Asian girls, but I had no real idea with westerners anymore.

"Hey, that's not a polite, Englishman kind of question. I'm still a long way from the big three 'O'." She made her blue eyes look sincere and inviting and her tone was mocking. "Don't tell me you really are as rude and unfriendly as your friend Julian makes out?"

"I am, generally speaking. But I haven't eaten yet. That's when I'm still mellow. How long have you lived here?"

"One and a half years in Pattaya. Six months in this place. It took me some time to get it right. I wanted it to be uncluttered, you know. When I was a little girl my Mom made me share a room with my sister. Our room was always full of things. I love having my own place and arranging everything just the way it suits me." She explained the difficulties she'd had finding what she wanted, breaking into slices of autobiography once in a while. I filled myself another glass and she told me to feel right at home while she got to work in the kitchen.

I snooped around the flat tentatively. There were two big bedrooms decorated in the same taste as the lounge. I got the impression of a country girl done good. Opening up her clothes cupboard the variety of evening wear surprised me. There must have been over thirty pairs of shoes - more expensive than the sort you saw in the Marine Disco on a Friday night.

When she called me through to eat, her steaks were succulently perfect. I'd asked for mine to be well done which had caused her to call me a faggot. In the end I agreed to a bit of pink. We made idle conversation, telling each other whatever lies we wanted the other person to believe. Gently, I prodded her with questions on her lifestyle and the people she knew around town.

"Three types of men come to the Bolthole: The local smart set; the regular members from around Asia who come to relax and play golf; and businessmen who use it to butter up their clients."

"What's the main attraction?"

"It's not my gym, honey. I can tell you that. The food's wonderful. You saw the menu? I spend a lot of time with Jean-Fabrice sorting out the healthy dishes. He's a great cook but he's gay. There's a lot of that around here, I'm sure you know. Then there's the other side, the unhealthy food that most of the members prefer to eat.

What they call classic club fare. Your British colonial dishes."

"You can still eat sensibly, and well," I said, pointing to our plates with the end of my knife.

"That's true, but the Bolthole is a business, and it supplies what rich people are prepared to pay richly for. It's peaceful and sophisticated but the bottom line is still the girls. Sometimes I feel sorry for them, they're so adorable. Always coming to me asking about what clothes to wear when they go up to Bangkok. Do they make some money, these little dolls! Makes you think twice about doing a real job instead of selling your ass." She chortled. "They tell me it's all well managed. Regular check-ups and safe sex. You like these skinny Asian women?" Her eyes betrayed that this was an important question for her.

I smiled insouciantly over the curve of my fork. "They have their charms."

"Don't you get bored of talking baby talk with them all the time?"

"I haven't reached the age yet where I look for intelligent conversation in a woman," I said provocatively but tempered it with a cheeky wink.

"Don't you miss a real woman? Someone who has personality and who knows how to talk back at you, instead of just lying there until you're finished and are ready to hand her the money."

"Most of the men who come to Thailand are trying to get away from their modern, aggressive women. They want to be pampered and waited upon by a sweet little thing who only gives and doesn't demand constant attention."

"I guess that's true. But it's kind of sad."

"It's the reality in the Far East. You should have realised that by now."

"As a modern woman you can never really accept that kind of thing."

"You mean the answer to the question: why have a woman for free when you can pay money for her?" She decided not to take my words seriously, rolling her eyes in mock irritation.

"Let's sit on the sofa. Finish off that second bottle, Bill."

We moved and she came and placed herself at the far end, tucking her bare feet under her buttocks, coyly playing with her half full glass.

"So what about all these Germans you see running around town?" I asked her.

She frowned for a second then replied: "The Germans? They give the place character. They run most of the go-go bars with that German efficiency. Kind of a cross between the Gestapo and the Hell's Angels. I like the Germans. They know what they want and get on with it."

"You like men who go out and take what they want?"

"Doesn't every woman?" She smiled coyly.

This was the moment that her left strap chose to slip and, because she was leaning forward on her arm, the material fell forward revealing one bare sun-tanned breast like a ripe fruit on a market stall. She looked embarrassed, recovered the strap and said hastily, "That wasn't meant to happen."

"It's okay, I didn't look."

"You did too."

"I looked but I didn't see anything."

"Yeah, you smoked but you didn't inhale."

"I inhaled, but only briefly."

She laughed, spilling some of her red wine on the white Lycra pants. "Bill," she said looking straight at me, "you're not the typical stuffy English creep I meet at the Bolthole. I find you damn attractive." I studied her liquid blue eyes and dropped my gaze to the skin on her arms. There was a pleasant aroma of Chanel that hung about her.

"Some people say the Germans run this town and if anyone gets in their way, they are dealt with."

Mandy shook her head with irritation. "Whatever people say, it's mostly stories. Don't change the subject, tell me more about yourself. You're an investment consultant, single and with lots of little Asian girlfriends?"

I smiled vacuously without replying.

"I know you were in the police with Julian. That must have been exciting?"

"Mostly we just got drunk and wrote reports full of bad grammar. Then he turned into a complete poofter, settled down and got married."

"I've never met his wife. I heard she's Thai."

"Yeah, that's true."

"Was she a bar-girl or something?"

"She was a flight attendant for Cathay Pacific," I said. I didn't elaborate but filled our glasses again.

Mandy wanted to know more about Hong Kong and I went into auto-pilot telling her of the strange city colony with the uncertain future and its fascinating rude, industrious, people. I was beginning to get bored and when she stood up to fetch me a brandy, sneaked a look at my watch and decided it was time to leave or get laid.

After a short struggle with myself, I decided to stay a bit longer. I was in two minds. There were two controlling forces within me - my upper brain and my lower, much smaller one. The first didn't want complications and aggravation; the second just wanted to dive in, have fun and sod the consequences.

Mandy changed the tape to some slow, seductive, blues and handed me a balloon glass. This time she sat very close. So close I could see the hairs in her nose. I must have looked irritated because after a moment she said:

"Bill, am I coming on too strong?"

"No, not at all. It's different."

"Not you're regular little Thai girl?"

"Shut up." I helped her to obey my order by putting my tongue in her mouth. She tasted fresh, a minty Listerine taste mixed with the sweetness of the cognac. We explored each other's bodies and I had her breasts in my hands and then between my teeth. She arched her back and a minute later I was stripping the Lycra pants from her hips. At first I was shocked by how much hair she had but she was a natural blonde.

"There, yes, suck harder, yes. God, I love it when a man licks my pussy, just don't stop or I'll scream," she panted in between deep breaths, as I ran my tongue along the folds of her pussy.

Twenty minutes later I sat back. We were both naked on the sofa. Mandy was stretched out, her head hanging off the edge nearly touching the floor.

"I'm sorry," I said. "Must have been the wine."
She sat up and looked at the misshapen form of the condom which covered my limp member.

"Don't worry. It happens to all men. I shouldn't have opened the second bottle. Hey, look on the bright side - at least you made me come with your tongue. That's more than I managed to do for you."

"It's been a long day."

"So what do the cute little Thai girls do when you can't get it hard for them?"

"Give you your money back, I guess."

Mandy gave me an odd look, not sure if I was being serious or not. She passed me my brandy. "I'm just gonna take a shower."

Removing the offending piece of latex and dumping it in the bin, I used her spare bedroom shower to wash the sweat and smell of sex off my body. It had been fun. Her body was firm and fit and her breasts had been a rare pleasure to knead. But somewhere in my brain a lever had been thrown and the hydraulics were out of order. It was probably just as well.

We sat and talked for another ten minutes and then I got up to leave, pleading exhaustion.

"It was fun, let's do it again whenever you're up for it," Mandy said without, I hoped, intentional irony. The way she said it made it clear that she wasn't expecting a replay. She hadn't fallen for the 'too much alcohol' excuse. She must have sensed that my heart wasn't in it. Perhaps it had happened to her before. I kissed her on the cheek and patted her rump, thanked her for the steak and a fine evening and rang for the lift while she watched pensively from the door of her flat.

26

I walked back to the Kawasaki and kicked it into life. From the hubbub and neon of the strip it took less than ten minutes to be enveloped by the quiet blanket of the night. The town faded into the distance and I was alone except for the sullen growl of the engine.

Back inside the grounds of The Bolthole, I ran up a gentle slope before turning the corner behind which sat the chalet. I rode the big beast carefully with only the light from its headlamps showing the way. The gravel crunched like frozen snow on Christmas morning.

A car was parked outside the chalet. I recognised its outline. Kronk was back. I clicked off the headlights and killed the engine on the motorbike, letting the wheels roll until the momentum was gone. On either side of the wooden porch were windows covered with heavy wrought iron bars. Black-out curtains hid the light coming from inside.

I tugged the Kawasaki cautiously back onto its stand and slipped the Glock from its holster. I was about ten feet from the boot of the Mercedes. My eyes gradually adjusted to the night. The car was empty. I tried the driver's door. It opened. Inside, the smart upholstery and the smell of fresh plastic told me the car was not long off the assembly line. The keys glinted shyly at me, so I pocketed them, then moved on without shutting the door properly.

The front door of the chalet was locked from the inside. I put my ear to the wood and made out voices. I skirted the edge of the building, stepping in soft earth and pushing through dense undergrowth. This would be a bad time to encounter snakes. The ground began tilting downhill. My senses tried to pick up every rustle, every smell, every shadow.

Just as I got to a point where I could see the edge of the veranda my left foot slipped suddenly, sending me slithering down on my rear. Digging my heels in arrested the movement. I froze wondering if I had made too much noise. Nothing happened. I pulled myself up on the stem of a small tree. Three yards above my head, the veranda jutted out. Light spilled out over it but not much beyond, so I was still in good cover. I managed to get close without slipping again, although the going was slow, then reached up for one of the supports. The French windows were not fully shut and there seemed a five-inch gap where the curtains were only partially drawn. I holstered the automatic and pulled myself up, rolling slowly over the banister and crouched in the corner of the veranda. Steadying my breath, I listened. The sound came clearly through the thin glass.

"I don't know," Simone said in a frightened, uncertain voice, in response to a question.

"Where he go?" Kronk demanded.

"I really don't know." There was a pause then she gave out a small scream.

"Where he go?"

Simone didn't answer this time. Kronk spoke to her in Thai.

There was a slap and an exclamation of pain.

Simone spoke a few low words in Thai. Kronk said something to another person whom I presumed to be his sidekick, Toothless. They both laughed coarsely. I leaned forward as carefully as I could to peer into the room. Simone was sitting on the sofa. She had no make-up on and looked unhappy and vulnerable. Toothless held a snub-nosed revolver, a brother of the gun I had removed from his partner, carelessly pointing down at the floor.

Kronk was leaning over the girl. He had the tip of his hunting knife resting against the end of her chin while his other hand ran pensively over the generous curve of Simone's left breast. I didn't like what I saw, but now I knew his boss was Harry Bolt's business partner, putting a slug into Kronk's temple was no longer a viable option. I checked again the way Toothless was holding his revolver, made my decision, then stepped into the room moving the French windows back with a quick shove of my left hand while covering them with the Glock in my right.

"Don't move. Anybody. Drop the weapons on the floor." I closed in fast on Toothless, dominating the situation, keeping Kronk in view. There was a moment of hesitation and then the revolver thumped to the floor. Kronk could have used his knife on the girl, but that was one of those calculated risks that you deal with as they come up. Creating and maintaining the aggressive momentum was vital. The knife followed the revolver to the floor.

"Hands on your head. Kneel down. Kneel fucking down," I barked, when they were slow to move. They adopted the position. Kronk gave me the same crooked smile I recalled from our first meeting. I released my left hand from the butt of the Glock and kicked both revolver and knife out of the way.

"Get up, turn around and walk out slowly. Understand?" They didn't reply but obeyed. I followed them, keeping over an arm's length behind Kronk and we trooped out into the hallway, the sights of the automatic aimed between his shoulder blades. It was academic I hoped, but a shot at this range would have sent the bullet out the other side, nailing Toothless through the back as well. I explained this to them as we walked in case anyone got any mad ideas. We came to the front door and Toothless unbolted it obediently.

We paused in the rectangle of light thrown onto the gravel by the Mercedes. Kronk half-turned. He didn't look as angry this time. Perhaps he was getting used to being humiliated by me. Or he might have been thinking 'third time lucky'. Cautiously I leaned back and pulled the front door shut. What I had to say was not for the ears of the girl in the living room.

"Listen carefully," I said. "Tell General Charoenchati that I am not here to give him trouble. Tell him I am a friend of Mr. Bolt. I know he wants a German man called Schwartz killed and I will do it for him if I can. We are not enemies. That's all."

Kronk looked puzzled so I repeated my words again. They wouldn't be goons if they weren't mentally challenged. It was worth explaining again slowly.

"Understand? Yes."

"Mr. Bolt?"

"I am a friend of Mr. Bolt."

"You kill the German?"

I nodded. Kronk exchanged sentences with his partner in Thai while I waited for the penny to drop. My gun hand didn't.

Eventually Kronk smiled and put his hands together. A light of understanding seemed to have gone on somewhere in the empty house of his skull. I tossed the car keys at Toothless who fluffed the catch and had to bend and pick them off the ground. They got in the car and at the same time I retreated into the cover of the hallway. I wasn't certain whether they had understood. If not, there was always the possibility that they had another weapon stashed in the glove compartment and might come back to even the score. I watched them drive off then listened for a while.

When I returned to the living room, Simone was still sitting where we had left her, but now a cigarette burned between her fingers.

"I'm sorry I was so pathetic just now," she said.

"You were fine," I said, and meant it. I put a light hand on her shoulder, which trembled slightly. A tiny tear of blood had congealed on her chin like an unsightly pimple ready to burst. "They're gone now, and they won't be back. I hope."

"How can you be certain?" She looked at me, inquiringly, taking another hurried drag of smoke. I shrugged.

"Not much in life apart from death that is certain. But I don't think they will come back. There's no point."

She looked at my hand and the Glock in it.

"Where did you get that gun from? You didn't shoot him? No," she said, processing her memories, "there was no noise."

"Not this time. I explained some things to them which should change their perspective. They'll have to go back and discuss it with their boss. But it should put an end to their urge to kill me."

It would be nice to have Kronk off my back. His attempts at running me off the road, spearing me, and assaulting my girl had been, all along, inopportune.

"What did you tell them?" Simone now wanted to know, perking up.

"Later. I'll tell you later." I wasn't going to tell her later, or at all. While I hadn't admitted to Kronk that I was the Reliable Man, a cleverer brain than his, such as his employer's, might put two and two together. I hoped it was enough that the General would believe that Harry and I were on the same side and I wanted to help Harry's business partner. He knew that, even as plain old Bill Jedburgh, I had more than enough in me to kill Schwartz.

"Tell me now. Please."

"Later," I said firmly. There was still something I couldn't work out. Tang and the General ought to be on the same side, but they clearly weren't. That was odd.

I took a bottle of Perrier from the minibar and watched as she killed her cigarette and went to light another from the crumpled green and white packet. Something glistened on her cheek.

"Are you all right?" I asked, as gently as I knew how. Women took a lot of patience and understanding. With Simone I wanted to make every effort I could. She merely shook her head and stared at the wall, lost in the maze of the female psyche. I wondered if it was the personal proximity of physical violence that had suddenly jolted her into a clearer realisation of what she was involved in?

"I'm confused," she said finally. "I don't know what I am doing here." I wasn't sure whether to slap her or stroke her, so I ignored her and sat down in the armchair opposite her. Whatever she was thinking, whatever she wanted to speak about, would come if the time was right. I had to find the right way to encourage it. Lines of tears began coursing down her face. She worked on the cigarette with venom until it was gone into smoke and ashes.

We sat in silence for many minutes. I felt like a hunter waiting for dawn to break and a doe to appear at the edge of the clearing. Finally, she spoke:

"I shouldn't like you in the first place. You're too selfish, too self-contained. Everything revolves around you and your needs. Nobody else matters to you."

I reached out and put my hand on her shoulder. She was right. I was selfish. Ordinarily I didn't care, but tonight was different. She pushed me away.

"When I look in your eyes, I see no feeling for anyone there except yourself. There seems to be frost in your eyelashes. Uncle Tang told me to be careful, that you were a dangerous man. I suppose I just laughed because I misunderstood him."

She wasn't looking at me but at the manicured red fingernails of her left hand.

"Why did he want me to come out here?" she asked, tears in her eyes. "You don't want, or need, anybody to help you."

"Tang didn't trust me so he wanted you to keep an eye on me," I said. "He trusts you."

"I've tried my best," she said, "but I'm not sure he can trust me to do my job properly," she sighed. "You're not his friend, I know that. Can I be your friend, which I want to be, without being Uncle Tang's enemy? Things get so confusing sometimes."

"Life is not always that clear cut," I suggested.

"I shouldn't be feeling like this. I shouldn't be telling you this. Just forget what I said. Just forget everything. Okay. Please?" She looked me in the face and said: "You don't trust me, do you?"

I shrugged. I wanted to tell her that it was impossible for me to trust her completely given the circumstances under which we had met, that getting on with a job was always the most important thing and that women were best kept clear of the game until the work was completed. Wisely, for once, I held my tongue and instead held her tight.

After a little while she said: "I'm not finding it easy. I like things to make sense. This is too complicated." The tears welled up again from beneath her long black lashes and dripped into her lap. I hugged this lost little girl, hugged her firmly and said nothing that could change her uncertainty. Then I took her to bed and made love to her as caringly and intensely as I could. I had wanted her since she had walked into my room in The Oriental, a vulnerable girl hiding behind a veil of worldliness.

A few hours later I leant on the balcony, anticipating the glimmer of the orange daybreak. Simone was fast asleep. There was a smile on my face.

My mind kept going back to the hour before when Simone, for reasons complex and inexplicable to a simple, insensitive, emotionally blunted man like me, had finally succumbed to my desires.

The physical pleasure of being inside Simone had been intense. I had marvelled over her strong generous breasts when she asked me to rub them and suck them. The panther-black fur nestling between the cream of her thighs. I loved the vulnerable sound she made when I entered her, the smell and texture of her skin and the taste of fresh summer meadows when I kissed her in the softest and most intimate cleft of her body. When I ran my moist tongue along her neck, turning her around enveloping her as I tickled the nape of her neck and she had melted in my arms like a woman deprived of tenderness for far too long. By the end, my movements had become gentle and caring until she dug her nails into my back and sighed a long wistful sigh before falling asleep in my arms a minute later, tranquil and exhausted.

Running over the memory, I felt aroused again, but cynically wondered how long it would be before the pleasure became less intense, less memorable. I knew it would get better the next few times, then the tension and excitement inevitably would tail off into something mildly pleasant or into a boring chore. I knew myself too well, I had lived with my urges too long.

Yet for the moment I was content and triumphant that she had given her body to me. I turned to go back to bed, to hold her tight while the small hours of the night crept past.

Suddenly I became aware that Simone had woken up. Her smell rose into my senses and I knew she was standing behind me. I expected a kiss, a hug. There was no warning. I had no premonition of danger. Nor did it make sense until later. A hard object swung strongly against the side of my skull and the world disappeared from my grasp. There was not even an instant in which to curse womankind for being irrational. I must have hit the wooden planks hard, but I didn't feel any pain. That came later.

27

I had a hangover worse than Armageddon. The pain woke me and I wondered if I had been dumped in the knacker's yard. It hurt me to think. Every little spark of a neuron emitted an insufferable agony. Even when I willed my eyes to open I seemed to be underwater without goggles, so I rested for what had to be another hour or two and tried moving again.

I was on the bed in a dressing gown, but things did not look familiar. With whom had I been drinking? I needed a gallon of mineral water and an export carton of Alka Seltzers. This was the worst it had been for a long time.

Finally, I commanded myself to sit up. The pain tempted me to vomit. Gradually it dawned on me that this was not the alcohol poisoning, de-hydration, morning-after-a-heavy-session, sort of headache. The agony was specific, coming from an area at the base of my skull. I eased myself around on the mattress and found blood on the sheets. Going to the bathroom, I tottered unsteadily on incompetent feet, accidentally ramming my shoulder into the doorjamb. Examining my head in the two-way reflection between the mirror on the wall and the one hanging from the back of the door I found the impact point and touched it tenderly. Nerves screamed. I whistled tunelessly to bear the pain, jumping around the bathroom until it became bearable.

Simone had gone. Her suitcase was still there, but she had taken her necessities and left. I had made love to her with an unusual honesty and she had smacked me over the head with something hard and then disappeared. I called down to the main building for the house doctor. He would come quickly, I was told.

It was the humiliation which hurt most. I felt a fool and hated the feeling. I thought by now that I could weigh up a person's character with a good deal of accuracy. Both the army and police force had taught me that, a mixture of experience and instinct, which advises you whether someone is telling you the truth or playing you for a fool. Admittedly women had never been my strong point, but I could usually tell a slut from a nun. It looked like I'd got it all wrong with this girl.

I thought I had her in the palm of my hand, uncertain of her loyalty to Tang, but more sure of her feelings for me. Then, when I least expected it, she had sapped me from behind. Prowling around the house I found the heavy brass ashtray that she had used. It still had my blood on the rounded edge.

Someone once said that women are the triumph of emotion over reason and it was hard for me to disagree with that as I held a plastic bag of ice cubes against the wound. The doctor arrived and smiled sadly when I told him I had cracked myself against a cupboard door. He was a slick young Thai with an American accent and he wore a dark blue suit. He put four stitches in, gave me a box of yellow and blue Ponstan painkillers, some pink anti-inflammatories and other instructions that we both knew I'd ignore, then wished me a less troublesome day, the likelihood of which was slim.

At least she hadn't taken my gun. The Glock lay where I had placed it in the bedside drawer along with the ammunition and its holster.

Her note was left on the bedside table. It was written in an even, rounded hand that looked as if calligraphy had been one of her favourite subjects at school. The capital letters curled and looped with unique flourishes, which helped to confuse the issue. It read:

My dear Bill,

I am so sorry. Please, please, please forgive me. Things are very difficult for me. I don't know if what I have done is the best thing for me to do but I hope so and I hope that you are all right. Please believe me that I really honestly sincerely meant it when I said I like you. I don't know why I slept with you, but I don't regret it. I know you are tough and your head is tough. I am going back to Bangkok to see Uncle Tang and ask him to let me go. I heard you talking to the two men outside the door and about you knowing about Charoenchati and wanting to kill someone called Schwartz. I have to warn Uncle Tang that things are not the way he planned it. This I have to do because it is my duty. I don't know what you are up to and I don't want to know but PLEASE believe me that I care for you whatever I have done!! I hope you can understand.

Anyway, Love (whatever that means)
Simone

I crumpled and tossed the cream-coloured Conqueror notepaper onto the floor and called her a bitch. Next time we met she would regret the day she had walked into my room at The Oriental, floating on a cloud of Estée Lauder, making me throb with desire and slip my brain into neutral. Being a woman and unsure of her loyalties was no excuse for abusing my trust. Keller had learnt that the hard way.

They had finished serving breakfast by the time I got to the Main House, so I sat on the terrace and ate a chicken sandwich. Staring moodily across the empty pool, I worked out the ramifications of this new development. They were mainly bad and all irritating. I fumed at myself that I had let her know so much, that I had allowed her to meet McAlistair and Bolt and she had managed to find out that matters were not entirely as I wanted her to think.

By now she'd be sitting on Tang's lap spilling the beans. I didn't want to think of her as being calculating and hard hearted. The letter told me as much. But she posed not only a threat to me but, unless she decided to keep her promise and not give Tang all the information, to my friends. There was no point in asking a man who had so spectacularly misjudged his lover, what she would do next.

There was little else to do. I had to take the cards dealt to me and play them. I wasn't a man to throw down my hand because the game had changed and the value of the aces had switched from high to low. She might not have understood properly that it was Charoenchati who had commissioned me to kill Otto Schwartz even before Tang had hit on the idea of using me as a scout to find his forger. But Tang might think it through and then I couldn't be sure what his next move would be.

Consuming two more coffees, I mulled over, like an indifferent chess player, all my various moves, evaluating each for likelihood, threat and counter-threat. In the end I kept on returning to the conclusion that I would go ahead and meet the Germans and find an opportunity to kill Schwartz as Charoenchati had commissioned me.

It was another beautiful day as I rode my

bike gingerly back into town. My headache had dulled a bit. The Sport Resort swimming pool and the café were busy with the usual crew of holidaymakers. I was early for my meeting with Gruber, so I stepped into the gym. A Thai girl with skin virtually charcoal sat on a stool and sipped a milkshake. She was a reminder that Thailand had seen a lot of Rest and Recuperation during the Vietnam conflict. Only her mother had been Thai. Her boyfriend, a skinny Westerner, was punching out curls on a sit-up bench. There was no sign of Wim or anyone else I knew.

I walked out again and found Gruber's office, which was empty. From force of habit, I glanced through the papers on his desk keeping an ear out for his return. But all he was handling were mundane hotel matters.

"What happened to your head?" Gruber asked jovially when he found me sitting at a table outside.

"The bathroom cabinet."

"I am sorry. I hope it is better than it looks. We will just wait for Wim and Harald to come in the car."

"Does Wim have a regular girlfriend?" I said idly. Gruber shrugged.

"Who needs a girlfriend in Pattaya? You can buy a new one on every street corner. But I think he has a thing for little girls, you know, really young ones. And little boys perhaps, what does it matter anyway, eh?" He leered, the mask of the urbane hotelier slipping momentarily.

"How about you? You like the Thai girls?" I asked.

Gruber considered the question carefully as if it were important not to be misunderstood on the topic.

"I don't mind them. But my taste is more traditional. I prefer bigger women, real women, with hips and breasts and generous, as you say, lips. I like German women with good figures that tell you they can take care of you and give you babies. I was married once but it did not work out. But here..." He shrugged and went on, "there are always some lonely tourist ladies, divorcees..." He looked almost apologetic that he preferred his own race.

We talked about places in Germany that we knew, which was easy for me. We discussed beers and the best vineyards. Later Wim and Harald arrived in a white BMW 520i and we were on our way. Both commented on my injury and being reminded of it made my head hurt again. The nagging pain was still there, despite the medication, which was supposed to numb all feeling. Harald drove north past Wong Amat beach, and out of town along the coast.

It took another fifteen minutes before we turned off and came to a dirt road. We followed this for ten minutes and reached a wooden gate that had 'Private - Keep Out' written in big red-stencilled capitals in English and presumably the same in Thai. A barbed wire fence stretched out on either side. Harald hit the horn twice and the gate opened. We drove in and found two Thais with Uzi submachine guns and Motorola radios waving us through. Two hundred yards on we came to another gate, this one was solid steel and on either side of it stretched a 5 metre high wire mesh fence.

"Electrified," Gruber said, noting my interest. "Herr Schwartz likes his privacy." Harald hit the horn again and rolled down his window. There was a pillar with an alcove that housed a video camera and a two-way microphone.

"*Komm schon Fritz, Du Arschloch*, I'm waiting." Wim yelled at the contraption. The second gate rolled back and we drove for another five minutes until we arrived at a long white-washed bungalow that was flanked by four smaller single-storey buildings.

Half a dozen vehicles were parked outside the main house: jeeps and station wagons and a stretch Mercedes limousine that needed a good wash. On top of the bungalow roof, like an enormous boil, was a dome at least thirty feet high and fifty feet long, attached to which were two satellite dishes, making it look like an outsize butterfly. By the front door another Uzi-touting Thai lounged in a chair, leaning forward and squinting through Ray-Bans, trying to determine who was behind the BMW's tinted windows.

The door swung open as we came up onto the porch revealing a woman who must have been fashioned inside one of Gruber's wilder wet dreams. She was a Brunhilde of Wagnerian proportions. Her age was indeterminate, between thirty and sixty, and her dark blue apron looked as if she had starched it that morning. She reeked vaguely of cooking pots and Sauerkraut. Her arms were the size of Wim's, though there was little muscle.

She nodded coolly at the men, examined me with the tiniest of interest and then marched off in the direction of what I presumed was the kitchen. I had the odd sensation of being summoned to Berchtesgarden for a quick conference on the Final Solution.

Harald led the way down cool, chalky corridors decorated with stills from black and white Hollywood movies. I recognised a few, mostly the ones with Humphrey Bogart and Cary Grant.

The room underneath the dome was a vast vaulted chamber which could have held a century of legionnaires. At one end of the chamber the owner had built himself a full size indoor miniature golf course on which he was currently honing his skill. Putting uphill into a model of a revolving Dutch windmill was a man who could only be described as obscenely fat - any other word was an understatement for Otto Schwartz. The entire Moscow ballet company could have put on a performance of Swan Lake across the expanse of his stupendous gut. His white trousers billowed out like a spinnaker in a force ten gale, held up by black braces.

He swore under his breath when the ball refused to enter through the hole on the moving blade, bouncing off instead, rolling back down until it came to rest an inch from his ridiculously small moccasin clad feet. He dropped the putter on the fake green grass voicing an obscenity and walked over to us.

"*Willkommen*, Herr Graunitz, welcome to my home. Let us have some cocktails on the terrace." Otto Schwartz spoke with a thick Berlin accent. He took my hand in his, which had the small bloated fingers you always find in an obese adult, squeezing it, then suddenly letting it slip from his grasp.

Wim and Gruber stayed behind by the minigolf course, leaving only the three of us. Schwartz and Harald were clearly the grownups. We walked past a full-size white concert piano, a dining and conference table, a billiard table, three sleeping wolfhound puppies, an ensemble of linen covered furniture on one of which reposed an elegant Thai woman painting her fingernails as she read a magazine with one eye and watched a bank of six television monitors with the other, and out through the ten-foot-high French windows that extended the length of the room onto a veranda which was surrounded by a low wall.

A set of stairs led down to the beach, which was so secluded it could not be seen from the house. Over a low wall the ocean stretched out into the distance. We sat in rattan chairs and sofas and a maid appeared and took our orders. It was all very civilised and for a moment I forgot that I had come here to kill this man and re-possess his ill-gotten gains.

Schwartz did not speak. He regarded me like an anthropologist uncertain whether the bones in front of him were genuine, or an ingenious fake. I returned his gaze like a physiologist unsure whether his bones were capable of carrying three hundred pounds of blubber around on a daily basis, or if he was a freak of nature.

"I have a gland problem. In case you want to know why I am so fat," he said. "You are much younger than I expected, Herr Graunitz."

I thought it impolite to reply that he was much fatter than I had expected.

"This estate is worth over seventy million Baht," he said conversationally. His hair was thin and slightly greasy, combed across from left to right with the vanity of the balding middle-aged man. His nose was a subtle bump compared to the horror of his three chins, which allowed no separation between face and neck. I sipped my beer appreciatively. It had been a dry ride and my head was still pounding from the after-effects of a brass ashtray.

"It's a lovely place you have, Herr Schwartz.

How long have you lived here?" I asked.

"What is it, Harald, now? Three years?"

"Four years next January."

"How long have you been in Asia, Herr Graunitz?" Schwartz asked.

"Ten years."

"You like it?"

"I feel comfortable here. I don't know if I could live in Europe anymore."

"I could not live in Europe," the fat man said. "Can you imagine the taxes? I pay taxes, for appearance's sake, but not taxes like people pay in Europe. For a young man like you, Asia is the place to be. If you know the right people and have courage, you cannot help but get rich. Now then, you have a business proposition for me?"

At that moment the housekeeper appeared on the terrace. She held a long wooden spoon in one hand and in the usual peremptory way of the Germans demanded how many people there would be for lunch. Schwartz held up podgy fingers to indicate we were expecting one more guest apart from our group and the woman painting her nails.

"Frau Wertheim. The best cook in the whole of South East Asia," Schwartz said when she had left. Judging by his size I did not doubt him. Gland trouble or not he looked like a man who took second and third helpings. There was a tangible aura of greed that hung about him.

"So," he demanded. "Business."

28

One way or another, as a copper or as a punter, I had spent a lot of time in the fleshpots of Hong Kong, so my business plan was simple and mostly true. The Wan Chai district of Hong Kong contained a whole string of girlie bars similar to the Patpong and Pattaya go-go bars. They were owned by triad-connected syndicates and their main business came from expats who had ugly, boring wives sitting at home and more money than sense.

The clubs were nicely decorated. The girls were hired as dancers on a six-month contract, which was an easy visa to arrange. They worked an evening shift dancing, talking to the customers and wheedling for drinks and they lived together under the supervision of aged Cantonese mama-sans who watched them like hawks. They were permitted no social life, which meant they sat at home eating and the foolish ones quickly grew plump. Even more foolish, but horny, men coughed up the two to three thousand Hong Kong dollars bar-fine that permitted them to take out the girl, bring her home or to a love-hotel and have sex with her. For that sort of money, you could buy a return plane ticket to Bangkok or Manila, which was where the girls mainly came from.

Every time I had drunk in a Wan Chai bar, I had wondered why they set the price so high. I assumed they either did not want to find themselves without dancers at nine in the evening, were content to make a healthy turnover from drinks, or perhaps they could just get away with it because every other bar charged the same.

What I suggested to Schwartz was simply my idea of better marketing. Fly in attractive but experienced girls who were primarily whores, set them to work and turn them over faster for bigger profits. To make this idea work well one needed someone permanently handling the recruitment in Thailand and who better than Otto Schwartz who appeared to be the Grand Master of Pattaya's sex industry.

When I had finished my pitch, Schwartz sat back for a minute and looked at me through piggy eyes. They were cold, calculating and like little black pearls.

"What you are talking about, is very small fry business," he said. "One bar, perhaps?"

"One, maybe two. For you it might be small fry but not for me. I want to make money and I do not have your overheads," I gestured around the estate. "Do I take it then that my proposition doesn't interest you?" Schwartz considered for a long minute.

"I am interested, a little bit, because you interest me. Every opportunity to make money must be considered. I am certainly interested in Hong Kong. But I'll tell you something, I don't feel comfortable dealing with the Chinese. They are tricky people. Hard to control." He swirled the remains of his drink in the glass.

"You seem to be a man of enterprise and, I suspect, violence. You don't expect me to believe you hit your head on a bathroom cabinet, do you?" He laughed, and as he did so his three chins vibrated in different directions. "Why don't you work for me and I'll pay you a commission to keep an eye on our affairs in Hong Kong?"

"There are other partners involved in this club," I said, as if I was thinking through the implications of the offer.

He said, "I presume you mean local partners. It's difficult doing this kind of business in Hong Kong without them. Everybody knows you have to square things with the Triads. People here are more understanding with western investors and really want to oblige. Especially the police. They all want to improve themselves, build a house for their family. Send their children to school."

"I couldn't agree more," I said. "The Police in Hong Kong are not easy to bribe these days. That makes it harder for new competitors to enter the market. I understand it was easier twenty years ago, before they cracked down on corruption."

He shifted his big bulk in the chair and the wood creaked dangerously. "I love making money. I love having a product that everybody wants and will pay a lot of money for. That's why I like to sell girls. Everybody loves girls. Or drugs. You can't go wrong. Now I have a new product which costs me nothing to make and which I can sell for a high price. I think it will be a very good one to sell in Hong Kong."

"What's that? Ice, Ecstasy?"

"Those are wonderful products too, but I have something else. I will show you later, maybe, when we know each other better. What I am saying is, I am negotiating to sell my new product in Hong Kong and I want a trustworthy man, a German like yourself, to act as my agent and keep an eye on my interests. Everybody knows you can never trust a Chinese. They would sell their grandmother for profit. They will cheat their best friend and then sleep with his wife. That's why I was interested to meet you today. I don't mind supplying ten girls every two or three months for your bar, but I have more interesting ideas. Like this we could get to know each other better. Build up some trust. I have to find out more about you first. But Harald here said you had the look, and if Harald says that..."

I took my time answering. Schwartz must be talking about selling forged passports, which would be a good business but not a game-changer for a man who already made millions from drugs and girls. Perhaps he had another angle. If he liked me, which he seemed to, he would come up with more details to persuade me. Details which could be of some use. Knowledge was always power.

"Lunch!" Frau Wertheim commanded from the French windows and disappeared again.

"Who suggested that you speak to me about dancing girls?" the fat man asked.

"I would rather not say. He had only heard your name. He is connected to the 14K Triad," I said.

Otto Schwartz looked pensive and ran a finger, a little overstuffed Frankfurter sausage, along his triple chins. He said, "I shall be checking you out. There is no need to be afraid to mention names."

"By all means ask about me. For myself I think it is usually better to be discreet about information." I had no worries about them calling people in Hong Kong. Provided they weren't working with Tang and Sebastian Tse, which seemed unlikely, there was nothing to link Bill Jedburgh, the ex-police inspector, to a man calling himself Graunitz in Pattaya. By the time they had discovered that nobody in Hong Kong appeared to know me, I intended this business to be over.

"I am not used to fencing," Graunitz said. "Let

us have lunch." With some effort he levered himself out of his seat and lurched off in the direction of the domed chamber.

At the other end from the mini-golf was a solid mahogany dining table that seated twenty but had only been laid for seven. I wondered who the missing guest would be. Wim and Gruber abandoned their golf game and joined us.

The Thai girl with the fingernails was already at the table. She neither smiled nor expressed interest in anyone else. She could have been in her late twenties, sitting tall, aloof and well dressed in a black blouse. Nobody introduced us or spoke to her.

"Where's that slut of yours, Harald?" Schwartz growled. "I have never met a woman so dependably late. *Punktlichkeit ist die Hoeflichkeit der Koenige*, punctuality is the politeness of Kings. Either sleep with German women, like Gruber here, or stick to Asian whores who know they are not needed at the lunch table."

His lieutenant looked uncomfortable and got up saying he'd go and see. The Thai girl, who I presumed was Schwartz's mistress, looked unmoved by his implied insult.

Wim drank beer while Schwartz asked me if I would try some white wine from Wuertemberg. He proffered a green bottle as Frau Wertheim brought in the pea soup. She looked displeased that not everybody was present. The soup, in a heavy terrine, smelt wholesome and made my mouth water. It brought back memories of my time in Germany.

"Herr Graunitz, do you eat much German food in Hong Kong?"

"Not as good as this. We have some bars that serve traditional German food."

"We will begin," Schwartz said imperiously. Gruber sitting next to me passed a pannier of warm, recently baked bread that crackled in my hand. Wim slurped his soup with the same obscenity that he had demonstrated the night before. I watched the fingers of the mistress, heavy with Thai gold, which is yellower and softer in texture, tear a bun apart with genteel precision. The first spoonful of the thick vegetable soup justified Schwartz's opinion of Frau Wertheim's worth.

"I don't know where the stupid woman is," Harald said, returning to the table. He tucked into the soup to make up for lost time.

The main course was a delicate veal slice covered in a thick mushroom sauce with potatoes and vegetables. The wine, a *Spätlese*, surprised me since I had always understood that it was drunk by the locals and never exported. Schwartz explained that his brother had married into one of the vintner's families. The wine did not travel well, since it lacked the chemical additives that other more commercial offerings were laced with, so every week a case was sent by DHL from Frankfurt and picked up by his driver from Bangkok airport.

"Let me tell you about my new little venture," he said leaning forward conspiratorially, a splurge of gravy on his cheek. "I have found a man, he came to me actually, he and his partner, a forger. His father was a forger and he learned at his knee. Then graduated from some university in computer sciences or something. This man has designed a machine, or a computer or something - I am not a technical person - that is a million times more accurate than a Xerox machine. This machine produces documents, passports, bank notes, share certificates, anything of value you might imagine. Think of how much money people will pay for access to such a machine. Do you need a passport? Do you need American currency? Fifteen minutes later we have it all ready, authentic, perfect." He gave a fat man's belly laugh, dropping his cutlery onto his empty plate with a ceramic crack. "What do you think, Herr Graunitz?"

"Very clever. Potentially worth a lot of money. This forger of yours is German?"

"No, he is Hong Kong Chinese, as is his partner. They came to me because they needed protection from the Hong Kong Triads. They wanted to run their own show here in Thailand, but everybody needs protection, eh, Harald? That is our watchword here in Pattaya 'Everybody needs Protection.' Except me of course, I *am* the protection."

Even my battered head was starting to put things together. The Forger was on the run from Tang. Tang had been right, he had not been betrayed for a German, but for a fellow Chinaman. My brain was telling me I had the key to this somewhere in my memory, but my head was shaking too much to let me fit it in the lock.

"I have a potential business partner," he continued, "a Hong Kong Chinese. Underworld connections, of course. He has expressed interest in being my representative in Hong Kong, the Philippines and China. Those are the big markets for forged documents and currency. But, as I said, who can trust the Chinese? I am willing to do business with him but not to trust."

"How come you are trusting me with this information then?" I asked.

"Oh, I don't have to worry there, Herr Graunitz. You are German. You are a little bit crooked but then, here at this table we are all crooks. Even my girlfriend there, she is a crook. Aren't you, *mein Liebchen*? Always stealing my money to go shopping in Bangkok."

He put his hand on her head and ruffled her hair in a proprietorial manner that barely elicited a response. I hoped for his sake she made more of an effort in bed. We had been speaking German since my arrival and the way she looked at him proved that she did not speak the language. Schwartz said in heavily accented English:

"I voz jost saying how bootiful you vere."

She gave him a smile that was turned on and off like a lamp, returning her attention to her plate. Schwartz tapped her once again on the thigh. I looked at the odious man and decided that the world would be a better place without him. He continued in a more menacing tone, addressing me:

"If I find out that I cannot trust you, Wim here will explain to you what a mistake you have made. He may not have good table manners, but there are some things he is very, very, good at."

"Sorry I'm late," a familiar American voice said. It was as if someone had thrown a bucket of iced water over my head. Instantly my heart rate hit a hundred and eighty, which was more excitement than I had managed the last time we had met. I looked up from my plate and found Mandy standing at the top of the table eyeing me with undisguised surprise.

29

The Glock jumped into my hand because I had no other option. Mandy knew me as Bill Jedburgh, a friend of McAlistair's, a former police officer from Hong Kong. How could I have known she was sleeping with Harald? My cover was blown leaving me with the only option of killing Otto Schwartz right now.

He was fast for a fat one. He saw the black thing coming up in my hand and threw himself backwards in his chair. I fired at where his head had been an instant earlier and missed. Then Gruber punched me in the kidneys and Wim was over the table with surprising speed, dropping his bulk on top of me and sending us both crashing to the floor.

The gun went flying from my grasp and I felt like a container of nuts and bolts had landed on my chest. The back of my head, where my wound was, cracked hard against the tiles and he butted me in the face. In my current state I wasn't capable of a fight with a 300-pound wild gorilla. It would have been touch and go even under normal circumstances so I couldn't really blame

Simone for that, but I did. He pinned down my arms in an instant and I found myself looking up into the unusual barrel grooving of my own weapon.

"Bring the handcuffs from the armoury," Schwartz ordered as he came to stand over me. Wim's knees were on my biceps, his butt on my chest and his hands around my throat, the fingers digging into my constricted windpipe.

"Shall I kill him?" he asked. "Just say, boss, and I'll kill him now."

"No," Schwartz spoke firmly, as if to a child. "Just hold him down. I have to know who he is and what he really wants."

Mandy came to stand next to him. She was white with fright; the bullet must have passed close by her face. She frowned at me. Harald brought handcuffs and they rolled me sideways to snap them on. I heard the ratchets, felt them digging into the flesh of my wrists until they could go no further. My head wound had reopened and there was wetness dripping down my neck. Wim heaved me to my feet, trussed like a turkey, and threw me carelessly into a chair. My head whipped back like in a car crash, but I managed to keep it from striking anything this time. The only thing striking, was a bell in my head.

"So, Herr Graunitz, you are a spy in my camp, a viper in my bosom. Who are you? Who sent you to spy on me?"

I said nothing. He turned to Mandy, who still had not spoken, and asked her in English: "Do you know this man?"

"His name is Jedburgh," she said. "He used to be a policeman in Hong Kong. I met him at the Bolthole." I glared at her and she looked uncomfortable. This was beyond her normal experiences. She was embarrassed and she was frightened.

"You're not German at all," said Schwartz, processing the information the girl had given him. "But you speak perfect German. You are English and a Hong Kong policeman? I suppose it makes sense. I had expected the DEA or FBI. What is this? A joint operation between the Hong Kong Police and the Americans?"

I remained sullen and silent.

"*Tja*, we'll soon know who you are. Harald go and find Victor. See if they have finished their lunch yet. They eat such terrible shit these Chinese, chickens' feet and pigs' intestines."

Schwartz's voice had been relatively pleasant. Then suddenly without warning he began screaming at Harald like a berserk Cossack. "You didn't search him? How can you let an armed man near me. You idiots. Unforgivable. Stupid. Insane. Incompetent." He stomped off onto the terrace with surprising speed, waving his arms and ranting to himself.

There was a sudden movement in the corner of my eye and a clenched fist struck me hard on the right cheek. It was Wim's fist and he was grinning at me. Then he hit me again on the left cheek. My head rocked first in one direction then in the other. A moment later came the pain. God, did it hurt. My cheeks would be bruised and the colour of prunes if I got out of this alive. I waited for the next blow, the next pain. Take every blow individually. Prepare yourself mentally. Accept pain as the normal course of events, I told myself. We had gone through interrogation procedures during army training, not enough because there is only so much you can do without making it dangerously real.

Wim hit me a few more times until Harald told him to stop. My lip had split in two places. The spice of my own blood gathered in my mouth. I passed out and came to looking at my lap. Only Wim was still standing beside me like a German Shepherd waiting for a command. The others had moved away and were talking in voices too low to make out. Frau Wertheim was clearing the lunch table, darting uncertain glances at me from time to time as she piled the plates onto her tray. I thought it might be amusing to smile at her. It was a futile, trivial thought. Wim would have hit me again. I wanted to marshal my reserves of resistance for later. Because there would have to be a later.

At last there were footsteps behind me and my hair was dragged back to show someone my face. My brain had finally worked out who it would be. It made a lot of sense. I found myself staring up into the moon face of Victor Mok Bun. He had always had long eyebrows and an ugly permanently puckered mouth. The first time we met he was still a Senior Inspector posted to CCB, the Commercial Crimes Bureau. He'd shone the right shoes and got drunk in the right messes and been appointed Chief Inspector in charge of the counterfeiting division. They sent him off on courses with the FBI and the Metropolitan Police and after a while he succeeded in appearing knowledgeable about his special subject. Being the only senior officer in the counterfeiting division, he had become quite indispensable. His expertise was rarely put to any real use, except to give evidence in court as an expert witness identifying forgeries and to lecture at the Police Training School.

There was little comradely warmth for a former colleague in Mok Bun's eyes. He turned to Schwartz who was chewing on a knuckle and said: "This is Bill Jedburgh, I know him in the Hong Kong Police. I think he worked in some of the Headquarter Units. But someone told me he resigned a few years ago. He's not German. What's he doing here?" His harsh Hong Kong accent echoed his concern. It bothered him to find me here.

"We think he might be part of this DEA operation your friends in Hong Kong warned you about."

"Maybe. They do some joint operations. Sure.

Once a policeman always a policeman. For the *gwai lo* anyway."

"This is Victor. Your former colleague. Now he is working for me and we are going to make a lot of money together, eh?" Schwartz told me with malice in his voice.

"Fucking chog scumbag. *Ham Gar Charn*, may your family all die," I heard myself say but the words did not come out as clearly as they were in my mind. Wim slapped me hard and a tooth dropped onto my tongue. Along with a mouthful of blood I spat it out and it splattered onto Victor's shirt.

"*Ach*, all this is boring me," Schwartz said. "Take him to B block, Wim, and I'll think about what will be done. Harald you better make sure your girl keeps her mouth shut or I'll arrange to have her dropped into the sea with a motorbike tied to her feet. You heard what I said, girl, whatever happens here is nothing of importance."

"He's nothing to me, Mr. Schwartz, if the guy's a cop then who cares," Mandy said somewhere behind me. I heard the fear underneath her brash reply, which I filed away in the 'things to be dealt with later if I get a chance' folder.

It could have been a success, my foray into the enemy's camp. It might have been, but for Mandy. One of those unpleasant coincidences that can seal the fate of nations and destroy the careers of statesmen. Well-laid plans foiled by the thrust of misfortune. Life had a way of pulling the rug out from under your feet if you started becoming too cocky.

30

It could have been an hour or a day. I had no concept of time, my mind was addled from the blows to my head but slowly the confusion cleared. The room looked like a cell in a prison for the criminally insane. The floor, walls and ceiling were spotless as was the bunk and also the chain that manacled both my wrists to a point a foot above my bed. A fluorescent tube threw a harsh chilly light into every corner of the room. I pondered my situation and listened to the pain which thumped in my temples, my forehead, my whole head.

I lay there thinking and waiting. My watch told me it was five thirty. It could have been the same day, or the next. I watched the wall, pretending it was a view from a mountain, the sort of view that made one feel small in the general order of things. I promised myself they would all die. Mandy would die, Schwartz would die, Wim would die. It would give me pleasure to kill them.

A long time later there was the faint noise of a well-oiled bolt being drawn and the door swung open.

"I can't let you leave here, Mr. Jedburgh, until I know why you are here and who sent you. If you assist me in my enquiries, I might let you go," Otto Schwartz said, gargantuan in the doorway. He made my English surname sound like an abomination practised by cannibal tribes. Wim had brought two folding chairs, one for me and one for his boss and what looked like a handyman's toolbox.

"Fuck off," I said with easy eloquence, using the English phrase because the German one contained less venom.

"I simply need to know what you are doing here. Let's be polite and reasonable."

I gave his words some consideration then decided to tell him to sod himself instead. He looked puzzled for an instant, perhaps not familiar with the English vernacular. Wim interpreted. He was more familiar with acts of self-abuse.

"I see: rudeness, resistance. We have had men like you in this little cell of ours before. Not so tough after some time. Let us be patient, Wim. Let the needles do the talking."

The large man opened his box of tricks and took out a sewing kit. He laid it aside and grasped my left wrist firmly. I was too weak to twist away and he had been lifting weights heavier and for much longer than me. He produced two thick belts of nylon containing Velcro fabric with which he securely fastened my forearms to the chair. From the sewing kit he extracted a shiny and sturdy needle, which he aligned carefully under the nail of my right index finger. Then, with a strong push he rammed the piece of metal into my skin. It slid in with little resistance. The searing agony was intense. My teeth clamped shut over a scream and I bit my tongue.

Wim pulled out the needle, which was covered with my blood and then slid it into the soft skin under my middle finger while putting his weight on top of my hand to stop me squirming away. My scream bounced off the walls again. How in God's name had men ever resisted torture? It was impossible to carry on like this for too long.

"Nasty, eh?" Schwartz gloated. "Wim read about it in a book about the Gestapo. Or did your grandfather teach you what he used to do to the KZ prisoners, Wim? History is still the best teacher."

What was the point of being defiant? After two more fingers with the same needle and with blood choking me from the split tongue, I told them part of the story. Slowly, so they could believe me. That I had been minding my own business in Bangkok when Tang came to me with an interesting and lucrative proposition to infiltrate the German syndicate in Pattaya.

"So you are not on official business? You really are retired from the Hong Kong Police?"

Schwartz regarded me like a headmaster who is undecided whether the pupil caught with drugs was intending to sell or simply keep them for his own consumption

"Wim, *noch einmal*, once again," he ordered and the needle stitched deep into my flesh.

"I don't truly believe what you just told me," Schwartz said. "Perhaps some of it is true, but you're a stupid arrogant English idiot who thinks he can outwit a German. You must be lying to me. Wim has a very big toolbox and there are lots more interesting and painful tricks in there. A little needle. That's only child's play."

He heaved himself out of his chair. There was a manic glint in his eyes as he passed in front of me. Then he was behind me and hit me hard on my open head wound.

This time I fainted. Withstanding torture is not something that can be taught in any classroom. It comes from within. Some people find the strength in unknown places and others are simply human.

Smelling salts, stinging and offensive, brought me back to consciousness.

"Tang sent me," I tried to say.

"I know Tang. There is no need for him to send you. And this stupid story of me stealing the forger from him. Now a better story this time. Preferably the truth, if you wish to die quickly." He'd given up on the fairy tale of permitting me to leave.

"Oh, go fuck your fat German arse." I regretted the words as soon as they were uttered. Not that they were proper words, only loud, hoarse whispered grunts. Wim applied three needles this time.

Schwartz rested his elbows on the enormous set of thighs that propelled him about. He explained why he did not believe me. I tried hard to listen.

"Mr. Tang from Hong Kong is the man your old colleague Mok Bun suggested I contact to reach an arrangement for distributing our products. I don't trust Tang, of course, but that doesn't mean we cannot do good business. Why would he send you here and tell you a story about me stealing his forger? You met Mok Bun. Is he here unwillingly? What you are telling me is rubbish. Rubbish I will not accept. You don't seem very smart to me. Brave but a bit stupid."

I wasn't brave, I didn't think, but I had been stupid. Tang had used me. Simone had been the carrot and Suvilit had been the stick. Tang was considering doing business with Schwartz and decided to use me in order to provide more information on the German's operation. He wanted a mole in the organisation before he set up a deal with Schwartz or perhaps with a view to cutting out Schwartz and dealing directly with Mok Bun and the forger. After all, the Chinese always preferred to deal with other Chinese rather than foreign devils.

There was silence in the little torture chamber. Schwartz pondered. Wim breathed heavily, waiting for his next command. I decided that a nice peaceful house on the beach would be something worth living for. Now I understood the meaning of eternity. It meant forever. Is this what hell would be like - endless pain without relief?

Schwartz said, "See if he knows anything else. Tell me if he does. I have to go. I have an important dinner appointment with a potential mainland Chinese partner at the Peninsula Hotel in Kowloon the day after tomorrow. Karl Graunitz might have joined me. What a pity he never existed."

He left, giving me an evil smile and shaking his head as if uncertain what to do with me. Wim didn't smile, he simply glowed with happiness. He had me to himself. His only instruction, albeit unspoken, was to keep me alive for the moment.

"I bet you'd like to be going with Herr Schwartz to Hong Kong this evening," he said in his lisping German. "Not tonight, not ever, *mein Kamerad*. Now the boss has left, we can get on with some real torture. I think I will start with your eyes. You like your eyes? No more eyes. No more women." He said conversationally, bringing out a thin sharp knife with no cutting edge. "Are you Scottish? I killed a Scottish man yesterday. Or the day before. I cannot remember. He was a small fat drunk Scottish man and he wet his pants when we made him drink a bottle of whisky and then take a handful of pills. I think I'll make it easier for you. No need to waste any good whisky. Just a needle in your arm. Pure heroin. We've got a lot of heroin here. It's cheap. Maybe I'll put an air bubble in the syringe. When the air hits your heart you are dead. *Kaput, Ende.* Think about that, hey?"

He paused and watched my reaction. He'd been moving the blade of his knife around the edge of my eyes and I was holding my breath in terror in anticipation of the incision and loss of my sight. A man can easily lose a limb, but his eyes are something special. When the blade moved away, I wet myself in relief.

"On second thoughts, I'll leave your eyes and make your death fast and easy if you tell me the real truth. What do you think? Am I not a nice, reasonable guy? You want to keep the eyes, or not?"

"Why should I worry about my eyes if you're going to kill me anyway?" I heard a cracked voice say, which I presumed, was mine. Wim paused for a moment. The thought struck him as curious, and then he saw the logic. He shrugged. He dropped the pointed tool back into the box and found a Swiss army knife instead, along with a packet of salt.

"I've never tried this one." He took my right arm, opened the largest blade and neatly slit a three-inch gash into my bicep. It cut the skin but mercifully didn't get into the muscle - not yet. When the salt landed on the open wound my senses went berserk. My body jerked and leapt around in the chair partially freeing one of my arms from the Velcro binding. My eyes fuzzed, watered. I bit my tongue again. I yelled with anger, fear and frustration and cursed his whole existence.

"I like that. A good reaction." Wim laughed and his feet crunched in a pile of salt that had fallen to the ground. "That hurt, eh? Think of how many other places on your body I can do that."

Wim had forgotten the purpose of the exercise. He was as happy as a child who had received a chemistry set for Christmas. He wanted to experiment with the tools in his box and watch my reactions. I had forgotten how many sick and sadistic creatures there are in this world.

"Have you ever killed anybody, *Bulle*? Will they pay your widow a lot for dying on duty?" He grabbed the same arm again and was about to make a cut in my forearm when the door opened and Harald popped his head in.

"Kill him now, says the boss, OK? Make it clean." The door closed again. Wim shrugged. He looked disappointed although I may have been wrong. His brow was wrinkled and he studied me for a moment. Finally he reached a conclusion.

"If I must kill you, we will have some fun

first," he said. He filled a syringe with white liquid from a small medical bottle. It had to be his supply of high-grade heroin. Then after he had snapped shut and locked the toolbox, he placed the syringe on top of it and unwrapped the Velcro straps, unlocked the manacles that held me. While he was doing this he maintained a tight grip on my windpipe that restricted my breath and movement.

"We will fight to the death. You and me, policeman. To the death, your death."

Releasing his stranglehold, he stepped quickly back with an impressive agility for such a muscle-bound man. He picked up the lethal syringe with a quick movement. He made a hand gesture indicating for me to get up and come at him.

He was giving me a chance, albeit a small one. I willed every ounce of adrenalin and every scrap of self-control, every ounce of anger and passion, every morsel of hate, and all my instincts for survival to come to my aid. I put my feet on the ground and shakily pushed myself upright.

"Komm schon mein kleiner, komm schon. Come little man," he said.

I came at him with vengeance, but his left fist stopped me dead in my tracks, blocking my blows. To remain alive was the only object in my mind. I had a chance to live. He did not see it like that. It was just a little game for him and that's where he made a critical mistake.

I came at him again carefully, with a tactic that had to work. It was the needle I wanted. No blow or kick, especially in my weakened state, would drop him. Feinting, with a punch that he easily deflected, I managed to get a good hard foot into his groin. He winced without budging an inch. Yet for an instant he was off guard, enough for me to knock the syringe out of his hand and see it spinning along the floor. Diving on it, I grasped the tube and was just rolling away when Wim's whole mass landed on me for the second time in one day. I lost the wind from my lungs. His weight was crushing me. An arm slid around and underneath my chin. He got me in a chokehold from which there should have been no escape.

Before the lights started going out in my head, I arched my spine as far as it went. Reaching back to get a hold of his hair gave me an idea of where his face was. I drove the needle backwards and hard into his face. His scream was like the screech of tyres on hot tarmac. I let go of the syringe, elbowed him in a kidney and rolled out from under his mass.

Scrabbling to my feet I got to the syringe before he did. I pulled it from the vile jelly that had been his right eye. Only a red and white pulp remained. Without mercy, I seized the advantage and jabbed his remaining eye. I smashed the plunger of the syringe fully home, toppling backwards as his flaying arms swiped me away.

Twenty millilitres of deadly heroin shot directly into his brain.

It wasn't long before he stopped twitching and hyperventilating. I approached the muscular body with caution, checking the artery in his neck for a beat. There was none. I regarded the sad, blind creature that had been a human being, albeit one on the lowest rung of humanity. I felt no remorse. Victory and revenge were mine.

31

I ripped off his T-shirt and used it as tourniquet around my injured arm. The remaining material I wound around my head wound. Thankfully the Ponstan painkillers the doctor had given me were still in my own back pocket. I dry swallowed a couple and hoped they would help, because there was pain in every part of my body. I felt faint from my exertions and the loss of blood.

I needed a weapon. I searched Wim's pockets, but he didn't have a gun, although I took his wallet. What I did find in his torturer's box was an awl with a six-inch long shaft sharpened to a vicious point. I didn't like to consider where Wim might have used it on me. It would have to do until I could find something better.

Outside, the corridor was empty. I took a couple of deep breaths before moving and reaching a set of stairs that led up into a room that was stacked wall to wall with cardboard boxes. Curious, I ripped open the top of a box and found stacks of gold Visa Credit Cards sealed carefully in plastic pockets. Another box contained Gold

Mastercards, American Express Cards, Diners Club Cards, all looking pristine and perfect to my layman's eye.

What was missing on all of these cards were the name, serial number, expiry date and other particulars usually embossed on the front. Provided they knew what they were doing – which usually involved duplicating the stolen numbers of existing cards - anyone presenting one of these could walk into a shop and leave with a solid gold Rolex or Cartier, an Armani suit, or even a brand new Ferrari. It was a simple scam and as effective as robbing a bank. It would take at least a week for the real owner to notice someone else was siphoning off his cash and that might only happen once his credit limit had been reached.

Another box yielded a crispy, crackling stack of US dollar notes. They smelt good. I pocketed a two-inch-thick wad, certain that I could find a use for it. The storeroom gave me food for thought. This wasn't simply selling passports for money, but the whole gamut of counterfeiting. If marketed well, particularly in Bangkok, Manila and Hong Kong, product of this quality represented serious income. Otto Schwartz was stepping into the big leagues.

I could see why it made sense to partner with a man like Tang who could handle all the distribution. It also made sense that Schwartz would have liked a fellow German, a fellow white man, sitting in Hong Kong keeping his eyes and ears open and reporting on how honest his sales agent was being. Not that anyone who undertook this job would survive very long. Tang would not permit it.

The windows were barred. It was already dark. In the courtyard the cars were still parked as they had been when we arrived, but the stretch limousine was missing. The main building sat pale and silent, while all the lights burned in the barred windows of the bungalow next door. I decided to move on and see what I could find.

I had two options: get out fast without being spotted, or get out fast after causing a lot of damage. I realised the first option was the more sensible, but I preferred the second. The guard sitting outside the front door of the main building was asleep, his head on his chest. Opening the door a foot I slid out on my belly and crawled, using elbows and knees as I had been taught years ago. My fingers ached from the punctures under my nails.

Pausing by the wheel-arch of the white BMW, I listened and looked. Then I moved on, until I reached the bungalow. I raised myself up quietly and stared through a window. The room beyond was empty, so I took a chance and went through the door, slowly. I found myself in a room filled with more cartons and beyond a staircase that led down into a basement. I descended cautiously.

On the other side of a sliding door lay what was clearly Schwartz's production facility. A dozen computers stood wired together. There were colour printers and copiers the size of small filing cabinets. Most of the famous computer brand names were represented in some form or another. It was state-of-the-art stuff. Whirring, humming noises came from several of the machines. The hardware contained in this underground room was worth a fortune.

In the far corner were two more machines. They were plastic injection moulders with large hoppers into which the PVC granules would be poured. Piled messily on the floor were stainless steel moulds the size of footballs. These, once slotted into the injection moulding machine, would create the desired form as the hot liquid plastic shot into its cavities. There was a bin containing crumpled and misshapen cards, deformed siblings of the perfect products I had viewed earlier.

Against the walls someone had piled several yards of paper, which I assumed was to be used in the high-tech colour copiers. On a desk stood two small racks, neatly labelled, holding official stamps for use on the passports, specimens of which were strewn over an adjacent workbench. Further along I came to a corner that had been set up like a miniature photographer's studio. I admired several Hasselblads and a Nikon with an impressive lens.

I paused in my exploration and that was when I heard him. He came out from behind a stack of boxes holding papers in his hand. He was a flaxen-haired youth still innocent of the danger in his occupation, judging by the way he panicked as he saw me. His blue eyes opened wide, even wider as I leapt the three yards between us, held him by the shirt front and drove my awl up through his chin into the brain, transfixing his jaw. His eyes rolled up and away, as he gasped a few last breaths, then he slackened and fell backwards. I put him down gently, tugging the bloody spike out of his chin and made my way back out of the bungalow.

There was about twenty feet between me and the main building. Outside, the guard had not moved. I studied the shadows and found a route in darkness to crawl towards the house. When I reached it, I got to my feet and inched along the building. The guard's face was in profile, but when I was a couple of feet away, he lifted up his head, sensing danger. He tried to pull up his Uzi but I butted him in the face. The cartilage in his nose cracked and I jammed my weapon into his throat.

His wooden chair crashed to the floor. I caught the Uzi just before it fell to the ground. I inspected the weapon. It had been years since I'd fired one because the RHKP favoured the Heckler & Koch. They were the Israeli equivalent of a Kalashnikov. Simple, effective, but inaccurate at longer range. The Israelis used them for bunker clearing, and I reckoned that was what I needed. The 15 round magazine appeared full. I cocked the sub-machine gun, hearing the satisfactory snap as it fed a round into the breech. I flicked the safety off expecting to use the Uzi any second. There had been too much noise.

Nothing happened.

The guard gurgled, not yet completely dead. In the twilight I could see a dark puddle growing beneath him. I left the awl in him, now I was armed with a better weapon. I moved on and found the door locked. As I was retracting my fingers from the handle the door started opening from inside. I brought up the Uzi.

Harald appeared in the doorway. His face registered astonishment and sudden fear for his life as he saw the evil eye of death less than a yard from his chest. He gawped only for an instant. His right hand disappeared behind his back. A short devastating blast from the Uzi froze his movements forever.

32

The hail of fatal projectiles punctured Harald's face, chest and arms. He flopped messily against the wall. I gave him another vengeful burst until the magazine was empty.

From his dying fingers I pulled the Glock 17 that Julian McAlistair had given me. Finding it undamaged, I tossed away the now impotent Uzi. The Glock welcomed me like an old friend, confidence and energy surging into my gun arm. I looked around with uncertainty. Should I go forward or try to lose myself in the gloom of the night?

The decision was made for me when suddenly Mandy appeared white-faced from a side door. She was wearing a cotton blouse, or one of Harald's shirts, and nothing else. Her jaw was slack with fear, but I couldn't fault the firmness and muscularity of her body. A whiff of her perfume mingled with the baser smells of terror. I crooked my index finger and said, "Come here, you little bitch."

She shuffled over obediently. I stared for a second at the dark diamond at the apex of her thighs then I grabbed the back of her neck, pulling her close until the metal of the automatic touched her left breast an inch below her erect nipple. She was cold and afraid. The flesh dimpled, turned red, as I applied pressure.

"Where's Schwartz?"

"What... what do you want?" Her voice cracked and rose an octave as she answered.

"Listen to me, bitch. Where the fuck is Schwartz?" She opened and closed her mouth, but no sound came from it. Time was running out. From outside came the noise of panicking minions. I backhanded her hard across the face sending her staggering against the wall. She slipped to her knees dripping tears onto the polished tiles that began to mingle with an exploratory rivulet of blood travelling from Harald's riddled corpse.

"One last time. Where's the fat German bastard?" I said, surprising myself with the fury in my voice.

"He left already, half an hour ago. He left..." Her laboured response emerged at last. A movement caught my eye and a head popped around the doorjamb, and then disappeared like a frightened rodent. I sighed, turned back to the girl who hadn't moved and decorated her forehead with a scarlet bullet hole. I needed to move on and she really hadn't been altogether helpful.

The room she had come out of was sparsely decorated with chair, desk, bed and a reproduction Picasso on the wall. Clothes were scattered around as if the couple's relationship had still been at an early stage of passion. What I really needed to know was how many other guards with Uzi machine guns were still out there. A look through the window told me nothing. No movement was visible.

I decided to leave the house by the terrace to the beach and stepping over the bodies carefully made my way through the interior of the building, retracing the steps we had taken when we first arrived. Only a few corridor lights were on and the walls resounded eerily with my footsteps. There seemed to be nobody around, only a hollow sepulchral echo. The silence of the walls made me wary. I took every corner with caution, tension in the trigger finger, trying not to let it and the pain slow me down.

I entered the vaulted chamber that served Schwartz as living room, dining room and playroom and listened. There was nothing to hear except the muted drone of Thai voices on a television. The room was in shadow except for a lamp and the kaleidoscopic flicker of light from the TV. It seemed possible that the girl sitting silently had not been able to hear the commotion and the gunfire. The walls were dungeon thick and the doors solid. She did not notice me until I was beside her.

"Where's Herr Schwartz?" I asked. She looked at me curiously, with no more emotion than she had deployed in the presence of her master.

"He go Hong Kong." She was not lying to me. She had no need or inclination. She simply wished to live. I explained to her that I wanted to leave with as little trouble as possible and needed her help. She got my meaning pretty quickly. I had no intention to harm her. There had been enough killing already and the dead were people who deserved their fate. Descending the steps to the beach I placed one hand on her shoulder. I asked her if she was Otto Schwartz's wife. She snorted as if the thought were an insult. I gave her the benefit of the doubt but kept my gun hand alert. Placidly, almost unemotionally, she led me through the soft sand and onto a little path through the low heather. We came through a scanty collection of trees and found ourselves at the side of the main building in what looked like Frau Wertheim's vegetable patch. I needed to get back to the cars. I had no intention of being pursued on foot through the darkness of Otto Schwartz's estate with dogs on my heels and only one magazine in my Glock.

Suddenly a flash illuminated the night and tracer bullets arced towards us in a hyphenated line. The girl caught most of them. As her bad luck would have it, she had been shielding me almost completely. In death as in life she made no sound, except for an intake of breath as the metal sliced into her body. Then she stumbled, fell on her face and died instantly, another casualty of this odd war I had started.

There was only one gunman and I could see him clearly in the moonlight. He had learnt little from his national service, crouching silhouetted against the wall, shouting wildly at someone else. He kept pumping bullets into the night, forgetting that all good things come to an end and that muzzle flashes, tracer rounds and moonlight, can be a fatal combination. When the breech locked on the empty magazine, I jumped up, ran ten yards, sighted with both hands in the classical firing stance, held my breath and snapped two rounds off. He was fiddling with the new magazine. One of my rounds hit him in the chest and he fell to the ground.

I wasn't sure if I had killed him. It was really too dark to be certain. I pushed the Glock into his chin and made sure. My fist was instantly wet. I pulled his Uzi from a slack grasp and moved on, a weapon in each hand.

There were three of them crouched behind the BMW. They seemed to be arguing in loud whispers, which drifted across in snatches like a row between lovers in the house next door.

The Israelis have a talent when it comes to the implements of war and the Uzi was an efficient and pleasant assault weapon. It was small, rugged and deadly at close range, but I rarely used one in my new profession, favouring accuracy over brute firepower. The group by the

BMW were barely within its effective range, which was not much greater than twenty yards. I wanted the vehicle bullet-free and with its petrol tank intact, so I decided to save my ammo and get in closer.

I studied the available cover. Years previously someone had told me that I had a sound eye for ground and used it well. It had probably been a casual compliment, but it was the sort of praise that sticks in your mind when you are young and keen to make a mark.

A shout came from the group by the car. I recognised the coarse accent of a native Cantonese speaker.

"Don't shoot".

The demand was repeated and somebody stood up, holding his arms high in the air like a cowboy in a spaghetti western. I crawled into a new position and observed his attempt at surrender. The other two were trying to pull him down and the occasional word reached me. It sounded like an argument, half in Thai and half in English.

"Walk forward," I called out and instantly rolled away from the spot from where I had spoken. Just as quickly bullets smacked the ground where I had been lying a second earlier.

The man with his hands up kept walking. His face crossed a patch of light spilling from the open front door and I recognised his buck teeth, accountant's face and frightened features.

It made sense that a man who thought of himself as a craftsman and had raised counterfeiting to an impressive blend of science and artistry preferred not to be caught in a moonlight firefight.

The adrenalin was wearing off and my body was starting to scream out for rest and peace. I concentrated on my legs, jumped up and got them pumping, sprinting for cover into to the doorway of the closest building. The two remaining Thai gunmen were no longer protected by the engine block of the car. I could see them clearly. They had only one Uzi between them. They squirmed in panic, unsure where to move. The range was perfect now. I fired a three second burst and ducked back into the doorway. There was a scream of contact and someone returned fire. Taking advantage of a break in the firing, I popped up with another burst that hit home again. The light was better and my hand steadier than theirs.

I waited five seconds, decided where next to move and sprinted out towards the closest vehicle, a station wagon. Firing from the hip as I ran, to keep their heads down, I hit the deck, slamming my shoulder against the front tyre. There were no gunmen left standing, only the frightened Chinese forger still reaching desperately for the stars.

I got to my feet warily. Now there was a stillness to the night. Nothing moved except for the sea down by the beach. I sniffed the night. It smelt of cordite. The BMW's bodywork was a mess. An eruption of acne had appeared across two of the doors, but all the windows and tyres were intact. Nothing seemed to be leaking and the key was in the ignition.

I called the Forger over, patted him down and frog-marched him rapidly back inside to the room beside my former cell. There were a couple of duffel bags in the room which I encouraged him to fill with the fruits of his labour. Ten minutes later and I'd locked him and the bags in the boot of the BMW, slammed the lid down on his protests and was wheel-skidding the big German sedan down a bumpy track, hoping my luck would hold. The Glock was in my lap and the Uzi lay on the passenger seat.

There was no resistance at the first gate, nobody to stop me except the gate itself, which looked too tough for the bonnet of the Beemer. I had faith in Bavarian engineering, but I would have needed one of Guderian's panzers to defeat it. What the car did offer me, however, was a Faraday Cage, and the electrical fence presented a weaker flank. I slewed off the road and gunned it towards the wire. For a few heartbeats the rear wheels of the BMW slid all over the place, screaming for traction in the soft earth. Thankfully the bonnet of the car parted the fence and its momentum carried me through. I ducked involuntarily and gritted my teeth, battling with the servo steering until all tyres got a grip on the earth and the car returned control to me.

My head smacked the padded roof as we leapt over the last bump and made it onto the tarmac. A moment later the second wooden gate loomed up in the headlights. Nothing complicated here. This one was flimsy. I still ducked when we hit. The sound of the wood cracking was louder than the breaking of a thighbone, but then the windscreen shattered. Glass slivers showered over me. I threw up my hand and stamped on the brakes. The car slowed abruptly. I used the butt of the Uzi to hack out a hole the size of a briefcase which allowed me to see through the shattered windscreen. I squinted into the slipstream striking my face as I pressed my foot down on the accelerator again.

Five minutes later the estate was far behind. I fought with every nerve to remain conscious. All the aches and pains of the last few days came seeping back like relatives at a rich man's funeral demanding attention. Finally, I pulled the BMW into a lay-by and opened the boot to check on the Forger. He was knocked out cold and his glasses had fallen from his face. A smell of excrement rose from the confined space. I found a pulse in his neck, faint but steady. Fetching the Uzi, It fired two rounds through the lid of the boot to let more air in. Then I rearranged his limbs, placed his head on the holdall, pillowed from the cash within, and shut him back in again.

33

When I finally reached the Bolthole, all I wanted to do was sleep for a week. I had remembered the route as best as I could and managed to find the main road in the end. I shoved the weapons under the seat, hoping that no policeman on a motorbike felt like stopping a *falang* driving a car with a smashed windscreen.

I was standing in the main room of the chalet, washing down three more Ponstan painkillers with a bottle of Perrier, when I heard a knock on the door. I went for the Glock in my waistband.

"The guard told me you'd just arrived," Harry Bolt said. He was dressed in a lightweight suit. He must have had a meeting with someone important as he rarely dressed up. The overhead light made his bald head shine.

"My God, you're in a bad way," he said when he took a closer look at me.

"Yeah, well I wish I could say the same thing about Otto Schwartz, but the bastard got away."

"You've got cuts all over your face and what the hell happened to your arm?" Bolt asked, as he picked up the bottle of pills and examined it.

"Have you been waiting for me?" I asked walking into the bathroom and looking at a face in the mirror that could have belonged to my grandfather.

"You and events. We'll go up to my suite when you're ready."

"I thought you'd gone back to Bangkok?"

"Change of plan. The girls like it better here."

"What happened to 'no women in the main building?'"

"They're not women, mate, they're the Four Seasons. Anyone asks, they're staff, until some idiot tries to touch them, then they're in big trouble."

"God, I'm tired."

"Did you win?"

"No, but I've put a few goals in the net for our team." There were at least ten bloody nicks. It looked as if I'd been trying to shave while drunk. The soap hurt and the alcohol from the aftershave burned like buggery.

Bolt stood in the doorway silently. I showed him the little puncture marks at the end of my fingers, then poured some Listerine into the wash basin and dipped my hands into the solution. It had originally been invented as an antiseptic until somebody was stupid enough to swig it. I swore, but my body had endured so much pain that it made little difference.

"What was the body count?" he asked, twirling the tip of his waxed moustache between forefinger and thumb.

"In single figures."

"Are the police involved yet?"

"Not that I know of." I'd finished bathing my fingers.

"Show you something," I said as we stepped from the chalet some minutes later. His eyes took in the pitted bodywork and the state of the windscreen.

"No resale value on this motor," he commented, running a finger through a jagged puncture in the driver's door. I turned the key on the boot and lifted up the lid.

"Is he alive?" Bolt asked.

"Should be. Yes, still breathing," I said, putting two fingers gingerly to his neck. "Just knocked around a bit, like me."

"By you or the car?"

"Didn't lay a finger on him."

I extracted the two duffel bags. "Got any handcuffs?"

"The girls have. Who is he?" I decided not to query why the Four Seasons possessed handcuffs.

"He's the man who made what's in here. The man that Tang calls the Forger." I slapped the man in the face several times and he groaned without returning to consciousness.

"He'll be all right," Bolt said "Leave him in there for now."

I relocked the boot and we walked down to

the main building and took a lift to the second floor. As usual Bolt had done himself well. It was a suite with five connecting bedrooms, fit for the president of a small African nation. Two of his girls were playing chess; the other two were lying by the television but leapt to their feet and began fussing over me when we entered. Autumn rushed off to fetch their First Aid box and Thai herbal balms.

Unzipping the bag I dumped its contents onto the sofa. The girls gasped.

"That's about half a million U.S. dollars," Bolt said, casting an experienced eye over the bundles.

"Forged."

"I'm impressed." He was examining a bill. "I like it. This is great stuff. What do you want to do with it?" I could see his mind was leaping around at the possibilities. He had a weak spot for cash and profit. More so than most men I knew.

I shrugged. He picked up the passports and then some of the gold credit cards. "Top quality gear. It would be a shame to throw this stuff away. I'll send it to the Caymans and have someone launder it discreetly. We'll get a thirty percent return on it provided the quality stands up. I'll take ten percent as a commission, the rest for your retirement fund."

My damaged face hurt as I smiled. "I don't see why not."

"Right you are, son. Spring, go and get those handcuffs you keep on showing me." He turned back to me. I noticed a sly glint in his eyes. "General Charoenchati is on the way here, to discuss business. You'd better tell me what happened before he arrives. I've known him for a long time and he's a cunning old fellow. Don't want him to get the better of us. Important thing is he'll be able to smooth out any police problems you might have caused."

I gave him the whole story. He didn't interrupt. He listened carefully and nodded every now and then, his mind considering the facts.

"So the Wertheim woman will be able to identify you, and so will Gruber."

"I can deal with Gruber now. He'll be at the hotel."

"You'd do better to leave Thailand as quickly as possible. If Gruber calls the police it won't take them too long to come up here checking on you."

"I've got at least a day or two. Not many people know I'm bunking here. That's why I've got to get to Gruber immediately, then I'll leave. Pass me a cigarette."

"It's a bit of a mess. But nothing that can't be solved with cash or alcohol," Bolt said. I wasn't sure if he meant the situation or my face.

Spring came up and placed a set of handcuffs in a black leather holder on the table. "Thanks, darling. Leave us alone now." Bolt ran his hand affectionately through her long sleek hair. She smiled mischievously and walked off.

"Why's Charoenchati coming here?" I asked. I still felt he had a hidden agenda. He might not be as rich as Bolt, but his corruption came with the power of the Thai military behind it.

"He didn't say much, but there have been some developments at his end and he wanted to speak to you. It seems you told his goons that you were on this job for their boss, so he's keen to meet you in your official capacity. Then there's the other contract I mentioned to you. He's the other party with an interest in it."

That didn't surprise me. Risking the General learning my secret, had seemed the only way to get Kronk and Toothless off my back. After three attempts to kill me I hadn't wanted to take any more risks with them.

"Remember, Harry: I told him I'd kill Schwartz, I didn't admit to being the Reliable Man. See if you can finesse things. I've got to go and get Gruber. After that I'm on the first flight out and I'm going after Schwartz in Hong Kong. I don't really want to hang around for your general." I took the handcuffs off the table. "I'll leave the forger with you. Charoenchati can have him if he's interested. I don't suppose that sort of thing is really your scene."

"Not really. But it's tempting. Keep him locked up in a dungeon somewhere, feed him chicken's feet and make him churn out piles of fake banknotes." Bolt's eyes looked dreamy. I got up to go.

Before I reached the door the telephone rang. I paused.

Bolt said, "The General is here. Stay and talk with him first."

When they arrived he had someone else with him. Captain Suvilit, whom I'd last seen looking mean and moody with Tang Siu Ling was now with the General. Kronk as usual was in attendance. Suvilit wore the same jeans and bomber jacket he'd worn before. Charoenchati was elegant in a white patterned silk shirt. Kronk looked like he'd been shopping in a thrift store for hired muscle. His eyes flashed at me.

"Bill," General Charoenchati said and shook my hand. "Our first meeting got off on the wrong footing. Let us put it behind us. Things have changed and I have been talking with our mutual friend Harry here." His smooth barely lined face became quizzical. "Have you killed Otto Schwartz for me?"

"Not yet. He will die once I can track him down. He's gone to Hong Kong. I've taken out most of his operation here."

"I heard reports on the police radio that there has been some trouble at a farm near Chonburi." He turned to Bolt and said: "The Germans are finished in Pattaya. They have no more power. I finally reached an agreement with the Police General in Bangkok today. We will stamp them out and kick them out. Like the vermin they are.

How did Schwartz get away?"

"He left the compound before I could stop him. It's a long story. Tell me what Suvilit is doing here?" It was becoming clear to me why Kronk had been able to find Simone and me so easily, so often.

"Captain Suvilit is one of my associates. He has been supplying me information about the dealings of that Hong Kong criminal Tang who thinks he can come to my country and steal money from me and my friends. As you can guess, Captain Suvilit told me that Tang planned to blackmail you into coming to Pattaya. I wasn't paying attention. I should have realised that you were the man Harry here had recommended to me for killing the *falang* gangster Schwartz. That's why I ordered Kronk to kill you when you angered me by ignoring my advice. But that is in the past. I know what sort of man you are now. Crazy and dangerous. Take it as a compliment. But you still have to prove to me that you are a reliable man." He paused. "You must finish off Schwartz for me."

"I am reliable," I said, "but I am not The Reliable Man". There was a pause, and Charoenchati smiled.

"If you wish to play it that way," he said, "then I will be $88,000 better off when you kill him." I swore inwardly. He was a wily operator. It hurt me to admit that my anonymity was worth more to me than money, especially now that I had a personal reason to kill Schwartz.

"He killed some of my friends. That has made me very angry," I said.

"You hear that Kronk?" the General said, "he is not that different to you. You have made Kronk look foolish so often Jedburgh that it has become a matter of honour for him to kill you. I have told him to forget you, but it might be best if you avoided him in future." I shrugged to show my acceptance. Unless he came looking for me, it was unlikely that we would frequent the same restaurants or nightclubs.

Charoenchati turned to Bolt and said, "We still have a small problem. When the girl Tang sent to accompany Jedburgh went back to Bangkok, she told him a lot of things. As a result, he no longer trusts the Captain here. I need to know the latest developments before I can plan ahead."

I told the General what I knew, which was now more than he did. He looked pleased. "Now I have finally reached the agreement with our Police General there will be no real investigation into any dead Germans in Pattaya. We'll keep your name out of this."

I had to admire his confidence. These kinds of deals were done in the Far East. Influence and hard currency smoothed over a lot of rough edges. It was, as always, simply a question of business.

"Kronk will take care of Gruber for you this evening. I no longer need you to do my work in

Pattaya. This is a Thai matter now. I will arrange for all the things to be cleaned up. The police will take the credit, unofficially, for destroying an extortion gang. Some of the senior police officers here will be gone by next week, posted to some poor province by my friend in Bangkok. Most of the Germans will leave because they will quickly realise that their time is over. Perhaps the Philippines will have them." He laughed.

"My brother-in-law in the Immigration Department will revoke Schwartz's visa so he cannot come back. You will finish your job in Hong Kong if the Fat Man is there. Your fee will be my gratitude to yourself and Harry."

Bolt, lounging on the sofa amidst the counterfeit goods, spoke for the first time. "We have got the Hong Kong forger. I'm willing to let you have him. If you want to make a little deal." He handed the General a bundle from the pile of money, cards and passports that both Thais had politely been ignoring.

After he had studied it for a while Charoenchati passed over the wadge of money to Suvilit who turned it over in his hands and held it to the light. There were also some Thai Baht in the bag. I proffered those. The two men exchanged words in Thai. They were impressed.

"Captain Suvilit says he's never seen anything so perfect. I heard about this man. And I am interested. What Schwartz has left behind should now belong to me, don't you think?

Finders keepers, loser weepers, isn't that how the saying goes?"

"Then you'd better get up to the estate and salvage all the equipment," I suggested. I explained about all of the computer hardware and the state-of-the-art copiers. He instructed Suvilit sharply who went off to make some phone calls that would ensure Charoenchati's continued control over the situation.

"What do you say," Bolt the businessman proposed," to giving me full control of the Bolthole in return for the forger?"

Charoenchati gave him a cold smile. "Is that a good deal for me? This resort makes too much money. And anyway, the main shareholder has to be a Thai."

"My girls are all Thai, they still have nationality. You sign over your share to them. This deal's a gift. Think how much money this quality product can make you." Bolt scooped up a handful of American Express cards and held them like a rice merchant bargaining with a buyer.

General Charoenchati didn't reply, simply looked at the stack of passports he held in his hands. Then he shook his head slowly.

"I'll go and get the merchandise," I said, unwilling to stand around while they haggled. I knew the General would go for it eventually, but he'd take his time because he didn't want to appear easy.

Picking up the handcuffs I walked out of the

room. Kronk followed me all the way to the car. I made an effort to smile at him wondering if he wanted to fight me. My head ached furiously. One could never be certain with Asians, however Western their manners and speech. For generations their minds had circled in different patterns than us simple foreign devils. There was always the possibility that Kronk would risk the wrath of his boss to get personal revenge.

The Forger was moaning and the whites of his eyes showed when Kronk pulled him out from the boot and onto his feet. I snapped on the superfluous handcuffs and the ugly Thai flung his skinny burden over a shoulder. We walked in hostile silence.

"He's just been bumped around too much." I explained when we got back to the suite. "He'll be all right soon." The Forger's face was bruised and his lip had split. Apart from this there seemed to be no visible damage. The buyer ordered Suvilit to inspect the merchandise. Ten minutes later they agreed on the price. The Bolthole would be Harry's except for ten percent but in turn he'd have first option and a big discount on any units in a new shopping and condominium complex the General was building on Sukhumvit Road in Bangkok.

"Now what about the other job, General?" Bolt prompted, once they had shaken hands on their deal.

"Yes," Charoenchati turned to me looking

grave, "We have one more job for you. You must kill one more man for me, for us. Outside Thailand."

"I hope it is whom I think it is."

"It is, Bill. Will you do it?" Harry Bolt said with a smile.

I nodded. "It will be a pleasure," I said smiling. "But this time I will require a fee."

34

In Thailand business disputes are frequently settled with guns and bullets instead of lawyers and writs. General Charoenchati had decided that his position was now strong enough to settle his differences with Tang Siu Ling once and for all in the ancient, final manner.

Schwartz had been powerful, with strong connections but only in the Pattaya area. Tang's position was much more deep-rooted. He enjoyed the support of many Chinese Thai businesspeople in the kingdom. To do away with him was a bolder move than to eliminate the fat German gangster. Because if the timing was wrong, there would be men coming after Charoenchati to avenge the murder of Tang. But that was not my concern. I was simply an instrument of extraction, removing a foul-smelling abscess from the gums of the person who paid most and paid first.

I added more detail for Bolt and the General about the connection between Schwartz, Mok Bun and the Hong Kong Triad. Charoenchati listened carefully and nodded.

"You are right," he said. "Schwartz had become too powerful and people were complaining to the Minister. He asked me to help. I find that Schwartz is also having some connections with this Hong Kong man. Some of my other friends persuaded me it was a good time to protect the interests of Thai people. No Germans, no Chiu Chow bandits..." He ran a hand across his neck in the cutting gesture. He made it sound unselfish, yet it was Charoenchati who stood to benefit.

"The fee for Tang will be split between the General and me," Harry said. "The contract comes from both of us. It'll be nice to see the bastard dead. I know you'll enjoy it."

The General opened his briefcase and pulled out some cash. He handed it to Bolt explaining that since both jobs would probably be done in Hong Kong, it made sense for Bolt to have his half of the contract now. I saw Harry count it out and noted he had passed over $44,000. My protestations that I wasn't the Reliable Man hadn't convinced him, but he was going to take his freebie on Schwartz just the same. Business was the same the world over. Catch a break, you take it.

The General spent the next ten minutes on the telephone talking in Thai, beginning to sort out the mess I'd left. He sounded like a man reporting to his partners on a successful take-over bid, and that was exactly what it was. I was pretty sure that General Charoenchati was in league with some highly influential people - a Government minister here, a property developer, some police generals. He would be the lynchpin heading up a cartel of greedy, powerful men.

I'd decided to leave immediately for Bangkok. I needed to lose myself in the big city and get some rest. I could backtrack on any loose ends before they caused me problems. And Simone was in Bangkok. But before I left, I needed some information from the Forger. The slight Chinese man had not uttered a word and looked in shock. I spoke to him in Cantonese. He looked surprised.

"What are the names on the passports Schwartz and Mok Bun are using to travel to Hong Kong?"

"I don't understand." He looked confused.

"*Diu lei lo mo* - fuck your mother," I swore at him. "*Lei mo chuen ngoh* - Don't be cheeky with me." My knee shot into his groin. He jack-knifed forward and made retching noises. "Mok Bun cannot come into Hong Kong on his real passport. He'll be on the stop list. What passports did you make for them?"

He hesitated, fearful of further assaults on his testicles.

"The names or I'll break your fingers." I grabbed his hand. He was too slow to snatch it away.

"For the *gwai lo* it was an American passport Mr. Hank Gutfreund, Mok Bun used the name John Chan," he stammered. "They were very good passports." He then surprised me by remembering the passport numbers. He was proud of his work. I noted them on a scratch pad next to the phone.

"Can I give you a lift anywhere?" Charoenchati asked. "I am going into Pattaya. Kronk will deal with Gruber and guard the Forger. I am going to spend the night with a friend." The way he said it made me think she was female and that he paid the rent.

"Thanks, but I am going to return the Kawasaki I rented then get a car to Bangkok." Charoencheti shook hands with Bolt and then left with Suvilit and Kronk, who ushered out the Forger at gunpoint. I stayed a few minutes longer to say goodbye to Harry and the girls and to transfer some of the Forger's goodies into my luggage. As I was doing so, Winter came from the bathroom and handed me a vial of capsules. They were red and grey and I recognised them for what they were - amphetamines. I kissed her on the cheek and gave her a wink. Smart girl.

"See you in Hong Kong. You really do look terrible. Get some sleep tonight or they won't let you in," Bolt said and gave me a kind of hug, the way good friends do sometimes.

"Take care of my money," I replied.

When I got down to where Charoenchati's limousine, a red Cadillac, was parked, I pulled Suvilit aside and asked him what had happened to Simone.

He shrugged. "She go home. Tang tell her she

work good and give her present."

"Was she happy?"

He thought about my question. "No," he decided, "she not happy." He smiled, a man of the world. "Maybe you confuse her. She looks like the woman who has a big heart."

"You know where she lives?"

"Sure." He gave me the address. "You want to take her for yourself. You like her but she's dangerous for you."

"She knows too much."

I strapped my bag onto the back of my bike. Toothless, sitting behind the wheel of the limousine, eyed me warily. I gave him a wink.

Mounting the bike was hard work. Simply getting my leg up hurt like hell. I kicked the beast into life. The familiar throb was comforting and somehow the rhythm was soothing. The limousine crunched off down the drive and I followed at a snail's pace.

We passed a lay-by that I had noticed before. Vaguely my brain registered that a vehicle was parked in the spot. Its headlights were off. After we'd passed the lay-by, a sudden glance in my side mirrors warned me that the dark car had come to life. The sixth sense that I had developed in the army and the police and perfected as the Reliable Man started to penetrate my dull brain. It began to feel wrong.

I turned and tried to see what was happening behind me. The headlights blinded me. It was impossible to make anything out except for the sombre threatening outline of a big saloon car.

The Kawasaki increased its tone and I overtook the limousine on the next bend. I was making hand signals, trying to indicate the potential threat. They didn't seem to comprehend my warnings and anyway it was too late. The car speeded up until it was level with the General's car. I saw the muzzle flashes through the open windows as the guns spat fire into the Cadillac.

We were half a mile from the main road, no other car in sight, a ditch on either side and the odd tree. I could hear all too sharply the chatter of rapid death, spitting destruction at the red Cadillac. There was nothing to do. Perhaps Charoenchati's limousine was armour plated and bulletproof, but I wasn't.

I gunned the Kawasaki. The throttle was all open, the engine was screaming, the sudden acceleration hit me in the chest like a flying anvil. I held on and was thankful that the rest of the road was straight with only one last bend at the end. I tore blindly into the shadows while the sound of murder faded rapidly over my shoulder. Charoenchati, who half an hour ago had been so proud, commandeering, scheming, victorious, was no more. It must have been Tang who had somehow got wind of what was happening and made his move first. That was the only logical explanation.

It was nine fifteen when I got to the rental

store next to the bus station. The owner, sitting by the food stall, was surprised to see me back. I tossed him the keys and he grudgingly returned my deposit with a shrugged apology that I had booked for an extra week that he couldn't refund me. There was a bus waiting to leave for the capital. Thais and tourists were boarding so I decided there was no need for a car. Ninety Baht got me the second last seat, next to a Buddhist monk in saffron robes who smelt of sanctity and garlic. He smiled and nodded, which was the last thing I noticed before closing my eyes. My fingers touched the Glock that was still tucked against my body and the comforting hardness lulled me into sleep.

My biological clock woke me before we reached the terminal at Ekamai. My whole system was moving like the Chao Phrao river after the rains had brought down a lot of mud. My neck was stiff. I had slept awkwardly. The air-conditioned bus was not Raffles Class on Singapore Airlines. It took a supreme effort to get to my feet and stagger down the steps. The monk was still nodding and smiling when I dragged my carcass past him looking for a *tuk-tuk*.

I found one and agreed to a foolish price. The man slammed his foot down on the gas and I went flying. My head jerked forwards again as he slammed on the brakes and then speed forward again to get past a cluster of cars. I thought of the way Harald had jerked, when the bullets did their fierce work. I decided that somewhere dark, discreet and anonymous would be a good place to spend the night. Then I would be ready for more revenge.

I chose a dubious guesthouse on Sukhumvit Soi 9. I'd never stayed there but someone had recommended it: the sheets were changed daily, the showers had good pressure and the landlord could supply girls. It was up three flights. They had ten rooms. I paid in advance. A middle-aged Caucasian man in flip-flops was leaving with a short fat girl who was very ugly. Each to his own.

The room had a double bed, a mirror and a fan. I showered quickly and around my feet the water turned grey. My mind began moving again. I considered Simone and my need to finish what she had started by bringing down a brass ashtray on the back on my head.

What would I do when I confronted the girl? I did not know. I didn't want to hit her. I wanted her to tell me what plans Tang had made and where I could find him. The girl knew too much. She didn't know everything, but she could suspect a lot. Given the wrong set of circumstances she could point a finger and put a noose around my neck. I had to be rational, professional, cold. But first I needed sleep.

Using a small shaving mirror I examined the wound on the back of my head. It was a strong head the doctor had said, barely any concussion. There was no sign of the pinpricks Wim had made in my fingers, only a septic ache that reminded me of days in muddy trenches while on army exercise. The rest of my body was covered in so many bruises it made me look like a leper. I put a big new plaster on the cut in my arm.

I wasn't going to sleep now. I got out the amphetamines Bolt's girl had given me and swallowed two with a glass of water. With shaky movements, like an old man, I dressed myself again in fresh clothes. Then, I cleaned the Glock. I studied the little copper cased rounds, and after polishing them carefully, clicked them, all seventeen, into place. I ejected the magazine and worked the action, watching and listening to it, making sure that everything glistened with the oil that would ensure smoothness in delivery. I laced up my shoes and resisted the temptation to lie back on the bed and forget everything for a few hours. Sleep would have to wait. Often enough I'd been called out of bed in the middle of the night and worked twenty hours without rest. This was no different. After a while I felt the magic pills kick in and my mind became sharper and my body lighter. I knew it would only last an hour or two.

35

It was midnight as I left my room. The heavy honeyed smell, of the clammy polluted night air, mixed with the choking smoke which came off the food hawkers' stalls. A taxi with an aircon that worked took me down Wireless Road and then turned off into a quiet, moderately expensive, residential area.

The houses appeared about thirty years old with five or six stories and were divided into apartments. A Thai concierge doubling as a telephone operator sat on her feet watching an ancient television set. She didn't glance up as I passed into the forecourt where two new Japanese hatchbacks and an older BMW indicated the middle-class tone of the building. There was a satellite dish on the roof and a swimming pool which hadn't been cleaned for a while, judging by all the leaves floating in it. A cardboard sign with felt tip markings indicated the apartment numbers.

There was a yellow hall light, not very bright, outside the flat that I wanted on the fifth floor. A heavy grille protected the door. I examined the design. The wooden door inside looked flimsy and once past the grille it would give me no problems. I knew about grilles from my days in the police. Most Hong Kong flats have their doors barred in this way to prevent burglars and I had taken down many doors during drug and hostage raids.

The grille had a central panel of steel with bars running up and down from it. Only a child could get its hands between the bars. Opening the grille from the inside was a simple matter of pulling back the latch. If it were locked from the outside the latch would not move, if it were bolted from the inside the grille would not open. I checked around to be sure that no one was observing me. Nobody was visible in the dim light.

I unthreaded the belt from my trousers, leaving the gun tucked into my waistband. I fed the belt through the top bars, let it dangle down and retrieved it through the bottom bars.

This was how Sergeant Yan had taught me. He had been my first Detective-Sergeant when I was twenty-two. He'd taught me sensible police techniques: how to avoid paperwork, increase my arrest record, not leave marks or bruises on suspects being interrogated and how to get into premises with the least bit of fuss and without a search warrant. He had been a practical man who knew that the letter of the law was less important than catching the bad guys and locking them up.

The trick was to snare the latch with the belt. It took a delicate pendulum movement until the leather strip was correctly in place but even then it tended to slip off easily. One had to be patient and to concentrate. After a minute or more the sweat was beginning to form on my face and my arms ached. I stepped back, rested for an instant and tried again. A sudden click and the grille opened outwards and moved towards me. I let out a sigh of relief. Simone had failed to bolt the door which was quite common as the latch gave the impression of being secure enough.

The door had the sort of handle you turn to open and a Yale lock that had seen better days. Sergeant Yan had his system for Yale locks too. One could try a piece of celluloid but the distance between jamb and door had to be absolutely correct and the plastic strip could not be too rigid, nor too soft or it would neither curve around easily nor lever the tongue of the lock backwards properly. With experimentation I'd found that an electronic key card from a Hilton hotel, borrowed once from a flight attendant I was visiting, worked best.

I took it from my wallet. No light shone under the door. I knelt and slipped the plastic into the gap at the bottom of the door, then worked it around the edge of the wood and up the side. Getting around the edge was the hardest part, where the card had to bend without breaking.

It took some wiggling and shoving and pressure against the door to make the gap larger. Once around the edge the plastic slipped upwards effortlessly. I moved it with care lest it come out or made too much noise. I had to hit the spring lock and force it back. After some more gentle pushing and wriggling the latch gave way and I was in, finding myself in a darkened living room filled with shadowy furniture. The kitchen was part of the room. A refrigerator hummed and faint music seeped in from somewhere.

I listened and waited.

There was no doubt I was in the right flat. A hint of her scent drifted into my nostrils, discomfiting me. Testing each step, I moved around the apartment. Two closed doors with light seeping through from behind the left one – I presumed they were bedrooms. The unlit one yielded to my turning hand.

Did she share her flat? Only, it appeared, with a collection of clothes and shoes extending around the edges of the room. Although her bedroom door was locked, it proved flimsier than the front door. I took a deep breath, rested my shoulder against the door and thrust hard. With a crack the plywood fragmented ripping away from its hinges and the door leapt open. I followed in fast as she screamed in terror.

She was sitting on the bed in a pink silk nightgown that came halfway down her thighs. She had been painting her toenails and the bloody scarlet bottle had tipped and was leaking its contents onto the bed sheets. She dropped the brush in horror and made as if to wrap her arms around herself. She still had make-up on and I couldn't help wanting her as I stood there.

"Were you going out?" I asked. It was a girlish room, cluttered with knick-knacks that a man would never buy. There were fluffy toys, extravagant picture frames, a fan on the wall, a full-length mirror, a vanity chest that didn't quite match the bed - a solid dark affair which probably creaked when one moved on it too rapidly. A baby hi-fi stood on a dresser surrounded by perfume bottles, body lotions and discarded tapes. It was playing a song by 'Simply Red'.

"What do you want?" she asked defiantly. "I didn't think I'd see you again."

"I wasn't sure I wanted to see you again after what you did to me." I indicated the back of my head.

"You're a big tough man. You can take it. What happened to your face?" It was the coldness with which she chose to defend herself that annoyed me most.

"A windscreen exploded in my face."

There was a flicker of concern, but she suppressed it quickly. She said, "At least you didn't get killed."

"Some other people did." I advanced a step closer. "I need to ask you some questions."

Simone slowly shook her head. "I don't want

to talk to you. How did you get in here anyway? I thought the door was locked."

"Did you know that Tang was going to have me and Charoenchati ambushed?" I asked sharply

A shadow of unease slipped across her eyes. My lips were dry and I felt a constriction near my throat because it was becoming painfully clearer to me what had to be done. I was trying to sound reasonable, but it was hard to look at her. I tried to blame myself for letting her find out too much and hoping that she could change her loyalties. I had fallen for this girl and that had been unwise. For as long as I was the Reliable Man it would always be unwise to trust any person.

"You're crazy. Why don't you leave?" she said.

"Simone, relax. I just want to talk. I need you to explain a few things for me."

"There's nothing to explain."

"You don't want to explain to me why one moment you make love to me and the next you crown me with an ashtray?" That hurt her. I'd touched a raw nerve and it pleased me.

"It was a mistake."

"What? Making love to me? Hitting me over the head?"

"Starting to like you."

"Sure it was a mistake. And I've learnt my lesson," I said and noticed the bitterness in my voice.

"You don't understand," she said avoiding my

eyes, looking down at the patch of red nail polish on her white sheets.

"No," I sighed, "men never seem to understand."

"No," she said vehemently, "you don't understand my life. For you things are easy. You have choices. I don't. There are some things that I have to do, whether I like it or not."

"Like betraying my trust? As a result of what you told Tang, several people have been killed. They were ambushed, machine-gunned. I was lucky to get away."

At last the frigid mask began to melt. A single decent tear coursed down to her chin, followed by another. Inside her a struggle was taking place but I didn't know what it was really about.

I spoke softly, soothingly now, sorry for her because I was starting to understand her situation. Her whole life she had been trapped between a rock and a hard place.

I said, "It was my fault. I screwed up. I should have known that your duty and loyalty would always be with Tang."

"Didn't you read my letter?" she asked.

"So?"

"Nothing." She shrugged, giving up.

"What did you tell Tang?"

"Will you just go away and leave me alone," she demanded, her eyes flaring with a sudden defiance.

"Then tell me what you told him."

"OK, fine, yes. I told him what you were doing. You know," she said with impatience, "seeing all those people, your friends. I didn't tell him their names, though. I told him about Charoenchati. I knew he was a man Uncle Tang had been having problems with. When I overheard you telling those men you were working for him - the window was open - I couldn't take it anymore. I wanted to leave and have nothing more to do with all this." Her voice disappeared into a whisper. "Just like now. I want to close my eyes and wake up somewhere else. Why is my life always so screwed up?"

She hugged her thighs to her chest and shut her eyes as if she really could open them and reappear in a different place and at a different time.

"Charoenchati is dead now," I said.

"I don't want to hear you telling me it was my fault. I had to tell Uncle Tang, don't you understand?" She looked resigned.

I shrugged and asked, "So what now?"

"Uncle Tang said I could go to New York next month. I want to study acting." The thought seemed to cheer her up.

"You did well with me. I doubt you need training, but Uncle Tang's rewarding you. Where is he now?"

"I'm not sure." She sobbed, wiping again at the wetness on her cheeks. "I think he went back to Hong Kong. To meet the German man from

Pattaya. They have reached an agreement and will settle things. The matter is over. Please, Bill, just forget it and leave. Get on with your life and forget about me and Uncle Tang and those Germans."

"Simone. I get paid to kill people. You are wrong when you say I have a choice. Sometimes I have as little choice as you do."

"You're crazy," she said, shaking her head.

"No, it's a cruel, selfish world. Bastards like Uncle Tang and Charoenchati make it worse. I'm just the rubbish bin collector who comes along and gets rid of the mess that people make in their daily business."

She shook her head. "Go away... please?"

Her eyes shone brightly from crying. She began vainly dabbing at the spilt nail varnish with tissues from a box on her side table. The liquid had already hardened and the patch of colour was fixed on the sheets.

She had been weighed by me on the balance and found wanting. Now was the time for reason to triumph over emotion. She had betrayed my trust. A long-forgotten line of schoolbook learning drifted out of the lumber room of my mind: 'And all men kill the thing they love... the coward does it with a kiss, the brave man with a sword!'

When I left, she was dead.

It took me five minutes to find a taxi and agree on a price. I slumped onto the sticky plastic of the rear seat and checked my pulse. It was cantering. I hated myself for this lack of control, this pathetic weakness of my emotions. In the past I had worked so hard to be in command of all my feelings and actions. My hands were shaking. But the deed was done. A loose end had been dealt with. But it hurt me worse than all the injuries I had sustained that day.

36

It was 2.05 a.m. and I was in a club called 'Supergirls'. I was drinking to forget, and I had already forgotten what I was doing. Minutes earlier there had still been naked women swaying in front of me. A line of shaven, pink pussies had faced me as I addressed myself to a drink that had now completely lost its flavour. Now they were all gone because the party was over. Slowly they began to reappear wearing clothes. A girl with short hair that had once been long, judging from a single strand that still hung down to her shoulder blade, was checking her purse. She'd been working at the club for six years and she still had the looks and the shape to make money dancing. If she was smart, and she seemed smart, she would have bought a condo or two by now.

She gave me a cool, impersonal look, the sort a butcher employs on a rack of meat he is about to slice. A middle-aged man with tattoos on his forearms and close-cropped grey hair joined her, then they left together.

The Mama-san came and asked me if I wanted anybody. I shook my head. With great care I made my way down the narrow stairs, slipping once or twice. At the bottom, three ladyboys stood around smoking long thin cigarettes, hands on hips, still on the prowl. Men like me were their target. Men who had lost the ability to judge. They eyed me like hyenas, wondering if my flesh was for them or for the vultures. I shook my head, staggering on.

Girls were mounting motorbikes sitting sideways and *tuk-tuks* vied for passengers. The street stalls had been dismantled and were packed, along with their goods, in enormous metal chests on wheels. I stood hunched with hands in pockets wondering where and what next. I realised I was swaying from side to side and my vision was coming and going. The glitz of an hour earlier had been turned off and only pockets of depravity remained. A few touts fingered me for late night drinking bars, "Nice girls, you come with me." Was there still such a thing in the world as a nice girl? Simone de Marelle had removed that concept from my mind.

Now was the hour of the hounds and they were baying for me in the distance. I was drunk and high but not ready for the kennels yet. At the end of the road there was always 'Peppermint'. The manager had paid his subscription to the Police Widows and Orphans fund, so at least there the beat went on. Briefly I paused at the corner of the side road that leads to Patpong Two. The 'King's Lounge' also stayed open late. Across the road, tables and chairs had been placed on a dais.

I studied the people hanging around the entrance and lolled against a chair. At this time of the night no one really cared about drunks. I could feel the heavy throb of the bass from the speakers upstairs. The vibration rode down my spine.

A fat girl with big breasts stopped to ask me for a light. I looked at her and tossed over my plastic lighter. She wanted to say something, but I wasn't interested. The lady-boys from earlier trawled past, flicking their long hair with slender hands, and swinging their hips more than a real girl would. They looked good. It would have been easy to forget what they'd once been.

All of a sudden, El appeared in front of me, staring up into my face. Her nose wrinkled in distaste because she could smell the liquor. She had seen me in a bad way before, but probably not this bad. There was another girl with her in sloppy jeans and T-shirt. Not my type. El was wearing a skintight pair of shorts, matching top in gold and black and on her feet chunky high heels. My type. I smiled at her. She yanked my nose.

"Why you no have lady?"

"Waiting for you," I said lamely.

El turned to her friend and spoke, then back to me. "We go eat now. You come?"

I nodded. She took me by the hand and led me to Suriwongse Road where we got a *tuk-tuk* which drove us to the New Trocadero Hotel, a popular eating-place for partygoers who'd finished with Patpong. The restaurant was full of young Thais slumped in stupor, even drunker than me, but the music was still loud and fast. I watched the two girls eat, refusing every time when they offered me a spoonful. I sipped from a glass of Coke, puffed on a couple of El's Marlboros and let my mind wander in an alcoholic haze. After a while I began to sober up a bit. The amphetamines were still in my blood so I wouldn't be able to sleep easily.

I was idly watching the boys and girls come and go. When Gruber walked through the swing doors accompanied by two swarthy, well-built Thai men, it took a few seconds for my drunken brain to register. The sudden recognition sobered me like an ice bath. We were sitting in a dark corner near the toilets, but if he went to take a leak he couldn't fail to notice me. Slowly, leaning forward and under cover of the table, I reached for the Glock which was miraculously still in its holster. The girls were too busy chattering for them to notice that both my hands were out of sight. I blinked rapidly trying to focus on the men. The place was intentionally dark with a huge video screen providing most of the illumination. It meant that the shadows constantly shifted.

Gruber and his companions sat down at a table about twenty feet away from us. He turned and looked for a waitress and our eyes met.

I had to give him credit. He was quick. His hand dived under his pale linen jacket and reappeared with a small black automatic. His companions went for their guns. I kicked over the table in front of me and the sound of two rounds cracking filled the crowded room. Pandemonium broke loose, chairs and tables went flying, panic-stricken youngsters dived for the doors and the floor. I dragged the two girls to the tiles.

I crouched behind the overturned table and pulled El's friend over to me. Half a bowl of *Tom Yam Gung* had hit her in the face and she was frantically trying to wipe the spicy soup from her eyes. El lay next to me, screaming hysterically. I stroked the trigger gently with my index finger and wondered what to do next. I risked a look around the edge of the table. Most people had stopped screaming and were flat on their faces or trying to crawl towards the exit. Nothing like the fear of death to sober you up. All my instincts were against having a gunfight in this crowded room.

A sudden movement of cream cloth told me Gruber had no qualms about opening fire. He must have been told about what had happened at his boss's house. I wished I had followed my instincts and killed him before leaving Pattaya.

The mirror above my head shattered. A waitress yelled in terror as a sliver of glass penetrated her arm. I sighted on the table where I had seen Gruber duck down. Wooden tables are not bullet proof. My Glock spat twice and I rolled off to a different location, over bodies twitching with fright. Briefly I noticed the look of terror in a young man's face as the muzzle of my gun brushed his cheek, then my knee gouged his back as I moved again.

A strange hush descended on the room. Three bullets slammed into the table where I had just been lying. The top of El's head was only inches below the ragged splintery hole that had appeared in the overturned tabletop. Sirens started in the distance.

I was cautiously working my way around to a better location when suddenly Gruber stood up, only ten feet from me. Once again, we fired at the same time. His bullet cracked past me. My two brought him down. I was the better shot, drunk or sober. He went flying backwards, the fragments from my hollow-points ripping through his spinal cord. I jumped up, slipping for an instant on a man's shirt, and ran forward. Gruber was still wriggling. His companions fired from behind another table. I put two more rounds into Gruber's torn shirt and managed to hit one of his men in the shoulder.

Then I was down again breathing heavily. Gruber's glazed and empty eyes, not a yard away, stared past me into the void.

A voice shouted: "No shoot, no shoot." The

other man got to his feet holding up his empty hands. I plugged him in the neck for good measure and he fell back down. My reservoir of mercy was expended. It was the wrong time to surrender.

I dashed back to my table and grabbed the reluctant girls by their hair, dragging them to their feet. We stumbled out through a back exit into a rat-infested alley and ran for five minutes. On Silom Road I grabbed a *tuk-tuk*, shoved the girls in, jumped between them and slapped the driver hard on the shoulder. He got the message and dropped the clutch with a scream of sudden acceleration.

Waking up was terrible. I was dehydrated, my joints ached and I wanted to slip backwards and die to get away from the agony of the hangover. My shirt was soaked with perspiration. A table fan standing on a chair whirred. Hot sticky air came in through barred windows that had no curtains to keep out the noisy, glaring Bangkok morning. It was a big hard bed with no top sheet and there was a girl on either side of me. I struggled off the end and found a cubicle in the corner of the room, which had a washbasin, a showerhead and a squat toilet. I looked in the mirror and then looked away. It was a stranger's face, all bruised, cut up and haggard.

My back ached nearly as badly as my head. The only thing to drink in the room was a large bottle of Pepsi. I drank half of it, took two painkillers from the packet in my jeans pocket then crawled back between the two brown bodies. Both were naked. El's skin was soft as a mother's heart. I brushed a hand over her sparse black pubes. There were no stirrings of lust in my loins. I simply felt exhausted, ill and in need of a great deal of rest. I curled the threads of pubic hair around my finger. The girl tried to brush my hand away in her sleep without waking up. The other girl shifted and buried her head under a pillow.

Mekong whisky hangovers are the worst in the world. Two hours later I surfaced again. El and her friend, who now had her hand casually on my crotch, hadn't moved. The heat was more oppressive than an unexpected tax bill. By the bedside sat a photo of El's Italian boyfriend. He grinned a cocky Latin smile in my direction. I went for another leak, drank more Pepsi and took two more Ponstan for the pain. I had one tablet left in the mangled blister pack. On a small chair wrapped up in my shirt I found my Glock. It was impossible to recall what had happened last night after the shoot-out beyond the random fragments of an unfinished jigsaw.

I looked around the bare room that these ladies called home. They shared a rack for clothes. Twenty or more pairs of high-heeled shoes jostled each other neatly on the olive lino floor. I placed two thousand US Dollars next to the photo, in anticipated loyalty and for their silence, and made my way out, down a gloomy corridor and five flights of stairs. The taxi driver wanted a hundred Baht. I didn't argue, simply got in, because I had no idea which part of town we were in.

In the store below my guesthouse, I bought two big bottles of distilled water. Sitting on the edge of my bed I took my final painkiller and emptied one of the bottles bit by bit until my belly felt bloated like a Buddha. Then I went outside and called Cathay Pacific, booking myself on the evening flight back to Hong Kong. I also tried reaching Harry Bolt, but nobody knew where he was. That concerned me.

At the back of my guesthouse was a 'klong', a stagnated waterway that had provided cooking and washing facilities in less polluted times. The stink was bearable but the slime on the surface would deter anyone from putting a hand into the frothy liquid. I looked around, checking I was unobserved and alone. I took out the plastic bag into which I had stashed my Glock. With a casual flick of the wrist, I tossed the deadly piece of equipment into the polluted brew, certain that it would never be found.

I had a shower, scrubbing the cordite off my face and fingers and went back to bed. The sheets, cold from the rattling air con, soothed my naked skin. It was the pressure from my bladder which eventually woke me. A few hours later, still feeling terrible, I checked out.

Down the road I called the Bolthole again. Bolt was in and alive.

"I can't talk long but I'm on my way to Hong Kong," I said. "You know what happened after we left?"

There was a pause at the other end. He said, "I assumed you'd got away. I wasn't sure. Are you okay? Where are you?"

"Bangkok. It was a bad thing. Tang had Charoenchati followed and machine-gunned us as we came down the road. Did you see the bodies?"

"Yeah, the Pattaya police had me identify them. I told them who to look for, but they didn't seem to be very interested in doing anything about Tang."

"He's got a lot of people on his payroll. Am I going to be clean in Pattaya?"

"I'm not sure, but I spoke with one of Charoenchati's associates. He's trying to get the Police General in Bangkok to do something about Tang. We're having a meeting this evening. I'll let you know how it goes. Clout or no clout on their part, it looks as if the police will sweep the whole thing under the carpet. It's easier that way."

"The press might care," I said carefully into the mouthpiece.

"No, it's not like that in Thailand. It's live and let live. A good Buddhist ethic."

"Or let die."

"Life goes on. You don't have to stop breathing just because someone else has."

" I've got to get the hell out of Thailand," I said. "I'm going after Tang. He's in Hong Kong with Otto Schwartz."

"I'll be there in a couple of days so get in touch with me then. Don't do anything mad. Stay professional. I know all this has become very personal for you."

There was nothing to say, because he was right.

"Don't worry," Bolt said confidently, "I'll sort things out here. You go ahead and do what you're best at. Hey, I heard on the news that somebody got shot in a restaurant near Patpong."

"Yeah, some German tourist."

"You?"

"I couldn't say. Just turned up by chance. The way things are sometimes."

"Okay, be careful. Tang will be expecting you."

"The thought had crossed my mind."

"Let it cross it a few more times and come up with something slick. I have faith in you. You've always been a lucky bastard. Napoleon would have liked you." He rang off and I made my way to the airport, getting stuck in traffic as always. It had started drizzling by the time we finally arrived. The terminal was crowded and smelt of unwashed bodies.

I got stuck in the check-in queue behind a party of weekend golfers who looked tanned and relaxed. Their conversation revolved around the numerous holes they had scored during their trip.

My main worry was that someone had got hold of my real name and given it to the police. However much I doubted their efficiency, it was possible that there could be a stop at Immigration. My nerves prickled for an instant when I pulled out my real passport and waited for the man in the tight brown uniform to finally deliver the stamp that meant all was well. He didn't comment on my bruises. Damaged tourists leaving were not that unusual.

At security a girl rubbed a hand-held metal detector over my body. It beeped for my keys and some change and that was all. I smiled happily at her and walked down to the departure lounge, which was already empty.

37

I hated flying. Ordeal by aviation. It didn't seem right that several bits of metal spinning at high speed from the pressure of burning fuel could lift three hundred people thirty thousand feet into the air. The other thing I did not like was sitting in a metal tube at the mercy of three fallible men and some computers. It was a feeling I loathed, this complete reliance on another human being, but it was an unreasonable fear so after several drinks before take-off, I blanked my mind as best as I could.

The Senior Purser, wearing her uniform badly because it was designed for a slimmer lither figure that she had lost a decade previously, pointed me in the direction of my seat. I stepped around the galley and a hand grabbed my arm.

"What are you doing here?" the voice attached to the hand said venomously.

I looked around and began to smile. "I'm going home." Asia can be a small place if you travel a lot.

"Why do you have to be on my flight? I don't want to serve you," the voice said. "Where are you sitting?" I laughed at the young Malaysian girl who, unlike her boss had the right figure for her uniform. I showed her my boarding pass.

She studied the row number grimly. "I'll talk to you later," she said, studying my pass to see my seat number. "You look terrible, you know. As if you've been in a fight." She got on with her work filling glasses with orange juice and nasty sparkling wine.

Ruth Lim and I had enjoyed each other's company and caresses once upon a time. Then she stopped seeing me, convinced that I wasn't serious about her. All her friends had warned her against me, probably with due cause. But she'd been wrong. It wasn't that I hadn't been serious about her, simply that work had taken up too much time.

My seat was on the aisle. I arranged myself as best as I could, buckled myself in, then watched people and especially Ruth. She had always moved well, vertically and horizontally.

Finally, everybody was settled, the last screeching Hong Kong tourist strapped in and the machine heaved itself laboriously into the skies.

On the whole it was a smooth flight once we reached cruising altitude. The girls were swift and polite, going about their service, dragging their trolleys along the aisles and filling the plastic glasses not quite more than half. I drank water. Some of the other girls were worth watching too. With Ruth it was a reliving of memories. With the others I could make up little carnal fantasies as my eyes closed and I drifted in and out of sleep.

"Did you have too many bargirls in Bangkok?" Ruth whispered facetiously into my ear. I looked up at her, standing next to my seat.

"That's not fair. I went on business."

She gave me one of those knowing sarcastic looks that former girlfriends always use. I sniffed her perfume. It was a scent I didn't recognise.

"How are you? Still with that banker bloke?" I asked when the trays had been cleared and she stopped for a moment to chat.

"No. Finished with him. He was seeing a Filipina as well as me." She shrugged stoically as if unfaithful boyfriends were just one of life's trials, like bitchy Senior Pursers and demanding Indian passengers. "All men are slime anyway," she added.

"Most of us are, yes," I said.

"Still going out drinking all the time?"

"Not that much. Been traveling a lot for work."

"No serious girlfriend?"

"I have too bad a reputation for anyone to risk getting serious with me."

"I pity any girl who wants to get serious with you. She'd need her head examined." She was bending over me with her arm resting on the back of the seat so that my neighbour could not overhear our conversation. "So, no love in your life?"

"Not at this moment. I happen to be --"

"Don't tell me. You're in a 'state of promiscuous bachelorhood waiting for the right woman to jolt you into committed monogamy.' You told me that one before. A long time ago."

"Did I? Who's that cute looking Singaporean working on the other aisle?"

"No one you'll ever get to know or meet," she snapped.

I laughed. "I'm a reformed man these days. How about a drink tonight?"

"Read my lips. N-O. I'm busy washing my hair every day until Christmas. Got to go."

She patted me affectionately on the head with what I hoped was a wistful warmth and wandered off to answer a call button further down the plane.

I slept for the rest of the flight and tried not to dream of Simone. I'd never been so close before to anyone I'd killed. As the Reliable Man, I had approached my assassinations as an intellectual exercise. I was beginning to realise that the reality was going to be a lot messier than that. I'd been wrong to regard myself as a precision tool. More often than not I was going to be a blunt instrument. On reflection, that didn't really bother me enough to consider changing my chosen profession.

When I woke up, we were in final approach. The territory sparkled below like the spoils from Ali Baba's cave. Somewhere below were Stonecutters' Island, Mei Foo San Chuen, Cheung Sha Wan. We skimmed over the illegal roof structures of Sham Shui Po, over Kowloon Tong where the love hotels and kindergartens were; the plane twisted in the air on sighting the Chequerboard beacon by the Urban Council swimming pool, hopped over the Robert Black Methadone Clinic, San Po Kong Magistracy and then the Australian captain slammed the ten thousand tons of American steel down onto British soil. Traffic control put us out in the car park.

I twitched a smile at Ruth Lim when we passed. She ignored me pointedly. I waited until the bus was full then got on. Last on meant first off. Kai Tak airport consistently got short listed for the 'most shoddy international airport' award and that status was fully deserved. As the gateway to an Asian hub city like Hong Kong it was appalling and an embarrassment, from its filthy, crowded facilities to its rude Immigration officers, it was an ordeal that could take hours.

I produced my regular passport again as well as a Hong Kong Identity Card. For a brief moment the woman hesitated. I looked around the busy hall nonchalantly. The keys on the computer clacked as she entered my ID card number. Then she tossed the passport and card back at me. Everything was fine, which proved a relief. I knew the extent of Tang's influence.

Telling the Customs Inspector that I'd come from Bangkok provided a spark of interest for the bored individual. I put the bag on his bench. He unzipped it, pulled out a few dirty T-shirts and a pair of smelly socks. He dropped them rapidly, opened my toilet case, an elegant black item that folded open. A Christmas gift from whoever. He studied my Gillette razor, the tube of Colgate, the bottle of Eno's liver salts, the Antaeus after-shave. He ignored a couple of Montblanc pens hastily shoved in the wrong receptacle.

I saw Ruth and her colleagues in the distance wearing their red skirts and pulling their trolleys with the blue crew bags. Women in uniform were always a fine sight.

I turned back to the man and raised my eyebrows.

"Go on," he barked and waved me on, moving to the next applicant. I hefted the bag back onto my shoulder. It had been a constant companion on my travels for the last two years. He like, every other customs officer before him, had failed to spotted the discreet hiding place beneath the floor of the bag, where this time I had concealed the wads of counterfeit money and three blank American passports. It had been a risk, but I wanted the stuff with me.

Half of Hong Kong seemed be standing in the Arrivals hall expecting their relatives. I barged through them roughly, as is the custom in this city. An elbow in the temple of a five-foot high grandma, a knee in the back of a hyperactive child, just part of getting on in this aggressive colony. Outside, the air was humid and hot, but it lacked the sweet heaviness that typified Bangkok's atmosphere. The taxi driver cleared his throat and spat out of the window indicating that he hadn't clearly heard the address I'd given him. I repeated myself in Cantonese.

Tang had not been wrong when he said the rent was overdue on my flat. But my landlord had emigrated to Vancouver and so he wasn't chasing for payment yet.

Officially I made my living from giving financial advice to expats, selling life insurance and pension plans which gave me a commission that permitted a moderate lifestyle and a realistic tax return. Anyone who makes money illegally should avoid showing off their true wealth. I had taken great care to ensure a convincing cover. There were lots of ex-coppers in Hong Kong barely scraping a living. I didn't touch any of the money that had accumulated in my bank accounts in Luxembourg, Liechtenstein and the Caymans unless I needed it for assignments, and then only under assumed identities. Mine was a lucrative profession. For murder and mayhem, people were willing to pay.

I'd been thinking of moving. Perhaps leaving Hong Kong finally. The financial consultancy cover was becoming tedious, although it explained my travelling and flexible lifestyle. It was something I'd have to speak with Harry Bolt about.

I lived on the top floor of an old building on Cloud View Road. It took some time to get to from the airport but, once on my balcony, I had a spectacular view of the runway, planes landing and taking off, the harbour and its ships below me and the whole array of high-rises on Kowloon side, backed by the mountain rage of the Nine Dragons with is peak at Fei Ngo Shan.

The territory of Hong Kong was a peculiar growth. It represented a capitalist wart on the smelly rear of Communist China that had gradually grown into a fully-formed, cheerfully wagging, tail. Which was why the Central Committee planned to assimilate it, when the lease for part of the land ran out. The predominantly Chinese population on the whole abhorred the foreign *gwai los* which most expats didn't realise because only policemen bothered to learn their vile dialect. The city was in many respects very modern, in others frustratingly Asian - a mixture of British administrative incompetence and Chinese industry. In my professional opinion it was the ultimate capitalist nirvana, a perfect temple for the worship of mammon and the divinity of greed. My experience of living and working in Hong Kong over the previous decade had made me the man I was today

Sadly, the chances were that the ripe fruit the PRC had been eying for decades in their neighbour's garden would taste very sour indeed by the time they took over the orchard. The gardeners would all have left and taken the freshest produce with them to other markets.

I looked out of the taxi window. It was nice to be back. After all this was still home. Traffic wasn't as bad as in Bangkok. People had become too affluent in Hong Kong and could afford cars too easily, but the roads were being constantly dug up and improved.

After the tunnel we passed Victoria Park, where the old Queen sat stolidly and guarded the basketball players and old men practicing *Tai Chi*. The red cab shot up onto the flyover, and up Tai Hang Road, winding along until we finally reached the heights of my building, itself surrounded by many others similar in build and height. Paying the driver with a hundred dollar note, I grabbed my bag and climbed from the cab.

38

My flat was average in size by Hong Kong standards, but I paid for the view not the space. I pushed the metal grille aside and entered cautiously. I was banking on the fact that Tang believed I had died during Charoenchati's execution but best to be careful.

The flat was silent and peaceful. The *amah* had been in and the place smelt of Pledge and floor wax. I liked that. The bare, slightly slippery parquet floor gleamed. The bolt had become rusty since my absence and it groaned as I slid it home and locked it tight.

There were three bedrooms, the master and two smaller ones, which served as office and dressing room respectively. Two black leather sofas stood at right angles to each other facing a 25-inch TV set and a Bang & Olufsen stereo system. I liked the place to be neat and uncluttered. The only mess was the pile of dirty laundry and dishes that the maid cleared away three times a week. Some enlarged photos from my days in the Royal Hong Kong Police Force and the British Army hung on what an American might call a vanity wall. They showed me looking younger, in and out of uniform with other men who had been friends and colleagues.

On another wall was a framed Singapore Airlines advertising poster. The smiling girl had once smiled at me in real life, but she'd been wearing fewer clothes.

A bottle of Stolichnaya, Watson's water and a six-pack of *Tsing Tao* beer were the only thing permanently in my fridge. A girl had once told me that it was my fridge that had made her decide to break up with me.

After making myself a cup of tea, I got changed and emptied the contents of my bag onto the hard unmade guest bed in the dressing room, then carefully removed the items hidden in the secret compartment. Upstairs on the roof was where I kept things that would cause me trouble with my former colleagues in the Force. Because it was included in my tenancy agreement, only I had access to it. The steep stairs were just outside my front door. In two years, I had never once met my neighbour who seemed to be another one of those Chinese men who lived half their lives in Vancouver or Sydney.

My hiding place was simple yet clever like all the best things in life. Behind the structure that hid the lift mechanism, out of view from all neighbouring buildings I shifted a large flowerpot, which only contained sand. Removing a roof tile, which had taken me several days to scrape loose, gave access to a small space. At the moment all it contained was a Heckler & Koch HK33 Assault Rifle with a collapsible stock and an old Walther PPK that I had managed to pick up from a Filipino businessman who wanted some cash, ammunition for these weapons, and an elegant display box that contained the rest of my Montblanc fountain pens. I went to replace the ones I had taken with me to Bangkok, but decided to keep one back. I had a feeling I might need it.

I stashed the money and credit cards, replacing the tile and sprinkling the edges with sand from the flowerpot. Tomorrow I would find a more permanent location for them. There were other hiding places where I had stashed weapons and ammunition; mostly banks and hotel deposit boxes because they valued the confidentiality of their clients.

All below me, as I sat on the balcony in my old rattan chair drinking tea, lay the magic of Hong Kong at night. The city glittered and glistened, thousands of structures, encrusted with jewels from a pirate's hoard.

I went back into the living room, powered up my NEC cellphone, and started ringing hotels, hoping to find where Schwartz and Mok Bun were staying. Since Tang lived in Kowloon side, I believed there was a good chance that they'd be in one of the hotels in Tsim Sha Tsui. I started with the major ones: Holiday Inn, Shangri-La,

Regal Meridian, Peninsula, Kowloon. I found Otto Schwartz eventually booked into the Regent Hotel under his assumed name. For about fifteen minutes I sat thinking what to do next. I began having an idea, risky, yet I didn't have time to waste.

A while later my phone rang. It was Ruth sounding breathy and a little embarrassed. It pleased me to hear her voice. She obviously remembered my cellphone number. I must have liked her. I gave it out only to a select few of the women I had slept with.

She was going to JJ's, the trendy nightclub in the Grand Hyatt, for a drink with her flatmate. Did I want to come? Could I bring a friend? Somebody decent, because her flatmate had only just started flying and was a nice girl. I agreed and suddenly I remembered something that I shouldn't have forgotten, something Schwartz had said to me, flippantly expecting me to be dead within the day.

The telephone operator at the Peninsula Hotel transferred me to the restaurant. The maître D' at Gaddi's who answered the phone sounded haughty. Yes, indeed there was a reservation for the gentleman that evening at nine, four people. My thumb hit the End button before he'd finished speaking.

I paged Kenworthy and he replied within five minutes. Certainly he was free. A fresh young Cathay Pacific stewardess who needed consolation? He'd be delighted. His existing date was with an Indian girl, but she was old news. He could easily blow her out.

"Where do you want to meet?" he asked.

I hesitated for an instant, wanting him to believe that I had to give it some thought.

"Why don't we start early? Couple of beers in 'Someplace Else'. About nine o'clock."

"Over on Kowloon side? Don't you live on Hong Kong Island?"

"'Someplace Else' on a Friday evening is always good for women. If we find a couple we like, we can always leave the other two for another day."

"You're right. I'll see you nine."

I checked my watch. My plan hinged on the assumption that Schwartz, with customary German punctuality, would leave his hotel ten or fifteen minutes before his dinner and cross the road to the Peninsula. There was only one path to follow and it should, with luck, put him directly in the crosshairs of my Heckler & Koch. Should he be coming from another direction I still had the option to take him out in or around the restaurant.

Rapidly, I ran upstairs to the roof, shoving the flowerpot aside, dragged up the tile and took out the weapons. Downstairs I dressed hurriedly, splashed after-shave on my face and assembled my arsenal, checking it carefully, loading magazines, working the actions. Finally, I pocketed the Montblanc pen in case the plan went wrong and I had to approach Schwartz in a public place.

When all was ready, I wiped down the weapons with a damp cloth. I used a solution of witch-hazel. It was the most effective way of removing fingerprints from metal. I planned to wear thin leather gloves when I fired the rifle. Once I had done so, I would dump it. No weapon with a bore that could match a fired bullet should ever remain in the hands of the assassin.

When I left the house carrying a nondescript blue rucksack it was 7.45 p.m. A cab ride and the MTR across the harbour meant I should be in Tsim Sha Tsui within twenty minutes. The underground system operated by the Mass Transit Railway is one of the marvels of Hong Kong: fast, reliable and, above all, unbelievably clean. At this time of the evening the carriages were still crowded. Casually I squeezed myself into a corner. I had decided to wear a dark grey linen suit with a red speckled tie, so I looked no different from many other homeward bound office workers.

Shoving past a fat lady, and three Chinese youths in turn-up jeans I exited by the Holiday Inn. This was the principal tourist shopping area. I was on time, but the going was slow due to the frantic bustle on the pavements.

At the end of Nathan Road stood two major hotels: the Sheraton on the left, the Peninsula on the right. Salisbury Road formed a T shape with Nathan Rd and diagonally across the former stood the Regent, with a magnificent view of the Hong Kong skyline across the dark busy harbour.

On the left of the Sheraton was a multi-storey car park that had seen better days. This was my first destination because the higher floors controlled an excellent view over the front entrance of the Regent Hotel. My second destination would be 'Someplace Else', a lively and popular venue in the Sheraton's basement, where I was meeting Kenworthy.

The lift took a long time to come, finally disgorging what seemed like a small Chinese wedding party. Another six people crammed into the foul-smelling space behind me. I could barely turn and press the button. By the time I reached the top level of the car park floor, there was no one else in the lift. It was mainly reserved for long staying parking permits and the cars in evidence were shrouded in dust sheets or covered by accumulated dirt. It was quiet and dark and some of the overhead lights were broken, perfect for what I had in mind. The door to the staircase stood open. That's where I would make a rapid exit after the hit. It was going to be quicker than the lift. I checked my GMT Master. It was just after 8.30 p.m.

Parked in the far corner was a white minivan with rust in the wheel arches. The next car along was covered with a dirty tarpaulin. If I stood behind the minivan, I was hidden from the rest of the car park. Directly in front of me I looked down over Salisbury Road. The brown facade of the Regent Hotel rose up ahead. A ramp about fifty yards long led upwards from the main road, culminating in a small roundabout where the hotel's fleet of pompous Rolls Royces were parked.

Walking back to a red Toyota Corolla, I donned my thin black leather gloves and smashed the rear window, leant forward and unlocked the driver's door then returned to my vantage point behind the white minivan.

I began unzipping the small rucksack, producing the Walther which I slipped into an ankle holster that was easily hidden by the slight flare of my trousers. That was for back-up. The Heckler & Koch HK33 came out next. Two quick movements had the stock extended and the telescopic sight fitted. Then I carefully screwed on the noise suppressing cylinder, which was nearly a foot long and slightly unbalanced the weapon.

Hidden in the gloom of the car park nobody from the building opposite could see me. The distance to the glass doors of the Regent was a hundred and fifty metres, give or take. Effective range for the HK33 was up to four hundred metres. There were better weapons for precision shooting, but I was a very good shot, we'd used this model in the police and it would do the job. More important was the quality of the telescopic sight. Good quality optics were expensive, often more expensive than the rifle, but they made the sniper's job much easier.

I rested my elbows on the ledge and snuggled down to a comfortable firing position. My right foot rested against the partially deflated wheel of the minivan. The palm of my hand held the pistol grip firmly, pushing the butt sideways into my shoulder. I closed my left eye and fitted the right one to the soft rubber on the sight. The front of the building jumped into my face.

I studied my killing zone. I took in the white gloved hands of the doorman, the chubby face of a guest as a bellboy dumped his luggage with little care, the slight spray coming off the fountain that stood in the middle of the roundabout. All around me in the car park was silence, broken only by noise from the busy street below. It was unlikely but I didn't want to be surprised from behind. I had to split my concentration to remain alert.

With my left hand I extracted the mobile phone from my back pocket and punched in the telephone number of the Regent Hotel. I asked for Schwartz by his cover name and waited, hoping that the man would pick up. It rang five times, then I heard a guttural German 'Hallo?'. I cut the call.

Ten minutes later Otto Schwartz emerged at the front of the Regent Hotel and placed himself plumb in the middle of my sights. For an instant he hesitated, maybe considering if he should take a taxi, then he stepped forward. I would never have a better chance. I took a gentle breath and held it, then applied the slightest of pressures to the trigger. I wished Schwartz a tough time in hell.

The Heckler & Koch twitched once. The fat German lay splayed on his back holding his hands to his chest. It had been a clumsy first shot. The weapon hadn't been fired for half a year. One had to follow through, as in golf and tennis. I didn't move. I fired again. Schwartz's head vanished as the next 7.62 mm round flew true.

The whole execution had taken five seconds. I dropped the weapon from my shoulder, crouched down and dismantled the sound suppressor, took off the telescopic sight and packed all three components away into the rucksack. I stripped off my gloves and stepped out from behind the minivan.

It was 9.05 p.m., barely an hour after I had left my flat in Cloud View Road. Already I could hear the sirens of the ambulance alternating with the howl from the regional Emergency Unit car that would be rushing to the scene. From experience I knew there would be panic and pandemonium for fifteen minutes before a senior officer with his head screwed on started getting a grip of the situation and began working out where the shots had come from. By that time, I would be sipping a beer in 'Someplace Else'.

I walked briskly towards the stairs. By the red Toyota I paused for a second to ensure I was unobserved and stashed the rucksack underneath the passenger seat. Then I reached through the broken window and locked the car from the inside. With luck my nearly new Heckler & Koch would not be found for weeks, unless some very smart constable noticed the broken rear window and exhibited an outrageous amount of initiative.

I was ten yards from the stairs when out of a darkened car that I had not noticed, jumped four men. A baseball bat hit me in the stomach and sent me gasping to the floor. I put up my hand knowing there was another blow coming. The tough wood brushed off my forearm and the pain on my bone was intense. I rolled onto my back only to find a figure standing over me, Asian features twisted grimly as he rammed the end of the same bat into my guts. I started retching and fighting for breath.

The next thing I knew was being hauled to my feet by two powerful arms. The fight had been knocked out of me and I slumped, my legs transformed to jelly.

39

By the time I had regained my senses, my hands were strapped and my mouth had been covered with heavy-duty tape. A dark hood smelling of mothballs had been pulled over my head and I was being held down on the floor of the car. It was an uncomfortable ride. I concentrated on breathing through my nose, grateful that my nasal passages were clear.

My assailants were speaking in low Cantonese voices and I could not make out what was being said. Once, the car stopped, probably for a roadblock, but we quickly started moving again.

I assumed in the course of the short journey that these were men associated with Tang. But I realised that this was not the only alternative. They were just as likely to be members of the Organised Crime and Triad Bureau. Whoever they were, my situation was precarious. I cursed myself for having walked into a set-up. The only way they could have known that I would be on the top floor of the car park was if they had followed me, which meant they had been watching my house.

The car moved slowly through the evening traffic. There was no way I could work out where we were heading. The men's feet rested on my body. My stomach muscles were bruised and I wondered if my head wound had opened up again because there was dampness around my cheek. I could only wait patiently until the end of the car ride and hope that they were not taking me to a quiet place for a swift execution.

At our destination, a hand pulled my collar, choking me. Other hands grabbed me and yanked me roughly from the vehicle. I could hear the noise of a busy street close by through the hood. The hood was a good sign. If you intend killing someone, you didn't bother with such niceties. I assumed we were somewhere in Mong Kok or Yaumatei, parked in a side street. We had not been travelling long enough to be in the New Territories.

I stumbled forward blindly, being pushed and dragged up some steps and into a lift. We stood in silence for a couple of minutes as the old elevator rattled upwards. At the top they deposited me in an armchair. I could hear the sound of a television and there were men talking around me. The armchair was surprisingly comfortable. Patiently, I waited for developments, forcing myself to remain calm. I had no other choice.

It was a good half hour later and I must have dozed off. The hood was whipped off my head and I blinked in the bright light. I was sitting in the lounge area of a luxurious massage parlour. Three men stood facing me, while in other armchairs around the room, not bothered by the spectacle of a foreigner tied up, were half a dozen Asian men of different ages relaxing and chatting, dressed only in bathrobes.

Somebody ripped the tape off my mouth, dragging parts of my stubble along with it. I suppressed a gasp of pain. My attention focused on one man. He was perched on the arm of a chair and probing one of his ears with a cotton bud. He smiled, continuing the digging movement with some vigour.

"I'm getting sick of meeting you in massage parlours, Sebastian," I said.

He laughed. He too was wearing a fluffy bathrobe. It had a little embroidered gold crest on the breast pocket. He dropped the cotton bud, its end now covered in slimy brown gunge, into an ashtray and blew his nose on a tissue. The other two men with him were wearing jeans and casual shirts. They were grinning at my discomfort.

"You know, Bill, this isn't the sort of dirty massage parlour we found you in last time. This is a very clean, high-class establishment. There's no sex for sale here," Sebastian Tse said.

"I'm surprised. Not even a hand job at the end of a rub down?"

"If people want sex they can go to a nightclub. The women here are expert at easing the tensions from a man after a hard day's work in the office."

"Will you send one over? I've got aches and pains all over my body. It's just what I need. And I'm getting tired of sitting on my hands."

"Always the cocky one, Mr. Jedburgh. But you really are a black horse aren't you? You've been killing all these people in Thailand from what we hear and now, almost in front of our very eyes, you shot our good friend Mr. Schwartz. Not really our good friend. Mr. Tang had decided that the fat *gwai lo* was an unnecessary embarrassment. Bugging your phone was a sensible move. When you enquired so persistently after Mr Schwartz, it became clear what you planned to do. Of course, Mr Tang knew exactly where to find him and where he planned to eat. Which is why we could predict exactly where a skilled marksman like you would choose to fire from. I've spoken to Mr. Tang already. He's busy playing *mah-jongg* tonight, but he thanks you for your good work." Sebastian chuckled with pleasure at his own humour.

"You will also be pleased to know we retrieved your rifle from that abandoned car. Careless to leave it there. I suppose though that there would be none of your fingerprints on it, although we could assist the police in this matter. What do you think?"

"Whatever you have in mind. I'm all ears," I said grimly, holding down the anger at my own stupidity. He settled himself in a more comfortable position and folded his arms.

"You're not in the best situation here," he gloated.

"Do all these people work for you?" I asked.

"Sure, some of them. It's a private club here. Over there is Mr. Wong. He owns a big trading company. That old man is Siu Mo Liu, he is a famous producer of movies. Not that you would know his name. They are all close friends of Mr. Tang."

"You mean," I said bluntly, "They are all members of your Triad organisation?"

"Friends, only friends."

"Triads."

"That's a rough word. Do these people look like common street gangsters?"

"Wolves in sheep's clothing."

"What a hypocrite you are. You just murdered someone in full view of many witnesses."

I shrugged. He had a point. Everybody lived according to their own rules. In my profession it was foolish to be too judgmental.

"Mr. Tang is more interested in what exactly you were doing in Thailand. The girl's information was confused and what she said was not very clear. What we understand is that you were working for either Charoenchati or this man called Bolt, whom we know very well. Correct?"

"Maybe."

"Then you agreed to work for Mr. Tang?"

"He didn't give me much of an option, if you remember. Anyway. it amused me to play along and see what the outcome would be."

"But what was your task for the Thai general and Harry Bolt?"

I considered the question and decided that, given the circumstances, I would have to tell him a version of the truth. For the moment I did not want to spoil whatever chances I might still have of getting out of the place alive.

"Charoenchati wanted me kill Schwartz," I said calmly. "Bolt wasn't involved. But he is, was, one of the General's business partners."

"Charoenchati is dead now," Sebastian said. "Why did you still kill Schwartz tonight if your paymaster is dead? Did Bolt ask you to?"

"I was paid in advance."

"So you kill for money? I wish we had known that before. If we pay you will you kill people for us?"

"No," I said quietly.

"No? Once in a while we need to have troublesome people removed. It's always hard to find men who will do that sort of work."

"You've got plenty of little followers who will do dirty work for you."

"Yes," he sighed. "Mostly they mess it up. We Chinese are good at business, extortion, gang violence, but not assassination. Our guys are too sloppy. Then we have to pay their legal fees and look after their families while they are in prison.

Better to have a professional. Like you, it seems. Trained by the Royal Hong Kong Police."

"I would be expensive."

"You'd give us a good discount I'm sure."

"Sebastian, you know why I wouldn't work for you or your boss. It's personal. I don't like Tang." As I said it, I realised I wouldn't really have had a problem working for Tang. Except one. I had been contracted to kill him and the Reliable Man never allowed himself to be bought off when he accepted a contract. It was bad for business.

He laughed. "Suit yourself. I'm trying to think of a good reason why Mr. Tang might be persuaded not to have you thrown into the sea with your head and hands cut off."

"How about I'll think about working for you," I said. That sounded more sensible, I thought. No need to be too proud when you're tied to a chair and negotiating for your life.

"He smiled. "Much better. But don't think about it too long. Mr. Tang is not a patient man."

"He's a slimy crook," I could have bitten my tongue off. I just couldn't help myself. I would need to work on that in future.

Sebastian tut-tutted, still smiling, and lit a cigarette from a box on a side table.

"In your place I would not insult him or anybody."

"You're right," I said. "He's a successful businessman with a charitable side that I would like to appeal to. Now could I have a massage and we can discuss this more comfortably afterwards?"

His cellphone rang and he reached behind him to pick it up.

"*Wai*?" He listened for a while then said in Cantonese: "Fine, at JJ's then, tell the Manager that you are my friend. I am well-known." He put the phone away, looking at me pensively.

"Yes, Mr. Jedburgh. No time for insults now."

"What happened between you and Schwartz then? Was there a disagreement?"

"No, mainly we wanted the software. The Forger never really worked for us. He was a partner with Mok Bun. Mok Bun for some crazy reason thought Pattaya was a safe area for operation because the Germans would protect him. He knew of course that if he wanted to sell his merchandise around the Far East he had to reach some agreement with well-connected people, like Mr. Tang." Tse turned around and reached for another cotton bud which he turned around his fingers as if it were a pen. "Mr. Tang is a successful businessman, as you said. His profits are higher when he eliminates middle-men. When Mr. Tang realised you were in Bangkok, he thought it would be a good idea to use you to find out more information before moving in for the kill, so to speak. It was very bad luck that the Forger got killed at the same time as General Charoenchati."

"How about the software?"

"Well, we have it now," he said casually.

"Schwartz foolishly placed it in a safety deposit box at the Regent while we were negotiating. The concierge opened it for us this morning. I'm sure we don't need the Forger; there are other people who have knowledge on these things. Passports, credit cards, counterfeit money. It's a big, big business."

"Would you have got rid of Schwartz if I hadn't shot him?"

"Probably. He was no longer influential in Thailand. The Thai police have started to clear up all his operations. We guessed it was you who went to his farm?"

I shrugged.

"With Charoenchati dead and Schwartz's operations destroyed, Mr. Tang plans to expand his interests in Pattaya."

"That might not be as easy as he thinks."

"Don't look down on us Chiu Chow people. We are influential. Even in Hong Kong we are getting to be nearly as powerful as the 14K and the Sun Yee On." He looked at his watch. "I'm leaving now. There's no decision yet on what to do with you. It depends on what use we can gain from you. We could kill you right now, or maybe hand you over to the police along with that expensive looking assault rifle. Or maybe we can reach an agreement?" He smiled coldly. "I think you could be very useful to our organisation, providing you are willing."

"I am beginning to feel much more willing already," I said.

"Yes, be smart. You will live longer."

"I'll take your advice."

"Don't be sarcastic, Jedburgh. I will have you killed just like this," he snapped his fingers, "if I think there's no benefit to us in keeping you alive."

"Keeping me alive would be of real benefit to me," I said.

Sebastian laughed with genuine amusement and went off to get changed. When he returned, he instructed the two toughs in Cantonese to take me to the laundry room, lock me up and guard the door until tomorrow when he'd call with further orders. Then he left, looking like any slick businessman who was off for a night on the town.

Nobody in the room looked in any way perturbed or curious as the two men led me past the other customers and down a dimly lit corridor, past dark massage rooms with couches and racks on the ceiling which the masseuses used to support themselves while cracking vertebrae with their toes.

Two female attendants passed us in the corridor, carrying sheets and towels. One of the guys opened a door with a key and shoved me into a room that was full of fresh laundry. I fell into the corner onto a pile of towels. I decided to take it easy. The smell of fresh citrus from the sheets was quite appealing. If they were going to lock me up and leave me overnight, I would have opportunities to escape. They checked my hands, taped over my mouth again so I could not scream, turned off the light and left me.

I sat in silence in the freshly laundered darkness and marvelled at a most amazing piece of stupidity. Still strapped into my ankle holster, undetected, was my Walther PPK and, although I could not reach it because my hands were bound closely in the small of my back, my proximity to the weapon gave me hope.

40

My shirt was drenched because the air conditioning ducts were blocked by the laundry bags piled up to the ceiling. Sweat ran down my face. The room was as stuffy as a Kwun Tong factory in the height of summer and I wondered how long I would have to wait before they decided what to do with me

I'd just made myself moderately comfortable and managed to maintain the circulation in my hands when suddenly the door opened. Only about half an hour had passed. A dark silhouette stood framed in the doorway.

"What the fuck are you doing here?" the man said in Cantonese. In his hand was a radio that hissed and sighed. I tried to make some noise in reply through the adhesive tape that covered my mouth. In the gloom he stared at me curiously then, surprised that I was a white person, he turned abruptly and called down the corridor.

"*Wai*, Choi-sir. There's a *gwai lo* all tied up here." Footsteps approached and several other figures appeared.

"Who is he?" They continued in Cantonese.

I saw plastic cards hanging from their shirt pockets and hoped that this really was the cavalry. I banged my feet on the ground and shouted into my gag until they got the message.

"He seems all right. Better free him, Chan-jai."

"Yes, sir."

Another silhouette had arrived. "What's going on, sir?"

"We found a *gwai lo* tied up, Sergeant."

"Is he alive?"

"Yes, I'm alive. Thanks, and the hands," I said.

"I'm Inspector Choi of Shamshuipo Special Duty Squad. What are you doing here?"

"I've been unlawfully imprisoned by the management of this massage parlour." I'd managed to get to my feet using the shoulder of the constable who had cut the tapes from my wrists with his sharp penknife. My legs felt ungainly and I limped forward into the light of the corridor. The Chinese Inspector was young, about twenty-five, and looked as if he hadn't slept much lately. He seemed unsure of the situation and blinked at me from behind his thick glasses, trying to work out what they'd found. Massaging my bloodless hands I glanced at the squat fat man standing next to the Inspector.

"Sergeant Lam. Do you remember me?" I said.

The fat man's puzzled look turned into a grin. He nodded. "Yes, I know you. You Senior Inspector Jedburgh from SDU. We work together before, Choi-sir." The sergeant and I shook hands.

He told the inspector rapidly where and how we'd met, during a hostage siege situation three years before where a demented mother had threatened to kill all her children because her husband had gone to live with his mistress. In the end the police negotiator had persuaded her to drop the knife and the firepower of my team had not been called on to resolve this family dispute.

The inspector looked at me with sudden respect. I was a fellow officer, he thought, one of the elite from the Anti-Terrorist Squad, probably senior to him and with his sergeant's stamp of approval. But he still wanted to know what I'd been doing locked in a laundry room. I had no intention of being taken down to the station for a statement. There was a danger I'd be searched and found armed. Since I was no longer in the Force that would take some explaining.

Had there only been the sergeant there, a jaded veteran, I would have taken him aside and told him a story about gambling debts or getting involved with a Triad boss's girlfriend, asking him to forget that he'd seen me because it could cause me trouble and embarrassment if my superior officers found out. He would have undoubtedly considered the suggestion and then made it clear that there would be a big favour owed to be repaid at some point in time. It was the way of the street, closing a blind eye when circumstances demanded.

The young, academically gifted, Chinese inspectors that the Force favoured had always been black and white in their interpretation of the laws and procedures. This one looked no different, frightened to do things that were questionable because it might harm his career. I thought the chances of that routine working on him were slim. With a serious expression he asked me again to explain my odd presence. Knowing the ways of the Hong Kong Police I decided to go confidently for the big bluff:

"As Sergeant Lam says, I used to be in SDU. I'm currently attached to NB for an undercover operation, targeting the gang behind this massage operation. Somehow my position became compromised and the suspected dealers grabbed me and brought me here. How come you raided these premises?"

"Routine W&J check. We opened a file on this massage parlour five weeks ago. An informer said they have been offering illicit services. We can't get any snake into the place, the owners are too clever, so we decided to give them a licence check to cause them trouble."

"Not a good idea, Mr. Choi. This is one of the hot target premises under observation in our operation. Many senior Triad members have been meeting here."

He looked confused. "Then why don't we have notification from PHQ to avoid this premise?"

I smiled at him paternally. The Special Duty

Squads in a district are plain clothes, anti-vice units whose members are attached for a short stint to work on routine street vice. Each District would have a squad for prostitution, under powers accorded by the Woman and Juvenile Ordinance known as 'W&J', for dangerous drugs and for gambling. The inspector generally did a six-month tour, after he'd gained some experience in uniform branch on the beat. The intricacies of the work done by Headquarters and its Serious Crime formations such as the Narcotics Branch, 'NB', would be a total mystery to him at this stage of his career. They had been to me when I was a young *bom baan-jai*. It would be no different for him.

"These kinds of operation are highly confidential. If we informed any local District about our activities, the information could very easily pass into the wrong hands," I carried on with my deception.

He looked puzzled. In his simple world, all policemen were still honest and loyal. The sergeant nodded knowledgeably. The police work of the Special Duty Squads verged on the amateurish. The constables were inexperienced but enthusiastic. On the street, although wearing plain clothes, their short-back-and-sides haircuts often gave them away as police officers. But there were also highly professional departments in the Force that pursued serious and intricate, long-term investigations into the upper levels of organised crime.

I told the inspector, with an element of command in my voice: "This operation may be blown. I need to get back and discuss this with my superior officer as quickly as possible. The best thing you can do is finish your licence check and leave. Avoid it for the next few weeks until told otherwise. If not, you will run across our operation again. Not good for you, right Sergeant?" I turned to the older man who saw the sense in that. He explained briefly to his callow boss that it was best not to interfere with NB investigations. My Cantonese was still good enough to follow the gist of this. We began to walk along the corridor and Inspector Choi gave orders to his six men and the dumpy woman constable who, wielding a wooden clipboard, had been taking down the ID card numbers of bath-robed patrons who seemed to take this kind of interference in their stride.

Outside on the street a battered van was parked on a curb, transport for the Vice Squad. I thanked the sergeant and inspector for freeing me, cautioning them again to stay clear of my hypothetical investigation. The inspector nodded gravely, we shook hands and I jumped into a passing taxi. They would go on to raid another ten suspected or actual vice premises before their shift came to an end in the early hours of the morning. It was not surprising the inspector looked tired and relieved that no documentation had been required on finding me trussed up in the laundry room. He was already starting to learn that it was best to keep complications at arm's length. Once the sergeant had recognised me, Choi never doubted that I was a police officer involved in some intricate plot designed to ensnare elusive drug pushers. There were so many Western inspectors floating around in the specialist crime formations based in Police Headquarters in Wan Chai, it was hard to keep track.

I straightened my tie and brushed down my hair. A thick crust of blood sat on the crown of my head. A shower followed by a day in a soft clean bed would have done me the world of good, but this kind of luxury was beyond me now. I was running several hours late. I leaned over and touched the hard metal that still rested firmly on my ankle. Snapping the popper I slid the Walther half an inch out of its holster, then pushed it back into the hard leather. It felt good. Unexpectedly, I was back in the game.

41

There was only one really classy nightclub in Hong Kong at the moment and Sebastian Tse was obviously a frequent and well-known visitor. It was a popular venue for airline stewardesses and the glittering crowd that loved partying. The taxi took half an hour to negotiate the busy streets of Kowloon, shuffle through the tunnel and take me back to the more cosmopolitan environment of Hong Kong side and the Wan Chai waterfront.

Status symbols on wheels were pulling up outside the Grand Hyatt Hotel at the rate of ten a minute. Prancing from expensive German and Italian motors were the radiant young things of the Hong Kong social scene. Armani and Chanel were lining up all the way to the main road anticipating entry to the hot club. They called them 'Chuppies', Chinese yuppies - the stockbrokers, bankers, property agents, young executives and heirs to their various family businesses.

It wasn't my type of nightlife, but a suit and tie permitted me to blend in with the crowd.

I walked past the queue for 'JJ's' and through the glass doors opened by valets into the lobby of the hotel, passing men in dinner jackets and women with bare shoulders, probably attending a charity function. In the toilets, a crinkled retainer watched me relieve myself, wash my face and hands and then comb cautiously at my hair, bringing some greater respectability to the tired scratched features that stared back at me from the mirror. I needed a drink badly.

In the champagne bar a manageress seated me and took my order. This was the only place I had discovered that sold Madeira. A Rutherford & Miles - sweet, brown and earthy - warmed my stomach. I rolled the nectarine substance around my mouth, let it trickle down my throat and soon ordered a second glass. I listened to the Filipina girl who was crooning from the American songbook. It was well after midnight now and the nightclub next door would be packed with people.

Outside the line had diminished substantially. The bouncer, Jim, knew me from the days when he worked a seedy Tsim Sha Tsui club called 'Apollo 18'. Since then, he had graduated to a better class of venue. His ponytail had gone and his T-shirt been replaced by a dinner jacket that looked impressive on his broad frame.

"Just the one of you is it, Bill?" he said shaking my hand.

"Have you ever seen me arrive with a bird?"

"No, son. Never seen you leave with one either," he said with a wink and I tried to remember if he was right. "Go right up." He clapped me on the shoulder, as bouncers do, and lifted up the rope for me. I ignored the lift, walking up the stairs to the first floor. The heavy bass of music could be heard in the background.

The decoration was sombre, with dark wood on the walls and a baroque flight of stairs. Renaissance style paintings were lit with spotlights and there were many little dark corners in which one could hide. I rammed my way through the layers of men and women, an equal mixture of self-conscious Westerners and Asians, then finally found Kenworthy in the place he had made his regular spot.

"Sorry, mate. Ran into a customer and he had a problem so I couldn't get to 'Someplace Else'." I made my excuses.

"You could have paged me," he said, but he had already shrugged it off.

He was staring at an attractive Japanese girl whose legs were unusually long and straight. After generations of sitting on their feet it seemed that most Japanese girls had bandy legs. I could see Kenworthy puzzling over this specimen.

In Hong Kong, the man dressed like a rising corporate lawyer and affected an air of sincerity and maturity by wearing half-moon spectacles. He was already drunk, his eyes sparkling with animation. His hair was slicked back and no one in the room would have placed him as an off-duty policeman, which was precisely the effect he was trying to create.

"Are those breasts stuffed with toilet paper or what?" he mused, then leant across the bar and managed to attract the attention of a barman who had so far given the impression of being slightly blind, as well as completely deaf.

"Those fucking bastards at PHQ. Have I been shafted or what? They're posting me to the mother of all admin jobs. Miscellaneous Sub-Unit Commander, Airport Division. The job comes with a full packet of razor blades with which to slit your wrists from boredom." He looked disgusted and I tried an expression of sympathy. "What happened to your face?" he asked. "Had an argument with your *amah*?"

"Fell off a Kawasaki on my last day in Thailand," I said.

He shook his head. "So you just got back? Wish I could have stayed for a few weeks longer. But, well, you know...Where's this fanny you promised me? Not having much luck at the moment. Going through a bad patch. All the women I fancy are avoiding me as if I had leprosy or something." He looked rueful. "Most of them have got boyfriends. French, German, Dutch blokes. All these bloody foreigners shagging our nice Asian birds. What's the matter with these women?"

I nodded in sympathy and we swapped stories about the days when we'd popped two new women a week. The game of conquest had always been Kenworthy's favoured topic.

Ruth Lim and her flat-mate were probably on the dance floor, or upstairs where a live group from America rocked the cosier atmosphere of the band room. We decided to seek out the girls, which would give me the opportunity to check if Sebastian Tse was in the club. All along I had been glancing around in case he suddenly appeared.

We moved slowly through the heavy throng, working hard at not spilling our beers. The girls were on the edge of the dance floor, looking slightly aloof, a trick that Ruth had perfected even before I knew her. So far no one had summoned up the courage to approach them. Ruth knew how to make heads turn and her flat-mate had been taking lessons from her mentor.

They were both in black, simple elegant dresses that stopped a hand-spread above the knee and started just below the shoulder. Her flat-mate had short-cropped hair, with a dimpled boyish face. I envied Kenworthy his date. Ruth was old news. I liked girls with short hair. A bare woman's neck is more sensuous than a bare thigh. I enjoyed the envious looks of men who had been wondering how to approach them, only to see us comfortably moving in. I kissed Ruth on the cheek and briefly put a proprietarily hand around her waist to show any predators that this deer was taken.

The other girl was called Prudence and came from Sarawak in East Malaysia. She had only been a stewardess for six months and was still flushed with the glamour of her existence. After two years the girls became jaded and began wondering what they would do with their lives if they didn't succeed in marrying a passenger from first class who conveniently combined wealth with good looks.

Ruth was playing elder sister, but I could see that Prudence was impressed by Kenworthy. A good-looking boy, after all. In his smart suit he really was a wolf in sheep's clothing. If he played things right, and the girls hadn't heard about his reputation with other colleagues, this could be his lucky night.

Ruth sipped her white wine, leant over to my ear and said: "Surprised to hear from me?"

"I was."

"Prudence wanted to go out. She still enjoys going to discos and meeting good-looking men." She made it sound as if the whole social process was a terrible sacrifice that she was making on behalf of her lonely flatmate. But her eyes were shamelessly darting around the edge of the dance floor, making sure that there were good-looking men and that they were noticing her.

"Yes, it's a real bother going out and meeting people," I said.

"I've met more than enough handsome men,

what I'd like to meet for once is a sincere, honest man."

I shook my head. "None of those around. Sincere, honest, decent are words alien to men in Hong Kong. You should know that by now."

"I should, but I live in hope. What about your friend? Is he a drunken, sleaze-bag like you?"

"Nah, he's a nice guy. Just split up with his girlfriend." I lied twice in the same sentence. There was a certain code of honour to be obeyed when out with a mate. Kenworthy was a slime-ball but he was always honourable to his mates.

Ruth came from a wealthy family; she was smart; she'd studied at university. It was a form of rebellion that had made her join the airlines. She offered me a Marlboro Light. I stuck two in my mouth, lit them both with my Dunhill lighter and handed one back to her.

"Last time we spoke, you told me you were going to quit," I said.

"Did I? No, must be one of your other girls."

I smiled. Looking at her legs sheathed in raven stockings I noticed they were longer and slimmer than Simone's. Her eyes were feline, more enticing as well. Life wasn't so bad. The Madeira followed by beer on an empty stomach was taking the edge off things.

"What's that knowing smile for?" she demanded. I simply continued to smile inanely, and she laughed.

I turned around and found that Kenworthy

was also making Prudence laugh. A good thing. Make them laugh in the first minute, then tell them a secret and you'd have them in bed before the evening was done.

Finally, by the entrance, I thought I spotted a familiar figure. I shifted to get a better look, but it wasn't Sebastian after all. Maybe he'd left already or wasn't planning to come tonight. I hoped not because I wanted to use the element of surprise which would be gone if I had to go looking for him and Tang the following day.

The girls suggested we go upstairs. We ascended a metal spiral staircase that overlooked the jostling, leaping figures on the dance floor and went into the band room. The band's trumpeter and saxophonist were side-stepping in unison and the sound was upbeat and professional. The girls smiled at each other and began moving their elegant shapes in time to the music. I forced myself into a space between two diminutive Japanese men and lit a cigarette. I began thinking. It might not be a good idea to return home tonight. They'd been watching my place.

"You're not very talkative tonight." Ruth leant against me and told me what they wanted to drink. Although her game plan was always aloof, she became very affectionate after three glasses of wine. I guessed they must have arrived earlier than me.

"You've heard all my lines. Nothing left to say.

It's nice to be here with you again, though," I heard myself saying.

Ruth Lim was not the sort of girl to say the word 'bullshit' out loud, but the look on her face spelled it out. She was still willing to accept the compliment. If a woman likes you, she wants to believe you are sincere.

Ruth and Prudence disappeared to the toilet. Kenworthy moved up to me and ordered another two beers. He was grinning.

"What a little slapper, eh. Lives in Whampoa Garden. I know my way around there. Might have to invite myself up for coffee." He ran a hand through his slicked-back hair and took off his banker's glasses.

"So you got shafted by the bosses?" I said.

"Just the usual. I'm not exactly Mr. Low Key. I got people's backs up in Vice."

He took a long pull from his bottle of Carlsberg then put his hand on my shoulder. "All these vice raids are just a waste of time. Close one place down and the big Triad brothers just open up another one on the floor below. They should legalise it, like they do in Australia. There's an excellent brothel in Whampoa, same place where all the stewardesses live. We should go there sometime. They even have a couple of very fit Singaporeans. Expensive though. Six hundred for half an hour. Lots of coppers go there. Sort of semi-legal. High-security, show your I.D. card and they have a bloke on the 'phone who calls up someone at Regional Headquarters who is part of the scam and checks the PONICS computer to see if you're legitimate. If these girls here blow us out we can have ourselves a little rub-down. No need to go without."

"Sure," I said. The notion sounded appealing although the last time I'd agreed to a similar suggestion from a copper I'd got myself into more trouble than I'd bargained for.

"Just going for a piss." I shoved through the crowd not too politely. I wanted to have another glance at the dance floor. On the cast iron spiral staircase, I paused to survey the people below me. It was a good vantage point. Sebastian was nowhere to be seen.

Carefully, because the steep stairs were unlit and the alcohol was making itself felt, I descended, pushed past a couple fondling each other and made my way through a line of young executive types in striped shirts with their jackets off drinking Corona beer from the bottle. I checked the toilets but the man I was looking for wasn't to be found.

It was when I stepped out from the Men's Room that a surprised voice behind my left ear said: "*Diu lei lo moh*. How did you get here?" I swivelled around fast before he could run, grabbed him by the collar and rammed him through the door, which led into a dark annex with telephone booths.

42

We tripped over each other's legs, but I was heavier and had the angry momentum to keep pushing him forward. A girl leapt to her feet, terrified, dropping the receiver of the payphone she'd been murmuring into. It was a room ten feet in length containing three phone alcoves. The girl, fearing a fight, fled out into the club and the pneumatic door shut itself as I pushed Sebastian to the far end, against the fire door. I pulled down the shoulders of his jacket, trapping his arms and kneed him in the groin. While he gulped with pain, I reached for the Montblanc pen in my inside pocket. A sign above his head warned that opening the fire door would sound an alarm.

"Okay, Sebastian," I said, twisting off the tip of the pen and jamming the nib into the side of his neck. "This pen contains a nerve agent that will give you an instant heart attack." He looked unconvinced

"Don't risk it," I said, pushing him harder. "It's a nasty, quick death. It was made by the Russians for KGB hit squads." His struggling lessened but my grip held firm. He seemed to believe me now. I made a quick decision. Going out through the fire door would be swift and safe but I didn't know where it led. I decided to take a riskier route.

Tse was a careful man. He knew that foreign devils were wild and illogical, and our recent history gave me cause to be wilder and madder than the rest. He didn't want to die. A deal could always be worked out. It was the Chinese way.

"Now listen carefully," I said, in a quiet menacing tone, we're going to walk out of here, arm in arm, retrieve your car from the valet and go and have a nice civilised talk. If you twitch or make any sign to someone else, I'll kill you. All I'll do is press this point here and you'll be dead in minutes. Is that clear?"

"Yes," he said softly.

"Let's do this nice and sensibly. I don't want to harm you. I just want information." I stepped back, allowing him to free his arms and straighten his jacket without letting him get away from the deadly nib.

"Careful now, Sebastian. Your mother would be devastated if her nice boy had a heart attack at such a young age. Give me your hand."

He did so, curiously. With a sudden movement I pulled the nib from his neck and pressed it into the fleshy palm of his hand. It would be equally deadly if I injected him there but we could move more easily without it being obvious that I was holding a weapon on him.

"Don't let go of my hand. It works just as fast," I warned him. "Don't worry if we look gay. It's better than being dead."

We stepped out from the telephone annex and a few people in the corridor gave us curious looks. We moved like an unwilling pair of Siamese twins, forcing ourselves through the crowd and down the stairs that led to the entrance. Jim, the doorman, looked at me enquiringly. I smiled and said:

"Be back a bit later. My friend's having some heart palpitations." He must have noticed the look of pain on Sebastian's face, but it wasn't something he would interfere with. He thought I was still a policeman and he knew that Sebastian was involved with organised crime. He'd been in Hong Kong long enough to smell a Triad, however well-dressed.

Since he was a regular and valued customer, Sebastian's racing green Jaguar XJS was parked fifty yards down on the main road instead of somewhere in the underground garage. The parking valet gave him back his key and I tipped him a hundred dollars. We walked awkwardly and in strained silence down the slope. When we reached the car I told him to open the passenger door. He got in first and I followed, holding his wrist tight as he manoeuvred himself over the gearshift. Quickly I switched the pen to his neck again.

"Where you want to go?" he said.

"Where is Mr. Tang tonight?"

"I told you. He's playing *mah-jongg* with Mok Bun and some important friends. How did you get away from the massage house?"

"I had some outside help."

He looked puzzled, even worried for an instant, then his naturally bland features reasserted themselves.

"You can't win against us. Why don't you understand that? We want you to work for us. You can make a lot of money," he said.

"Okay, enough bullshit. We will discuss that later," I snapped and he visibly relaxed. "I want to see Tang now, so tell me where he is." Sebastian stared ahead at the windscreen and into the darkness that was the harbour.

"Where's your fucking boss?" I could see a vein standing out on the Chinaman's temple, indicating the tension underneath his apparently calm features.

"'Officer help, my friend's having a heart attack,'" I suggested, pushing the nib of the pen hard into his skin.

"They are at his mistress's house," Sebastian said at last.

"I'm a bit of a gambling man myself and I'll wager you he won't be winning much tonight. Drive me there."

His lips were pursed and he wore a mask of malevolence that made his feelings clear. He loathed me for who I was, for the colour of my skin and the fact that I had managed to turn the tables so unexpectedly. The centuries-old superiority of the Chinese race was so ingrained in his being, genetically and culturally, that the thought of me outwitting him made him seethe with inner fury.

"The address," I snapped. I began boring the metal tip into the side of his neck making him bite his lip in pain. Then he gave in, telling me the location. It was right at the top of the Peak. I knew the building, often shrouded by mist. Four stories, an old house, one of several, converted into eight luxury flats, much higher up than the Peak Tram terminal. I reduced the pressure on his neck.

"Okay, let's go," I said. He leant forward and started up the car. With my right hand I reached down and pulled out the Walther PPK from its ankle holster. His eyes flickered sideways in surprise.

"I'll poison you and shoot you in the heart if you try anything foolish. Remember. You'll only die once, but I will have twice the pleasure"

He nodded, probably thinking that there would be opportunities for escape later. At heart Sebastian was no more than a functionary. He was not a man of action used to spitting danger in the eye. He preferred caution and negotiation to wild risky action. That was where we differed. That and our views on racial superiority. In my world all men were equal in death.

It took about twenty minutes to wend our way up the mountain. Hardly any cars passed us and the only noise was that of the tyres as they complained on each bend. When I saw the odd-shaped towers of the Peak Tram terminus, I ordered Sebastian to pull into the deserted car park. He'd been quiet up to now, concentrating on driving. He glanced at me swiftly and brought the Jaguar to rest. Up here, it was desolate in the middle of the night. One could hardly imagine that spread out below was the commercial heart of Asia's busiest metropolis.

There was an unlit path, which led all the way around and afforded impressive views of Victoria and Kowloon in the daytime. And a road, marked for residents only, that went further up to the top.

Sebastian had outlived his usefulness. I'd never liked the man. I rested the pen nib against his chest, and when he realised with a shocked Chinese yelp what I was about to do, I pressed the nipple. There was a little hiss, like a man discreetly passing wind. Too late, he tried to push the pen away but the tiny needle had already shot its way through his shirt and buried itself deep in his chest. He looked at me in fear. His hand clutched his heart. His mouth opened so wide I could have stuck my fist into it without touching the sides. The muscles on his face began to twitch, spittle drooled from the side of his mouth and his knees beat hard against the steering wheel. He tried to grab me, but his arm ran out of strength. Then his eyes glazed over and he was gone, slipping sideways into the door, his head banging against the glass.

Pocketing the spent Montblanc, I looked out of the window. There were gentle swirls of mist eddying around the car park. I checked the glove compartment but there was nothing of interest beside a pair of driving gloves. It took some effort to get them over my chunky hands but finally I managed. With a handkerchief from my top breast pocket, I wiped the door handle and everywhere else I had touched.

Outside, the air was damp on my lungs. Taking a deep breath, Walther in my hand, I jogged up the steep access road. It took me ten minutes.

43

My inclination was to walk in shooting, but even Billy the Kid must have known the benefit of scouting out the lay of the land first. I leant in the shadows of a stone gatepost, getting back my breath and looking out for a watchman's hut. Above my head was a brass plaque giving the number of the house, which matched the one Sebastian had given me. There was a small forecourt in front of the buildings but no gate. Tang's metallic blue Rolls Royce Silver Spirit outranked the other motors, although they were all expensive European models. I checked the action and the magazine, which was full. Then using my handkerchief, I wiped it down, because later I would have to lose it.

The watchman, like all of his kind in Hong Kong, was an old man who slept on the job. Often, they were simply employed on a risible salary to comply with a clause in the insurance contract. No one expected watchmen to physically prevent robbers or thieves, and they regularly became deaf, dumb and blind when interviewed by police officers. But with murder it was best not to take a chance. I poked him in the ribs until he started waking up, then clocked him on the temple with the gun butt before he opened his eyes. I hoped that he had a strong head and might live. Real life concussion was a lot worse than it appeared in the TV shows. A trickle of blood ran over the counter where he'd been resting his head. From his pocket I took the set of keys that opened the front door. I wedged it open with the Welcome mat.

I chose the stairs over the lift. The building had been thoroughly renovated. It smelled of recent paint and fresh pine. It had probably been built for some cunning commercial buccaneer at the turn of the century.

Arriving at the top floor I paused to get my bearings. The stairs went on to the roof and the room housing the lift machinery. Two doors faced each other with identical doorbells. Flat A was the one. I put my ear to the wood. The ritual cracking of *mah-jongg* tiles on the table told me that a game was in full swing. The Chinese loved games of chance - gambling was in their blood from birth. Anything with odds would make their eyes pop with excitement. I'd seen men gamble away a month's salary on the turn of a card, heard of housewives losing their husbands' life savings in 24-hour marathon *mah-jongg* sessions. Far more than substance abuse, gambling gripped the Asian character and twisted and turned its victims with glittering promises, which were often fulfilled and denied in the space of hours. The tiles were slapped down in rapid succession and the games might continue well after the sun rose again.

I studied the door. There was no heavy metal grille. Probably the designer felt one would detract from the rejuvenated artistic integrity of the building. In any case, this area had surprisingly few burglaries. The affluence of the owners probably frightened the run of the mill housebreaker. The rich were powerful in Asia, and well connected. Only a fool messed with the wealthy, unless they were a professional like me.

There was a single lock on the door, but not the sort that would yield to my trick with the supple plastic card. I tested the lock by leaning against the door. The door was not fully flush and there didn't seem to be an internal bolt. Sergeant Yan, veteran of many drugs raids with me would have been proud. Three hard kicks exactly over the door handle loosened the jamb, then a run against the whole panel and the doorframe released it with a crash. I staggered into a well-decorated hallway. Regaining my balance as I tumbled forward, I covered the hallway in a second, went through the dining room and had my back against the wall with an eye on every exit, covering the four people around the dealing table, as well as the woman sitting on the sofa. My knees were bent, the Walther was up, steady, my breathing controlled, I took in the surroundings. With luck I had about ten or fifteen minutes to do what was needed.

The room was around 800 square feet and decorated with taste by a professional who knew how to make a place feel warm and friendly. Tang, fat and prosperous as usual, flushed with brandy, sat in shirtsleeves, a mauled cigar in an ashtray by his elbow. Facing me sat Mok Bun and two other men in their late thirties, both in pale shirts and loosened ties. The girl was just decoration. Probably a model or minor actress, somebody who had been one of the runners up in the Miss Asia-Pacific contest. A girl who had legs, breasts, a pretty pouting face and the other accessories that made a man enjoy being seen with her. There were thousands like her in this big city. If they didn't get that acting contract with ATV or TVB and weren't willing to shed some clothes in Category III movies, being a rich man's mistress was a cosy way to live. Chinese men were generous to their women and the rich flung sports cars and condos around as a matter of course.

Everybody had paused and was looking at each other.

"If the girl screams, I'll shoot her," I said, as her painted mouth was already open and the lungs were pumping for air.

"*Sau Seng*," Tang snapped at her. She slumped as if hit by an iron rod. I had little time. 'Get in, get out, stay alive' they'd taught us. When you're inside, control the situation. I was controlling it. I was less than twelve feet from all of them, easier than popping pigeons.

"Who are these two men?" I demanded.

Tang seemed calm, considering his situation and what he knew of me. "One is Mr. Wong, he is a well-known businessman, and the other is Mr. Chan. He is a barrister. Why don't you put down your gun and we can discuss matters. I'm sure there are many misunderstandings. You used to be a policeman. Don't you remember the penalties for what you are doing? I always thought English people are careful and calm about what they do."

At the Police Training School they had taught us that while arresting a man he must be told what his offence was and what his rights were. On the streets you learnt it was bollocks, you grabbed the guy, hit him hard and told him to shut the fuck up. But this time, I wanted to tell the criminal why he was being punished and then watch his face as the sentence was pronounced and effected.

I said, "Tang, I am the Reliable Man and there's a contract for your death. Some important people would prefer you dead. You have upset too many people. And you've upset me. Mok Bun, you double-crossed Otto Schwartz. You think you can get away with that?" From the look on Mok Bun's face, he thought he had but was rapidly reconsidering.

"As for the rest of you. Bad luck. But I'm judging you by the company you keep." I noticed a damp patch appearing on the trouser leg of one of the men. Fear of death plays havoc with the bladder. He was regretting his decision to play *mah-jongg* with the dubious Tang Siu Ling.

Tang saw the intent in my eyes and waved his cigar in a calming gesture. "No, no, Jedburgh, don't be foolish. I can make you a rich man."

"I'm rich already. You can't buy the sort of satisfaction I get from killing scum like you and Schwartz."

"Don't be rash," yelled the man who was a barrister. I ignored him but out of the corner of my eye I was watching Mok Bun carefully. Once he'd been a good copper and carrying a gun would feel natural to an old CID man even when he'd crossed to the other side of the fence.

The *mah-jongg* tiles went flying as the table tipped. Mok Bun had a fancy shoulder holster and suddenly he had in his hand something modest yet deadly. Deadly for him, because my first bullet shattered his nose and ploughed on into the brain behind.

I'd already decided on the order when I entered the room - the renegade copper, the gangster, the witnesses, the girl. Not much louder than *mah-jongg* tiles, the small, classic automatic cracked, dealing out its destruction. The girl was halfway over the sofa but I got her twice in the back of the head.

For a split second I paused and surveyed the carnage. I jogged around the bodies. Tang was still gurgling; the entry wound two inches below his left collarbone. I dragged his head up by the thinning hair, looked into his limp black and confused eyes, angled the muzzle into his mouth and took off the top of his head.

The job was done.

The nice things about handguns is that, in real life, they don't sound at all like they do in the movies, especially this small .22 LR calibre I was using. At four in the morning, dampened by thick colonial walls, the shots would sound odd, but more like firecrackers, to the law abiding neighbours. Trusting to speed was better than trusting to luck. My time on the premises was up.

I calculated it would take half an hour for an Emergency Unit Land Rover to respond to a 999 call up to the Peak. The local police station had no C-shift mobile patrol. But there were no guarantees. The last week had seen me take too many risks. I was running out of luck.

I sprinted down the hill unseen and opened the driver's door of the Jaguar, pressing the Walther firmly into Sebastian's flaccid fingers. The arm flopped back into his lap. It was a five-minute jog down to Mansfield Road. There was still no sign of any police car, although once I had to leap into the undergrowth as a Mercedes swept uphill.

Senior civil servants and policemen lived in the spacious but crumbling blocks of concrete on Mansfield Road. It was a typical collection of deteriorating government quarters. Opposite, on the junction with the main road down to the city, was an all-night petrol station.

After ten minutes a taxi arrived and two drunk English schoolgirls rolled out giggling. I stood in the darkness between blocks, and lit a cigarette waiting until the cab had reversed. The driver, a testy old lad, grumbled in Cantonese about the smoke. I told him to shut his mouth. Then he cheered up and asked me how come I spoke such good Cantonese. I told him I was a policeman. "Ah, a *gingsi*," he assumed and was impressed. I had to be at least a superintendent to be living on the Peak, probably on my way to work. As his red Toyota set itself in motion, the first sirens began wailing tentatively a long way off. Taxi drivers never talk to the police. They don't want to be involved. And what had a *gwai lo gingsi* to do with a shooting between Black Society members? Just in case, I made a mental note of the taxi's number and his name, marked on a dashboard panel.

We took the long way down from the mountain, through Wong Nei Chung Gap and eventually reached Wan Chai where the girlie bars were still trading. It was half past two in the morning. 'The Old China Hand' fried up the best pre-hangover breakfast in the territory. I was ravenous.

Munching on the sausage, mashing the potatoes, I went over events to see how the evidence looked. No one had seen me. None of my prints were at the scene. The immediate assumption would be that there had been a falling out amongst Triad members. Sebastian's corpse held the murder weapon. His symptoms would be those of a heart attack brought on by the adrenalin rush associated with murder. Jim, the doorman would keep *stumm* about having seen me leave with Sebastian. It was part of the job description.

If the investigation did find its way to me, there would be no forensic evidence to link me and no apparent motive. OSCG would not contemplate the idea of a hired hitman operating in Hong Kong. It was unlikely that OSCG would bust their balls investigating a case that so neatly disposed of a major Triad figure, a bent copper and their associates. It was too pleasant a gift horse for them to look closely in its mouth.

The only other possible area of concern was my meeting with the Shamshuipo Vice Squad. However, my knowledge of Hong Kong Police procedure told me there was little danger there. The OSCG investigators would never canvass other stations for information. It would take a stroke of misfortune for someone, out drinking with colleagues, to mention the curious case of the *gwai lo* Inspector imprisoned in a linen cupboard.

Of course, Tang's minions might point the finger at me. But even they would not be able to say for sure who had killed Sebastian and Tang. I'd need to keeping a low profile for a while. I figured it would be best to pack up and leave Hong Kong for a while. Perhaps it was time to try Singapore.

I'd contact Harry Bolt the next day and confirm that my job was completed and get him to transfer my money directly. There was only a fork full of baked beans left on my plate. I had no desire to go home just yet. My body was wide-awake, still buzzing with adrenalin from a mission fully accomplished.

44

It was easy to get a Kowloon Taxi back across the water. Whampoa Gardens was a middle-class housing estate bordering the tourist area of Tsim Sha Tsui. It seemed to be popular with up-and-coming Chinese families who had the sort of children that get between your feet on Saturday afternoons. Apart from them, in a honeycomb of neat, box-like flats one could find hundreds of Cathay Pacific stewardesses from diverse Asian countries for whom it was an easy cab-ride to the airport.

Ruth's voice didn't sound sleepy when I rang the buzzer. Curious, mainly. When she opened the door to me it was obvious they had only just returned from clubbing. Kenworthy was sipping the proverbial hot mug of coffee. Prudence sat next to him looking flushed, whether from drink, anticipation or both. I took in her fluffy Garfield slippers and the location of her left hand.

"The mysterious Mr. Jedburgh reappears," said Kenworthy. "And me thinking I could have both girls for myself."

"Shut up," Ruth said sternly. "So what happened to you?"

"It's a long story. Did you miss me?"

"They forced me to go to 'Club Soho'," Kenworthy said, "which, as usual, was full of gays and weirdoes." Soho was one of the few clubs that managed to stay open until dawn.

"You want a coffee?" Ruth asked, resigning herself to my presence. I nodded. "Then you need to explain why you abandoned me without saying anything?" Abandoned, I liked the sound of that.

"It's very simple, you were in the toilets somewhere and I bumped into an important guy who I'd been trying to sign up as a client for ages. We got talking and he suggested we have a few more drinks in a Wan Chai girlie bar..."

"And you just dumped us to go drinking?"

"It was business, Ruth. I live on commissions. This guy could pay my rent for the next six months."

"I think it's incredibly rude," she said sternly.

"However charming and enjoyable your company is, and it is very enjoyable, it's a hard fact of life that bills need to paid. You wouldn't want me starving on the streets, would you?"

"This is a hard fact of life too," said Kenworthy patting his crotch with a smirk which made Prudence squeal in mock horror. His slurred vowels told me that he'd had a good night so far.

"At least you could have told us you were leaving," Ruth said, not giving up her case yet.

"It was impossible."

"Well," she shrugged. "What made you think you could come around here in the middle of the night after leaving us like that?"

"It's hardly the middle of the night. It's practically dawn."

"Is it?" said Prudence with surprise.

Ruth turned on her slippered heel. She had not changed out of her dress yet and even without the heels she looked tall and delectable. If need be, I intended to grovel.

"Did you sign him up?" asked Prudence, swallowing my little tale like a yearling trout.

"We're having lunch next week to sign the papers," I replied and flopped myself into the other armchair.

Kenworthy gave a shrewd smile. He thought he knew what had really happened - I'd spotted another girl I liked better than Ruth. When she had blown me out, I had come here to rescue the evening. I wasn't going to correct his assumption. It had happened before.

"Come," I said to Ruth when she returned with my coffee, taking her arm and pulling her gently into the master bedroom. "I need to talk to you about something."

"We can talk out here," she said, putting up notional resistance.

"It's private. And these two don't want you around. Prudence is a big girl now." We were already in her room, all fluffy pink bed quilt and useless ornaments.

"She's not, you know. She hasn't had a boyfriend before except back home. They just broke up." I was already closing the door.

"Perfect then. She needs a handsome fellow to tell her how sexy she is and make her tingle and shiver all over. Now let me tell you how sexy you are and..."

She leant back against the closed door with a determined expression on her face. If she hadn't had a few drinks herself she would have booted me out of the house by now.

"I didn't ask you out this evening to have you come home with me, Bill Jedburgh. I'm not that desperate." She had to make her point, of course.

I pushed out my bottom lip and sat on the bed, kicking off my shoes. She sighed.

"All right, you can stay the night, but we're not going to do anything." She came over and began stroking my hair. I grabbed her by the waist and nuzzled her chest, which was scented with perfume and perspiration. I thought of the money that I'd collect the next day. I thought of the dead lying on the Peak covered in blood. But I didn't think of Simone because that was different. Those events were over, and I would box them up and never think about them again.

"You smell funny," she said.

"I had a full English breakfast with the client. It's that cheap cooking oil they use."

We fell back onto the bed and dozed fully

dressed in each other's arms. When the sun came furtively through the pink blinds she pulled me on top of her, her eyelids flickered with desire and her strong hips began moving sensuously against mine.

END

Afterword
The Story of 'The Reliable Man'

When I started to co-write with Julian Stagg, we agreed that it would be sensible to revisit the earlier books in The Reliable Man Series and took a decision to change the name of the first book in the series and also tighten up the plot and the language.

The novel was originally written longhand in exercise books in the late 1980s based on stories I'd been told by my better half and his policemen friends.

It was turned down by an editor at Hodder Headline who said nobody was interested in reading books about single men 'shooting and shagging' their way around Asia. He advised me to concentrate on writing romances with strong female leads and an element of jeopardy, which is what I did for the next few years.

With 'The Reliable Man' I'd set out to capture the world of Asian expats as we knew them. Life for young, especially, unmarried Caucasian men was then just as drunk and debauched as my books depict. To those who think I must be exaggerating, I simply say: ask anyone who was there at the time – preferably when they are out of earshot of husbands, wives and children – and they will admit that it was often even raunchier.

I've been frequently asked who the model was for Bill Jedburgh. In truth he is an amalgam of many people we knew who were in the RHKP. I ask all former members of the Force to forgive me for the outrageous suggestion that any of their number would become a contract killer. But what if...?

Pattaya in its current form owes its genesis to the Vietnam War, when a sleepy seaside resort became an R&R location for the U'Tapao Air Force Base at Sattahip, just thirty minutes from Pattaya, and for the troops who flew into it from Vietnam. After the troops departed, the town became a popular destination for sex tourism and cheap package tours in the 1970s and 80s. By the time of this novel it was home to a large contingent of expatriate Europeans, Americans and Australians. The idea for the plot came from a friend of ours who regularly visited Pattaya and told us the true story of how the German 'mafia' were run out of town by the Thai authorities who hired two off-duty Filipino police officers who were moonlighting as hitmen.

Valerie Goldsilk, 2021